# FIREBIRD

Bob Holt

outskirts press

Firebird

v5.0

This is a work of fiction. Names, characters, businesses, places, events, locales, and incidents are either the products of the author's imagination or used in a fictitious manner. Any resemblance to actual persons, living or dead, or actual events is purely coincidental.

The opinions expressed in this manuscript are solely the opinions of the author and do not represent the opinions or thoughts of the publisher. The author has represented and warranted full ownership and/or legal right to publish all the materials in this book.



Outskirts Press, Inc.
http://www.outskirtspress.com

Paperback ISBN: 978-1-9772-2528-3
Hardback ISBN: 978-1-9772-2539-9

Library of Congress Control Number: 2020904601



PRINTED IN THE UNITED STATES OF AMERICA

*Dedication*

*I am forever grateful to my wife and soulmate, Margarite, for her never-ending support and advice. But I also must single out some special people who without their encouragement and involvement, this story would have not been told. Captain Scott Self and his wife, Jan, first introduced this West Texas boy to sailing and inflamed my passion for the life. Dearly departed David and Sally Haase, godparents to our daughter, Robyn, spent many hours with me in the British Virgin Islands, brainstorming this story, and sadly passed on before its publication. They are missed and will never be forgotten. Plus, my good Colorado Elk friends, Dan Duffy, Rick Sloan, and Jon Harshaw, who read an early manuscript, then nagged me to get it published. And last, but not least, my Texas critique group, Novel Crafters, a talented bunch of published writers who won't let you get away with being lazy in your writing. Thank you all.*

*Sadly, I just learned today, April 4, 2020, that the best-selling writer, Patricia Bosworth, died in New York of the Coronavirus. I met Patty in 1983, and we spent many hours discussing the art of writing and organizing my stories such as "Cowboy" and "Firebird." She encouraged me and introduced me to many helpful people in the publishing industry. I will never forget her.*

# PROLOGUE

June 1969

Hugh Blaylock, a wide grin on his sunburned face, gripped the helm of the big sailing yacht as it tacked back toward the western shore of Lake Michigan. The Stars and Stripes on the stern popped in the stiff breeze while the crew cranked in the large genoa on the starboard winch. A glance at his Rolex told him it was past four o'clock.

It was hard to believe that two years had passed since he contracted for Firebird's design and construction at the Palmer Johnson yard on Lake Michigan. His dream of designing and building a highly engineered boat to sail around the world was now a reality. After being delayed by decades of life, he could now see it and damn well taste it. By the end of day, the engineers from the boatyard would complete her final sail tests.

Hugh flexed his fingers on the stainless-steel wheel and squinted up into the sun to check the luff of the mainsail. The ketch had caught a building breeze on a close reach and its eighty-four-foot hull powered forward. The swooshing sound from the bow indicated a "bone in her teeth," the white frothy wave pushed away from the hull as it drove through the water. "Dammit!" He slapped an open palm on the wheel. *It's even better than I imagined!* He felt the fresh wind on his face and relished Firebird's ballet over the sapphire blue water.

Bill Therry, the marine architect at Sparkman & Stephens, dragged a large sail bag forward and passed it off to the foredeck crew. He waved back at Hugh on the wheel. "Bring her about when you're ready and fall off. Let's set the spinnaker and see how she moves with the wind on her stern."

Hugh's eyes sparkled. "Ready about!" He paused a moment to let the crew prepare their lines.

"Hard alee!" He spun the wheel to port. Sheets eased, dumping air from the main and mizzen sails. The bow crossed the wind, and the foresail flopped to port. Firebird completed her tack and picked up speed. Hugh turned downwind with sails full as the team on the spinnaker cranked the winch and tailed the line. A silky plume rose out of the bag at the bow and writhed like a waterspout toward the top of the mast. The nylon chute caught air and billowed out. In the center of the white spinnaker, the towering figure of a scarlet Phoenix drew everyone's attention. The mystic bird with wings spread, seemed to lift the boat out of the water.

"Wow! Feel that?" Hugh tightened his grip on the wheel. He noticed every man around him grasping to hold on as the giant sail yoked the wind and moved Firebird forward like an arrow shot from a crossbow.

Late in the afternoon, people on shore watched them motoring through the harbor toward the boatyard. All her sails were furled, sheets and halyards secured, and gear stowed away, leaving nothing out of place to break her graceful lines. High above the deck, the two raked-back masts reminded one of a cocked-pistol, while the setting sun on her white topsides made her look like she was plated with pure gold.

When they entered the yard's marina, Hugh steered into her berth while the crew tossed lines to hands on the pier. He saw his daughter and son-in-law at the outdoor bar and waved to them. That's a pleasant surprise, he thought.

He stood on the dock watching the crew put things away, when someone slapped him on the back.

"So, Hugh." The manager of the boatyard was checking his clipboard. "Ready to take possession?"

Hugh smiled. "She exceeded all my expectations. I'm ready to sign the papers whenever you are. Your people put up with a lot of my crap over the past couple of years."

"Your crap is better than most people's." The manager smiled and pushed a pen back in his shirt pocket. "I think my boys will miss her when she leaves the yard."

Hugh laughed as they turned and walked up the pier toward the yard office. "My sweet wife often informs me that two years is enough time to build one sailboat, but she doesn't understand the most important part was the previous forty years of dreaming about it. And since I turned sixty today, I'm giving myself one hell of a present."

"Happy birthday, Daddy." Suzanne Blaylock Prouty met her father at the top of the ramp and kissed him on the cheek. Hugh frowned at the odor of bourbon on her breath.

"Oh Daddy." She looped her arm through his. "The flight from Chicago was terrible, and my dear husband here gave me no sympathy. Did you, Delvin? Your company president was a very bad boy." Suzanne laughed loudly, winked at the yard manager, and squeezed Hugh's arm.

His son-in-law fingered his silk tie and then picked at some phantom lint on his navy-blue suit as they trekked across grass toward the office. Hugh noticed everyone sported rubber-soled boat shoes except for his son-in-law. Delvin Prouty's Gucci's reflected the setting sun like a signal mirror.

"And are you joining your father on his circumnavigation?" The yard manager's wife refilled Suzanne's champagne flute. Darkness had settled in, and dock lights created circles of light on the wooden walkways.

"Oh no. I'd much rather spend that time at our villa in the south of France," Suzanne said. She sipped champagne and winked at a sun-bronzed boy watching from across the dock. "Daddy's been obsessed with this since he was in school. After college, he wanted to go to sea but had to manage the family business when Grandfather died."

"Aren't you glad I did?" Hugh slipped his arm around her and squeezed. "Blaylock Industries provided you and your mother a good life, and you a handsome husband." He nodded at Delvin who stood off to the side between two dock lights.

"And paid for your little toy over there." Suzanne cut her eyes toward Firebird, causing everyone to laugh. "No, Daddy, dear. This is *your* dream. Even Mother had more important things to do today like getting her hair highlighted, but she sends hugs and birthday kisses and hopes you love her half as much as you love your Firebird."

Hugh smiled while everyone laughed, but his daughter's joke had hit home. Boy, he wished Maureen had been out on the lake with him today. Just this one time.

Ten minutes later, he found himself cornered at the food table by several of the yardmen.

"Sir, when do you plan to take her to sea?" a young fellow near his elbow asked. "And what size crew will you have?"

Hugh nodded. "I want to be out of the Great Lakes and in New York City by Labor Day," he said, "and we designed her to be handled by just two people. It's the challenge. You know—man versus the sea."

A bit later he stood alone under a light at the end of the dock, staring into his empty glass when a young man approached carrying a fresh bottle of champagne. Hugh recognized him as one of the foredeck crew who set the spinnaker that afternoon.

"I like her name, Mr. Blaylock." The boy reached to fill Hugh's glass.

Hugh studied the bubbles rising in his flute. "The Firebird is the western version of the Phoenix, the mythological bird that burns itself to ashes every five-hundred years then rises to live again." He looked at the boy. "When I was your age, my dream to sail the world turned to ashes when my father died." Hugh gestured toward the ketch in its berth. "It's now resurrected in this marvelous yacht you all have built."

The young man raised his glass. "To you, sir, and to Firebird."

Hugh swallowed the lump in his throat and met the boy's flute with his own. "And to your dreams, young man."

Bill Therry stepped into the dock light. "I'm heading to the hotel. What time should we meet in the morning?"

"Sleep in, have a leisurely breakfast, and I'll meet you around ten o'clock," Hugh said.

"I can use the extra winks after this past week. You looked pleased today."

Hugh nodded. "Couldn't be happier. Have a steak on me and get a good night's sleep."

Watching his designer walk away, a feverish shiver raced up Hugh's spine and sweat beaded his face. God, he thought, tasting a salty flavor on his lips. *I'm having a hell-of-a-rush.*

Suzanne and her husband dropped him at his hotel in town and promised to pick him up in an hour for a celebratory dinner.

He stepped into the bathroom and turned on the shower. With his son-in-law in place at the firm, they could get along without him for a couple of years. The old man would be proud, Hugh thought, as he stepped under the spray and soaped himself. His breathing sped up and his body tingled with the rushing sensation experienced earlier. He stepped out of the shower and gulped fresh air. *Damn.*

The white-tiled room spun dizzily, and he sat on the toilet. *What the hell?* He put his face in a towel and closed his eyes. After a few moments, he stood to rinse off when a shattering pain rocketed up his arm, smashed across his chest, and knocked him face down on the bathroom floor. His mouth opened and closed, but there was no sound. At least nothing he heard. Another searing pain stung his heart and slowly dulled. The tile floor felt cool against his face. His eyes closed, and the final thing he saw was Firebird rocking quietly in her berth at the dock.

# CHAPTER 1

AUGUST, 1998

Sam Berrenger's eyelids felt glued shut, and the sour odor of vomit hung in the air. Morning sunlight warmed his face, and the hard slats of a park bench pressed into his back. He thought about sitting up, but his ribs hurt too much. Events of the previous night rattled around in his head, a jumbled mess of places and faces, all unpleasant, ricocheting around in no particular order. A wave of nausea rolled over him, and he put his foot on the ground to stop the spins. One eye creaked open, but the other one seemed damaged. He lifted a hand and tested the puffiness around his bruised cheekbone. All evidence pointed to a fight, but he couldn't remember where, when, or with whom. But that was just him. Other men kissed their wives and children before they went to bed. Some had a glass of warm milk or read a book. After a few shots of whiskey, Sam usually got his lights knocked out.

He couldn't recall last night's pugilistic particulars, but he did remember getting thrown off the island steamer he had been working on for the past six months. They'd sailed to Puerto Rico from Key West several months before and had done a good business hauling toilet bowls and Sheetrock from San Juan over to the Dominican Republic. At least until yesterday morning, when he'd been fired with no notice. The captain had accused him of coming on to the ship's cook. It was a crock. The whole crew knew the little guy was the captain's darling, which explained why everything served up from the ship's galley tasted like crap. Growing up, his old man had warned him about working hard and keeping the boss happy. He'd always followed that advice, at least that he could remember. Anyway, it'd been a lousy nothing job.

"Ugh!" He groaned at the pain in his ribs when he pulled himself up to a sitting position.

His old man had said a lot of things when the family lived in that shabby little rental house overlooking the Houston ship channel. Most of it, Sam didn't remember, or pay any attention to. The old drunk had spent his life humping heavy pipe around gasoline cracking plants at Texas City. That'd never seemed so smart to Sam.

Two small boys in the grassy park across the street pointed toward him and spoke Spanish to their mother who was buying them cream sodas from the umbrella cart at the corner. She was a pretty, little thing and for a brief-moment reminded him of Darlene. The woman's dark hair glistened in the morning sunlight as she handed the boys their treats. She looked toward Sam and rattled off something to them. Probably a warning that they'd end up like him if they didn't behave. He smiled to himself. The day had just begun, and he'd already done a good deed, even if it was only to serve as a bad example.

Sam closed his good eye for a moment. The familiar image of a teenage girl crowded everything else out of his thoughts: faded jeans, white sleeveless blouse, long dark hair. A familiar wave of guilt numbed him. He should've listened to his old man when he tried talking him out of getting married right after high school. It wasn't that his dad had been so against Darlene. He thought Sam should live life a bit more before settling down to one woman and a string of minimum wage jobs.

They'd exchanged ID bracelets in the fourth grade and were never apart a day after that until he went to six months of National Guard training. After that, he was lucky to land a job with a drilling company. She was a petite, girly, spark of passion that he would wrap up in his arms and cuddle like a puppy. She'd liked that a lot. He liked it too. But in the end, his old man was right. If he'd listened to him twenty years ago, he wouldn't have awakened this morning out of work and homeless in San Juan, Puerto Rico.

Glancing down at the ground, he saw his faded duffel bag next to the park bench. It was no great comfort to know all his worldly belongings were within easy reach. Not much to show for forty years, but he valued the freedom. Made it easier to move on without dragging around an anchor of mortgage payments, insurance premiums, phone bills, and all the other stuff of normal life. Money was never plentiful, but he had enough to get by. A drilling accident in the Permian Basin soon after Darlene's funeral had gouged a four-inch chunk of muscle from the upper portion of his left arm. Small children stared at the ugly scar when he didn't wear a long sleeve shirt, but the oil company paid him a thousand dollars each month for the rest of his life for the inconvenience. Right now, he wished he'd spent some of it last night on a hotel room.

Rows of aluminum masts at the marina across the way rocked and clanged in the breeze. Sam reached for his bag and stood up. A shower and shave, a toothbrush, and a few minutes on the toilet would brighten his day. A Bloody Mary at the marina bar, and a paying job with a dry place to bunk would make it even better.

After showering in the locker room just off the marina dock, he donned fresh clothes and entered the air-conditioned bar and restaurant. Booths and tables were all occupied with chatty morning diners. The room was hazy with smoke from cigarettes and burnt bacon grease. He nodded to the young surfer-looking bartender. "Morning, Donny."

"What'll it be, Mr. Berrenger?"

"Something spicy to kill the beast," Sam said, pulling out a barstool and dropping his bag at his feet. "One of your special bloods with twice the Tabasco would be a good start."

While waiting for his drink, he surveyed the many customers in the restaurant at this late hour of the morning and decided they were an eclectic bunch of live-aboarders in the marina, and a few park bench aboders, like himself.

"Looks like you had a rough night," Donny said as he punched holes in the top of a large can of tomato juice.

"Should've seen me before I got cleaned up." Sam leaned forward with his elbows on the bar. "Actually, it's good you didn't. You would've called the morgue."

Sam had on his last clean T-shirt, the one that had ***I SLEPT ON A VIRGIN island*** printed across the front, and a pair of chinos worn only once since they were last laundered. Lifting his baseball cap and brushing unruly hair out of his eyes, he glanced in the mirror behind the bar. He needed a haircut. Seeing the ugly scar exposed on his upper arm, he covered it with his right hand.

The young bartender placed the tomato juice and vodka on a bar napkin in front of him and started washing glasses in the sink. He paused a moment and dried one on a towel kept flung over his shoulder. "Almost forgot, Mr. Berrenger, Mrs. Zavalla asked about you last night."

"Call me Sam. Mr. Berrenger was my old man."

Donny shrugged. "Anyway, she and her sister from New York were in last night having some drinks. She wanted to know if your freighter had returned to San Juan for the weekend."

Sam raised a brow. "Her husband with her?"

"Nope." Donny glanced up from the sudsy sink and grinned.

Movie stars would kill for his straight white teeth, Sam thought.

"I heard Captain Zavalla's running a tanker to Kuwait for Hess Oil," Donny said, drying another glass. "That trip should take him weeks with the way things are over there in the Persian Gulf."

Sam took a big swallow of his Bloody Mary. The spicy liquid burned just right going down. His empty stomach greeted it with a little rumble. "Maybe I'll call Mrs. Zavalla and see if she needs my assistance while the good captain's away." He winked at Donny and took another swig of breakfast. "You know how little things can build up around a house without a man to tend them."

"I think she had something like that in mind." Donny nodded. "She said if I saw you, to tell you to come on over to her place. You needn't call or anything, just stop by."

"Hey! Hey, Sammy. Just the man I want to see."

Sam turned on the barstool and saw the harbormaster threading his way between tables toward him. Gerald Diaz—Jerry, to everyone who knew him around the marina—was a squat friendly fellow in a khaki uniform. He'd retired a few years before from a career in the U.S. Coast Guard. Sam didn't remember where or when they'd first met, but the popular harbormaster frequented most of the bars and gin mills around the docks. Sam waved. "How's it hanging? That wasn't you I traded punches with last night, was it?"

"Nope. Not me." Jerry sat heavily on a barstool beside Sam. "And from the looks of that bruise on your face, I'd guess 'traded' is only your assumption." He nodded at Donny and pointed at the Bloody Mary in front of Sam. "Gimme the same."

The harbormaster nudged his elbow into Sam's sore ribs. "A little bird told me Captain Bligh tossed your butt off his boat yesterday cause he didn't like the dewy look his cook gave you every morning while dishing out your gruel."

Sam shrugged. "Wasn't said in so many words, but the result's the same."

"So, looking for a new job?"

He took a long sip from his drink, and wondered what Jerry had in mind. "Might be. Any ideas?"

The harbormaster remained silent a moment, folding and unfolding a paper napkin on the bar in front of him. He turned on his stool toward Sam and spoke in a low voice. "If I could lose forty pounds, ten years, and three bratty kids at home, I'd pursue this one myself." He looked serious and Sam didn't interrupt him.

"There's an interesting ketch moored over on the far side of the harbor near Tobias' boatyard. It's tucked in some mangrove trees. She's a big one, eighty-four feet with an eighteen-foot beam and an aluminum hull. Looks in pretty bad condition but can be bought cheap."

The bartender set his drink in front of him, and Jerry paused to sip it. Sam waited for him to continue; his interest piqued.

"Some Rastas were living on her for a couple of months, smoking their bongs and howling at the moon or whatever they do," Jerry went on. "U.S. Customs ran 'em off and impounded the boat. They put her up for sale, but no one's expressed any interest. They approached me about towing her out to deep water and scuttling her. They offered to pay me a thousand dollars for the trouble. That's why I know she can be bought cheap. I'm guessing a thousand dollars together with a promise to get it out of the harbor in a reasonable number of days would probably buy a fellow a damn yacht."

"A sinking yacht's not worth a thousand bucks." Sam drained the rest of his Bloody Mary. More people had come into the restaurant, and he figured there were too many ears around with a thousand dollars. He looked at the harbormaster and nodded toward the door. "Let's take a walk."

Outside on the dock, Sam tossed his duffel bag into Jerry's Boston Whaler tied up by the gas pumps, and they motored across the harbor to have a look at this mysterious boat. Her tall mast could be seen above the mangrove trees when one knew where to look. Jerry said he didn't have time to go aboard her now, but they could see plenty from the water. With the little Whaler's engine at idle, they circled. The ketch's long graceful hull and tall masts had once been painted white. The teak decking looked in need of repair and a good cleaning. All the paint was chipped and flaking but the hull seemed solid. Several places had rust stains from the corroded steel fittings. Saltwater and the fierce tropical sun had done a lot of damage over the years when no one cared.

"Check out her bow." Jerry pointed toward the front of the boat.

Sam saw dark streaks trailing down the white hull from two rusting anchors. They looked like tears. *The old girl's been weeping*. As they continued circling, Sam studied her rounded stern and two raked back spars. The main and mizzen sails were roller-furled, but outside rather than inside the masts. He had never seen anything like it. Whoever built her had done so with a lot of thought and even more money. He glanced back at Jerry at the wheel. "How old did you say she was?"

"I didn't," Jerry answered. "To my knowledge, there's no documentation on her, but my friend at Customs thinks she was designed by Bill Therry and built at the Palmer Johnson yard sometime in the sixties. She's one of the first ever constructed with roller furling sails outside the spars like that. Those were pretty new ideas back then."

Jerry slowed the throttle, and they drifted along the ketch's starboard side. "The Customs office said she was sailed up from South America, Rio or Caracas, someplace like that, and spent some time over in Jamaica. Evidently the Rastas lived aboard her down in Kingston for a while before setting sail on a mission to spread ganja and Bob Marley. They made it this far, then something broke. It's been parked on this mooring ever since. That's not much history to help you with your decision, but hey, man." Jerry grinned broadly. "It's only a thousand dollars."

As they passed the stern, Sam looked up. Someone in her recent history had given her a name. It wasn't even centered. *CRUSIN CANNABIS* looked like it had been painted on by a ganja believer with black paint, a bad brush, and an unsteady hand.

"It's almost noon now, and I've got to get back to the office," Jerry said. "Tomorrow's Monday. Let's come back out in the morning with my friend from Customs and go aboard for a better look."

"Why are you doing this, Jerry?" Sam's gaze was still locked on the big ketch as they drifted around her.

"Hell, I don't know." Jerry turned the Boston Whaler away and eased the throttle forward. "Guess maybe I can do a double good deed here." He reached over and slapped Sam on the back. "I can get an abandoned boat out of the harbor and a homeless person off the street." Jerry laughed, but Sam didn't.

As they motored toward the marina, Sam's thoughts stayed with *Crusin Cannabis*. The old girl looked like she'd been born to better things, and like him, had lived a hard life.

During the years that he'd worked around ships and harbors, he'd often thought about buying a boat. But something much smaller, maybe a thirty-footer made of fiberglass that didn't make many demands. An eighty-four-foot ketch was a damn yacht and a lot of responsibility. On the other hand, Jerry was right. He was homeless and jobless and didn't know of any thirty-foot boats that could be bought for only a thousand dollars.

Sam tossed his gear up onto the pier while Jerry tied the Whaler to a dock cleat. "Call 'em in the morning and make the appointment," he said. "I'll be here by eleven." He reached back to shake the harbormaster's hand. "And Jerry, I really appreciate your help. Who knows, maybe one day I'll operate the classiest charter yacht in the Caribbean."

Jerry let go of Sam's hand. "You have a license for that?"

"As a matter of fact, I do," Sam said. "My last company sponsored me to get a Masters License in case something happened to the ship's captain. They paid for the course and even gave me a small cash bonus."

"Well, if you decide to do it," Jerry said. "I can help scrounge parts for you. I'm a sucker for old dogs, old boats, and the homeless on hard times. I'll meet you here in the morning." He untied from the cleat and looked up as Sam walked away. "And don't forget to bring your checkbook."

# CHAPTER 2

Anna Neeson opened her eyes and stared up at the ceiling. A sigh of relief escaped her lips when she saw the familiar wicker fan blades stirring air over her bed. Somehow, she had made it safely back to her own bedroom after another booze-filled night on the town. She extended an arm and felt about the bed, making sure she had come home alone. Finding only downy covers, she grasped a handful, rolled herself up in the bedding and lay staring out the window.

The wooded hillside in the distance beyond her curtains was still a velvet green with a few special maples already turning to a pulsating red and yellow. It was the first week of September. In less than thirty days, the whole of New England would look ablaze. Anna closed her eyes and tried to remember where she had been the previous night. And more important, with whom?

She vaguely recalled cocktails with her friend, Louise Banks, at the Hyatt in downtown Boston. She had known Louise since high school, and they had much in common. One major difference was that Louise's husband was waiting for her at home in Brookline. Anna's husband died a long time ago.

The boyish handsome face of the previous night's graduate student flashed through her memory like a strobe light. She took a deep breath and held it a moment until the numb feeling of regret passed. She couldn't remember his name, but he'd claimed to be twenty-five. She wanted to believe it since it made him older than her son, Ian, even if only by three years.

"Mrs. Neeson." The Irish housekeeper's clipped voice came through the bedroom door. "Your father-in-law is waiting breakfast for you in the dining room. He said he has to leave early for a meeting in Providence."

"Okay." Anna groaned through her pounding temples. "Okay, okay, okay...."

She pushed the covers away and sat up. She rubbed her eyes and shook loose her red shoulder-length hair. The taste in her mouth made her frown.

Twenty -two years had passed since she moved into her father-in-law's white colonial mansion on the outskirts of Cambridge. The same day the government notified her of Daniel's accidental death in a downed fighter jet while training in Florida. She was just eighteen and seven months pregnant.

Anna traced the stitched outline of a flower on her bed comforter and wondered where the years had gone. She had just passed her fortieth birthday, but in many ways still felt like the naive Irish Catholic girl from South Boston. She had met Daniel at a dockside bar right after he graduated from flight school. She had borrowed her sister's ID to get in. He was home on leave and celebrating with some friends. She never expected to meet, much less fall in love with, a handsome Boston Brahmin like Daniel Neeson.

She closed her eyes and saw his laughing eyes shaded by the polished brim of his navy officer's hat. He had taken her breath away, and later that night in his hotel room by the harbor, he took something else. A whirlwind courtship, too fast for her widowed mother's approval, and a grand wedding provided by Daniel's father in one of Boston's great cathedrals convinced her that fairy tales did indeed come true. But the day the navy commander arrived at her door in his spotless white uniform and nervously read the letter expressing the president's regrets, her life went on hold. Sometimes it seemed like a hundred years ago, but most times, it seemed like yesterday.

Ian, her son, had grown up during those years she remained stuck in limbo. Next May, nine months from now, like his father and his grandfather before him, he would graduate from Cornell University with a degree in engineering.

Remembering her father-in-law was waiting, Anna pushed up off the bed and took a robe from the closet. She stopped at her vanity and opened an aspirin bottle. Finding only the cotton stuffing, she cursed under her breath. In the bathroom, she rummaged through the medicine chest with no luck, then turned on the shower. While waiting for the water to get hot, she let her robe drop to the tile floor and carefully inspected her body in the mirror for any souvenirs from the night before. Turning this way and that, she was relieved to find no bruises, no telltale marks. Everything looked trim and proper and in its place. She also noticed her summer tan had begun to fade.

Almost a month had passed since she and Ian vacationed at the family's summer place on Martha's Vineyard before he went back to college for his senior year. Their time together had been strained. Something was troubling him. He had long, hushed phone conversations with his grandfather but refused to discuss it with her. When he drove away a week ago for his last year at Cornell, he had seemed angry.

Anna fingered a freckle on her left breast and made a mental note to see if Louise would go with her to the vineyard for a couple days of refresher rays. They could visit the nude beach for one last all-over dose of sun. Her father-in-law wouldn't like it, but then he never approved of anything she did.

She had always thought she would one day leave Turloch Neeson's house to make a new life for herself and her son. As the years passed, there had been opportunities—young men courted, bedded, and said they loved her. But her capacity for new love had been numbed by regret, despair, and too many vodka martinis. Her wealthy father-in-law's stone and clapboard castle provided comfort and security. It had become too easy to depend on him even if she despised his efforts to control her. After Daniel was killed, her father-in-law took on the responsibility for making her and Ian's lives worry-free. For all these years Turloch Neeson had single-mindedly devoted himself to the task.

A second-generation Irishman, Turloch had built one of the

more successful highway-contracting companies in the northeastern United States. After his wife died giving birth to their only child, he never remarried. Daniel had planned to return to Boston to work in his father's firm when he got out of the navy. Now her son, Ian, stood next in line.

After Ian's birth, her father-in-law had charted his grandson's life the same way he engineered his bridges and turnpikes—with mathematical precision, detailed blueprints, and absolutes. Deviations were not allowed, which was the source of considerable conflict between Anna and him. She looked every day for little ways to rebel. To fight against the maddening control exercised over her and her son. At the same time, it had become the opiate that kept her there.

The salve for such slow asphyxiation had usually been a bottle of iced vodka, a handsome young man, and a hotel room with expensive linens. All of which had been too easily available over the years. Now her depression had become a dark chasm, sucking all hope into blackness. She had often thought about restarting her life. Perhaps having a career of some sort. Maybe even attending college. There had always been plenty of time. There was always tomorrow. But tomorrow came and too soon turned into yesterday.

After her morning shower, Anna wrapped a fresh bath towel around herself, padded barefoot into her dressing room and rummaged through a drawer for a pair of panties. She lifted a nylon slip and uncovered a bottle she didn't remember hiding. It was half full.

"Mrs. Neeson, are you all right?" The maid's voice came through the locked bedroom door. "Your breakfast is waiting in the dining room. I could—"

"I'll be down soon. Please let me get dressed in peace."

"Yes, mum."

Anna unscrewed the cap and sniffed at the vodka bottle. The pounding in her head rang in her ears like an iron hammer against an anvil. *What was that boy's name last night?* His cologne was "Polo" by Ralph Lauren, and he had reminded her so much of Daniel, even if it was only for a few hours. She raised the bottle to her lips, and the familiar liquid stung her throat. She closed her eyes and swallowed. Someday she would not have to dress in the dark in a strange man's bedroom and race home to beat the sunrise and her father-in-law's spying maid. One day she would live in her own place and maybe find a nice young man who would love her. *Like Daniel loved me.*

When she came downstairs and entered the sunlit dining room, she saw the maid clearing away the breakfast dishes. Her father-in-law's chair sat empty at the end of the long mahogany table.

"Mr. Neeson left for his meeting." The maid didn't look at her as she continued picking up dishes. "He said to remind you about your doctor's appointment this afternoon. He wanted you to tell the doctor about—"

"Thank you," Anna said. "But I know what to tell my own doctor. Please get me an aspirin and a glass of orange juice. I've got a splitting headache."

She picked up a stack of mail from beside her plate and thumbed through it while the maid disappeared into the kitchen. A smile creased her face when she recognized Ian's handwriting on one of the envelopes. He had promised to call when he got back to school, but it had been over a week and she hadn't heard from him. Her son had never given her cause to worry. He had probably talked to his grandfather, and the old fart failed to mention it. On purpose, too, she thought. Just to torment me.

Setting the rest of the mail aside, she opened the letter. The aspirin and glass of juice on the table in front of her went ignored.

*Dear Mom,*

*I know this isn't what you wanted to hear, but. . . .*

# CHAPTER 3

The taxi let Sam out in front of Maria Zavalla's pink stucco house in the Condado Beach area of San Juan. Captain Zavalla made good money moving tankers around the world for the oil companies, and Sam figured the captain spent most of it keeping his hot little wife happy. Flowering plants and green shrubs grew lush around the well-trimmed yard, and water tinkling in a fountain somewhere in the courtyard could be heard over the high wall. The heavy wood front door swung open as soon as Sam pressed the bell. A slender attractive woman with long dark hair and honey brown skin returned his stare. She smiled. He smiled back.

A light breeze lifted her gauzy transparent wrap. He could see she wore a tiny string bikini underneath; that and the sheer loose shift, black heeled sandals, and expensive jewelry.

"Is Maria here?" Sam almost choked on the words. He held his hand over his mouth and cleared his throat. "I'm Sam Berrenger. I think she's expecting me."

The woman said nothing but stepped back and motioned him to enter. He dropped his bag on the floor in the foyer and followed her down the hall. Long toned legs ran all the way up to her heart-shaped rear, and her heels clicked a samba across terracotta tiles. He figured this must be the visiting sister that Donny said accompanied Maria to the marina bar last night.

She led him into a sunlit courtyard full of flowering hibiscus and stopped at a towel-draped lounge chair. An open book lay face down on the small table next to the chair. She turned to him, slowly moistened her lips with the tip of her tongue and smiled. "Maria's busy in her room right now, but you can wait out here with me if you would like while I get some sun." Her long fingers untied the flimsy sash, and her gauzy cover floated to the ground. Stepping out of her heeled sandals, she donned a pair of Ray-Bans and lay on her back in the sun. A mirthful smile lingered on her lips. Manicured fingers toyed with the book beside her. He could tell she was enjoying her little tease.

Sam pulled a lounge chair over and sat facing her. He stepped out of his Topsiders and pulled his T-shirt over his head. Two can play this little game he thought to himself. He wondered how far she wanted it to go. Besides, what did she mean Maria was "busy in her room?"

Her accent had also made him curious. She didn't have one. At least not like her sister. Maria talked like the girls in *West Side Story*. This woman, lying in front of him without a hint of modesty, reminded him a lot of the actress, Rita Moreno—petite frame and toned dancer's legs. He figured she was in her late thirties. Clues included the sway of her breasts, the hint of sun lines around her eyes and glossed lips, and the trace of tendons in her brown hands and feet.

He wondered what she thought of the jagged scar on his left arm. Dark glasses hid any sign of her thoughts.

Her smile widened. Was she pleased or amused?

He thought he was in good shape even though he had passed his fortieth birthday two years before. Lots of manual labor including plenty of lifting and hauling, not to forget fighting, had kept him hard and lean. More like a swimmer or long-distance runner than the muscled Hulk Hogan or Arnold the Terminator.

"Well, well, well." Maria's voice made them both jump. "I see you 'ave met. Fine, I don' 'ave time, anyhow. Sammy, make my seester 'appy. She dumped her ass'ole 'usband in New York." Maria wore a bikini, strappy high heels, and jangling jewelry. His gaze followed her as she crossed the patio back toward her bedroom. A figure greeted her and closed the double French doors behind them. For a moment, he thought he'd seen the Hulkster.

"Personal trainer off a cruise ship," Maria's sister said. "I think she'll be tied up for the rest of the day. I'm Evelyn. My sister has told me a lot about you."

"Sam Berrenger." He pushed up from the lounge chair, stood over her and held out his hand, palm up. "How 'bout we go inside, Evelyn, and have a couple of stiff rum and cokes? I'd like to get better acquainted."

Sam woke the next morning with the sun in his eyes, the big white sailing ketch in his dreams, and a hand between his legs. He glanced down and saw it was his own.

The bed shifted as Evelyn pressed her bottom against the small of his back.

He lifted the covers trying to keep from disturbing her and stepped out to go to the bathroom. On the way back, he saw his bag in the foyer. He found the laundry room and put his dirty clothes in the washer. Evelyn was awake and waiting for him when he went back to bed.

"Good morning," she said, laying her head on his chest. She sighed and stretched out beside him. "You were just what I needed. Maria knew what she was doing when she called for the cavalry."

"What do you mean, 'needed?'" He kissed her bare shoulder.

"Oh Sam, you don't know it, but this was a big risk for me. I've never been with anyone other than my husband. I needed to find out what it was like. I'm glad you came along yesterday. Maria worried about me." Evelyn reached up and brushed hair away from his eyes. She smiled. "So, big boy, what are our plans for the rest of the weekend?"

# CHAPTER 4

"Jerry Diaz, this is Evelyn Lerner," Sam said. "She's Maria Zavalla's sister. Mind if she goes out with us?"

The harbormaster held the Boston Whaler close to the dock. "My pleasure." He nodded at Evelyn. "Watch your step coming down. The harbor's a little choppy this morning."

Evelyn removed her sandals and held on to Jerry's hand as she stepped into the rocking boat. She sat on the seat and gathered her skirt around her bare legs while Sam untied the painter and followed her aboard. The little skiff plowed through the water toward the mangrove trees on the far side. Once again, Sam could pick out the unusual raked-back masts across the way.

"Ralph from the customs office should be on board waiting," Jerry said over the outboard motor. "He's bringing papers with him in case you decide to buy."

They tied up next to a gray inflatable secured to the boarding platform at the stern. Ralph Martinez was waiting for them in the cockpit, smoking a cigar and sipping a cup of coffee.

"Good morning, Geraldo." The custom agent smiled behind a thick mustache and waved as they stepped onto the deck. Introductions were made and his eyes twinkled when he shook Evelyn's hand.

"Please, take all the time you want to look around," he said. "I have nothing more important to do today than sell this boat."

Evelyn followed Sam to the bow to survey the ketch's condition while Jerry stayed back on the stern, chatting with Ralph. When the harbormaster later joined them, the first page on Sam's clipboard was already full of notes.

"Nothing major up here yet," Sam said, handing Jerry the list. "Needs a ton of elbow grease, some new cotter pins, a few gallons of Naval Jelly to arrest the rust, a lot of new marine paint, and major sail repair. One of the most difficult jobs will be breaking the windlass down and getting it to crank again, at least manually if not with the electric motor. It's crusted with salt and frozen solid. Ten men couldn't handle all the chain and those heavy anchors by hand. The windlass has got to work."

Jerry studied Sam's notes a moment then passed them back. "Ralph says the steering is broken somewhere between the wheel and rudder which is why the Rastas couldn't leave after they got here." He paused while Sam scribbled another note. "Could be something major, or just a severed cable."

"What does Ralph say about the engine and electronics?" Sam asked as they both started back toward the cockpit.

"The engine runs," Jerry answered. "Probably needs fresh diesel and some TLC, perhaps even an overhaul, but it turns over. The batteries hold a charge, but you'll want to replace them at some point. All the navigational electronics are a rusted mess. The wheel compass is in good condition, but you'll need a new knot meter, a wind speed indicator, and a depth meter. There's no radar, SSB or Sat Nav aboard, nor a working VHF radio. I've an extra one stored away somewhere in my garage you can have. You'll need it just to get out of the harbor."

They sat in sun in the open cockpit and surveyed the stern area. Sam continued making notes. The outside storage compartments held rusted tools and parts, decayed life preservers, and other corroded, unrecognizable objects. The lines, sheets, and extra halyards hanging in the line locker were mildewed and stiff. He had made four pages of notes, and they still hadn't gone below. He gazed at the long list and shook his head. "I don't know. Maybe it's too much."

Sam put the pad down and looked at Evelyn. Her eyes were hidden behind her ever-present dark glasses. Her glossed lips parted, showing him a line of white teeth. He was thinking about how those teeth had felt nibbling on his body when she drew one brown leg up under her, flashing him a bare thigh and something else. He swallowed. She must've shaved this morning. Evelyn laughed and pushed her skirt down between her knees. Sam wondered if Ralph or Jerry had noticed.

"Hope you have more paper to take notes on when you go below." Ralph's mustache fluttered when he talked. "Looks pretty bad down there, but a lot of soap, metal polish, and about six coats of varnish on the wood will make a big difference. As will new cushion upholstery. There's some water leakage around the ports, but silicon caulk and new rubber gaskets should fix that."

After going down the steps, Sam left Evelyn at the salon table, thumbing through an old *People* magazine while he and Jerry poked around in the dark engine room. Ralph remained on deck, smoking another cigar. The engine and batteries seemed to be in reasonable working condition. The 16-kilowatt Onan generator was burned out, but Sam had rebuilt several such generators when he crewed on freighters. He was pleased to see plenty of standup and walk around space in the engine room. The Customs Department had brought out a portable generator on a weekly basis to keep a charge in the batteries to run the bilge pump. The bilge looked surprisingly dry, indicating minimal leakage at the stuffing box where the prop shaft passed through the hull.

Old magazines littered the floor in the main salon, along with empty juice cartons, bottles, and other live-aboard trash. The spacious cabins received good light through side ports and deck hatches, and fresh air circulated below from two large dorade funnels on deck. The salon table on the starboard side sat ten people. Across from that to port were two stuffed armchairs with a small table between them. Underneath the debris covering the floor, the teak sole needed a good sanding and new varnish.

The layout was basically traditional for a yacht this big. An ample but dated galley forward of the main salon had a small crew dinette for four. To the right of the steps, the navigation station preceded a passageway leading back past the engine room to the owner's stateroom. Sam found two more staterooms forward of the main salon and galley with private heads and two smaller crew quarters. He counted twelve sail bags in the sail locker. Three of the bags were empty. Probably for the main, mizzen, and foresail that are furled up top, he thought. He made a mental note to do a full sail inventory and inspection later. In the bow, the chain locker held several hundred feet of rust covered anchor chain.

Headed back into the main salon, he again wondered where the old girl had been. What her story might be. There were more than a bunch of dreadlocked Rastas in her past. The stories she could probably tell if she could talk.

Sam sat at the dinette table in the galley to write more notes. She was a lot of boat for a thousand dollars—maybe too much. He also didn't have the money to return her to mint condition. The few thousand bucks he had in a money market account in Miami was supposed to be for his old age. Now that he was out of work, his only source of funds was the thousand dollars he received every month from the oil company. The eight hundred dollars in his pocket needed to last three weeks until his next check arrived. A hand-to-mouth existence.

And what about the freedom that'd always been so important to him? If he bought her, he couldn't just pick up and walk away. *This big boat will be my responsibility. I might as well have a kid.*

On the other hand, he didn't own a pot to pee in. And the few thousand dollars in the bank wouldn't provide anyone much of a retirement. Maybe it was time he did something different. It'd take a lot of work, but maybe that was her destiny. Maybe it was his destiny. The idea of owning a real charter business in the Caribbean made him smile. He needed to talk to Jerry.

Sam found him at the bow, wiping sweat from his face with a folded white handkerchief. A nearby mangrove tree was alive with seabirds. Hundreds of 'em were fluttering from branch to branch and chattering at one another.

"Damn, its hot this afternoon and not much of a breeze," Jerry said as Sam approached. He stuffed the handkerchief in his pocket.

"Well, what do you think, Cap'n? Is this old boat gonna be a new home for you, or one for the fishes?"

"What do you see as the priority items, Jerry?" Sam wanted to see if the harbormaster's list was shorter than his.

"First, you don't have a lot of time to work on her here in the harbor," Jerry said. "They want you out right away. Ralph's supervisor said to give you three days."

"Three days?" Sam shook his head. "What can I get done in three days? It's impossible and—"

"No, it isn't. Here's what we do. We only need to get her moving under engine and her sails. The rest of the stuff can wait till you get to where you're going to do the work." Jerry paused a moment. "Maybe you should take it over to Saint Sebastian. The island's only forty miles away, less than a day's sail, and there's plenty of inexpensive skilled labor. It has an independent government, not part of the American nor British Virgin Islands, but it's close enough for easy access to the prime charter areas. The island also has a minimum of bureaucratic bullshit."

Sam knew a few things about Saint Sebastian. It was a pretty little island with a fresh water supply that the Virgin Islands didn't have, which made the people less anxious and more friendly. Its history, like the Virgins, was tied to sugar, slavery, and pirates. The island's few beaches and restrictive laws against outside speculators kept out the chain resort hotels and made the island a boating paradise.

"My list has gotten too long," Sam said, showing Jerry the pages. "I'm not sure what to do first."

"Pay the man and sign the papers, Sammy. That's what you do first. For all you know, someone else is back at Ralph's office, waiting to buy her. You can always take it out to sea later and sink it. That's always an option. And if you decide to do that at some point, I'll tow it out for free."

Sam stood with Evelyn and Jerry at the stern rail watching Ralph Martinez motor toward the marina with signed papers and Sam's check in his briefcase. Ralph had surprised them by giving him four days instead of three to vacate the harbor or pay a six hundred-dollar per day fine. Today being Monday, Sam had until five o'clock Friday afternoon to get out of town.

"First thing to repair is the steering," Jerry said, turning away from watching Ralph. "There's plenty of good cable in one of the storage hatches, and I have more ashore if you need it. Second, you should drain the diesel tanks and put in fresh. That's your first expense right there, about sixty dollars for thirty gallons of diesel. Do most of the work out here on the mooring to get her running and I'll let you tie up at the marina dock on Thursday to take on fresh water and fuel."

Sam lapsed into silence as they departed the ketch in Jerry's Boston Whaler and motored toward the marina. Evelyn sat on the seat across from him. She seemed to understand his silence and reached for his hand. "Congratulations. It's a new life for you," she said. "A terrific opportunity for a fresh start, even though the risks look immense. I know because I felt the same way when I left my husband in New York this week. The first day is scary, the second day is better, the third day I met you."

Sam looked at her and smiled at her pep talk.

"Look, I have an idea," she said. "I'll help you while I'm here."

"What?" Sam cocked his head.

"I know this is crazy," she said. "But I have two weeks before I have to go back to New York. My sister has her own plans, anyway. Why don't I help you get the boat in shape here in San Juan and sail it with you to Saint Sebastian on Friday?"

Sam started to say something but stopped when she pulled his hand up under her skirt. *Damn! How can I say no?*

# CHAPTER 5

Jerry Diaz was right about the steering problem being a broken cable. On Tuesday morning, Sam discovered it had frayed and jammed on a pulley underneath the wheel housing. He spent the rest of the morning installing new cable while Evelyn filled plastic garbage bags with trash from the galley and salon below and stacked them on deck. After lunch, they found a canvas awning stowed in the sail locker and positioned it over the cockpit to provide protection from the broiling sun. Knowing it would be hot, sweaty work that day, they had both worn the minimum for safety and comfort. Him, a pair of Nike running shorts, and her, the thong bottom to a bikini.

Sam spent most of the afternoon on his knees at the bow dismantling the frozen windlass. After removing the crusted salt, and greasing all the moving parts, it could be operated manually to raise the anchors, but rebuilding the electric motor would have to wait till they got to Saint Sebastian. It might even need replacing. After reassembling the windlass, he stretched out in the shaded cockpit for a short break. He could hear Evelyn down in the galley, Lysoling the cabinetry.

He hadn't slept much the night before. It had begun to weigh on him that he was now responsible for an eighty-four-foot sailing yacht. *Christ, how serious could I be about this if I haven't even named her yet?* Jerry and Evelyn agreed with him that CRUSIN CANNABIS was not a proper moniker for a classy Caribbean charter yacht.

Over dinner, he and Evelyn had made a list of possible names, debated each, but couldn't agree on a single-one. Wind Walker,

Sun Dancer, North Star, Bright Star, Orion, were on Evelyn's list and were all good names, but they also graced the stern of a hundred other boats plying Caribbean waters. Sam had argued that his boat needed a special name, a name befitting a thousand-dollar yacht. His own list had included Slammin' Sammy, Skip & Go Naked, Wet Dream, and a few others that Evelyn thought sounded like happy-hour drinks at a nudist resort. After dinner, they gave up making lists and had gone back to her sister's house. Sam figured he would know the right name when it came along. He felt no urgency to name her.

Perhaps it reflected his ambivalence. Putting a name on something implied commitment. It hadn't escaped him that it would be far easier to scuttle a boat named CRUSIN CANNABIS, or easier yet, one with no name at all.

After dropping he and Evelyn off at the boat that morning, Jerry had said he'd come by later to check on how they were doing. He also knew where Sam could pick up a cheap dinghy and outboard motor. He said he'd look into it and let him know.

As the afternoon waned, Sam met with Evelyn in the cockpit and worked together on shortening the long list of projects. He was finding it harder to keep focused on the task at hand. Watching her go barefoot, topless, and almost bare bottomed about the boat made his lips curl back over his teeth. It was going to be a lot harder to get work done with her around, but it would certainly be more fun.

Evelyn went below and returned with a cold beer and a towel to wipe his face. His upper body glistened with perspiration. They rested for a moment in the shade of the awning, enjoying a light breeze off the harbor. Evelyn sat opposite him with her bare feet in his lap and crossed at the ankle. Her toenails were painted a pink coral color. Sam put his beer down and started massaging the taut muscle in her arch. She closed her eyes. He leaned forward and she tilted her head for a kiss. He ran his tongue wetly over her lips. "Oh, Baby," he whispered hoarsely.

"We'll never get your old boat ready this way."

"Slave driver."

"Horny bastard."

By six o'clock he had drained the fuel tanks and had put in fresh diesel from two five-gallon cans they had brought out with them. Jerry's portable generator had given the batteries enough charge to turn the starter and fire the engine. The old motor burped, then ran, and water gushed out the exhaust hole on the stern. Sam was relieved to see the saltwater cooling pump working. The engine would run even smoother and cooler after a good tune-up. Cleaning the fuel injectors and replacing filters would also make her more reliable. Right now, the big Ford Lehman engine popped along, making Sam feel more secure about his thousand-dollar investment.

He left the engine running and went below to check out more of the systems. The motor heated fresh water in the hot water tank, and the alternator was charging the batteries. Charged batteries meant cabin lighting and running lights, plus a working auto-bilge pump and the ability to reliably start the engine. He decided right then to buy his own portable generator for emergency backup.

Several pulleys on the engine block were missing belts. Sam figured they were for refrigeration and freezer systems as well as other to-be-discovered capabilities that existed when the boat was new, and her owner had money. A new refrigeration system would cost thousands. His needs were simple. A solid non-leaking hull, a reliable engine, and charged batteries were all he required right now. Beer and other things that needed to be kept cold could be stored in a picnic cooler. Ice could be bought on shore at any marina.

Just before the sun dropped behind the mangroves, Jerry tied his Boston Whaler to the boarding platform and came up the ladder. Sam sat in the cockpit enjoying a beer and feeling smug at having accomplished so much on the first day. With an operating engine and steering system, the boat had new life. She could now move under her own power in any direction.

Jerry grinned when he saw Sam. "So Cap'n, got her runnin', 'ave ye?" The engine exhaust blew a steady stream of diesel fumes and water out the stern hole.

Sam pushed himself up to a sitting position. "Hey Evelyn," he called down the companionway into the shadows of the main salon. "We're done for the day. Come up and bring some beers from the cooler. Jerry's here and he's thirsty."

The portly harbormaster found a seat and wiped a handkerchief across his face. "It was a hot one today. This cockpit canopy was a good find. I worried about you two getting heat exhaustion."

Evelyn appeared on the stairs, balancing three cold ones on a tray. "Refreshments, anyone?" She had put on the top to her bathing suit and wrapped a sarong around her waist. Sam noticed not a hair was out of place. Fresh lip-gloss and a chipper attitude also didn't reflect the fact that she'd spent the better part of a sweltering day scrubbing on her hands and knees.

"You're a lucky man, my friend." Jerry paused to take a swig of his beer. "A running engine and batteries that hold a charge. Either could've cost you a bundle."

"And that steering problem could've been worse," Sam replied. Evelyn placed the tray on the cockpit table and sat next to him.

"Yeah, I'm glad it was a cable steering system and not hydraulic," Sam continued. "I used up a whole can of WD40 just on all the pulleys. Two of 'em will eventually need to be replaced, but the helm turns easily now. No binding like before. I'll dive under tomorrow to check the bottom and make sure the rudder moves with the wheel."

"Also looks like the bottom needs several coats of antifouling paint," Jerry said, lifting his beer bottle towards his mouth. "There's enough growth on the bottom to qualify you for a farm subsidy." He grinned at his own joke and took another long swig.

"I'll go in the water to scrape some of the hull each day before we leave on Friday. That'll get it cleaned up enough to sail over to Saint Sebastian," Sam said. He finished his beer and set the empty bottle on the cockpit table. "I don't want to spend money hauling her out now just for a bottom job. In a few weeks, I'll have a long list of things to do when we take her out of the water at Saint Sebastian."

Evelyn loaded up the tray with everyone's empties and carried them below.

"And what's with you two, Sammy?" Jerry winked at him. "Never figured you for a one-woman man, even though she's built like Aphrodite. How long she staying?"

"Evelyn's a good hand on the boat." Sam shrugged. "But she says she's going back to New York in two weeks, and I believe her."

Jerry shook his head. "Too damn bad. I motored by here this morning on my way over to Tobias' boatyard and saw her on deck moving those garbage bags around. I wasn't paying attention to where I was going and almost decapitated myself on another boat's anchor line." They were both laughing when Evelyn came back up with three more cold Heinekens.

That evening at Maria's house, Sam stepped out of the shower and went into the bedroom, toweling himself dry. Evelyn sat at the dressing table; her long hair pulled over one shoulder as she brushed it. He leaned down and kissed her exposed neck. She tasted fresh and the scent of bath oil filled his nostrils. "I'm all clean now," he breathed huskily into her ear.

She laughed and turned on the bench to face him.

He lifted her up in his arms and carried her to the bed. When he stretched out beside her, she turned onto her stomach and smiled at him. He trailed his fingers over her shoulder and down her back.

"So, why did you shave?" he asked in a throaty whisper. "You do that for me?"

Evelyn blinked and stared at him a moment. "No, Butthead." She laughed. "I did it for me." She then leaned up on one elbow. "You're a wonderful lover, Sam, a fun fling on a girl's Caribbean vacation, but that's all it can ever be." Another long moment passed before she continued, "Just think of me as some sailor in a faraway port. My ship leaves in two weeks and I'll be on it. In the meantime, you and I can have a lot of fun," she said. "We can even help each other out and—"

"What do you mean, 'help each other out?'" he interrupted.

"I mean I can help you get your boat to Saint Sebastian," Evelyn answered. "So, you can remake her into a wonderful charter yacht. And during that time, you can help me to feel like a new woman again. And that's all I want to say about that right now."

"Why won't you stay longer than two weeks?" He pushed himself up on one elbow. "Why the big rush to go back to New York?"

She leaned over and kissed him on the end of his sun-burned nose. "Sam, I've got two children at home and a big house in Forest Hills. It's a life I'm committed to and one that scares you to death. I can't stay here with you even if I wanted to. Besides, you can't support me. That takes a large alimony which I currently have, or a rich husband which you aren't. My monthly electric bill alone would make you ill."

Another long moment passed while they lay gazing into each other's eyes. Her fingertips rubbed lightly over his chest.

"So, okay," he said hoarsely. "I'll take what I can get."

The next morning Maria had vodka and orange juice, coffee and toast ready for them in the sun-filled courtyard before they left to spend the day at the boat.

"Hold the orange juice and pour me a double," Sam said, sitting next to Evelyn. The sweet scent of flowers from the surrounding gardens brightened the morning.

"So, Sammy." Maria smiled, handing him a small glass of straight vodka. "You and Evelyn 'aving fun?" She took a sip of her coffee and set the cup back on the glass topped table. The three of them wore white terry cloth robes that stopped at the knee. The words *Carnival Cruise Line* were embroidered on the upper left side. Maria sat across from him with her legs crossed, her robe partially open. Her toenails were painted a bright red. She extended her foot and pinched his bare leg with her toes.

"Ouch!" He pushed her away and rubbed the spot on his calf. "That hurt."

"Sammy likes it to hurt sometime. Don' you Sammy?" Maria lifted an eyebrow at him.

"Finish your breakfast, Sam," Evelyn huffed. She set her coffee cup down and stood. "We've got a lot to do today. Did anyone ever tell you that you drink too much?"

"Right on both counts, babe." Sam drained his glass and picked up a slice of buttered toast. He playfully pinched Maria's nose and followed Evelyn inside to get dressed.

When they met minutes later at Maria's car, Evelyn had on a pair of tan baggy shorts, leather sandals, and a yellow T-shirt with *SAIL NAKED* printed on the front. Sam assumed it belonged to Maria, as did the thong swimsuits Evelyn brought with her each day to the boat.

At the marina they met Jerry in his air-conditioned office. "Glad you're here. Let's go look at that inflatable dinghy I told you about yesterday." He stood up from his desk and stubbed out a cigarette. "She needs a few patches, but like I said, you can probably buy it cheap."

Fifteen minutes later, they were staring at a gray Zodiac lying upside down and limp on the end of the dock.

"Looks like a big condom the Jolly Green Giant used and tossed," Jerry said, laughing. "There's a small rip on that pontoon." He pointed to the right side. "And a couple more on the other one. The owner said his son took it out snorkeling over a coral reef a few days ago and it got away from him in some rough water. I think the owner is just looking for an excuse to buy a new dinghy to go with his new cabin cruiser."

"How much does he want?" Sam asked. "I've got a limited budget and—"

"Two hundred for the Zodiac, and another hundred will get you the nine-horse Johnson outboard that comes with it."

"Three hundred bucks for a leaking dinghy to support a thousand-dollar sinking yacht?" Sam shook his head, thinking this couldn't get any crazier.

By noon, he had cold patched all the visible leaks on the inflatable, and it had held air for over an hour. "Tight as a drum, see." He thumped the two pontoons to show Evelyn. The dinghy lay on the pier, its wooden flooring panels in place, keeping it rigid. The beat-up looking outboard was beside it, the shaft and propeller pitted from years of salt-water corrosion. The plastic motor casing also looked severely dinged, like it had been attacked by an angry chimp with an ice pick. Jerry had said the dinghy once drifted up under the dock and pounded the motor housing against the barnacles for a week before the owner found it. The old Johnson motor looked like hell, but after it had been installed on the Zodiac's transom and the gasoline tank hooked up, she started with one pull. That was good news to Sam. A dependable dinghy motor was almost as important as a reliable diesel engine in the boat. Some would say more important.

Jerry stopped by the dock before lunch to see how they were doing, and Sam took the three of them on a spin around the harbor in the new *old* dinghy. At full throttle and with everyone leaning forward, the twelve-foot inflatable gathered enough speed to plane over the surface. Waves slapped at its bottom as it skimmed across the water. Afterwards, he dropped Jerry back at the marina before motoring over to Tobias' boatyard to browse through the chandlery.

"I need at least one of everything in here," he said to Evelyn when she dropped a bottle of bilge cleaner into her basket. "Too bad you're not a rich old bitch that'll buy me everything I want in exchange for great sex."

She rolled her eyes and shook her head.

They stopped by a grocery store and picked up ice for the cooler, a case of beer, a bottle of rum for Sam and a couple of turkey sandwiches and chips for lunch. With a loaded dinghy, Sam carefully steered them across the harbor toward the big ketch. Passing by the stern, Evelyn wrinkled her nose like she smelled something unpleasant.

"What?" Sam asked.

"That name," she replied. "CRUSIN CANNABIS. It has to go. Even if you don't have a replacement for it, yet. At least paint over it. I'll get some white paint and do it this afternoon. Maybe you'll get more interested in choosing a name if your boat has a blank stern."

Sam spent the rest of the day under the awning with the big mainsail spread across the deck and his lap, making repairs with the new sail repair kit picked up at the chandlery. He'd unfurled all three of the primary sails and checked for condition. They were probably original with the boat but had been kept covered and away from the tropical sun. The main was the only one needing serious attention. After lunch, Evelyn maneuvered the dinghy around to the stern and stood on tiptoe, brushing a coat of white paint over the crudely written scrawl. When she showed it to Sam, he thought the old lady seemed to perk up a bit without the humiliating name blemishing her transom. The big ketch was now ready for a new name to go along with her new chance at life. Unfortunately, he still hadn't decided on one.

Late that afternoon, he and Evelyn waited in air-conditioned comfort in the marina bar for Maria to pick them up. They were enjoying a cold beer while Donny washed a sink full of bar glasses and bragged about his new girlfriend. She was a seventeen-year-old Puerto Rican girl who he claimed looked at least twenty-five. Sam glanced into the mirror behind the bar and saw Jerry coming toward them.

"Thought I'd find you guys in here. Come out to the dock. Got something to show you." He sounded as excited as a five-year-old about to pee his pants. Evelyn and Sam picked up their beers and followed him outside.

"This is your lucky day," Jerry said, rubbing his hands together. "I got you some good stuff over at the coast guard station where they'd just cleaned out an old navy landing craft. My buddies let me pick through the scrap pile and take anything I wanted. It was a damn gold mine."

Jerry's Boston Whaler sat low in the water piled high with a heavy cargo of nylon lines, bumpers, life preservers, dinghy anchors, and three hundred feet of galvanized anchor chain. The booty also included several boxes of cleaners, sponges, mops and brushes, and a case of red anti-fouling bottom paint.

"I always liked a white hull with a bright red bottom," Jerry said, holding up a can of the coast guard issue paint. "And look what else we have here." He pulled the flaps back on a large box revealing an assortment of galley supplies; pots and pans, lids, skillets, strainers, mashers, cleavers, spatulas, knives, and enough dinnerware to feed the crew of a battle frigate.

"Scrounging was my specialty when I was in the coast guard," he bragged as he opened another box revealing bright-yellow, foul-weather slickers. "Can you believe they were about to trash all this?"

Sam took a yellow slicker Jerry handed him and examined it. "They didn't happen to have a new eighty-four-foot sailing ketch they were about to throw away, did they?" He winked at Evelyn. "I'd sure like to find one to replace the old one I got now."

Jerry took back the slicker and stuffed it in the box. "There's enough parts here to almost build one," he said. "Dang it, man, this haul will save you thousands of dollars. Just the braided dock lines would cost you a thousand dollars to buy new. You can use these tomorrow when you tie up here at the marina."

Jerry was right, Sam thought to himself. He couldn't afford even half this stuff.

On Thursday morning, Maria drove him and Evelyn to the boat to lend a hand on their last full day in San Juan. Sam knew he would need another hand aboard when they dropped the mooring line that afternoon and motored over to tie up at the marina dock.

Maria stopped at a traffic light and turned the rear-view mirror to put on her lipstick. Sam sat with her in front, reviewing his things-to-do list while Evelyn read a romance novel in the back seat.

"I'd sail over to Saint Sebastian with you guys," Maria said, putting the cap back on her lipstick, "but the cruise ship returns to San Juan tomorrow night. Dennis es planning something beeg for me."

Still focused on her reflection in the mirror, She moistened her red lips with her tongue and quickly ran a finger over her bottom lip. The light changed, and several horns sounded before she flipped them her middle finger and drove on toward the harbor. Sam saw Evelyn had put her book down and was gazing out the window. He wondered if she was thinking the same thing--like what was the "beeg" treat Dennis had for Maria.

He expected Maria to be more of a hindrance than help, but she surprised him. After going on board, the two women took pails of water, sponges, and Pine Sol to clean below while he stayed on deck, measuring and cutting new dock lines from the large roll of nylon rope Jerry got for him. When he finished coiling the new lines, he laid them on deck by their respective cleats and went down to join the girls.

He poured himself a glass of rum and leaned on the galley counter to watch the two sisters scrubbing the floor on their hands and knees. The teak floor and walls sparkled.

"You girls have this place looking pretty good," he said. "Take a break and I'll treat you to cold beers on top."

Up in the cockpit they rested in the shade of the canopy, enjoying the fresh breeze that somehow found its way into the mangroves. Evelyn and Maria both wore short shorts and white T-shirts without bras. Maria's breasts rested high on her rib cage. Evelyn's swung full and free. They were eighteen months apart in age, but unlike Evelyn, Maria had not borne children.

"Oh Sammy, don' stare." Maria stuck out her chest at him in defiance.

"You love it." He laughed. "You all want great boobs and if you have 'em, you like others to see 'em. It's a known fact. . .even the parson's wife."

"Who? Who es thees parson's wife?" Maria glanced at Evelyn with a puzzled look on her face. "And 'ow you know she got beeg titties?"

"A figure of speech." Evelyn sighed. "Just one of his figures of speech."

"Oh, Sam's so smart." Maria wrinkled her nose at him. "He always says smart things."

"Yeah, I'm so damn smart," Sam said, shaking his head, "I've got a big yacht here that needs more money than God has just to fix her up so she can start deteriorating in the sun and saltwater again. I'm really damn smart."

"Well, I'm smart, too." Maria giggled and took a sip of her beer. "I'm smart enough to 'ave a 'usband who geevs me goot home, and cars, and credeet cards, and jewelry, and—"

"And the freedom to bed every guy that picks up your scent." Evelyn didn't look like she'd meant it in fun.

"Oh? And you are Mees Virgeen Mary?" Maria's eyes flashed. She said something in Spanish which Sam didn't understand, then she got up and went down the steps to the salon, leaving them alone in the cockpit.

"Sorry about that." Evelyn shrugged. "You know how sisters get jealous over the smallest things."

Sam looked hurt. "I hope that's just one of your *figures of speech*."

# CHAPTER 6

The five o'clock ferry carrying tourists had just left the harbor when Sam steered the ketch to its temporary berthing spot at Jerry's marina. The harbormaster stood on the pier and took the line Evelyn tossed him from the bow. On the stern, Maria threw another line to an assisting hand that almost missed it. Sam put the transmission in reverse, slowing their approach, then shifted to neutral when the rubber side fenders eased against the concrete dock.

Jerry and the dockhand took the lines and guided the boat forward on the pier and secured the lines to dock posts. Sam supervised the positioning of more bumpers between the hull and dock and set up two spring lines to keep her in place regardless of current or wind shifts. He then plugged in the shore power cord and was somewhat surprised to see they had electricity onboard.

A few curious people came over to inspect the boat. Most had heard about the mysterious ketch moored out in the harbor, but few had seen it.

"Jeez," a kid on the pier said to a friend. "That old tub's an accident looking for a place to happen."

"Yeah and you should've seen her a few days ago," Jerry said, removing the boy's baseball cap and mussing his hair. "Sam here and his crack team have cleaned her up good."

"I'd like to see her crack," the teenager smirked when Maria stepped off the boat onto the pier. Sam laughed when he saw her stick out her tongue at the two boys then seductively swing her hips as she sashayed down the dock.

Sam and Jerry filled the diesel tanks from the fuel pumps and flushed the freshwater tanks with a mixture of Clorox and water. They then put six-hundred gallons of fresh water on board which took some time with the small garden hose provided by the marina. He would work on getting the water maker working when they got over to Saint Sebastian. Word had gotten around that the strange ketch was tied up at the marina and a small crowd gathered to watch.

"Brasso will polish the scratches out of those Plexiglas ports and hatches," a male voice said.

"Yeah, and if you pour straight laundry bleach in the heads," someone advised, "don't leave it too long cause it'll ruin the rubber gaskets and connections." Everyone had advice on how to solve a problem.

"What's her name?" An elderly gentleman dressed in a white linen suit and smoking a slender cigar watched Sam holding the hose to the starboard water tank. "What is the name of your vessel?" he asked again.

"I'm sorry," Sam said, stepping to the lifelines. "Didn't realize you were talking to me." He took off his baseball cap and brushed his hair back. "Don't know her real name. When I bought her, she had CRUSIN CANNABIS painted on the stern, but I doubt that was ever her documented name."

"Cruzin' what?" The old man had a concerned look on his face. "No, I don't believe that's right," he said. "Don Antonio Melga never owned a yacht named Cruzin Cannybust." The old fellow scratched his chin and looked thoughtful. "No, no, one never forgets a yacht like this," he went on. "Don Antonio owned only the best, whether it was horses, yachts, or women. You knew him?" The old man looked at Sam like he should have but didn't give him a chance to answer. "No, no, Don Antonio was a proud man." He shook his head. "Too bad what happened to him, but what can you expect when you mix mistresses and blood family. Don Antonio knew better. He was a man of considerable experience. Someone told me the family sold Firebird after he was killed in Rio. Killed by his bastard son." The old man touched his forehead as if remembering something. "Firebird?

Yes, that's it. Firebird. I knew Don Antonio didn't name his beautiful yacht, Cruzan. . .whatever."

Sam started to say something, but the old man turned and made his way down the dock.

"Hey!" Evelyn's head shot up through the companionway. "Turn the hose off. Water is overflowing in the sink down here."

"Crap, I forgot," Sam said, pulling the hose out of the input and doubling it to pinch the flow. "Hey, Jerry! Turn off the water," he called toward the dock office. "The tanks are full."

Before it got dark, two of Jerry's dock boys wired portable flood lights up on the mast spreaders to light the deck for a farewell celebration party. When the floods were turned on, Sam thought his boat looked rather festive--if one would look beyond the rust, grime, and peeling paint. Maria brought a boom box and her collection of Salsa and Reggae tapes. Donny and the manager at the marina bar provided an iced keg.

By ten o'clock, the alcohol and pounding music had the small crowd dancing on the deck. Maria zeroed in on Donny who had left his new girlfriend brooding alone in the cockpit. Sam still wore his yellow running shorts. Evelyn and Maria were also in the same shorts and bathing suit tops they had brought to work on the boat that morning.

Sam felt Evelyn's hand on his bare back.

"Hi," she said, her fingers trailing down to the waistband of his shorts. "Can I get you a cracker with some of that Brie that Jerry's wife brought?" Her hand slipped further down and cupped a cheek. "I just love your hard, little butt," she whispered, and leaned forward to kiss his shoulder.

Sam looked down at her and smiled. "Are we going to initiate those new sheets you and Maria put on the bed today in the captain's cabin?"

"We could've if Maria and Donny hadn't beaten us to it." She grinned.

"Oh, no. Not Maria and Donny?" Sam looked incredulous. "Already? No wonder his little girlfriend has been watching him all doe-eyed."

After a while, Evelyn and Sam sneaked below to take a break from the revelry. They hadn't had a chance to talk much about their departure the next day, and he could tell she felt somewhat anxious. Going away on a sinking boat with a guy that walked into her life only four days before, sounded pretty risky to him.

At the bottom of the steps, he put his arms around her. "I'm glad we came down here," he said, looking into her eyes. "I'm not used to being sober at parties like this."

She raised up on her toes to kiss him and ran her hand through his hair. "Me too," she said. "Glad we came down, that is. And also, glad you're sober."

Evelyn went into the galley and put a pot of coffee on using shore power while Sam sat at the dinette table. "See," he continued, "The responsibility is already getting to me. Our sail to Saint Sebastian tomorrow has me all nervous. I worry that I'll do something stupid and we'll sink at sea or something worse."

"I'm glad you're worried." She took cups out of the cabinet. "I want my captain sober and worrying at least as much as I am."

She poured their coffee and sat across from him. "I took a peek at your list on the navigation table. It looks like the only things we have to do in the morning are replace the two propane tanks for the galley stove, pick up Jerry's VHF radio, and buy groceries."

"That's about it," Sam said, and sipped his coffee. It tasted like hazelnut. "We won't buy too much since Saint Sebastian has excellent markets. I heard a new Pueblo Supermarket opened near the harbor to serve charter boats. We'll put on a lot of ice for the trip. There's also one major spot on the hull left to scrape clean."

"God, this is exciting." Evelyn put her hand under the table and squeezed his leg. "It's like we're setting sail on a great voyage to an unknown place. Kind of like Jason and the Argo." She scooted around beside him on the settee and ran her hand over his chest. "How long will it take to get there?"

Sam wrapped her in his arms and licked the side of her throat under her ear. "Six hours if the wind holds steady," he said in a husky voice. "It's a voyage, but not a great one. We'll leave by eleven in the morning so we can arrive in Drake Town Harbor before dark. Jerry reserved us a mooring, but it's an unfamiliar harbor to me. I don't want to be groping around there after dark."

Maria and Donny came down to say goodnight. Donny had been following Maria around all evening like a lovesick teenager. His girlfriend had already left.

"I'll drop by in the morning to see you two off." Maria kissed Sam on his cheek and then hugged her sister. "Call me if there's anything you want me to bring."

"Thanks for all your help," Sam said and meant it. He winked at Evelyn as they watched Maria act exasperated as she pulled Donny's hand out of the back of her shorts.

Going up the companionway to the deck, Donny leaned forward and bit Maria's butt cheek. She squealed, whirled around on the steps and kissed him. Sam wondered how she planned to get him out of her bedroom before her cruise ship friend showed up on the weekend.

The party shut down at midnight. Evelyn readied for bed while Sam went up to unplug the floodlights and check the fenders and docking lines. Jerry Diaz and Ralph Martinez from the customs office were standing on the dock smoking cigars and looking over the boat. Ralph took the cigar out of his mouth when he saw Sam. "You decided on a name yet?"

"Still thinking about it," Sam answered. He pulled the electrical plug, dousing the floodlights. The moon hung low over the sea out past the breakwater. Just below it, he could see the red and green flashing buoy lights, marking the entrance to the harbor. "What about Firebird?" he asked.

"Firebird?" Jerry said. "Firebird," he said it again out loud. "Don't know of any other boats named Firebird. Kind of original."

"Still thinking about it," Sam said. He stood by the mast feeling the cool breeze blowing off the harbor. "I'm not settled on the name. Maybe something else will come up when we get to Saint Sebastian."

"Well then," Jerry said. "If we need to raise you on the radio after you leave tomorrow, we'll call you by your last name. Keep your radio on channel sixteen and listen for Berrenger."

"Now, there's a good boat name," Ralph said, taking a big draw on his cigar. "Berrenger. Sounds like derringer. You know, the little one-shot pistol?"

"Yeah, I'm not too keen on Berrenger." Sam scratched his bare chest with one hand and chuckled. "It's not much of a name for me, much less a classy charter yacht."

"See you in the morning, Sammy," Jerry said as he and Ralph turned and strolled down the dock. The red glow of their cigars marked their way in the dark.

# CHAPTER 7

Friday morning came too early. A rain squall had passed through just before dawn and everything below deck was soaking wet. Numerous ports and deck hatches needed re-sealing. Evelyn mopped up with towels while Sam worked at the navigation station, installing the used VHF radio that Jerry had given him. It wasn't anything special, but it was free. It had seventy-two channels and its distance was only line-of-sight, but at least they could monitor channel sixteen for emergencies at sea and not feel totally isolated. A Single-Side Band radio had to wait till he was making money in the charter business.

By mid-morning the remaining storm clouds blew away, and Sam took a snorkel and mask into the water to finish scraping the hull. Visibility underwater was much better with the sun directly overhead. He surfaced often for air. Seventy feet of hull at the water line and a keel drawing seven feet was a lot of bottom. He had scraped most of it while out on the mooring but had left a large area around the knot meter impeller on the port side. Leather gloves protected his hands from the razor-sharp barnacles.

As he pushed a wide blade putty knife down the hull, barnacles, green algae, and other hull-adhering creatures peeled away and slowly drifted down to the bottom of the harbor. When he surfaced for the last time, it was kind of clean. But without a fresh coat of bottom paint, he knew it would soon be covered again.

Sam dropped his mask and snorkel into the deck locker just as Evelyn arrived at the boat pushing a cart loaded with grocery bags. They were busy stowing the provisions away in the galley when the harbormaster knocked at the companionway. “Sammy, your propane tanks are here. I had ’em tested and filled.”

Evelyn continued putting things away below while Sam went up top to help. The two propane tanks were stored in individual sealed lockers at the stern with a vent in the bottom of the locker leading out the transom. An electric solenoid, controlled by a switch in the galley, opened and closed the tank. One tank was hooked up to the system, while the other provided backup. The separate sealed and ventilated lockers were an important safety factor. Propane tanks aboard a boat were like carrying bombs on board. The gas is heavier than air, and if a leak occurred inside the boat, the propane would settle down in the bilge where an electrical spark from either the engine or the bilge pump could ignite it. Most leaks were apt to occur in the tank locker which is why it had its own vent opening to the outside of the hull.

Sam would’ve preferred a less dangerous alcohol stove, but the boat’s original owner designed it to use propane. If she’d survived all those years with the abuse she’d had, then he’d give her the benefit of the doubt. Besides, a classy charter yacht needed more than a simple alcohol stove to provide gourmet meals to its guests. And he planned on serving his charter clients the best food in the Caribbean.

After hooking up one of the tanks, he and Jerry went below to test it. Sam flicked the solenoid switch over the galley sink and a red indicator light came on. He lit a match and turned the dial for the right-front burner on the range. Blue flame flared.

“Hey, we do good work.” He grinned at Evelyn.

Jerry then checked for line leaks by following the copper tubing from the galley back through the boat to the tank lockers.

“Nothing, nada,” he said when he returned to the main salon. “You might check it again after you reach Saint Sebastian.”

Sam flipped off the solenoid switch and watched the flame go out. He waited a moment, then turned the burner on again and lit another match. Nothing. No flame, no gas. “Good,” he said. “The solenoids are working. Now we can cook dinner and not have to exist on tuna fish and chips. By the way, what's for lunch? All this talk about food's made me hungry."

"Tuna fish and chips." Evelyn smiled. "But let's wait till we get under way. It's already eleven."

Sam took a quick shower at the marina to rinse off the salt from his morning dive and prepared to set sail. Showers aboard were not possible until he installed a new water pump. They could get water at the sinks in the galley and in the heads by using the hand pumps, but the flow was only sufficient for small jobs like shaving and washing dishes. Jerry had picked up two new electric water pumps from his coast guard friends, but like a lot of other things, installation would have to wait till they were at Saint Sebastian. One of the pumps was for the freshwater tanks and the other would pump seawater for outside showers and washing down the deck and anchors. It could also be used for fighting fires on-board should the need arise.

At exactly eleven thirty, they fired up the engine, pulled in the dock lines and motored away from the marina toward the mouth of San Juan Harbor. Jerry and a few friends from the bar stood on the pier waving goodbye. No one had seen Maria and Donny all morning. Sam wasn't surprised.

He steered at the helm while Evelyn rolled up the dock lines, took in the fenders and stored them away in the deck lockers. Before setting the sails, he wanted to remain under power for at least an hour to get the cobwebs out of the engine and put a good charge in the batteries. The sky had grown overcast again and a strong breeze blew from the southeast at twenty-knots. It would be a hard six-hour close reach to Saint Sebastian, so he wasn't in a hurry to turn off the motor and get the sails up. They would get in plenty of sailing before reaching Drake Town.

After passing the breakwater, he turned directly into a sea of rolling swells. The big boat plowed through them like a linebacker leading interference. Evelyn waved at him from the bow and he saw she, too, had a big grin on her face. He knew it pleased her that she'd been the one to talk him into buying this large boat. He doubted he'd have taken such a big step if she hadn't encouraged him. For a brief moment, he thought of Darlene and imagined her up in the bow. . .with the wind in her face. . .her long hair whipping around her eyes. . .waiting for him to come up and join her.

# CHAPTER 8

Sam kept the boat under engine power for two hours before he throttled back, turned the helm over to Evelyn and prepared to unfurl the sails. The sea had a slight side roll pushed along by the trade winds. Putting up the sails would steady the boat and make their passage more comfortable.

He loosened the mainsheet to take stress off the boom and began unfurling the mainsail. "Keep her pointing into the wind," he called back to Evelyn. "Yeah! That's it!" He waved a hand as the sail rolled out and flopped about on the boom. "Hold it right there!" After cranking the mainsail all the way out on its track, he winched in the sheet to tighten the big sail and take out the luff. The boat heeled and picked up speed.

The mizzen sail jammed halfway out. He fiddled with it a bit before leaving it to be fixed in Saint Sebastian. Enough sail was out to provide adequate helm.

"Fall off the wind till she's on a beam reach," he said, looking over at her.

She turned the wheel, watching him for approval. He released the foresail furling line and the big genoa caught the wind and rolled out with a thunderous boom. His muscles ached as he cranked it in on a port tack. In less than five minutes, he had all the sails pulling and the big yacht crashing through the waves toward their destination.

Evelyn smiled when he rejoined her in the cockpit. "You steer," she said, leaving the helm to him. "I'll put on a swimsuit. I want to lie in the sun and take a nap."

"Why bother wearing anything out here?" he asked as he

stepped behind the wheel. "I was thinking about dropping my shorts and letting the breeze tickle my fancy." He turned his baseball cap backwards on his head and flashed her a goofy grin.

"Because we're getting way too familiar," she said, blowing him a kiss before disappearing down the companionway.

Sam stared a few moments at the empty hatchway then turned his attention to driving the boat. He gripped the helm with both hands and felt the power of the sea flowing through the stainless-steel wheel. The morning clouds had given way to an afternoon sun that promised fair weather the rest of the way. From his position at the helm, he took a few minutes to study the sails and rigging to ensure nothing had busted loose. Everything looked in order. He smiled to himself as he thought about his new position in life, *yacht owner and charter boat captain*. She might not be the prettiest sailing craft in the Caribbean, but he had plans.

His attention was drawn away from the wind indicator at the top of the mast when Evelyn reappeared on deck wearing only the bottom to a white thong bikini. She had penned her long hair on top of her head. A few loose strands caressed her bare shoulders. His gaze followed as she made her way forward and spread a towel on deck in front of the mast. Sam rubbed his hand over his bare chest and smiled. A seaworthy boat, blue water, fair winds, a lovely semi-naked wench on the bow, and so far, it had only cost him a thousand dollars.

Four hours later, Sam fired up the diesel engine and furled the sails before beginning their approach into Drake Town Harbor on Saint Sebastian. It was just after five in the afternoon, and the sun had already gone behind the lone mountain that dominated the middle of the island. This side of the island was now bathed in shade even though there was still two hours of daylight remaining.

The trip over had been quicker than he'd expected, and Sam felt both lucky and relieved that nothing on the boat had broken. The mizzen sail furled back against the spar with no problems, but he still needed to find what caused it to jam.

A red buoy, marking the entrance to the channel, slid past to starboard. Sam looked around the harbor and saw two large marinas inside the breakwater, one on each side, like bookends. Twenty or so boats were scattered about on moorings in the open water between them. It was one of those moorings that Jerry Diaz had reserved for him when he called in a favor from an old coast guard acquaintance who had connections at the Virgin Cay Marina in Drake Town.

Sam appreciated Jerry's help and the good deal he had negotiated for him. The marina manager at the Virgin Cay had said he could use the mooring for free as long as he purchased all his supplies from the marina owned chandlery. Sam figured he owed Jerry for that one along with everything else he had done for him.

"Number twenty-nine!" Sam called to Evelyn standing ready at the bow with the boat hook. She had put on baggy shorts and a T-shirt.

"Twenty-nine," Sam said again. "The number is in red paint on the side of the mooring ball."

"There, near that blue boat." Evelyn pointed to port. Sam saw it, too. He turned the bow toward the mooring ball, shifted the transmission into neutral, letting the heavy boat drift toward it. After two attempts with the boat hook, Evelyn snagged the mooring line and lifted it up on deck. Sam went forward to help guide the line through the starboard chock and secure the looped end on the bow cleat. "Teamwork," he said, smiling at her. "We make a good team."

The heavy yacht drifted forward until the mooring line went taut, and the bow turned, eventually pointing out into the gentle trades. Sam went back to the cockpit to kill the engine. There was a loud popping sound when the big diesel stopped, and he saw a cloud of black oily smoke belch out of the exhaust. He hoped it was something simple like the points needed cleaning or a gasket needed replacing. Just then Evelyn stepped into the cockpit carrying two cold beers.

"Nice job, Captain." She handed him one. "This trip was almost too easy." Their green Heineken bottles clinked in mid-air.

"A good captain makes things look easy," Sam replied with a smug grin and lifted the bottle to his mouth for a long swig.

They tidied up the boat, put the dinghy in the water, and went ashore for something to eat and a hot shower at the marina. Since it was just after Labor Day there were only a few people around the dock and restaurant. Even though it was off season, the marina was nearly full of boats as it was home to a large number of yachts awaiting the arrival of their absentee owners who summered in Europe or in the states.

After showers and burgers, they returned to the boat and sat together in the cockpit enjoying a glass of wine and the quiet evening. As Sam gazed out at the dark mountain, the harbor town's twinkling lights blended seamlessly into the night sky. He spotted a shooting star and closed his eyes to make a wish.

"Were you ever married?" Evelyn had moved to sit across from him and put her bare feet in his lap.

He opened his eyes. "Yeah, once. Why?"

"I don't know," she said, taking a sip of her wine. "Just wondered."

Another moment of silence passed.

"It was a long time ago," he continued, massaging her arch with his free hand. "She died in a car wreck."

"Oh, I'm sorry," Evelyn said softly. "It must have been terrible for you."

"You get over it," he lied.

"And you never remarried?"

Sam swigged down the rest of his wine, put the empty glass on the cockpit table and began rubbing her feet with both hands. "Nah, never did. What kind of life could I give anyone? I haven't spent two months in the same place in the past twenty years."

He was glad she didn't ask him why. He didn't really know himself. After Darlene was killed, it just seemed like the thing to do. He should've known she couldn't wait on him. She was too young, just a kid, too scared to be left alone.

He blamed himself. Instead of six months away at National Guard training, he could've gone AWOL and run away to Canada like she wanted—even begged him to do. His old man would've gotten over it. . .sooner or later.

Evelyn moved back next to him, and he slipped an arm around her shoulder. She kissed him on the cheek. "I'm tired," she said. "Let's go to bed. We've had a big day." She opened her mouth and kissed him. Her tongue probed deep. "God, you are one sexy man," she whispered.

# CHAPTER 9

Sam woke late the next morning. He slipped out of bed without disturbing Evelyn and stepped naked into the head to splash water on his face and brush his teeth. After making a pot of coffee, he wrapped a towel around his waist and went up on deck to inspect the mooring line. Everything seemed to be in order. The twenty or so other boats in the harbor were all drifting aimlessly on their lines, waiting for the morning trades to pick up and put them in their place.

He leaned his elbows on the bow pulpit and watched the sun brighten the new day in a warm glow. A noise startled him, and he turned to see an attractive girl perched naked on the deckhouse of a boat anchored near them. She was brushing her long-wet hair. Sam figured she had just finished a shower and came out on deck to dry.

She waved. Sam lifted his coffee cup toward her and wondered if it was in bad taste to gawk. Content to do just that, he then saw a young man step out of the deckhouse and join her. He was rubbing a towel over his shaggy, sun-bleached hair, making his wiggly parts waggle. The girl said something to him, and he looked over at Sam and waved the towel. There was something primal about the young couple in their casual nakedness. He waved back at them and went below to see if Evelyn was awake.

"They're flying a Tri-color, the French flag." He buttered his toast while she sat opposite him at the salon table with her morning coffee. "I've heard this island attracts a lot of the European sailing crowd. The government doesn't hassle you. Jerry told me almost anything can go on here as long as it isn't noisy or hurtful to the resident population. It's all very British."

"Sounds very continental," she said, drawing her knees up to her chin and cradling her coffee cup in both hands. "Maria said there are some great nude beaches here."

"She'd know." Sam grinned. "We'll check 'em out in our free time. But first we'll need to make some progress on my long list of projects."

"Remember you have my help only till next Friday," Evelyn replied. "Six more days are all the time I can take off." She got up from the table and took the coffee pot from the galley stove. "My kids' sitter is expecting me back in New York a week from yesterday. So, what's on your list for today?" Evelyn poured them both a refill and went to put their dishes in the sink.

"The Customs and Immigration Office on the island is open till noon on Saturdays. We should clear the boat in so we're legal. Afterward, we can check out the town, buy some more groceries at the market, and restock our ice supply. This afternoon I want to try installing the new water pump for the fresh-water tanks. Being able to take showers on board will make life a little easier."

"Eeek!" Evelyn slammed a cabinet door and stepped backward into the main salon. "There's a cockroach in there as big as a Buick." She squeezed her eyes shut and shivered. "God, those things give me the creeps. I've seen them around ever since we came on this boat, and I've already used up three cans of bug spray. The big ones seem to like the damn stuff."

"Don't pay 'em any attention." Sam frowned. "They really don't bother me as long as they stay out of my bed. I can't tolerate bugs in my bed."

"Well, Buster." Evelyn looked serious. "Get rid of these filthy insects if you want me in your bed. There's not enough room here for me and cockroaches. It's either me or them."

"Boric acid, young man." The plump woman watched him studying the directions on a can of bug spray. He and Evelyn were in the Pueblo Supermarket in town.

"Boric acid. It's the only thing that works. Put some into jar lids, add a little flour and place them around in your cabinets and under the sinks. In a few days they'll all be dead. Been using it on our boat for years. Here, take this." The woman handed him a box of boric acid, took the can of Raid out of his hand, and returned it to the shelf.

"Yep, the little buggers eat that stuff like I eat fudge, then they go hide and die. The acid breaks down their hard, little shells to dust. No muss, no fuss, and no roaches." She nodded her head up and down.

"Thanks, ma'am." Sam smiled at her. "I'll give this a try. It's sure better than gassing us on the boat with those sprays."

"And they don't come back." The lady continued nodding while he and Evelyn pushed their cart down the aisle toward the check-out stand.

After leaving the store they spent an hour in the Customs and Immigration Office filling out forms and getting their passports stamped. The island bureaucrats were polite but slow. "Definitely on island time," he whispered to Evelyn.

They left Immigration just as the office closed at noon. After motoring the dinghy back to the boat, Evelyn busied herself putting things away while Sam set out jar lids with the magic white powder guaranteed to rid their floating abode of all wildlife.

"I don't know about this," he said, closing the cabinet door underneath the galley sink. "The directions on the box don't say anything about killing cockroaches. You better hope it works."

"Oh no." Evelyn arched an eyebrow. "You better hope it works, because if I see another roach on this tub tomorrow, I'm taking the next plane back to San Juan."

"It'll work. It'll work," he said, laughing. "The lady promised it would work. Let's give it a chance."

He took Evelyn back ashore for a late lunch and then they went exploring the area. Drake Town was the capital of Saint Sebastian and a quaint little island town that spilled down the mountainside to the water's edge. Wood and stone shops painted brilliant blue, pink, and bright canary yellow, lined the narrow cobblestone main street that followed the water's edge around the harbor. The ground floor shops offered Caribbean spices, beach fashions, hand-painted T-shirts, camera supplies, and island crafts to the tourists. Mixed among the retail stores along the harbor was an assortment of restaurants, outdoor cafes, and ice cream parlors. Away from the water were hardware stores, appliance shops, and department stores catering to the island's eight thousand residents. A sign in the immigration office said the last census was completed in 1980.

On Saturdays, the islanders gathered in town to shop, exchange gossip, and attend the seventh day adventist church. Sam and Evelyn strolled through the open-air market adjacent to the cricket field and watched housewives picking through piles of Levi-Strauss blue jeans and baskets of plantain, papaya, coconuts, bananas, and unidentifiable tubers brought to market by the island's farmers.

The farmers' fields could be seen as little green quilt patches covering the mountainside above Drake Town. Most of the crowd at the market were of African descent, as were ninety-five percent of the island's citizens known as "Belongers." The few white people shopping in town in various degrees of sunburn, included Evelyn and himself.

"When you goin' ta name dot bote?" A large black man in dark blue trousers and a white dress shirt approached them on the street as they walked back to the marina. The tone of his voice told Sam the man's question was more official than curious.

"Hello, I'm Sam Berrenger." Sam held out his hand to the man.

The fellow looked at it a moment then shook it with no enthusiasm. Nodding toward the white ketch in the harbor, he said, "When you name dot bote?" He didn't take his eyes off Sam. "You gotta name dot bote or it cannot be recorded in my customs office."

The old boy looks positively constipated, Sam thought to himself. "I'm sorry about that. Didn't realize it was so important and—"

"All botes gotta have a name," the customs official said, shaking his head back and forth.

"Ah, yes. But can you give me a week?" Sam asked. "I just purchased it a few days ago in San Juan. I haven't settled on a name yet, but I'm close and—"

"You get a name damn quick and come to da office and put it on da form. A botes not a belonger's, gotta have a name."

"Yes sir." Sam nodded. "Just as soon as I settle on a proper name."

The customs man turned up the street. He was a large man with wide shoulders, a large middle, and a bigger butt. Sam thought the fellow's bureaucratic trousers were about to bust.

They found their inflatable tied up at the crowded dinghy dock, and Sam took Evelyn on a water tour of the harbor before heading back to the ketch.

The Virgin Cay Marina offered slippage to about sixty yachts ranging in size from thirty feet to well over a hundred feet in length. Most were sailboats, but Sam also counted a dozen large powerboats, including one mega yacht. Most of the vessels had European homeports painted on their sterns. There was a mix of English, German, French, and Greek yachts with several from Australia and New Zealand. At least a dozen from South American countries. Most of the boats with American registrations were berthed across the harbor at the Caribbean Haven Marina. The boats at Virgin Cay were privately owned while most of the hundred or so at the other marina were managed by U.S. charter companies. The clientele frequenting each of the marinas reflected this. In the bar at the Virgin Cay, one heard many foreign languages spoken. At the Caribbean Haven across the way, it was all American hot dogs, baseball, and apple pie.

Sam liked both places. Each had a swimming pool located next to an outdoor bar. The bar and pool at both marinas stayed busy even in the month of August with paid crews waiting for the tourist season to start. Someone had said that from January to May, during peak season, tourists were stacked five deep at the bars. Sam thought that was good news. Hopefully some of those people would want to charter an eighty-four-foot sailing yacht to get away from the crowd and explore all the little anchorages around Saint Sebastian and the nearby Virgin Islands.

It was late in the afternoon when he and Evelyn returned to the ketch. She went below to nap while Sam studied the fresh-water pump problem. The old motor mounted in the engine room next to the fresh-water tanks was bolted onto rubber pads that absorbed vibration when the pump came on. A mess of corroded wires went from the motor to the boat's batteries and rubber hoses connecting the pump to the tanks.

He unpacked the new water pump Jerry had given him and studied the connections. There were a few differences in size and layout, but the concept was the same. It was a demand system. Turning on a faucet or shower automatically decreased water pressure, and a drop of pressure in any tank started the pump.

The rusted nuts holding the old water pump needed to be soaked in WD40 before he could budge them. He set the old pump on the floor and saw he needed new bolts. The old ones were far too corroded and were also too short to fit the replacement motor. He glanced at his watch and saw it was after six o'clock. Being Saturday, the chandlery had closed at noon. It would be Monday before he could finish installing the new pump. That meant showers ashore at the marina for the next two days.

Sam went up on deck and found Evelyn in the cockpit with a glass of wine, watching boats return to the harbor after a day out sailing. Crews scurried about bringing down sails and setting fenders and docking lines. The sun had long dropped behind the mountain.

"It's a beautiful evening," she said.

Sam sat beside her. A loud splash near the stern signaled a pelican's face-first dive into the water for a mouthful of sprat.

"That seems hard on the poor bird," she said. They watched the gray pelican surface, swallow, blink a few times, and glide away just inches above the water.

"It is," Sam replied. "They eventually go blind from it and die of starvation."

"Oh, that's terrible! You're kidding me, aren't you?"

"Nope." He shook his head. "It's their life cycle. If it wasn't supposed to happen that way, then God would've made pelicans smart enough to shut their eyes when they dive. I always do."

Evelyn studied him a moment then laughed. "I don't believe you."

He shrugged. "Your choice."

"Can I take a shower on board this evening?" she asked, changing the subject. They watched another boat coming through the breakwater, furling its sails.

"Not on this boat," he finally answered. "It'll be Monday before the new pump is working. I need a longer bolt."

"Oh?" She turned back to him and rolled her eyes. "And I thought your bolt was plenty long."

He shrugged.

"I saw the cute couple you told me about on that boat over there." She pointed toward the sloop flying the French flag on its stern. "They waved to me when I came up on deck."

Sam looked but didn't see anyone.

"They must be French," she continued. "He was wearing one of those skimpy little bathing suits that French men seem to like, and she was topless. They both looked so sexy. I think French people are sexy, and I think you'd look good in one of those little bathing suits, Sam." She sounded serious. "Why don't you wear one like that instead of those baggy shorts you always wear?"

"My bolt's too long," he said.

"They looked like young lovers." She went on, ignoring his joke. "God, it's the stuff of romance novels. A boy and his girlfriend living together on a sailboat in the gorgeous Caribbean." Her voice tapered off.

On Sunday, they spent most of the day painting naval jelly on deck fittings to remove the accumulated rust. By four o'clock the stanchions and lifeline fittings were all done as were the bow and stern pulpits. The newly polished metal gleamed in the late afternoon sunlight. After a brief rest and a cold beer, Sam made a tour down below to survey the toilets and make a list of parts to purchase when the store opened the next morning.

As he'd suspected, most of the gaskets in the toilet pumping mechanisms had dried out. Water leaked into the bowls and foul odors seeped back up through the system. The boat had holding tanks and through-hull options, but he was only interested in the through-hull capability. In non-U.S. areas of the Caribbean it was still legal for a private boat to pass toilets directly into the sea, and he wasn't ready yet to get into the condition of the holding tanks. He'd deal with those later. Right now, he only wanted to get the toilets working and to keep the sea from backing up into the boat and sinking it.

The head in the forward crew compartment had a broken pump handle, and all the wooden toilet seats on the boat were cracked and needed replacing. The porcelain bowls were solid and in good condition, so most of the problems looked like they could be solved with a few new parts. Sam checked his list one more time before joining Evelyn in the cockpit. She had brought up their towels and was waiting for him.

"Let's take our showers before dinner," she said. "We've done enough for a Sunday. When we come back, I'll fix pasta and a salad."

"Good idea," Sam said, "but I want to run the engine while we're gone to charge the batteries." As he started below, he saw the young couple on the blue boat step out on their deck, toweling themselves after what must have been their afternoon showers. Evelyn waved to them as Sam went down the companionway to crank the engine.

# CHAPTER 10

Sam waited at the front door of the chandlery on Monday morning when the manager opened for business. Evelyn had gone to the laundry in the marina to wash their bedding and a load of clothes. Sam found the long-threaded bolts he needed and picked up three toilet repair kits containing an assortment of gaskets and rubber washers. The replacement toilet seats, and pump handles weren't stock items and had to be ordered. Walking back to the marina, he saw the man from the customs and immigration office standing on the road, talking with a taxi driver.

The customs official looked up and saw him. "Hey, mon. You named dot bote?"

Sam waved and acted like he didn't hear him. He felt the man's eyes on his back as he continued on through the marina gate. *Yeah, yeah, mon. I'm working on it.*

He spent the next hour bolting the new water pump to its base and adding extra rubber pads. Then he hooked up all the hoses and the battery wires. Everything looked right. He stepped into the galley and turned on the faucet at the sink. A faint hum could be heard from the engine room and water gushed into the sink. He turned it off and smiled at his success. The new pump continued to run a few more seconds to build pressure in the tanks before shutting off.

Sam went to each head, turning on the faucets in the sinks and checking the showers. Water flowed, the pump hummed, and he discovered he had more gaskets and rubber washers to buy. *Damn!* Water leaked at every pipe and hose intersection. The pump came on every few seconds to replace lost pressure. He shut the pump off at the main switch and headed back to the chandlery for more parts.

On the way, Evelyn met him on the dinghy dock with her bags of fresh laundry. "Can I take a shower on board now?" she asked. "The heat from the dryers made me sweat."

"Give me a half hour to replace the washers in the aft head, then you can shower back there," he said, shaking his head. "I fix one part on this damn boat only to find what it's connected to is broken. I'll get that aft shower working as soon as I return." He had already decided the toilets could wait another day.

The rest of the week went by quickly. True to the old lady's prediction, the cockroaches disappeared shortly after they put boric acid out around the boat. On Wednesday morning, the young French couple dropped their mooring line and left the harbor. Evelyn and Sam stood in the bow with their coffee mugs and watched them sail away. After breakfast, Evelyn spent the day cleaning on deck while he worked below in the engine room repairing pumps and other mechanical items. Things with Evelyn had become very comfortable, and he hoped she was thinking about staying. It wasn't all work and no play. The days were filled with sweaty projects to repair or slow the boat's rot, but the nights were a mix of soft, sweet canoodling and hard, mudwrestling, elbow throwing, mattress-pounding sex. She liked it either way. He did, too.

On Thursday morning, Evelyn seemed pensive as they sat in the main salon eating a breakfast of toast and jam. Neither wanted to speak about it being her last day in the islands.

"I think I'll get all those old sail bags out of the locker and check 'em," he said. "I'm not sure what I have in there. Probably a mildewed mess." He smiled at her and spread butter on a slice of whole wheat.

After breakfast, she stood at the sink in her bikini washing dishes when he kissed her bare neck. She leaned back into him, and he wrapped her in his arms.

"Don't leave tomorrow," he whispered. "Please stay." His lips touched the top of her brown shoulder, and his teeth grazed her skin.

She sighed. "I have to go home. My children need me. And God knows I miss them."

"I'll miss you." He breathed into her ear. Her neck arched, and he felt her tremble. She turned and pushed herself into him. Her wet mouth traveled over his throat and up to his jaw. He picked her up and carried her to his cabin where he dropped her on top of the unmade bed.

Afterwards, she dozed next to him while he stared at the cabin ceiling. He knew she couldn't stay, and it wasn't fair of him to ask. Also, he wasn't so sure he wanted her to stay. For over twenty years he'd had no one to worry about but himself, and this damn boat was now more than enough responsibility. There wasn't room in his life right now for a full-time woman. He'd been there before with Darlene, and he'd screwed that up.

After a late lunch, Evelyn busied herself in the aft cabin packing her things, while Sam lugged mildewed bags out onto deck and piled them in the sun. He started at the top of the stack inspecting the boat's sail inventory. Halfway down, he pulled out a large blue sail bag with *Firebird* stenciled on the side in white letters. He dragged the bag up beside the mast and opened it. Inside was a white nylon spinnaker. He tugged the sail out and unfurled it on deck. The figure of a ferocious eagle-like bird with spread wings was sewn in the center. Though faded nearly to pink, he could see it had once been bright red. Much of the stitching needed resewing. He turned over the bag and looked at the stenciling. The old man in San Juan wasn't senile after all, Sam thought. *Firebird, Firebird,* he said it to himself a few times. *Must've been her original name. Everyone knows its bad luck to change a boat's name without a good reason. I think I like it.*

There were five bags of sails in all. Most were foresails of different sizes and sailcloth weights. There was a small storm jib, a one hundred, and a one twenty-five. In addition to the big spinnaker there was a robin's-egg blue drifter for light air. All of the sails needed a good cleaning, and a few were in need of new stitching. The spinnaker looked the most interesting.

"It's a Phoenix, dummy." Evelyn had come up behind him. She knelt on the deck to smooth the material out for a better look. "A Phoenix, you know, the bird that sets itself on fire and rises out of its own ashes. I think it's Greek, or Aztec, or something like that. It could use some work." She pulled at a loose thread and unraveled an inch of seam.

Friday morning, he carried Evelyn's bags from the dinghy dock to the taxi in the marina parking lot. The sky was overcast and threatening rain. They had gone to bed early the night before after a wonderful dinner Evelyn had prepared on board. They went through the motions of making love, but it wasn't the same. Maybe they tried too hard or—maybe they didn't try hard enough. Afterward, they lay awake in each other's arms, waiting for the sun to come up.

The island cab driver took her bags and plunked them in the trunk. Evelyn waited by the rear door, her dark hair pulled back and her face with just a blush of makeup. The hem of her pink cotton sundress brushed the top of her tan legs. Sam stepped in front of her and looked down into her brown eyes, trying to think of something to say.

"Thanks for a wonderful two weeks," she said, beating him to it. "I'll never forget it."

"Me, too." He smiled. "Every time I see a thong bottom, I'll think of your cute brown butt."

"And I'll never see a cockroach and not think of you and your old boat." She laughed. A moment passed while they just looked at each other. The taxi driver got behind the wheel and slammed his door.

"Call me if you ever come to New York and get a job paying more than two hundred thousand a year." A flicker of a smile danced in her eyes, or was it a tear?

"You're the first one I'll contact when that happens," he replied. "And let me know when you're down here in the islands again looking for a good time."

"I'm sure Maria will know how to reach you," she teased.

"Just get to a VHF radio and call for the yacht, Firebird. All us charter captains monitor channel sixteen."

"Firebird?" she said, smiling. "I like it." She kissed him on the cheek then turned and got into the cab.

The driver crunched the gears and sped away leaving Sam in the middle of the street watching the taxi wind its way up the mountain road. When it disappeared over the crest toward the airport, he turned to go back into the marina and almost bumped into the fellow from the customs office.

"You named dot bote?" The man's large arms were crossed on his chest.

"Firebird," Sam said. "Yes sir. Firebird is her name."

"You come to da office today and write it on da form. Okay?"

"Okay." Sam nodded. "I'll be there."

A part of him felt relief that Evelyn had gone home. He'd miss her company, her help on the boat, and the great times they had. But he also knew her departure equaled his own narrow escape.

# CHAPTER 11

It started raining at noon and continued intermittently throughout the weekend. Water leaked into the boat from every porthole and hatch, and around the mast, which kept Sam busy emptying pots, mopping the floor, and wringing out towels. He made a list of the leaks and noted their location since he couldn't repair them until the rain stopped. The ports needed new silicone caulking around the outside housing, and new rubber gaskets inside where the glass dogged down. The main mast and mizzen mast required new weatherproof wrapping where the spars passed through the deck. Canvas sleeves around the base of the masts would also help a good deal. Leaks are an inescapable fact of life on a boat, but with a sunny day and more than a few tubes of silicone caulk, Sam knew he could substantially reduce the volume of water finding its way inside.

Depressed about the constant rain, he stayed aboard Friday night and got drunk on rum and coke. He didn't mean to drink so much, but he missed Evelyn. Late Saturday morning, he pulled on a yellow slicker and a pair of rubber boots and sloshed through puddles to the customs office in town to register Firebird's name with the island authorities. The Chief Customs Officer wasn't there. A pretty island girl wearing tennis whites greeted him cheerfully when he walked through the door. She provided the necessary forms and gave him instructions in clear and proper English on filling them out. He must have looked surprised at her lack of island patois.

"I graduated from LSU last year in Baton Rouge," she said, laughing. "Go Tigers."

After filling in all the blanks, he handed back the signed papers, thanked her and stepped outside into a face full of tire splash. He took two steps backwards on the sidewalk, wiped muddy water from his eyes and watched a black Jeep Cherokee with darkened windows speed through the town's narrow streets, hitting every pothole. A hundred yards down the road it braked to a stop in front of Pussers Pub. Four men got out, and looked back at him, laughing. The tall one, wearing white linen trousers and a white silk shirt open at the collar, pointed and said something. More laughter followed. One of the other men opened an umbrella and held it over the man dressed in white who then led them into the pub. For a moment Sam considered going down to Pussers and using his fists to teach those jokers some manners. But he didn't.

Charlie Taylor, the manager of the Virgin Cay Marina, was sitting behind the reception desk when Sam stopped by to check for messages. He was hoping Evelyn had called to say she had made it home and was missing him. There were no messages from Evelyn or anyone else.

Charlie had been living on the island for three years now and had been managing the marina for the past two. Someone said he had been a Wall Street trader who lost his shirt along with the fire in his belly after the '87 crash. A month-long stay at a friend's house at Smuggler's Cove on Saint Sebastian had evolved into a new life. His spouse had returned home to Saddle River, New Jersey without him. Sam thought Charlie seemed like a happy man.

"Hey, how's it hanging?" Charlie nodded when Sam walked in the door. Charlie was overweight and balding and hadn't yet hit his fortieth birthday. Wire rim glasses were pushed back on his widening forehead as he sorted through the morning's mail. Sam liked the guy. He thought Charlie ran the marina with an MBA efficiency.

"Here's something you might be interested in." Charlie tossed a brochure on the counter in front of him. "You should enter your boat in the charter show on Saint Thomas in November. An event like that can make or break your year." His glasses slipped down a bit and he pushed them back up with his middle finger. "A good show can guarantee bookings for the whole season. If you miss it, you'll be lucky to get enough business your first year to pay your fuel bill."

Sam picked up the pamphlet off the counter and thumbed through it. The show started November 13 in Charlotte Amalie at the Yacht Haven Marina near the cruise ship docks and went for four days. Reservations could be made by mailing in the enclosed coupon. The brochure's photos of some of the fancy boats in last year's show reminded him of Firebird's current sad condition. This being early September, the show was a little over two months away, and there was still much work left to be done. Maybe this is just what I need, he thought to himself. *A deadline.*

"Thanks, Charlie," he said, putting some change on the counter to pay for the local newspaper. "By the way, who is the rude dude that runs around town in a Jeep Cherokee with the gaggle of bodyguards? Someone ought to teach him some manners."

Charlie's face creased in a scowl. His eyeglasses slipped from his forehead to his nose. He pushed them back up again and looked at Sam. "You met the Haitian?"

"No formal introductions were made," Sam replied, "but he splashed the contents of a mud hole on me over on Main Street. He and his friends got out of their Jeep at Pussers and had a good laugh about it. An apology would've been more appropriate. I don't like getting splashed with dirty water, but I especially don't like being laughed at."

Charlie's face relaxed. "They're a bunch of assholes, Sam. I don't know their story, but it can't be a good one. They showed up on the island six months ago and moved into the Dupont Villa on the hill overlooking Long Bay. They swagger around town like they own the island. Maybe they do. My advice is give them a wide berth. Fortunately, they haven't come around the marina here."

Charlie glanced over at his young secretary busy at the copying machine, then stepped closer to the counter and lowered his voice, "I spoke with a local constable about them after they shot up a cafe over at West End during an argument with the owner. The constable shrugged and said a belonger didn't own the café. My guess is the Haitian's paying someone off in the ministry. His name is Guy Mont Violet. Suggest you stay away from him, Sam. Ignore him like the rest of us do."

Charlie turned to look at a sailboat motoring down the channel toward the marina from the breakwater. He opened the office door and stepped out on to the dock. "Direct them to C-12," he called to the dock boy. The big sloop was going too fast. "Goddamn rookies!" Charlie lumbered off down the dock.

Sam slid the boat show pamphlet in his back pocket and headed toward the dinghy dock. Behind him he could hear the marina manager yelling at someone. He thought Charlie might've been a bit melodramatic about the mysterious Haitian. He'd like to think his getting splashed was just a stupid accident. The streets on the island were narrow and potholed, and it had been raining. He'd try to be more careful when walking about town during or after a rainstorm.

By Monday morning, the sky cleared, and the hot tropical sun came out swinging. Charlie sent a man over after breakfast to paint Firebird's now officially registered name on her stern. The ancient-looking black man wore paint-spattered overalls and a faded Red Sox baseball cap pulled so low over his eyes that the top was rounded against his skull. He stood in his boat at the stern and carefully hand-penciled in the letters on the hull. Sam went below for a cup of coffee and brought it up on deck to watch him work. The artist arched the placement of the letters to match the curve of the stern. Underneath the name, he centered the homeport in smaller letters. *Texas City, Texas* was the only hometown Sam ever had. It now belonged to Firebird.

After outlining everything in pencil, the old man carefully filled in the block letters with black epoxy paint. To Sam's amazement, he used no stencils or masking tape, but freehanded the entire job while swells in the harbor lifted and dropped his little fiberglass boat at irregular intervals. The old man performed microsurgery with a steady hand while his legs bent and extended at the knees, like coordinated hydraulic lifts.

When the job was done, Sam leaned over the rail to check out the finished product. The artist smiled up at him with a mouthful of yellow ivories. The job looked perfect. The letters were blocked, the edges machine-straight and raised with drying black paint. No runs, no drips, no smudges. Sam nodded his approval and the bill of the baseball cap nodded back at him. The old man's grin widened, and his eyes sparkled. "You like." He said it as a statement of fact.

"I like it very much," Sam said, smiling.

"Good. Good." The man kept nodding. His large teeth reminded Sam of the keys on his grandmother's old upright piano that he banged on in her parlor when he was a kid.

Sam paid him for a job well done and watched the man's knobby fingers work to untie from Firebird's toe rail. The skiff then drifted away with him bent over the outboard engine, attempting to get it started. It fired once, twice, a third and fourth time before catching and blowing out a cloud of blue smoke. The old man turned to sit on the seat and waved at Sam as he steered in the direction of the marina, the fifty dollars collected for the job clutched tight in his fist.

When the old man disappeared behind a fishing boat that was motoring out of the marina, Sam looked down at the newly painted name on the stern. The glossy black paint reflected sunlight bouncing off the water. He smiled to himself. A warm wind ruffled the American flag on the pole next to him. Waves from the wake of the departing fishing boat lapped at the hull. Firebird rested quietly on her mooring. The big ketch seemed happy with her name. If she'd been a cat, he was sure he would've heard her purring.

Having a real name and real homeport for Firebird made filling out the entry form for the charter show on Saint Thomas much easier. The show being just two months away didn't give him much time to get ready, but if he budgeted his time and pennies, and worked only on priority problems, he thought she could be presentable in time. It would be tight, but he thought it worth risking the five hundred-dollar non-refundable entry fee. Besides, Charlie was right when he said it could be the difference between a good year and a disastrous one. He needed a good one.

After lunch, Sam mailed off the entry form to Saint Thomas at the post office and was standing in his inflatable, untying the painter from the dock cleat, when he looked up and saw a good-looking kid walking toward him.

# CHAPTER 12

"Mr. Berrenger?" The boy flashed an All-American smile and extended his hand. He had a firm grip. Sam liked that. Said a lot about a fellow's character.

"I'm Ian Neeson," the young man continued. "The marina manager said you might could use some help on your boat." He didn't pause to take a breath. "I want you to know that I'm a hard worker, and I've been around sailboats all of my life, and I'd be a senior this fall at college in engineering except I took the year off, and well. . . ." He stopped talking and stared at Sam like he was waiting for some response. His pale skin and dirty blonde hair told Sam he had just arrived on the island. His wardrobe consisted of Levis, a white T-shirt, and tired looking Topsiders.

"What?" Sam looked at him from the dinghy and squinted. The boy took a couple of steps forward and stood between Sam and the sun.

"Uh, my name is Ian Neeson, and—"

"Yeah, I heard that." Sam retied the dinghy painter to the cleat and stepped back up on the dock. "What'd you say you wanted to do?" The boy looked like a good kid. Six feet tall and maybe a hundred and seventy pounds. A mite too nervous, Sam thought.

"I'm looking for a job on a boat and Mr. Taylor, the marina manager, said that—"

"What can you do on a boat, boy?" Sam crossed his arms across his chest like Yul Brynner in *The King and I* and looked him in the eye. For some reason he'd decided not to make it easy for him.

The boy blinked, dropped his gaze to his feet. He hooked his thumbs in his back pockets. "Well, sir," he continued. "I'm good with machinery and I know sailboats. My grandfather owned boats, and I won several regattas at our yacht club and—"

"Can you sand and varnish?"

"Yes sir."

"Can you repair sails and rigging?"

"Yes sir, I—"

"Can you work on pumps and motors?"

"Yes. I—"

"Can you cook?"

"Yes, well..., not really. But I can learn and—"

"Can you overhaul a diesel engine?" Sam figured he was now pushing it a bit.

"I can." The boy sounded a bit testy.

"Then I'll think about it," Sam said, turning and stepping down into his dinghy. "Meet me here in the morning and we'll talk about it again." He started up the outboard and left the boy looking frustrated on the dock. He'd been an ass about it and didn't know exactly why. The kid seemed nice enough. A college boy, Sam thought to himself. How about that? *A college kid wants to work for me.*

After a dinner of cold leftovers, Sam poured a glass of Cruzan over ice and took it up on deck for some air. The sky was full of stars and a gentle swell rocked the boats in the harbor. Halyards clanged against aluminum spars, and a reggae song could be heard from a taxicab across the way. He sipped the rum and felt it warm his insides. Drops of condensation fell from the rigging and a cold one surprised him on his bare back. He watched the red and green buoy lights at the entrance to the breakwater, blinking on and off and thought about Ian Neeson. Part time help had not been in his plans, but if he were to have a real chance of getting this old girl in shape for the charter show, some outside assistance would be necessary.

Firebird measured about forty feet too much for him to handle alone. At eighty-four feet, everything was just too big, too difficult, too complex, and too expensive. The boy hadn't said what kind of wages he wanted, but Sam thought he could afford to pay him maybe a hundred bucks a week. Add room and board and it would cost him maybe five hundred a month--about half of his monthly check. So, it might cost him a little over a thousand dollars to get her ready for paying charter guests. He decided to do it. Besides, since Evelyn left, he'd found himself missing the company.

Now that he'd decided to hire the kid, he spent the rest of the night worrying that Ian wouldn't be at the dock the next morning. Maybe he'd get a better offer from someone else. That's the way he'd always done things. He would be reluctant to do something and after torturing himself and finally making up his mind, he would worry that someone would step in and beat him to it.

# CHAPTER 13

Sam heaved a sigh of relief to see the boy waiting on the dock as he steered the dinghy toward the marina. The morning sun burned bright in a clear Caribbean sky. The air smelled fresh and clean. Ian wore denim shorts and another white T-shirt. Sam saw the bag by his feet on the pier. He looked anxious.

"Morning." Sam tossed him the dinghy line. Ian caught it in one hand and secured it with an efficient half hitch on the dock post. "Grab your things and let's go have a cup of coffee," Sam said, stepping onto the pier. His head still hurt from too much rum and worry the night before. Ian lifted his duffel bag and followed him into a dockside cafe.

"Yes sir. I got here a few days ago. Flew from New York." Ian carried the conversation while Sam finished his first cup of coffee. Sam also made an on-the-spot decision to cut back on drinking hard liquor after ten o'clock at night.

"No sir," Ian went on. "I got tired of my grandfather running my life. The old man insisted I go to Cornell and become an engineer like him and my father. I stuck with it for three years, and this summer, I confronted him and said I wanted to do something else. Something different. But he wouldn't listen. The old guy can be pretty stubborn. When I went back to college to start the fall term, I decided not to take it anymore. I wrote both him and Mom that I was leaving school to figure out what I really want to do with my life."

The waitress refilled their coffee cups and brought Ian a buttered bagel.

Sam sipped his coffee and watched the boy over the rim of the cup. "Why all the fuss with your grandfather?" he asked. "What's your dad say about it?"

Ian swallowed a bite of bagel. "Nothing." He paused a moment. "He was a navy pilot and died in an accident before I was born. We've lived with my grandfather ever since."

Sam studied him a moment. "I'm sorry." He didn't know what else to say. He finished his third cup of coffee, watching Ian pick bagel crumbs off his plate. He liked the young man, and that had to be the most important thing if they were going to live and work together in close quarters. Firebird was a big boat, but eighty-four feet wasn't enough space if two people couldn't stand each other.

"Seventy-five bucks a week and that's all I can afford to pay," Sam said after the last crumb disappeared from the boy's plate. "Seventy-five in cash, and room and board. We have just over two months of hard work ahead to get her ready for a charter show over on Saint Thomas. Then we'll have to wait and see how it goes after that. No severance, nor any notice, either. If I fire your ass, I want you off my boat ASAP."

Ian smiled and nodded. "Anything you say, boss, uh, Captain."

After breakfast, Sam took him out to Firebird and showed him where to stow his gear. He assigned him a forward cabin on the starboard side. After a quick tour and instruction on operating the heads, Sam left him with a broom and mop to clean up below while he went to the chandlery in town for a case of silicone caulk.

Just as he was crossing the street to return to the marina, he saw the black Jeep screech around the corner about a block away, clip an Island boy on his bicycle and send him sprawling on the pavement. The Jeep sped up and disappeared around another corner.

Sam ran toward the boy. By the time he arrived, several people including a uniformed constable were already in attendance. The boy's head lay in a growing pool of blood. The bike occupied the middle of the macadam, the front wheel still spinning, the rear spokes bent and broken. Sam watched the constable rifling through the boy's pockets. He assumed he was searching for some identification.

"Officer, I saw it happen," Sam said, trying to be helpful. "It was a Jeep Cherokee; I've seen it before. I didn't see the driver, but—"

"Move it on, mon." The constable stood with his hands on his hips and glared at him.

"But I saw the car and—"

"I said move it on, mon. Not your affair."

An ambulance braked to a stop in the street. Two attendants jumped out, lifted the unconscious boy into the back and took off, Sam presumed to the island's hospital. The group of islanders gathered around the scene spoke in whispers before breaking up and going on about their business. The constable continued glaring at him until he turned and crossed the street. As he headed into the marina he wondered about the condition of the young bicyclist.

Sam relayed the events of the accident to Ian while they went from porthole to porthole on Firebird, working the silicone sealant around the outside casings with a caulking gun.

"And the authorities didn't go after the guy?" Ian asked, reaching over Sam's shoulder and thumbing the white rubbery caulk smooth around a porthole.

"Not that I could tell," Sam said. "It's a small island. Maybe the officials know where the asshole lives and will pick him up in their own time. The constable didn't seem too concerned about it except that I'd volunteered as a witness. He obviously didn't want me or anyone else involved. Christ, the kid couldn't have been more than ten. Hope he makes it."

There was nothing about the accident or the boy's condition in the next day's newspaper. The big story on the front page of the island daily told about the release of a dozen flamingoes at one of the island's ponds to repopulate the endangered species. The other front-page story detailed fisticuffs between two island senators during a late-night legislative session called to enact a new tax on charter boats operating from the island. The subject of taxing charter boats caught Sam's attention, but the article carried none of the particulars about the proposed law. Instead it detailed the two senators' fight with a blow-by-blow analysis. At times, the reporter interjected both criticism and praise for the two lawmakers' boxing style and their gentlemanly sportsmanship after the event. The article read like the society column back home in the Texas City Gazette, where each article ended with "and a good time was had by all."

Following several long days of caulking, sanding, cleaning, painting, greasing, and polishing, Sam decided that Ian was an angel sent from heaven. He must've been crazy to have ever thought he could do it all by himself and be ready in time for the November show. At the end of each workday, they dove off the boat into the harbor to remove the sweat and surface dirt, then lathered up on deck and rinsed off with the salt water hose. Anyone on a nearby boat who happened to peek, would've noticed Ian was a big strapping boy. He had also browned a good bit in the tropical sun.

Dinner on the boat that first week for the two of them consisted of canned spaghetti with bread and a salad, or Ian made up a plate of sandwiches with whatever he could scrounge up. They also kept plenty of Pringles potato chips around to satisfy their craving for salt. Sam bought Pringles by the case at the store. They went with everything. After dinner, he and Ian usually went to shore for a few Heinekens at the Queen's Pub in town and challenged each other at the pub's dartboard. Most people thought them father and son even though Sam would've preferred them to think they were brothers. It was okay with him if they'd thought he was just the older sibling. He'd begun to enjoy the boy's company. Ian worked hard and earned his money. He was also fun to be around. He laughed at everything. The tropical sun had started to set the laugh lines around his eyes. His contagious laugh usually started out as a widening grin and then punctuated with a loud guffaw.

Other than the first morning at breakfast, Ian hadn't said much about his family back in the states. Sam could tell the boy worried he'd disappointed them by dropping out of college. Sam liked that in the kid. He wouldn't care much for someone that could hurt his folks and not be bothered about it.

# CHAPTER 14

Sam stopped in the marina office on the way back from the market to ask Charlie about borrowing a power sander while Ian went on ahead to load the groceries in the dinghy.

"Hey, get away from that!" Ian's voice broke through the calmness of the hot afternoon. "What are you doing?"

Sam heard a crunching noise like a cockroach caught under a hard-soled shoe, followed by a big splash. When he stepped out of the office to see what the commotion was about, he saw Ian treading water surrounded by floating cans of foodstuffs while two pony-tailed goons decked out in white pants and Hawaiian shirts stood on the pier laughing at him. One picked up a loaf of bread and threw it, hitting Ian on the side of the head. The shorter guy was about to hurl a can of beans at the boy when Sam grabbed his wrist from behind and twisted his arm behind his back. Sam jerked upward as hard as he could, and the thug fell to his knees. His partner whipped out an evil looking box cutter and snarled at Sam like a pit bull.

"Put the blade away," Sam hissed and jerked the guy's wrist upwards, dislocating his shoulder with an audible pop.

The man screeched like a barn owl and his free hand pounded the pier.

"Do it," Sam growled, "Or I'll wrench his freaking arm off and shove the bloody stump down your throat!"

The curved blade disappeared into the big guy's pocket. "Let him up," the man said grimly. "We wasn't doing nothing. Jus' having a little fun."

Sam glared at him a moment then nodded to Ian in the water.

"Help the boy out and give him fifty bucks for the ruined groceries." He squinted hard at the fat, ponytailed bastard in front of him and recognized him as the umbrella carrier for the Haitian. "Make that a hundred. Your little fun isn't going to be gotten at someone else's expense, especially mine or my friend's here."

"A hundred bucks for some beans and bread? No fuckin' way."

"Pay him the damn money," whined the slime ball on his knees.

Sam jerked his arm up one more time, making him yelp.

"Pay him the money, Albert! Do it! This was your stupid idea to come over here anyway!" The thug on his knees was panting like a German Shepherd on an August day.

At that moment, Ian pulled himself up out of the harbor and stood beside Sam. Saltwater puddled at his feet. Albert took out a leather wallet and handed the boy a crisp hundred-dollar bill. Sam looked at Ian and motioned with his head toward the dinghy. "Get in and start the motor." He then turned to the goon standing in front of him. "Now back your ass off this dock and out of this marina. I'll let your friend up when you're gone."

"I ain't leaving without—"

Get outta here, Albert!" the fellow on his knees screamed. "Do what he says! My arm is fuckin' ruined!"

The outboard engine fired up and Ian throttled fuel to keep it going. Albert started backing away, glancing over his shoulder to make sure he didn't fall into the harbor. When he disappeared through the marina gate. Sam pushed his partner face down on the pier and hissed through clenched teeth, "Don't think about moving, slime ball!"

The injured thug nodded, unable to speak through the pain.

"Let's go." Sam said as he jumped into the Zodiac. Ian spun the gray inflatable away from the dock and accelerated until they were skimming across the surface of the harbor toward Firebird. Sam looked back and saw the man stumbling down the dock, his right arm dangling at his side.

When Sam returned to Firebird an hour later with new groceries, Ian was on deck by the mast with the extra genoa spread out around him. He took a break from resewing the split seams and helped Sam carry the boxes down to the galley. With the hundred dollars, Sam had splurged on some sirloin steaks instead of just beans and bread. They needed to get used to preparing and eating gourmet fare anyway if he expected to operate a proper charter yacht for big-time paying guests.

Ian put the cans away in the cabinets while Sam emptied the cardboard boxes onto the galley counter and tossed the empties up into the cockpit. Roaches often made their way onto a boat in containers from the market, so he minimized the amount of time a paper bag or cardboard box remained on board.

"You see those guys when you were in town?" Ian glanced Sam's way.

"Neither hide nor hair." Sam shook his head. He could tell the kid felt responsible for what had happened at the marina. "But don't worry about it. Creeps like them don't fool with anything or anyone that bites back. After this morning, they know how sharp our fangs are."

Ian took a case of Pringles from Sam and began lining the tall cans up on a shelf. "I don't know why they jumped me," he said, shaking his head. "When I walked up on them it looked like they were fooling around with our dinghy. They could have been getting ready to steal it or just let it loose as a prank, but one of them definitely had the painter in his hand and was untying it. Those guys are too old to be doing high school stuff like that."

"Bullies are bullies, whether they're fourteen or forty," Sam said. "And a bully doesn't need a good reason to hurt someone. Makes 'em feel powerful, probably gives 'em a hard on. A kick in the balls is the best way to deal with a bully. I learned that in grade school from my old man. There's a guy in Texas City--four years older than me who sings high soprano in his church choir. I'll tell you about it sometime."

Ian laughed and tossed Sam the last empty box to put up on deck.

After a quick run to the dumpster behind the marina to drop off their load of roach condominiums, they spent the rest of the day on Firebird's deck drinking beer, sewing sail seams, and laughing at each other's bad jokes. Sam thought he should've been caulking more leaky ports before it rained again, but he figured the boy needed company. Ian still seemed a little shaken from their run-in that morning with Heckle and Jeckle.

The afternoon felt hotter than usual with no breeze which was unusual for the third week of September in this part of the Caribbean. So far, there had been no major storms or hurricane warnings even though they were in the middle of the season. For most of the past week Ian had worn swim trunks while working on board which had allowed him to tan pretty good. The physical work of restoring the old boat had also toned up his muscles and his hair had grown blonder in the fierce sun. Sam thought he looked like a teenage character in an old Frankie Avalon surfer movie.

During the afternoon, Sam kept an eye out for any strange powerboats moving about in the harbor. He wasn't too worried about it, but you never know about scum like the two they had encountered that morning. They might've gone and focused their toxic testosterone on some other unlucky person, or they might've spent the afternoon sulking over shots of tequila in a bar and plotting his destruction. He hoped for the former but was alert for the latter.

A cool breeze picked up as the sun dropped behind the mountain. They folded the sails and slid them back into their sail bags. The bottom seam on two bags had rotted and ripped way under the sail's heavy weight. Sam said to leave them on deck for the next day. It seemed impossible to finish one job on the boat without uncovering another one that was just as important.

Feeling hot, dirty, and hungry, Sam tugged off his sweaty T-shirt and looked over at Ian. The boy was putting the sail repair kit back into its leather case. "Let's go for a swim before cooking those steaks. I'll get the charcoal started, then after our swim, I'll grill 'em if you'll make a salad."

"You got it, Captain." Ian executed a graceful dive over the side into the water. Sam followed with a loud whoop and an awkward cannon ball. After dinner, they sat in the cockpit enjoying the clear night. Sam was on his third glass of rum and Ian was sipping a beer. The sound of a girl's laughter wafted across the water from a near-by yacht. There was a splash and more laughter. Ian seemed preoccupied. Sam figured he was still thinking about his run in with the two thugs. His ego had been bruised, but he'd get over it. Sam had had his own tail kicked more than once and figured it could be a good learning experience.

He was thinking about how good a Cuban cigar would taste when Ian interrupted the silence. "I wrote my mom and told her I was here."

Sam didn't say anything.

After a few moments, Ian drained the last of his beer and looked at him. "The worst thing was leaving her alone with my grandfather. He'll blame her for me dropping out of Cornell."

"Now why would he do that?"

"He's always on her case about something. He's tried to run her life ever since my father died and we moved in with him. At least that's what mom says. After she moved into his house, she told me he started complaining about her using makeup and said her dresses were too short. Hell, it was the seventies and she was just barely eighteen." Ian paused a moment. "The old man ran off the few decent guys she went out with. She introduced me to a doctor once that she was seeing, but he didn't hang around long. I think she's always been lonely." He lifted the beer bottle up to the light from the full moon to see if any was left. "I think that's why she drinks so much."

Sam finished his drink and reached for the near empty bottle of Bacardi. "We're all lonely sometimes," he said, leaning forward to set his glass on the cockpit table. "And sometimes we all drink too much. It's part of life, part of the 'covenant with the creator,' as my old man used to say." He realized he was slurring his words.

"Were you ever married, Sam? You have any kids?"

Sam rubbed his hand across his bare chest and watched the lights go off inside a sloop anchored across the way. The stars overhead looked so low that he could reach up and touch them. He didn't know how much he wanted to tell the boy about Darlene right now. Besides, he didn't feel like picking at that old scab on such a beautiful night and ruining a good buzz. "Yeah, I was married once, a long time ago," he finally answered. "But no kids. I guess we weren't in love that way. Not like your mom and dad."

# CHAPTER 15

"Hey Charlie," Sam nodded to the marina manager. Sam waited at the counter for Louise Marie, the manager's shapely assistant, to get his mail. "You need to put some poison out around the docks. Ian and I had to kick two slimy rats out of the marina yesterday morning. There's no guarantee they won't come back."

"Heard about that," Charlie said, shuffling through a stack of papers on the counter. He didn't look up. "Do me a favor and be more careful about who you piss off on this island. You could get yourself and some others hurt." He put the papers down. A weary look crossed his face. "Or worse."

Sam glanced at Louise Marie holding a handful of mail. "Who the hell are they, Charlie?"

The marina manager pushed his glasses up on his forehead and rubbed his eyes with his pudgy fingers. "Goddamn it, Sam, just be more careful, will you? This place was paradise until this morning."

Sam watched him go back into his office and shut the door. Louise Marie gazed at him a moment through expressionless eyes. She dropped three envelopes on the counter in front of him and slowly shook her head. Her father was a brother of the island's Chief Minister and Sam figured she had some idea about what was going on.

He thumbed open an envelope from his old oil company employer. His check was late this month and he'd been a little worried about it. A warm fuzzy feeling came over him when he saw the check. Slipping it into his pocket, he looked at Louise Marie. "Tell me something, did the Haitian and his thugs stop by to see Charlie?"

"No one's been 'round here this morning 'cept you." She cut her eyes to the back room. "He started actin' crazy like that when he came in." She shook her head, "White people always go crazy when they come here. It don't take long. Belongers should make non-belongers go home after a few weeks or require them to put up a 'crazy' deposit."

The phone rang, and she went to her desk to answer it. Sam couldn't hear what was being said. She glanced at him then turned her back to continue her discussion.

Maybe she's right, he thought to himself. He could think of more than a few locos he'd encountered in Puerto Rico, Santa Domingo, and Key West.

Sam took his mail and left the air-conditioned office. He looked at the two unopened envelopes in his hand. One letter was from a life insurance company and the other from an estate planning company. He assumed they thought he needed help spending the measly thousand dollars he received each month. Junk mail had caught up with him in paradise.

He stood in a slow-moving line to deposit his check at the island's branch of the Chase Manhattan Bank located in town between the Spice Shop and the T-shirt Emporium. The male teller behind the counter seemed in no hurry. He chatted amiably with everyone in front of Sam who seemed to be neighbors or family members and laughed loudly and spoke rapidly in his island lilt, which Sam found difficult to understand even though it was basically English. He found it a lot like listening to a record playing at forty-five rpm when it should have been at thirty-three and a third. When his turn came, the nattily dressed teller stopped smiling, recorded his deposit in a ledger and curtly handed him back a receipt.

Sam stepped outside onto the hot sidewalk feeling even more of a non-belonger and saw Ian disappear into the hardware store across the street. Dodging a speeding taxi, he entered the air-conditioned store after him. He found him in a rear aisle, studying a can of machine oil.

"It's almost noon," Sam said, patting him on the back. "I'll buy you a burger."

The boy turned, and a big smile creased his face. "Hey, look at this old ship's log I found on the boat." He handed Sam a tattered book. A coat of mold clung to the hard leather cover.

"I found it underneath the bottom drawer in the chart table this morning while following a cable to the on-deck electronics. It must've fallen out and been under there for years."

Sam thumbed the pages and saw it was indeed one of Firebird's early logbooks. The first entry was dated January 20, 1970. The last one had been made in December 1975. "Let's get something to eat and look at this," he said, feeling like he had just been handed a long-lost treasure map. "Maybe it can answer some of our questions about the old girl's past. Perhaps we'll find a clue as to why she's in such bad shape."

Sam paid for the can of oil plus a box of sandpaper, and the two of them headed over to the Buccaneer Bar and Grill at the ferry dock for lunch. During the day the place was frequented by the island's workers, mostly house builders and road pavers, instead of the tourist crowd. Hard hats and steel-toed work boots were the norm instead of ballcaps and flip-flops. The noise level in the place dropped a few decibels when they entered, and Sam felt several pairs of eyes watching as the pretty waitress escorted them to a table in the rear next to the busy kitchen. He didn't think they were just checking out her cute ass and felt the hairs prickle on his neck.

"Today's specials are pork chops with fries or plantain, and the fish is Mahi on a bed of rice." The freckled waitress spoke with a sophisticated accent that was either British or Australian. He could never tell which, and both were prevalent on the island. However, he could see that she and his young employee had already connected. Ian held the menu in front of him, but his gaze was locked on to the pretty blues of their tawny young waitress. A name tag with *Sarah* scrawled in black Magic Marker was pinned to her sleeveless blouse.

"What do you recommend?" Ian's smile widened, showing straight white teeth.

Sarah leaned over and whispered, "The burgers are best, and you have the cutest dimples."

"Then, two cheeseburgers," Sam said, saving Ian from saying something stupid. "With everything on them, and a couple orders of fries." The two weeks they'd spent working together had shown him that young Ian wasn't a match for an international flirt like Sarah.

"Two cheeseburgers coming up." Sarah smiled and took their menus. She playfully pinched Ian on the shoulder before heading back to the kitchen, her hips swaying sassily under her short skirt.

"Pretty girl," Sam said as she disappeared through the double doors into the kitchen.

"She's gorgeous!" Ian turned to look at him, his grin reached from ear to ear. "And she's definitely my type. You see those long legs? I dream about legs like those." He looked back toward the kitchen. "I want to ask her name when she comes back. Will she think I'm too obvious?"

"Her name is Sarah," Sam said, opening the logbook to the first page.

"How do you know?" Ian's brow furrowed.

"Trust me." Sam grinned. "I just know." He began to read the first entry.

*January 20, 1970, this day, Firebird became the property of Mid-Jersey Securities Corporation to be used for the business benefit of the firm's chairman, Mr. Eldred Meyerson, Founder and Chairman of Mid-Jersey Securities. The purchase papers were signed on board this afternoon. A cocktail party followed at the Pier 66 Club in Fort Lauderdale in honor of William Therry, Firebird's famous designer, and Stevens Yachts, the brokerage who assisted Mr. Meyerson in acquiring Firebird from Blaylock Industries of Gary, Indiana. The yacht was put up for sale last summer after the chairman of Blaylock Industries died of a sudden illness.*

*Firebird will winter in Florida and spend summers at the Meyerson estate on Martha's Vineyard. Her captain, along with four crew including our excellent gourmet chef, are happy to be aboard. Mr. Meyerson's orders are to spare no expense in her upkeep.*

*My lady, you are a very lucky yacht.*

*Nelson Owensby, Captain, U.S.C.G. Licensed*

Sam heard a deep rumbling noise and looked out the restaurant's window. The noon ferry from Saint Thomas was reversing its big diesel engines and easing its way toward the dock. Water churned at the stern, and a uniformed crewman stood ready at the beam to toss a line to barefooted help on the pier. A full load of passengers slathered with sun block crowded the port rail, cameras clicking.

Sam's attention returned to the logbook. So, Firebird was built by one rich bastard in Indiana and then sold to some other moneybags back East, he thought to himself. *Puts me in high cotton, as my old man used to say. Old Eastern money. Right up there with the Rockefellers and the Vanderbilts.*

# CHAPTER 16

Sam knew a little about Blaylock ball bearings. All the kids in his neighborhood around Hiram Hogg Elementary School on the south side of Texas City carried one or more in their pockets for shooting marbles. A Blaylock steely could shatter a glass cat's eye to smithereens if you hit it just right with enough thumb power. Those stainless-steel ball bearings could also turn a sling shot into a lethal weapon. Ask any squirrel in Texas City.

"Anything interesting in the logbook?" Ian interrupted Sam's thoughts.

"She's a countess, my boy." Sam winked at him. "The old girl is pure blue-blooded royalty. She's known champagne and caviar in her day and will again when we bring high society charter guests aboard. She'll make 'em feel right at home."

The kitchen doors swung open and Sarah carried out a tray of burgers in one hand and two cold Heinekens in the other. "Food's ready." She smiled. "You two probably thought I'd forgotten you."

She set one of the green bottles on the table in front of Ian and slid the other across to Sam. Two sizzling burger platters followed, and the aroma of grilled meat and onions made Sam's stomach rumble.

"This is an interesting old thing you've got here, Captain," Sarah said, picking up the logbook. "Mind if I take a look?"

Sam shrugged and bit into his hamburger. Ian hadn't moved, his gaze remained locked on their sassy waitress, a silly grin frozen on his face.

"Oh, it's about Firebird." Her eyes widened. "Isn't that the sad-looking boat moored over near the Virgin Cay Marina?" She smiled at Ian. "That wouldn't be yours, now, would it, laddie?"

Ian's eyes darted from her to Sam and back again. Sam almost laughed out loud, seeing the quirky smile still plastered in place.

"What do you know about Firebird?" Sam asked, wiping burger grease from his chin with a napkin.

"Oh then, it's yours?" Sarah set the logbook back on the table. "Everyone in town's been talking about it since it arrived in the harbor. Up close she looks a bit run down, but she's also the biggest sailing yacht on the island, so everyone's curious."

"Want to come aboard some evening for a beer or something?" Ian asked hoarsely.

Sarah and Sam turned to look at him. Sam took a swig of his beer to keep from laughing out loud. The boy had finally found his voice.

Ian averted the pretty girl's eyes. "I mean, if you're not married or anything."

"Cheeky boy," she said, and leaned over to whisper in his ear, "You asking me out on a date?"

Ian looked at Sam for help. Sam cocked an eyebrow and shrugged, "Yeah, kid. What's your intentions?"

"If you are," Sarah didn't wait for an answer, "pick me up in front of the Reef Boutique on Cane Garden Bay Road this afternoon at four o'clock. My shift here ends at three. I'll need an hour to get home and freshen up. My little apartment is on the second floor." She paused a moment to brush a lock of hair away from her face. "And my name is Sarah, Sarah Pendleton."

Seeing Ian was slow to respond, Sam stepped in. "I'm Sam Berrenger, and this talkative Casanova here is Ian Neeson."

Sarah shook hands with them both, and Sam noticed she held Ian's hand longer than necessary.

"Hey, honey!" A burly guy in a dirty undershirt and work pants waved to her from a nearby table. "You gonna stand over there gabbing all day or get us our lunch? We gotta be back on the job in an hour."

Sarah tore the check off her pad and placed it in the middle of the table. "Be there at four," she said to Ian in a hushed voice. "I'll show you a secret beach on the west end of the island. We can lie on the sand this evening and watch the sun fall into the sea."

Ian wolfed down his burger in silence while Sarah left them alone to serve the other tables. Sam paid the cashier, and they walked back toward the marina. Neither of them said anything. For some reason, Sarah's flirting with Ian had made Sam feel like an ancient hoary mastodon and put him in a grumpy mood. He was beginning to hate this getting old crap.

After a couple of blocks, Sam broke the silence. "So, you got yourself a date tonight. Well, good for you. I'm glad one of us still has some moves with the ladies, except I'm still trying to figure out what yours are. They're subtle but damn effective."

"You think she's married?" Ian asked. "She's too pretty—"

Sam stopped in his tracks. The boy's question irritated him. "That's the second time you've brought that up," he said, shaking his head. He lifted his baseball cap and ran his fingers through his hair. "Why in the world are you so worried about it? If she's married, then her old man is obviously off island, and what makes you think she's married anyway?"

"She didn't deny it when I asked?"

"She didn't confirm it either. Did you see a ring on her left hand?"

"No, but—"

Sam started walking again. "Then take the cutie to the beach this afternoon with a towel and a pocketful of protection and see if you can get lucky. Afterwards, tell me all about it cause that's the closest I'll get to the real thing before we get that damn boat fixed up. Just make sure you're back in the morning in time to do some work."

They had crossed the street to the marina and were passing through the wrought iron gates that led to the dinghy dock when Ian said, "I don't have any."

"Any what?" Sam asked, bending down to untie the dinghy.

"Condoms." Ian coughed.

"Then buy some," Sam snapped. "I pay you good money."

The buzzing of the dinghy motor irritated him even more as he steered the Zodiac out towards Firebird. Ian sat beside him. Sam didn't know why he felt so angry. It wasn't that he was jealous. The girl was cute but much too young and not his type. He liked 'em petite and girly. Like Evelyn, and like. . .Darlene.

# CHAPTER 17

Sam climbed up the ladder to the deck while Ian secured the dinghy to Firebird's boarding platform. "I'm taking a nap," Sam said. "If I'm not up when you need to go ashore for your date, wake me and I'll take you in."

For a moment, he felt bad about blowing off the afternoon. There were a lot of projects that needed to be done, but he just didn't feel like it. Right now, it could all go to hell. He owned the damn boat even though it sometimes seemed like the other way around. Before going below to crash, Sam saw Ian come into the cockpit, wiping his hands on an old towel.

"Is it okay with you if I start to take apart the old generator? That project will take more than a week anyway, and I could get a couple of good hours on it this afternoon before meeting Sarah."

"Knock yourself out, kid," Sam said, and went down the steps to his cabin. The room was dark, and the small wall fan sent a warm breeze over the rumpled bedcovers. He tossed the logbook on a shelf and promised himself he would read it later. Right now, he just wanted to sleep. He knew his bad behavior on the way back after lunch had troubled Ian. He couldn't even explain it to himself.

His nap was fitful with spotty dreams of well-tailored men and glamorous gowned matrons sipping champagne and nibbling canapés from silver trays on Firebird's deck. The yacht sparkled with festive party lights strung above her deck. All the women wore big floppy hats. A sprawling Victorian mansion could be seen high on a grassy hill above the harbor. One gentleman with oiled hair stood next to the helm wearing a cravat and blue blazer with brass buttons, holding forth about boats and bonds. Sam assumed it was his mental image of Eldred Meyerson. He'd never met an investment banker before. Several times during his nap he was aware of the sound of a hammer banging on metal.

Sam decided he didn't like any of the people in his dream. They were department store mannequins, expensively attired and hollow on the inside. Firebird's deck seemed to bow under their weight, and no one noticed or cared. Everyone was too busy clucking on about themselves.

When he finally awoke, he was covered in a sheen of sweat. His watch showed it was eight o'clock in the evening. He lay in the dark staring up at the ceiling. There was no sound on board, not even the hum of a cabin fan. Crap, he thought, either we've lost our batteries or Ian shut off the power while working on the generator and didn't turn it back on before leaving.

He felt in the dark for the lamp by the bed and clicked the switch. Nothing happened. There was no power, at least not in his cabin. After disengaging his bare legs from damp, wadded bedding, he found a flashlight and went naked into the main salon. The whole of the boat was quiet as a tomb. Feeling his way in the dark, he made it to the navigation station and found the master battery switch in the off position. Sam dialed the big knob to Battery Bank One, and the boat sprang to life. The brass lamp hanging over the dining table came on as did the two wall-mounted fans by the settee on the opposite side. Light from the bedside lamp in his stateroom spilled out the cabin's open door. He also detected the low vibration of the new fresh water pump, increasing pressure in the water tanks. The door to the engine room had been left open and Sam saw the old generator sitting in pieces on the floor. It looked like Ian had finished the hard task of getting the generator block out of the cramped engine room, so they could move it on deck to rebuild it.

Sam went up on top and felt a strong breeze blowing in his face. Firebird had swung around from its usual position of pointing into the southeasterly trades and now aimed her bow north which usually meant the strong probability of rain. A steel drum band played

Bob Marley at a dockside cafe and strands of colored lights over the dance area swung wildly in the gusting wind. Outside the harbor entrance, the sea was building and white caps breaking.

Over at the marina dinghy dock, Sam could just make out his grey Zodiac tied up amongst other inflatables. He gritted his teeth. The kid had left him stranded out there while he went off chasing some skirt. It was just the perfect ending to a lousy day. It wasn't like he had any plans to go somewhere. He didn't. But hell, Sam thought, he's a damn employee. He's not my son, so I shouldn't have to put up with the same kinda stuff I gave my old man.

Sam could hear his dad's voice, "Don't go taking the car without my permission." He'd said it a thousand times if he said it once, and Sam got his ears boxed every time he did. At least until that time he was seventeen, and his old man punched him in front of Darlene. The old man spent a thousand dollars on new teeth the following week. After that, he never hit Sam or told him what to do again. When Sam buried his father a few years ago, the mortician asked him if he wanted his dad's dentures as a family keepsake. Sam had told him to drop them in the casket if he couldn't get them back in his mouth.

At least here on Saint Sebastian, Ian can't take minors across state lines for immoral purposes like Sam did once in his old man's Ford Fairlane. We need to have a serious talk about this, Sam thought. I won't have a helper on my boat that I can't trust. Ian has some explaining to do.

Dinner was a can of Vienna sausages, a packet of saltines and a glass of rum. He didn't feel like cooking. Besides it wasn't worth wasting propane for just one person. After cleaning up his mess, he donned a pair of thin cotton pajama bottoms, took Firebird's old logbook and sat at the dining table in the main salon to read. He had left his glass in the sink and was sipping directly from the bottle. The wind howling in the rigging outside grew stronger. Every now and then he felt a hard jerk as the boat swung on her mooring line. He figured the smaller boats around him in the harbor were dancing a jig.

His inner core harbored a nagging worry about Ian and Sarah, but there was nothing he could do stranded out here. He thought about calling on the radio to the marina office and asking if anyone had seen them, but it was after ten o'clock and the office shut down at eight.

He focused on the logbook to keep his mind off the growing storm. The next several entries were cryptic notes, listing work done to the boat for her new owner. As best he could tell, Captain Nelson Owensby seemed to be a proper sailing master. He wrote very little that was personal in nature about his employer, the rich banker, Eldred Meyerson. Sam thought Eldred sounded like a character in "The Great Gatsby."

There were pages and pages of names of people who had visited on board and comments were written by guests in feathery handwriting about the beauty of the yacht and the graciousness of their host. He didn't recognize any of the names but then he wasn't familiar with the social register.

He'd known only one millionaire in his life, and he was a grocer in Texas City whose wife inherited a little farm near the gulf where Exxon poked a hole in the ground one day and discovered oil. The money didn't change their life much. The grocer still worked the cash register at the grocery store everyday while his mousey wife stayed in the back picking bad fruit out of the produce section.

No one would've ever known they had any money except for the new Rolls Royce Silver Cloud he bought every January. The old man and his wife drove to work each day in that fancy car that cost more than their customers made in a lifetime and parked it out back of the store in the sun next to the dumpster. Sam doubted either of them ever knew there was such a thing as a social register, much less cared they weren't in it.

Sam skimmed over most of the uninteresting details, but the log reported that the boat spent the next five years alternating summers and winters in the waters off Maine and Florida, entertaining Mr. Meyerson's wealthy customers. Her diesel engine was replaced in 1974, and new sails were added the same year. She was also dry docked once each year in Florida to paint the bottom.

He thought about the gallons of red marine paint Jerry Diaz had gotten for him from the Coast Guard Station in San Juan. The paint was stored in one of the lockers up on deck. He needed to cut a deal soon with the local boatyard to haul the boat so he and Ian could put a coat of anti-fouling paint on the bottom. While she's up on the hard, they would also inspect and replace many of the through-hull fittings where seawater is pumped into and out of the heads, and generator and engine cooling systems. The prop shaft should also be pulled, and new bearings and a new bronze propeller installed along with new zincs to prevent metal corrosion. When spending the money to take a boat the size of Firebird out of the water, Sam knew he'd better take full advantage of the opportunity. He figured she'd be in the yard for at least three weeks. He didn't want to think about the cost.

Toward the end of the logbook, there were several pages torn out and then the captain's last entry.

*December 18, 1975. The old man radioed this morning and said the captain and crew's services were terminated immediately. We are to be off the boat no later than sunset today. No one is surprised. This was seen coming since August when paychecks started bouncing at the bank. I asked Mr. Meyerson who I should turn control of the boat over to, but he refused to discuss it. We've been anchored outside of the shipping lane in Biscayne Bay ever since Halloween when the boat was evicted from the marina in Fort Lauderdale for non-payment. I don't like the idea of this lady being alone and unprotected out here, but I've done the best I can and it's time to move on. None of us would be too surprised if an insurance scam was imminent. We would hate it if this grand vessel wound up on the muddy bottom of the bay.*

*3:00 PM: Everything on board has now been secured. The sails were folded dry and stored in the sail locker. Propane tanks for the stove in the galley have been turned off and disconnected. Both the engine and generator ran for a few hours to ensure a strong charge in the batteries to keep the bilge pumps operable until someone comes aboard to look after her. The lockers on deck are all padlocked. We are removing the open foodstuffs and have turned off refrigeration and cleaned out the freezers. A launch is arriving in half an hour to take the crew ashore.*

*Dear Lady: It was a grand five years as your captain. You sailed the seas with grace and dignity. I wish God's blessings to you and Mr. Meyerson and send his wife and sweet daughter my prayers. I'm sure he will do his best to repay all those people that trusted him. Perhaps one day he will be able to pay the crew their back salaries. It's a shame what happened, for everyone concerned.*

*Goodbye, Firebird. I pray you find a new owner that can care for you as you've cared for us.*

*Nelson Owensby, Captain, USCG Licensed*

Wow, Sam thought, as he put the logbook down. Looks like the old girl's life turned upside down. He heard the wind howling in the rigging. The lamp over the dinette swung back and forth like a clock pendulum. Rain began pelting the top of the deck house, and he stood to pull the hatch doors shut. A check of his Seiko showed it was nearing midnight. He began to worry that Ian hadn't returned from his date. Perhaps they'd gone to Sarah's apartment to wait out the storm. He would've if he were smart – or lucky, Sam thought. Maybe he'll stay the night. On the other hand, Sam wasn't keen being alone on the boat in a storm without someone to assist should they drag the mooring or the line fray apart.

He grabbed a yellow slicker and went up to check things on deck. Horizontal sheets of rain were blowing from the north. Visibility was so bad he couldn't see any lights on shore, or any of the boats anchored nearby. Up at the bow, the two-inch mooring line ran taut in the chock and strained on the bow cleat. Water running over the deck, coupled with the strong wind blowing on the bow, made for a treacherous trip back to the cockpit. He went below and closed the companionway hatch behind him.

Sometime later, after the storm subsided and he had fallen into a rum fueled sleep in his berth, he felt something bump against the hull. He opened his eyes and blinked into the darkness. The rain had stopped, and he caught the unmistakable sound of a dinghy motor being doused. That was soon followed by the sound of hushed voices and the boarding ladder creaking. Little strobe lights started going off in his brain. Grabbing the flare pistol on the shelf over his bunk, he scrambled out of bed. He flattened himself against the bulkhead behind the door and tried to steady his ragged breathing. Detecting movement in the main salon, he figured the goons on the dock had shown up to reclaim their manhood. His thumb cocked back the flare gun's hammer.

The beam of his flashlight swept the salon, stopping on Ian's startled face. The boy's clothes were sopping wet.

"Wha. . . ." was all Ian could say before Sam swung the light to the second figure. The unfamiliar person, even more soaked and bedraggled, huddled behind Ian. Sam directed the beam around the salon to ensure they were the only ones who had come aboard. He switched on the overhead lights.

"My god, kid," he hissed. "Why didn't you wake me when you left this afternoon. I. . . ." He realized he was naked in the presence of a strange female. The two figures stared at him wide-eyed when he realized the wide barrel of his cocked flare pistol still pointed at them. Sam eased the hammer forward and placed the gun on the salon table. "Sorry. Thought you might be those desperados sneaking onboard looking for revenge."

No one spoke for a moment. Then the person cowering behind Ian stepped forward. Sam had never seen this one before. She was older than Sarah. There were faint bruises about her pretty face and her long dark hair was pulled back in a ponytail, making her look younger than she probably was. Her thin wet sun dress clung to a shapely body, her legs and feet were bare. She carried a pair of strappy sandals in one hand and a small clutch purse in the other.

Sam looked at Ian.

"Uh, this is my mother," Ian said, "Anna Neeson. And I wish maybe you'd put some pants on."

"Oh, sorry." Sam ducked into his cabin and grabbed his PJ bottoms off the floor. He returned to the salon bare-chested and nodded to the attractive woman beside Ian. "This is quite a surprise. I figured the boy wouldn't be back tonight with the storm raging and. . .well, with his lady friend and all—"

"I left Sarah's apartment around eleven and was in a cab back to the marina when I saw Mom on Main Street. I was bringing her back here when we were untying the dinghy and someone yelled at us from the street. I recognized that black Jeep, and we cranked up the motor and took off."

"They follow you?" Sam grabbed his flashlight and headed for the stairs.

"Don't think so." Ian followed him up on deck.

The storm had passed, and the stars cast pale gray light over the quiet harbor. Sam listened, but heard nothing unusual. "Just to be sure, we'll stand two hour watches up here till morning. I'll go first since I had a nap this afternoon. Clear our tools and stuff out of that third cabin. Your mom can stay in there. Get her into something dry and you two try to get some sleep. I'll come down to wake you in a couple of hours."

"Thanks, Sam. I don't know." The boy shook his head. "I found her wandering the streets alone in the rain. She said she arrived two days ago but won't tell me where she's been staying."

Sam gazed out over the water a moment. "You did right to bring her here. We'll sort this out in the morning. She say anything else after you picked her up?"

"Not really, other than she was relieved to have found me and kept mumbling that she was sorry. I figured she'd been drinking, but there was no alcohol on her breath and—"

"Okay," Sam said. "Get some sleep. I'll pull up the boarding ladder just in case. No reason to make it easy for them."

He let Ian sleep through the night. Things remained quiet around the harbor. Any sound could easily be heard across the water. He chose a seat in the cockpit that gave him a good view of the surrounding area and kept his flare pistol close by. He remembered Jerry Diaz warning about having a real firearm on board. "Every two-bit banana republic uses illegal weapons as an excuse to confiscate boats," he had said. "Keep an emergency flare pistol handy. Point a wide barrel flare pistol at any hombre, and he'll shit his pants. I kid you not. It don't just blow a big hole in a person at close range, but the phosphorus flare will cook a man's guts to chili real quick. Hell, man, you don't need no real gun."

Sam dozed off more than once, but his waking hours were spent contemplating two questions. First, what was the story on this new woman now aboard? And second, what happened to Firebird after Meyerson's business collapse left her stranded in Miami back in the seventies? The log gave no clue. He figured the first question would be answered in the morning.

# CHAPTER 18

"Mom's still sleeping. I hate to wake her." Ian sat across from Sam at breakfast. "And I apologize for leaving you out here alone. When it was time for me to leave, I shook you twice and boy, you're a heavy sleeper. I was about to give you mouth-to-mouth when you opened your eyes and told me to go on without you."

"Must've been out of it. I have no memory of that. Maybe Sarah didn't want me around and put voodoo in my burger yesterday at lunch." He picked his cereal bowl up to drink the rest of the milk. "Speaking of. . . .?" He raised an eyebrow at Ian who'd just filled his bowl with Cheerios for the second time.

Ian shrugged. "She's a nice girl. We drank some wine and watched the sunset at the beach. When the storm came, we had a good time playing chess in her apartment till it stopped raining, then I left.

"They call it chess, now?" Sam said. "We called it a lot of different things when I was your age... hide-the-sausage, park-the-car, playing doctor, but I don't remember 'playing chess.'"

"Sorry to disappoint you." Ian laughed. "Like I said, she's a nice girl."

"Oh yeah, she's a big flirt, and you're a nice guy," Sam said, pouring himself another cup of coffee. "So, let's talk about your mother. I noticed she didn't bring any luggage onboard."

"She told me not to worry about it. She was anxious to get away from downtown last night and didn't want to talk about it. She has her passport and credit cards and can buy what clothes she needs."

Sam leaned against the galley sink sipping his coffee. He wore a pair of nylon running shorts and a T-shirt—his usual workday outfit. "So, what should we do?"

"Let's see what she says when she gets up," Ian said. "I'm pretty sure she came down here to get me to return to college. My grandfather must've sent her. I've been expecting it. His spies in the house probably found the letter I sent her."

"And what will you do?" Sam asked, setting his cup in the sink. "Now that you've got that generator all apart—"

"Don't worry." Ian put his bowl in the galley sink. "I made a commitment. You have me at least until the charter show in November, and hopefully, you'll want me to stay on as crew for the winter. Grandfather also taught me the importance of keeping my word."

"Good." Sam nodded. "We need to drag that heavy generator block out of the engine room and up on deck to rebuild it. That's at least a two-man job. Let's do it first thing. The noise will probably wake your mother, but—"

"I'm not so sure." Ian laughed. "She can sleep through a hydrogen blast if she's had enough vodka. My grandfather used to—"

"I'll meet you in the engine room as soon as I put something on to protect my toes," Sam said. It made him uncomfortable to hear about someone else's drinking problems.

Just before noon, he carried the last box of old generator parts up from below and was returning to his cabin to dump off his work boots when he sensed movement in the salon.

"Excuse me," he called out into the empty room. "Uh, Excuse me. . . ."

The door to Anna's cabin opened a crack. "I'm sorry, but I don't have anything to wear. I just took a shower and can't put on this dress. It's still wet and—"

"Hold on. I'll find something." Sam dropped his boots on the floor and rifled through his closet. He found a few things that could work and carried them down the passageway. "Try these." He held the bundle of clothes out toward the door. A manicured hand reached for them.

"Come up on deck when you're ready," he said after the hand disappeared, "and we'll see about getting some lunch."

He wondered which choice she would pick. One was Evelyn's orange thong bottom and matching bikini top that she'd left behind, probably as a souvenir for him. The other outfit was a pair of navy-blue boxer shorts that he was sure would be way too big and the smallest T-shirt he could find in his drawer.

"Your mom's awake and getting dressed." He watched Ian clean grease off generator parts in a plastic bowl half full of gasoline. "How will we know which parts need replacing and which ones we just need to clean and put back on?"

"I've got a list," Ian said, wiping his hands on a rag. "A few of these are toast but most can be reused. New gaskets, plugs, and filters along with replacing all the belts should make her run good as new. I helped my grandfather rebuild a Chris Craft engine last summer at our lake house. Diesel engines aren't that complicated. Pretty simple, actually. I bet the Parts and Power Supply store in town has everything we need. How does my mother look this morning?"

They both turned toward the cockpit as Anna stepped out into the light of day. Sam grinned. She looked like a little girl wearing a pile of laundry.

"What—" Ian started to speak but was cut off by his mother's shrug.

"I see you picked the Ralph Lauren outfit," Sam said.

"I'm wearing everything you gave me," Anna sighed. "I would've worn a fur parka if it had been included." Her clean shoulder length hair had been brushed and framed her pretty face, hiding some of the bruises Sam had noticed the night before.

"I'm sorry those things are so large but—"

"I feel like a turtle in a shell." She laughed. "And this bikini I'm wearing under these shorts. Where's the rest of it? The church would burn me at the stake if I ever wore it in public."

"It was left aboard by a good Catholic girl, so what can I say?" Sam smiled. "It's got pedigree."

“If I make a list could you two shop for me in town?” She held out the hem of the baggy shorts.

“Uh, Mom, this is Sam Berringer, my boss and the boat’s owner and Captain.” Ian grasped the banter away from the adults. “And Sam, let me properly introduce my mother, Anna Neeson.”

“Yes, you said that last night.” Sam stepped closer and took her extended hand. “My pleasure, Ms. Neeson, and a proper welcome aboard. Hope you found your accommodations satisfactory.”

“So, so,” she said, winking at her son. “Do you perchance have some coffee on board? Or the makings of a good screwdriver? Either one will cheer me up this morning.”

“Coffee is below in a thermos,” Sam responded, leading the way down the steps. “I thought you might want some.” He noticed Ian stayed behind on deck to clean some tools

Sam poured several fingers of scotch into a glass for himself and sat across the salon table from her. He quickly did the math and decided she was in her late thirties, maybe thirty-nine, a year or so younger than himself. As she chatted away, fueled by the fresh caffeine, he saw she could play the role of a sophisticated woman or innocent schoolgirl, and both were real personas. Having lived in her father-in-law’s mansion like a pampered pet the past twenty years stifled her in some ways but had also protected her and Ian. What this meant, he didn’t yet know. “So, Ms. Neeson—”

“Please call me, Anna,” she said, sipping her second cup of coffee.

“Anna, okay then.” He took a big gulp of scotch and set the glass back on the table. “So, what brought you down here to Saint Sebastian? And, I was wondering what your plans—”

“Afraid you will lose your cheap labor, Mr. Berrenger?”

“Call me, Sam.” He smiled. “And no, I just want to know how long we’ll be accommodating you on board. Things are not yet in resort shape as you can see, but in a few months, we should have her ready to host the Queen of England.”

“Yes, I’m sure,” she said a bit too sarcastically. “The Queen will find the sail bag you call a mattress in my cabin quite comfortable.”

"But—" Sam looked confused.

"Don't worry about it, Sam," she said, rubbing a bruise on her arm. "I already see this was a terrible mistake. A decision made one lonely evening in a manic, martini madness. I'll collect myself here for a couple of days then return to Boston. It's happened before."

"Did something occur in town that we need to know about?" he asked straight out, not knowing any other way to address the subject. He hadn't forgotten the bruises.

She lowered her eyes and pursed her lips. "Just another bad choice I made. It's a habit, or maybe a character flaw as my father-in-law often reminds me. After arriving two days ago and not knowing where to find Ian, I encountered a suave talking man who whisked me away to his villa in the sky."

She raised her head and looked at him. "It seemed like a good idea at the time. I guess enough drugs and drink can make cutting off one's head seem like a good idea. Anyway, after two days of his kind of fun, I had to get away. My son, my knight in shining armor, magically appeared in the middle of the night and saved me. I'd hoped it was all just a bad dream until I woke this morning."

"Who—" Sam started to say.

"His name is Guy Mont Violet." Anna pulled a cigarette case out of her purse. "Mind if I smoke?"

"Yep." Sam grinned. "You can fart on board all you want, but smoking is forbidden, that is unless you're a charter guest paying me ten thousand a week for the privilege."

"Ten thousand dollars a week seems a bit much for all this." She put the cigarette case back into her purse and looked hard at him.

"But that also includes all the good scotch whiskey I can drink." Sam held up his glass. "You can smoke up on deck if you need to, but there are too many fumes down here from fuels, varnishes, and solvents. I haven't insured this old boat yet, but I'm thinking about it. So, does Ian know anything about—"

"These things have happened to me my whole life and, no, I've never discussed my private affairs with him. There are things a son should never know about their mother. Don't you agree, Mr. Berrenger. . .Sam?"

He watched her a moment before responding. "I think you'd be surprised about what he knows. Don't worry about me saying anything to break the spell, but you underestimate that boy. Anyway, we've had our own run in with Guy Mont Violet and his posse. So, what's he doing up there on the hill with his gang of thugs? Did you see anything or get a sense of—"

"I saw only the master bedroom suite. I can describe the duvet covers, the cut of crystal in the bar cabinet, and the brand of toothpaste in the bathroom, but the rest of the place was off limits. When I left, I went out the terrace window and ran to the road to beg a ride into town. I will tell you that he is an evil man, a very sexy, exciting, but evil man."

Sam pushed himself up from the table. "His thugs were hassling Ian the other day on the marina dock. I broke it up and almost threw their asses into the harbor. I figure they'll try to exact their pound of flesh if they see an opportunity. In that regard, you shouldn't go into town alone while you're staying with us. Okay?"

"I came here to find my son, Mr. Berringer. Every minute I can spend with him will be precious."

"I'm sure," he said, putting both hands on the salon table and standing over her. He was so close he could smell her. "But, also recognize we have a lot of work to do. We're under a tight time and cost deadline and can't play tour guide and or babysitter." Her face was only inches from his bare chest.

"Then I'll try not to be a distraction." She looked away: her breathing noticeably ragged. "You can depend on that."

"We'll see," Sam said, draining the rest of his scotch. "We'll see. And just between you and me, Ms. Neeson, I've seen how attractive that swimsuit I gave you looks on a good Catholic girl." He winked and turned to take the stairs to the deck two at a time.

# CHAPTER 19

Sam stopped by the deli in town to pick up a sandwich and chips for Anna. There was little to eat on-board, and she refused to leave the boat until they brought her some decent clothes to wear in public.

"Whatever you select will be fine," she'd said before he and Ian pulled away in the inflatable. "You have an eye for fashion. Just look at the good job you did this morning." She'd twirled showing off Sam's shorts and paint-stained T-shirt. They were so overly large on her; she could almost turn completely around inside them.

At a clothing store in town, they found the cotton shorts, tees, and blouses on her list. Ian also picked out a sundress and a pair of flip flops. The clerk charged their purchases to Anna's credit card.

"She can wear this into town and get whatever else she wants," Ian said. "She won't be here that long anyway. I bet she goes back to Boston before the end of the week. I'll meet you at the dinghy dock. I'm headed over to Parts and Power to see if they have those things we need for the generator."

"Before you do that, if you don't go in that shop right there and ask for those panties she wants, then I'll have to," Sam said, "and—"

"But you're a grown man," Ian whined. "I'm just a kid. They'll think I'm a pervert or something."

Sam laughed. "All twenty-two-year-old boys are perverts, or at least wannabes." He nodded up the street. "Look who's there."

Ian turned to see Sarah step out of the ice cream shop. "Great. We'll get her to do it. Hey, Sarah!" He ran off towards her.

Sam found a picnic table outside the grocery store in the shade of a large Tamarind tree and ate his sandwich. The bag with Anna's new clothes rested on the ground at his feet. He was thinking about her story and wondering if Ian would leave the island with her. His own mother had left the family before he was five, and for the next several years his father ran a steady stream of potential stepmothers through their house in Texas City. Nothing ever stuck.

The mother and son thing was unfamiliar to him even though he thought he might've been a better person having experienced it. A wild woman he lived with a few years back in the Florida Keys once accused him of being a woman hater. True, he had eventually hated her even if the blanket charge had been unfair. He later learned a lot of men had bedded, then hated that woman.

He also wondered how much of a delay Anna's presence would cause their restoration effort on Firebird. They couldn't afford to lose any time. There was too much to do to get ready for the charter show, and his schedule had no slack. He'd have to be a bastard about it. They had to give at least eight to ten hours a day to the project. She needed to fly back home as soon as possible. It was too much to think she could be of help. Her manicured nails and soft hands evidenced no experience in manual labor. And all the thinking jobs were taken.

He grabbed another cold Corona from the deli and returned to the table. He had just pushed the lime wedge into the bottle neck when he saw Ian and Sarah exit a shop and head his way. Her denim shorts showed off her tan legs. Her flip flops had yellow rubber flowers on top, and it looked like she'd torn off the bottom of her T-shirt, exposing four inches of her tan tummy.

Sarah held on to Ian's arm, and they were laughing. She whispered something in his ear, and it made him blush. He laughed that cheery laugh of a boy in lust.

"You get those, um, things?" Sam asked. They hadn't seen him at the table and almost walked past him.

"His mother will love these." Sarah held up a small bag containing the unmentionables. "But I'm not sure we got enough. I mean, four pair won't—"

"At one pair a day," Sam said, "I expect she'll be back home before she takes the tags off all of them."

When the three of them arrived back at Firebird, Anna was curtly polite as Ian introduced Sarah. Anna picked up the shopping bag and peeked inside. "So." She looked at Sarah. "Did you have a hand in selecting these, or did the boys—"

"Only these panties," Sarah said, holding up a small boutique bag. "I haven't seen what's in that one."

"I'm sure everything will be perfect," Anna said without smiling and took both bags below.

Ian and Sam exchanged glances.

"You have to get me back ashore in a couple of hours." Sarah turned to Ian. "My shift starts at three. The boss scheduled me for the dinner rush today instead of lunch."

Sam watched them go hand-in-hand up to the bow. He remained under the shade canopy and watched them whispering, their faces only inches apart.

"So, how does this look?" Anna stepped on deck wearing a new pair of navy-blue shorts and a white, wide-neck tee.

Sam cocked his head. All her parts seemed to be the perfect size and in all the right places. *Perky* was the word that came to mind. Her red hair had been brushed till it gleamed and pulled back into a ponytail that touched an exposed bare shoulder. Her cosmetic skills had been finely honed. She was striking, in a threatening kind of way. Her freckles made her look like she'd just stepped out of a "Come to Ireland" tourist commercial. She looked like Sarah's younger sister.

Anna smiled at his speechless response. "Ian?" she called to her son at the bow. The boy was up to his eyeballs in flirt. "Come see the things you brought me. Everything's a perfect fit. I'll return the panties," she said to Sam. "They were okay, but not my style." She looked back at her son and his new girlfriend. "Ian?"

"Coming!" Ian said, taking Sarah's hand and leading her back to the canopy. The sun was directly overhead, and the last cloud of the morning had burned off. It was hot and getting hotter.

Sam watched Anna. Her gaze never left her son. He wondered if her comment about returning the panties meant she wore nothing under her shorts. *Stop it. She's off-limits. Captain's orders!*

He stood with Anna at the rail and watched the two kids motoring away. He thought it cute the way Ian had been so polite and attentive, helping Sarah down the ladder and aboard the inflatable. Ian turned and waved back at them.

"And you let this happen?" Anna faced him. "I thought you were the adult in charge here. My god, he's a confused boy who just ran away from college, and you allowed him to shack up with that—"

"Stop it," Sam said with such strength that she was left speechless. "For god sakes, he's four years older than you were when you had him. He's still a boy, but he's also learning to be a man and—"

"Oh, you stop it." She turned to go below. "How do you know how old I was? Is there any vodka on this shitty tub? I need a drink."

"As do I," he said, following her down the stairs. "I normally don't drink during the working part of the day, but you're enough to—"

"Screw you!" she said. Sam saw the Absolut bottle in her hand before her cabin door slammed shut.

"Oh, yeah, well. . .well. . .You just wish!" He grabbed the bottle of scotch on the galley counter and took it into his own room. "And screw you, too!"

Ian was surprised that no one was up when he returned to the boat. It was still mid-afternoon, and he'd expected to find Sam busy sanding the two salon doors they had removed for varnishing. He went into the galley for a glass of water and saw the door closed to Sam's cabin. He knocked on his mother's door and heard a muffled, "Go away, Sam!"

Sam's door opened, and he stumbled out into the galley and leaned against the sink. He wore a pair of white Jockey briefs, his face looked puffy and his hair was mussed.

"Been napping?" Ian asked as Sam stared at him through bloodshot eyes.

"Yeah, something like that." Sam filled a glass from a large bottle of distilled water and gulped it down. "What time is it, anyway?"

"Four o'clock," Ian said. "I brought back those generator parts you wanted. Was going to start reassembling it. Unless you want me to do something else."

"Nah." Sam shook his head and scratched an itch on his chest. "That's good. Maybe the day won't be a total waste."

"Why, what happened?" Ian glanced back at his mother's door.

"Nothing. At least nothing worth wasting time talking about."

"I'll change into some work clothes," Ian said, and disappeared down the passageway to his cabin.

"Yeah, you do that," Sam said to no one. "I'm going back to bed. Somebody wake me when she's gone."

# CHAPTER 20

Late the next morning, Sam had one of the teak salon doors leaned against the mast and had just completed sanding it. Another door was ready for its first coat of varnish when Ian came on deck to take a break from installing the generator. The tropical sun beat down, and the town's lunch horn had just sounded.

"Hey, kid, I apologize for being such an asshole yesterday. Ought to assign you the job of locking up all the liquor on board. You could ration me a tot a day like they used to do in her majesty's navy."

"You seen my mom?" Ian asked, not responding to Sam's joke.

"Not yet." He rubbed the red scar on his left arm and gazed out across the harbor. "Not since yesterday when you took Sarah ashore."

"Did something happen between you two?"

"Nothing important." Sam faced him. "I don't think she likes your little girlfriend. She took off blaming me for letting it happen."

"But I—"

"I know. I know." Sam shrugged. "I said the same things. Pissed her off. She said some things, then I said some things, and we both grabbed our adult beverage of choice and went to hide in our cabins."

"I'd better go check on her," Ian said, stepping across the cockpit to the stairs. "You know how she can get when—"

"I do now." Sam turned a teak door over and picked up a sanding block. "Believe me, I know now."

"But Mother, I'm not going back; not now and maybe not ever!"

Sam listened to Ian and his mother in hot argument up at the bow. He bent to dip his brush in the varnish can. They had been up there whispering for over half an hour, ever since Anna came out of her room. She didn't acknowledge his presence when she swished past him, following Ian to the bow. Her hair was brushed and the new sundress she wore reminded him of a little girl dressed up for Sunday school. She also had the new flip flops Ian had picked out for her. Sam thought they made her brown feet look even more sexy. He heard her voice rise and looked up to see her arms crossed in frustration.

"So, what's the verdict?" He asked as the boy helped him carry the newly varnished doors to an out-of-the-way place on deck to dry. Anna had retreated to the shade of the canopied cockpit and stared out across the harbor, an iced drink in her hand.

"She wants me to go home when she does, but I—"

"Heard that," Sam said. "So, what's she gonna do?"

"Says she won't leave without me." Ian looked at him. "This could last a day or a week, but I don't believe she'll hang around too long. This is far from her natural environment."

Sam looked back in her direction. Their eyes met as she raised her glass to her glossy lips. "Can she handle a varnish brush?"

A broad grin stretched across the boy's face. "Probably not. But we should make her try."

"Okay," Sam said. "If she's going to take up space on my boat, then she'll need to pay rent. The only currency I take is labor and sweat."

"You are out of your mind, Mr. Berrenger, if you think for one moment, I'll—"

"No work means no food, no water, and no argument," Sam said, looking at her across the cockpit table. Ian had just cleared away the remains of their lunch of tuna sandwiches and Pringles. "We're under a tight deadline and have no time to host guests. Either help out or get your butt back home to whatever wonderful life awaits you."

"Hey, Sam, that's—" Ian started to protest but stopped when Sam glared at him.

After an awkward silence, Anna stood up. "So, what do you want me to do this afternoon?" Her voice heavy with resignation. "Men have told me all my life what to do. Why should things change now?"

"Don't give me that victim crap," Sam said, looking at her. "We need assistance. And I'm happy you're on board," he lied. "Your help would be valuable and appreciated."

She smiled. "Then I'll go change into something proper to work in. All you men ever have to do is ask nicely."

Sam saw Ian roll his eyes. "You'll find a bag of old shorts and T-shirts on my closet floor," Sam said. "Take what you want. They're clean, I think. There's sanding and varnishing that needs to be done while Ian and I handle the heavy lifting and equipment repairs. I'll meet you back up here in ten minutes and show you how it's done."

"Hey, take a look at this." Ian stood in the forward passageway, staring at the back of his cabin door.

"What?" Sam asked, joining him. They had spent the past hour removing cabinet doors and taking them up for Anna to refinish. The old varnish on Ian's cabin door had turned almost black, but traces of a scrawl could just be made out. Someone had scratched something on the inside of the door a long time ago.

"Looks like a name and—"

"Don Antonio Melga," Sam said. "I can read that, but the rest is too faded."

Ian swung the cabin door back and forth so light from the porthole illuminated it. "It's Spanish. You read Spanish?"

"A little. Mostly cuss words learned on the school ground at Texas City. This door needs refinishing, so take it off and bring it up to your mother. We'll copy the words and find someone in town to read them."

"I know how to do this," Anna said, studying the scratches on the door. "I mean I know how to copy it. Our Junior League goes to old cemeteries around Boston and makes rubbings from grave markers. I'll be right back."

Sam watched her disappear down the companionway. The deck was cluttered with evidence of her new learned proficiency with a sanding block and varnish brush. Hatch covers, hatch boards, and cabinet doors from the galley were in various stages of sanding, varnishing, and drying.

"We might have created a varnish fiend." Ian looked at Sam and grinned. "Who knew?"

"I'd keep an eye on your things if I were you," Sam replied, "or you might find them varnished."

Anna returned with a sheet of brown wrapping paper and a lead pencil. She spread the paper on the door and rubbed the pencil over it. Letters appeared, obviously the handwriting of a child.

*Don Antonio Melga*

*Un dia, Voy a matarte. Un dia, cabron.*

*Jorge*

"What does it say?" Anna held the paper up when she was done.

"I'll find out in the morning," Sam said. "I'm meeting with guys at the machine shop about an overhaul of Firebird's engine. There's a fellow there from Puerto Rico who can tell us what this says.

# CHAPTER 21

Sam killed the dinghy motor and tied up in front of the marina office. He left the dock and headed into town, carrying the rolled-up rubbing under his arm. His first stop would be the chandlery for some nuts and bolts, and then the machine shop to see if they could schedule work on Firebird's big diesel engine. He had just crossed the pot-holed street running by the marina when the Jeep skidded to a halt in front of him. The rear passenger window slid down.

"Get in," a voice said.

Sam checked around to see if there were any witnesses. The street was deserted. "And why would I want to do that?" he said to the shadowy figure.

A dark hand with several gold rings on the fingers extended from the window, palm up. "Why would you not?" the voice said. "Get in. I want to talk about the woman."

Sam didn't see anyone else in the vehicle other than the driver. He shrugged and went around to the other side and got in. "I assume you're speaking of Mrs. Neeson. What about her?"

Guy Mont Violet did not look at him but kept his window down and gazed out over the harbor. A few more moments passed before he spoke. "Return her to me," he said almost in a whisper. "We are not finished."

"Uh, sorry, pal," Sam sputtered. "But I think she's done. You sound like y'all were just playing cards or something and didn't end—at least to your satisfaction."

"Yes, playing *something*." The notorious Haitian turned to face him—his black eyes flashing. "Bring the little Irish candy back to me and nothing will happen to you, the boy, and— his new girlfriend."

Sam shook his head. "I don't know what your game is but keep it in your pants and away from my crew and my boat. You have no idea who you're dealing with here. It's not smart to jack with someone who has nothing to lose, who's lost it all more times than one can count and doesn't care."

The Haitian turned his gaze back out the window and said nothing.

"It's a small island," Sam continued. "I'm sure we'll see each other again, perhaps often. But trust me. You screw with me and mine, and you'll regret the day you were born. Ever lost everything that was meaningful to you?" Sam opened the Jeep door and put one foot on the ground. "You get used to it." He stood and slammed the door. The Jeep spun its wheels on the asphalt and sped away.

"There's no way we can get that engine rebuilt by the time you need it, Sam." The machine shop manager wiped his hands on a greasy rag. "We have a backlog of work and a couple of my guys are going on vacation at the same time. Couldn't really start until late December or sometime after the first of the year."

"But the charter show on Saint Thomas is in November. That's only two months away," Sam protested.

The shop manager shrugged. "It's what it is." He tossed the rag into a pile on the worktable.

"Did the Haitian say something to you?" Sam asked, raising an eyebrow.

"What do you mean? Why would he do something like that?" The manager turned away.

"Can you do anything to help us out?" Sam was now almost pleading.

"Ask me for what you need." The manager sounded sympathetic. "Maybe some parts and tools. We'll see."

Sam nodded. "I'll appreciate any help you can give. In any case, ready or not, I'll be out of here in November."

"Sooner rather than later will be better for everyone on the island." The machine shop manager looked at him. "I shouldn't say any more."

"I understand," Sam said. "That thug has everyone on edge. By the way – is Orlando around? I have something for him to look at." Sam unrolled the rubbing paper and held it up in the sunlight coming through the shop's front window.

The manager opened a door to the back room. "Tell Orlando to come out. Someone wants to see him." He nodded at Sam, turned into his office and shut the door.

"What's up?" Orlando appeared inside the work area. "Hey, Sammy. I heard you were here on a boat in the harbor. The last time I saw you was at the marina bar in San Juan with your face pressed into the tits of some glam New York chick."

"Yeah, I don't remember." Sam grinned. "There's a lot about San Juan that's still fuzzy. I've got something here I want you to see." He rolled the paper out on a table.

"Looks like someone pissed off a little kid." Orlando traced a finger over the scrawl. "Don Antonio Melga, Un dia. Voy a matarte. Un dia, cabron. Jorge," he read out loud. "Don Antonio Melga is a name I'm not familiar with, but it can be checked out. The rest basically says, 'one day I'll kill you.' Nice. The writing looks like a kid's scrawl. Not unusual. Hell, I once wrote 'I hate my father' on the window blinds in my room with a Magic Marker. It could only be seen when the blinds were down and closed. It's probably still there. I feel bad about it to this day."

"We found this scratched into the varnish on a stateroom door on the ketch I'm restoring," Sam said while he rolled the paper back up. "We were curious."

"Maybe this Don Antonio was a previous owner," Orlando said. "You have any history on that?"

"No, but now that you mention it, some guy in Puerto Rico told me before we left that a Don Antonio something was once an owner of my boat. Hey, I bet that's it. I'm learning more every day," Sam said. "She's got a lot of secrets. Wouldn't be surprised by anything. She's a big ketch. Built some thirty years ago, and abandoned in the harbor at San Juan. Jerry Diaz, the harbormaster, helped me acquire her from U.S. Customs. Let me know if you learn anything about it."

"Jerry Diaz, you say?" Orlando's eyebrow shot up. "Interesting. Did he say anything else? Anything about the yacht's history."

"Only that U.S. Customs impounded her from a bunch of dope smoking Rastafarians."

"Interesting," Orlando said again. "Jerry Diaz? Interesting. I thought he was still in prison."

Sam cut the engine and the dinghy drifted toward Firebird. He tossed the painter to Ian on the boarding platform.

"Any luck with scheduling the rebuild?" Ian asked while looping the line around a cleat. He extended a hand to Sam and pulled the inflatable sideways against the platform.

"Nope." Sam passed him a plastic bag of groceries. Anna had given him a list before he went ashore. "The shop is booked until January. We'll have to make what repairs and improvements we can do on our own. Where's your mom?"

"Cleaning up below after lunch. Did you eat in town? You see Sarah?"

"Yes and no." Sam grinned at the boy's anxiousness. "I grabbed something at the deli. Looked like a big crowd over at her cafe. Two water taxis had just dumped off their passengers. I'm sure she was very busy."

"Anything going on in town?" Ian asked, as they stepped into the cockpit.

"Nothing special," Sam said, wondering how much he should tell him about meeting the Haitian. "The shop manager said they might could get us parts and loan us tools if we did some of the engine rebuild ourselves. Oh, I saw Orlando about the scrawl on your cabin door. Said it was probably a kid of this Don Antonio Melga angry at his old man a lot of years ago. They'd both probably laugh at it today."

Ian went below with the groceries and returned with two cold beers. He handed one to Sam and they sat in the cockpit, listening to the sounds of Anna working down in the galley.

"Has your mother said anything about what happened here on the island before she found us?" Sam asked.

"Not really. I learned a long time ago not to ask about where she spent her time. Granddad hovered over everyone and everything in his domain, so I tried to respect her privacy. Why do you ask?"

"Nothing, really," Sam said, turning to look out over the busy harbor. "I was curious who she might have met here before finding us. It's a small town. I'll ask her about it if I remember."

"I'm going to see Sarah tonight after she gets off work at nine. Can I take the dinghy? I promise not to stay out too late."

"Sure, kid." Sam smiled. "I'd flip you the keys like they do in those cheesy father and son commercials, but I left them in the dinghy. That's probably not very smart."

After dinner, He and Anna stood at the rail, watching Ian motor away in the dark. It was a warm night. Anna was barefoot and wore a pair of loose shorts and a tank top. Her red hair was in a ponytail and held with a rubber band.

"I heard you tell him to be careful." Anna looked up at him. "Does he need to be? Is there something I should worry about?" Her sweet perfume made him dizzy. She touched his bare arm with her hand. "If there's anything. . . ."

Sam put his arm around her. He felt her shiver. She was a head shorter and petite like an Irish fairy. The sound of tires screeching in town and a constable's blinking lights along the causeway made him think of the Haitian. "I need to know what your relationship is, or was, with Guy Mont Violet?" He whispered in her hair while she leaned against him.

"What?" She stepped away. "What do you mean?" Her eyes flashed in the harbor lights.

"The Haitian stopped me in town today and requested, no, demanded, I send you back to him. Like I could do that even if I wanted. Said you two weren't finished. Now that's an interesting thought which begs the question—"

"What else did he say?" Anna wrapped her bare arms around herself and turned back toward town.

"Only that it was in my best interest—and yours, and Ian's, and his girlfriend's, if I took him seriously."

"Oh god." Anna dropped her chin to her chest. She closed her eyes and shuddered. Sam took a step towards her, but she held up a hand to stop him. "No. No, don't. I'm okay." She wiped her eyes with the back of her hand and turned to face him. "All right. Storm's over." She took a deep breath. "Now what do we do?"

They moved to the cockpit and sat opposite each other. Neither spoke and the darkness amplified the silence. Sam recognized this was sensitive territory and took his time contemplating his next question. He slipped off his flips, stretched out his long legs and crossed his feet at the ankles on the cushion next to her. It was warm so he leaned forward to remove his shirt and felt the air on his bare skin. They both sat quietly watching the other boats in the harbor. He reached down to rub a spot on his foot. "Must have bruised it today. It's really sore."

Anna pulled his foot into her lap and began massaging the muscles in the arch.

"Wow," he moaned. "Oh, God, that feels good." After a bit he opened his eyes. "So, what about the Haitian? There are no saints here, so don't worry about anyone judging. I'm just concerned about Guy Mont Violet and his threats. Should I be?"

She slid her fingers between his toes and gave them a good stretch.

"Oh, god. Don't stop." He groaned. "That feels so damn good."

"When I landed at the airport here," She set Sam's foot down and picked up the other one. "I collected my things in baggage claim and went outside to find a taxi. I had no plans but thought I'd get a hotel room and look for Ian."

"The cab dropped me off in town, and I went into the nearest bar smack into the web of Guy Mont Violet. He's a handsome man and there was something attractively dangerous about him. He had a brilliant white smile, and the open collar of his silk shirt revealed a broad chest. His dark skin, wavy black hair, and brown eyes with the longest eyelashes I've ever seen on a man were mesmerizing. He ordered us a couple of drinks and must've slipped something in mine because the next thing I knew, we were in his villa snorting lines of cocaine while his bodyguards stood outside the bedroom door. The rest of the time I was there has melded into a lump of fuzzy regrets."

After a short pause, she continued. "He liked to play rough, my bruises prove that, and he really likes his drugs. I woke up the evening of the second day, alone in the bedroom and no one around. I dressed, grabbed my purse and slipped over the terrace to flag down a car on the road. The driver let me out in the rain in town, and it was pure luck that Ian came upon me when he did."

She continued pressing her thumbs into Sam's arch. "This would work better if we had some lotion," she said. "Your skin is so dry."

He sat up. "I'd go get some, but I'd fall on my face since my feet are totally numb. Check that basket on the seat behind you. Will Coppertone work?"

Anna took the brown bottle and squirted a supply into her palm. "It's nice and greasy." She lifted his foot up off her lap. "You have big feet."

"And?" Sam cocked his head at her.

"Nothing," she said, rubbing the lotion between his toes. "It's just more work to give a good massage to someone with such big ones."

"I mean what else did you see and hear? Why is he called the Haitian?"

Anna worked the tight muscles more aggressively. "Said his mother was French and had an affair with the president of Haiti. Called him Papa something."

"Papa Doc?" Sam's eyebrows raised. "Papa Doc Duvalier, President for Life. A medical doctor who terrorized the citizens with his secret police—the Tonton Macoute. Read a book about it once. Supposedly used voodoo to control the people."

Anna moved his foot back to the cushion beside her. "Let's do the other one again with the lotion."

Sam lifted his left foot into her lap and watched her squirt another handful of lotion. "So, Guy Mont Violet is the bastard son of Papa Doc Duvalier?" He looked out over the harbor. "The cruel bastard's been dead about twenty years. His son, Baby Doc, was overthrown and went into exile in France. Wonder if he and the Haitian know each other?"

"I have no idea," Anna said, working the lotion into Sam's left foot. "Guy was charming the first day. His villa up on the hill overlooking the town is impressive with a large courtyard and gardens. He took me into the master suite and said to stay as-long-as I wanted. It was after dinner that first evening when he went outside with his men to talk business. He returned with lines of cocaine on a compact mirror. You can imagine the rest."

"Uh, no I can't," Sam said. "What happened?"

# CHAPTER 22

Anna didn't answer as she focused on digging her thumbs into the sole of his foot. Finally, she looked up and shrugged. "I'm Irish, but not a good Catholic, Sam, if that's what you mean. Things happen. I've done worse."

"Does Ian know about the "worse?'" Sam asked, almost in a whisper.

"I don't know what Ian knows or doesn't know." Anna stopped rubbing his foot. "What does any child really know about their parents? Let's say it was never discussed at the dinner table."

"Is there a lot to be *discussed* if the subject ever came up?"

"We're done here." She pushed his foot off her lap and stood. "Let's just say that a convent would have a difficult time accepting me, which is a suggestion my father-in-law often made. I think he wanted to have Ian to himself, and me out of the family picture. Now we're both out of his life."

Sam followed her to the stairs. "What do we do about Guy Mont Violet?"

"Your decision, Sam. I'll assist any way I can, but I'm done with him."

"Okay, so don't go ashore anytime without me or Ian with you. We'll finish this refit and get out of here as soon as we can. Hopefully, he'll forget all about this."

"I doubt it," she said, turning to go below. "I hope so, but doubt it."

Sam lay awake in his bunk listening for any unusual sounds. He couldn't sleep until Ian returned to Firebird. His conversation with

Anna had made him worry even more about the Haitian. His whole life had always been on the edge of falling into the abyss. *Why can't I have a boring life for just a few months like every other normal asshole?*

He pushed up on one elbow at the buzzing sound of an outboard motor. He reached for the flare pistol and swung his bare legs out from under the sheets. Naked except for his baseball cap, he went up the salon stairs to the cockpit and stood in the shadows. A dinghy killed its engine and floated to the side of the boat. A dark figure appeared coming up the ladder. Sam pointed the pistol and cocked the trigger.

"God damn!" Ian said. "You scared the crap out of me."

Sam lowered the pistol and released the hammer. "I thought those goons were paying us a visit."

"Saw them in town." Ian swung his backpack onto a cockpit cushion. "They were parked by the customs house chatting it up with a couple of constables and passing a brown bag of something back and forth."

"They see you?"

"Don't think so. They had a couple of girls with them, laughing and talking loud. They weren't paying attention to anything or anyone except the girls."

"Was the Haitian with them?" Sam asked.

"Didn't see him. Just three guys including the two that threw me in the dink. Why do you ask?" Ian picked up his backpack. "Are those assholes—"

"Not yet," Sam said realizing he was naked and turned toward the stairs. "Can't be too careful."

"She's so cool, Mom." Ian sat across from Anna at the salon table. She wore one of Sam's long T-shirts as a night gown. It came down to mid-thigh. Ian held a cold beer that Sam opened for him. "We hung out on beach chairs talking most of the night. She's had a very interesting life in England. She read French at school. The Brits say *read* instead of *majored*. I love her English accent. Sounds so smart and sophisticated."

"How long is she planning to stay on the island?" Anna looked first at Ian and glanced at Sam standing by the galley sink. He was wearing a pair of cotton boxer briefs.

"She says it's common for British kids to take a year or more during their schooling to travel the commonwealth." Ian eyes widened with enthusiasm. "She arrived at the beginning of summer with no time frame in mind and still doesn't have one. She could be here a year or a lifetime. Isn't that cool to be so free?"

"What do her parents say?" Anna furrowed her brow. "I mean—"

"I haven't asked," Ian lowered his voice. "She hasn't said anything about them, yet."

"And what has she asked about me?" Anna glanced at Sam.

"Nothing." Ian stood up. "I need to hit the sack. I've got to finish that generator tomorrow so we can start recharging our batteries. I told Sam I'd get the electric windlass motor working after I finish the generator. It'd be expensive to replace it."

"Then what have you told her about me?"

"Nothing," Ian said over his shoulder as he headed down the passageway to his cabin. "I told you, she didn't ask."

Sam smiled to himself as he watched Anna push out of the settee and stomp off to her cabin. *That boy's gonna keep poking the mama lion until - I don't know what. And neither does he.*

# CHAPTER 23

It was a while before Sam fell asleep. He couldn't get his mind off what Anna had told him about Guy Mont Violet and the hints about her past. Her little girl manner made her come across so innocent, the mother, the Madonna. He rolled over on his bunk, grabbed a pillow and hugged it against his chest. It felt warm and firm like when he held her on deck as they watched Ian go ashore. He could smell her hair and the heady fragrance of her perfume.

He turned over trying to find a cool spot on the mattress. He spooned into the pillow and gave it a couple of involuntary humps. The gentle rocking of the boat on its mooring finally put him to sleep. His dreams were a kaleidoscope of people and places. He saw Darlene running away from him on the school grounds, and Evelyn standing on a train platform in Queens. She was reading a newspaper and carrying a briefcase. When he woke the next morning, he remembered nothing about his dreams.

By noon, the tropical sun was blasting dry heat. Sam helped Ian install a refurbished fuel filter on the generator, and then they drug the heavy block into position in the engine room. Ian was on his hands and knees tightening bolts that held it in place. Sam had figured out the electrical wiring and was making the proper connections to the boat's batteries and the 110V system.

It was mid-afternoon when they had the fuel line for the diesel connected and were ready to test it. A new generator would have been preferable, but there was no money to replace it or even do a proper overhaul. The inside of the block with its crusted valves and pistons was left untouched. Hopefully, they weren't too bad. Enough new parts had been found on the island and together with a lot of cleaning and oiling, Sam and Ian agreed they had solved most if not all the problems.

"We ready?" Sam watched him replace wrenches in the toolbox.

"I think so," the boy replied. "Let's see."

Sam pushed the generator starter button on the engine room control panel. There was a sputter, two cranks, and the generator hummed smoothly like new. He nodded at Ian. "Good job. We should now have electricity out here on the mooring. Let's check out the 110V while it's running." He went into his cabin and plugged in a small travel hair dryer. It blew hot.

"It's a go. We've got all the current we need. Means we won't have to run the main engine every day to recharge the house batteries. It'll save wear and tear as well as fuel. We can also operate the water maker which takes a lot of power. Our tanks are about half full now so we can replenish what we're using." He looked at Ian standing in the doorway. "It's a home run, kid. Good job."

Ian saw his mother come out of her cabin. "We got it running, Mom. Now we can play the radio and the cassette player. You can dry your hair and use the lights in your cabin at night without worrying about saving battery power."

"And," Anna said, "I found an old portable electric sewing machine in the floor of my closet this afternoon. I suppose it was used for sail repair. Can't imagine anyone would've made—"

"Slow down, there." Sam joined them. "Life on a boat means conserving everything, especially electricity and fresh water. It's like living on a small planet. In Firebird's case, the planet is only eighty-four feet long and sixteen feet wide."

"Yes, sir," Ian said. "Sorry, I got carried away."

Sam laughed. "It's the crew's job to get excited about things. It's the captain's job to rain on everyone's parade. It's nature's balance."

No one spoke a moment as they listened to the generator's steady hum in the engine room.

"How long shall—" Ian started to ask.

"An hour a day to charge the house batteries, Sam answered.

"Then always start it up if you're going to operate something that will be a big drag, like a power tool or an air compressor."

He stepped over to the navigation table. "This switch turns on to convert battery power to 110V current through the convertor box mounted on the back wall of the engine room. We haven't run anything through the convertor since we've been here. I didn't want the extra stress on the engine to replace that charge. We live and die on a sailing vessel like Firebird by engine power. Hell is having no working engine. With the generator, we now have current to fire up the motor even if the batteries are dead."

Sam moved through the salon to the microwave oven on the galley counter. "We haven't used this or other appliances like the toaster, but now we can. That'll save propane for cooking. He put a cup of water from the tap in the microwave and turned it on for two minutes. The water was almost boiling when he took it out. "See? We can now offer paying guests real creature comforts on our classy charter yacht. Big steps, guys."

Later that afternoon, he and Ian were washing down the forward deck with the saltwater pump when Sam checked his watch. The hum of the generator could barely be heard at the bow. "You can turn it off now," he said to Ian. "It's been over an hour. Guests will appreciate its quietness. When the main engine is running, it's so loud you almost have to yell to be heard."

At dinner, the three of them sat at the salon table finishing off spaghetti and meat sauce prepared by Anna. She was obviously proud of herself. Sam knew cooking was not a skill learned in her father-in-law's Cambridge mansion.

He finished his third glass of wine and watched her clean the dishes. She wore the yellow sundress bought in town and padded barefoot between the galley sink and table. He noticed her undergarments were a string bikini. Another one of Evelyn's souvenirs left behind.

"I'm going ashore first thing tomorrow to see about a few things." Sam poured the last of the wine bottle into his glass.

"Want me to come with you?" Ian asked.

"Nah. I'd rather you stay out here with your mother. With those thugs around, I don't want either one of you left alone on the boat."

"But what about you going in by yourself?" Ian got up from the table and carried his plate to the galley sink.

"I can handle whatever they throw at me. I'm also not too worried about you. It's your mother I'm concerned about. You've seen what those creeps can do."

Sam took his wine into his cabin and shut the door. He couldn't get his mind off the bikini Anna wore under her sundress. He remembered how the thong looked on Evelyn. He pushed down hard on the front of his shorts. *Damn. One or both of us need to start wearing more clothes. I'm only human and a weak one at that.*

He stepped out of his shorts and stretched out uncovered on the bed. He wondered if Anna was aware of the effect she was having on him.

The next morning, a warm breeze blew over the harbor while Sam steered the inflatable towards the marina. He could see Charlie outside the office chatting with two catamaran captains who took guests from hotels and cruise ships for a day of snorkeling and a barbecue lunch. Most mornings, the double hull boats left the harbor with up to forty passengers each.

Charlie caught Sam's dinghy line as the Zodiac drifted toward him. "Hey! How's it hanging?" Charlie's grin was contagious.

"Low, hairy, and heavy." Sam laughed.

"Oh, probably because of that sweet thing you have living out there with you."

"It's a bad rumor." Sam took the line from Charlie and did a figure-eight on a dock cleat. "I'd say she's more like an angry wet bobcat than a sweet thing."

"Not what I hear in town." Charlie walked with him up the dock. "I hear the Haitian—"

"I know." Sam cut him off. "I've heard it, too. But I think it's more like the stuff we used to hear on the school yard. Janie Lou

Dumas in the ninth grade was said to be doing the varsity basketball team. She was a virgin when she married the Methodist preacher's son. I know. I always struck out with her in the back seat at the drive-in movie theater."

Charlie laughed. "It was Belle Ann Davidson at my school in West Orange. If the rumors had been true, I probably would've gotten my share in high school. As it was, I'm still trying to catch up."

Charlie followed him to the end of the dock where Sam stepped down into the marina parking lot. "I'll pick up my mail when I return," Sam called back to him. "I'd appreciate it if you'd keep an eye out for any strangers around my boat while I'm seeing about engine parts over at the machine shop."

Charlie nodded as Sam crossed the parking lot and headed into town.

"You going to the machine shop?" One of the charter captains Sam had seen at the marina office stepped along beside him. "Me, too. They're repairing a boarding ladder for me. I hope it's done, or I can't take folks out snorkeling without a safe way to get them on and off the boat."

"I'm Sam Berrenger." Sam extended his hand. "Which boat is yours?"

"Captain Meredith Ainsley, and I operate White Squall." The man shook Sam's hand. "She's a seventy-two-foot schooner rigged catamaran built in New Zealand. My late father sailed her to the Caribbean thirty-five years ago. We've been taking tourists out for day sails ever since."

They walked a block in town without saying anything more.

"You're on that big ketch out in the harbor, ain't you?" Captain Ainsley asked as they passed a bakery. The aroma of fresh baked bread was heady on the sidewalk.

"I am." Sam glanced at him. "Refitting her into a proper charter yacht and hope to be outta here in time for the charter agent's show on Saint Thomas in November."

Captain Ainsley nodded. "That's a good show."

"By the way." Sam paused and turned to the captain." Where do you guys go when you take tourists out for a day of fun in the sun? I don't know the waters around Saint Sebastian that well. I sailed here from San Juan to work on her and haven't left the harbor once. Was thinking it might be nice to take my crew somewhere for a picnic and a swim."

"There's several places we go with our guests. Each captain has his favorite, and we try to leave each other alone and not crowd up paradise," Captain Ainsley said. He stopped a moment and looked up the street like he was thinking about something.

"I usually head across the channel each day to Moskito Island. I had a mooring set there every year in the lee of the island, but there's plenty of room in the harbor for boats to anchor. Folks know the shallow anchorage near the beach is reserved for White Squall and leave it be. Every now and then I have to run off some idiot on a bare boat charter. The island has a protected lee and a secluded white sand beach about two hundred yards long rimmed by palm trees. My guests from Europe, mostly France and Germany, like to hang everything out on the beach, if you know what I mean." He chuckled.

"Sometimes it's enough to give the Pope a hard on. Other times, it's a real turn off. Too much wiener schnitzel, beer, and years of gravity can do terrible things to the human body. Know what I mean?" He chuckled again.

The front door of the machine shop was open as was the bay service doors. Captain Ainsley turned toward the open bay, and Sam went through the front door into the parts department. Orlando stood behind the counter.

"Hey, man," Orlando sounded pleased to see him. "I've got some information for you." He reached across to shake Sam's hand. "Spoke to my cousin in Argentina yesterday. He's been living there for thirty years and travels Latin America for Caterpillar Tractor in sales and service. I asked him if he knew a Don Antonio Melga. He laughed and asked me if I was kidding. Said there was a rich coffee grower by that name in Rio that was killed by his bastard son some years ago. The old man kept his mistress and the kid on his yacht in the harbor."

"No kidding," Sam said. "He remember the name of the yacht?"

"Nah, I asked specifically about that. He said the story was well known in that part of South America. One day the kid waited until the old man got off his mother, then slit his throat. Almost decapitated him. My cousin says everyone thinks the boy went to Columbia and joined up with the FARC rebels. Maybe he's dead. Who knows? Don Antonio's wife and real son then took over the plantations and sold the yacht. How's that for a story?"

Sam turned and looked out the open door. "Gives me a lot to think about. I haven't heard a good ending for one of Firebird's previous owners yet."

"Maybe, you'll be the good ending," Orlando said. "I have a feeling."

"Maybe. I need to call the marketing department at Palmer Johnson in Wisconsin. They built Firebird. Hopefully, they can shed more light on previous owners. Especially the original owner."

"Hey, Sam." Captain Ainsley stuck his head in the doorway. He carried his boarding ladder over his shoulder. "Nice meeting you today. And good luck with that big ketch."

"You bet." Sam waved to him. "See you around. We'll look for White Squall if we get out to Moskito Island."

"Lunch aboard is on me when you do." The Captain waved and shut the door.

"Best to go over there on a day a French cruise ship is in," Orlando said with a wide grin on his face. "White Squall is usually loaded with Frenchies wearing the skimpiest thongs you ever saw. And even those come off when they get to the beach. Seen it myself a couple of times. Definitely improves the marriage."

Sam stared at him a moment. "Oh, yeah, I almost forgot. I need to order an exhaust manifold for that big Ford engine on Firebird. The one on it now leaks and won't take another weld. Can't have charter guests dying from carbon monoxide."

Orlando made a note. "It'll take a week or more. Probably cost around a thousand dollars, including shipping."

Sam groaned. “Well, I need it and have no other options. I’ll go by the bank and bring the cash by tomorrow.”

“Oh, I almost forgot.” Orlando grinned. “The town Dock Master told me that a French liner is due in two days. It’ll arrive Friday morning and leave late afternoon on Sunday for Saint Martin.”

# CHAPTER 24

His walk from the machine shop to Sarah's café on the town dock took only a few minutes. Sam arrived there a half hour before the start of the lunch rush and found her wiping down the counter. "Don't want to take much of your time," he said. He glanced around at the few tables hosting the leftover breakfast crowd. "But there's something I need to tell you."

"Has something happened to Ian?" She tossed her rag into the sink. "What—"

"No. No. Nothing like that, yet." Sam removed his ballcap and rubbed his forehead. "It's just that there's been a ratcheting up of my bad relationship with the Haitian. I think it best if Ian and his mother not venture into town alone anytime soon. You heard about the event on the dock the other day with his thugs and Ian?"

"Yes, but I thought they were just horsing around. Ian didn't say it was anything serious."

"It was." Sam put his cap back on and pulled the brim low over his eyes. "I'll tell you more at another time. Just assume it's between me and the Haitian. No one else. I don't think anything bad will happen but—"

"I understand," Sarah said. "His men come in the café most days for an early lunch. In fact," She looked at the clock on the wall. "They could be showing up here any time now. They are a bad lot if you ask me. They give me the creeps the way they leer at me all the time they're here. I feel like a. . .I don't know, mostly a shower after my lunch shift."

"Let me know if something more than leering happens," Sam said. "Uh, Ian and I would enjoy you visiting on Firebird anytime during this, shall we call it a quarantine?" He smiled. "I think things should cool down fairly soon. Until then, when you want to come out to the boat, either he or I will pick you up at the dock by the marina office. Just call us on channel sixteen on a VHF radio. You can call from the marina office. It's open every night till eight."

"I can do that." Sarah sprayed the counter for another wipe down. "But we'd planned dinner tonight at my apartment. What did he say about that?"

"Uh, how about steaks on the grill on Firebird?" Sam said. "He told me to invite you to join us for steaks and good wine. So, what should I tell the young squire?" Sam stuck his hands in the pockets of his shorts and raised both eyebrows.

Sarah pulled a laminated shift schedule from a shelf under the counter and studied it. I'm off at 7:00PM. Pick me up at the dock at ten after."

"Great," Sam said. "We can play cards or a board game after dinner. It'll be good for you and Anna to spend some quality time together."

"Yeah, sure." She tossed the schedule back under the counter. "Tell Master Ian that I expect to spend some quality time with him after dinner."

"Really?" Sam said. Her frankness caught him by surprise. "Uh. I'll pass it on." He turned and headed out the door as a loud group of lunch customers came down the dock.

Sam walked back to the marina, thinking about how he could break the news to Ian and his mother about remaining on Firebird as a temporary precaution. He figured they wouldn't like it, especially Ian, and he couldn't tell the boy the real reason. *No son wants to know that much about his mother.*

He stepped off the sidewalk to cross the busy street into the marina. A speeding truck swerved toward him, it's bumper just brushed the hair on his leg. It was gone before he had a chance to yell out.

"Son-of-a-bitch," he mumbled under his breath. Shaken, he stepped back up on the sidewalk and tried to calm himself. *That was close.* The glass in the truck was dark and he couldn't see who or how many were inside. He looked around for any witnesses. No one paid him any attention. A shiver ran up his spine. He wasn't sure if it was an accident, a botched hit job, or an intentional warning. Whatever, he thought. *The battle's on, and I'm holding a losing hand.*

Sam secured the dinghy to Firebird's boarding platform and saw Ian waiting at the rail. "We need to finish up this refit as soon as we can and get the hell away from this island," he said in a lowered voice. "Where's your mother?"

"Taking a nap in her cabin. Why? What happened?"

Sam told him about the near miss on the way home and his escalating feud with Guy Mont Violet and his thugs. "It started a few weeks ago when I saw a kid on a bike in town get hit by his car. I berated the local constable on duty for not even questioning them. Later there was nothing in the local paper about it. I assume the Haitian used his influence with the island ministry to hush it up. They've had it in for me since I got here. I figure that's why his two men attacked you on the dock."

Ian shook his head. "Should've told me. I thought they were just being assholes."

"Well, that too," Sam said, and punched him teasingly on the arm as he stepped past him into the shade of the cockpit. "I didn't eat lunch while in town. You want anything?" He started down the stairs to the galley.

"Just finished a sandwich," Ian replied, following him. "What do you think is going to happen? I mean—"

"Yeah, I know." Sam took a loaf of bread out of the cabinet and started spreading peanut butter and jelly on two slices. "I've been thinking a lot about this. Hopefully, it'll blow over, but we still need to focus on finishing what work we can, and get over to Saint Thomas as soon as possible. For now, it's probably best if you and your mom stay on the boat and out of town. I'm sure they think they can get to me through you two."

"When I see Sarah tonight, I'll tell her to be careful. I don't want anything to happen to her."

Sam paused spreading jam and looked at Ian. "Oh, yeah. I saw her at the café in town and invited her out to Firebird this evening for steaks and your fun company. Don't want to get up in your business, but she said you were meeting at her apartment. I figured this was a better plan."

"Whoa." Does that mean I'm confined to this boat? I mean—"

"You can accompany me into town but don't go alone. Too risky right now."

Sam put the two slices of his sandwich together, grabbed a cold Corona from the fridge and headed up the stairs to the deck. "It's cooler up here in the heat of the day. The shade and a good breeze makes it tolerable." He pulled his sweaty T-shirt off, hung it on a lifeline in the sun, and plopped down on a cockpit cushion to eat his lunch. Ian sat in the shade across the cockpit from him.

"I'm concerned about your mom being out here alone if we're both in town. We'll have to be aware of our surroundings and use good judgement."

"What did Sarah say about tonight?" Ian rubbed his hand over his arm. "We were—"

"Yeah, she told me." Sam cleaned peanut butter from the corners of his mouth with a finger. "She gets off work at seven and will call us on Channel 16 when she gets to the dinghy dock."

Ian gazed out over the harbor. "I'm almost finished painting the engine room. You'll be able to eat off the floor in there by this evening. Tomorrow, I'm varnishing the woodwork in mine and Mom's cabins. I'll do yours, too."

"Good," Sam said. "That'll freshen everything up down below." He noticed the boy seemed a bit worried. "You can take the dinghy in and pick Sarah up at the marina. Just don't dock until you see her on the pier. I'll stay out here and get the charcoal going for the steaks. I'll put on some potatoes and get Anna to make a salad. Who knows, after a great meal and some wine, you may get lucky." Sam winked at him and finished off his beer.

"No chance with you and my mother aboard." Ian wiped sweat off his face with the bottom of his T-shirt.

"It's good training." Sam laughed. "Every kid needs to hone his seduction technique and skills in the presence of adults."

"Maybe," Ian said, standing by the stairs. "This was to be our third date, and I hoped it was going to be the night."

"We each are in control of our own destiny," Sam said. "I think that's in the *Prophet* by Kahlil Gibran. Or maybe it was Alfred E. Neuman in *Mad Magazine*. Not sure. The library on the last freighter I worked was pretty thin." He laughed as Ian turned and went down the steps.

Sam looked back toward the charcoal grill on the stern of the boat. They had used it a couple of times and the bag of charcoal looked half full. He thought about taking a nap before readying for their guest. He checked the time. *Yep – time enough for a nap. Anna won't like our plan but she, even more than I, knows the risk of crossing Guy Mont Violet.*

# CHAPTER 25

"See anything unusual at the marina?" Sam stood at the rail as Ian escorted Sarah up the ladder from the boarding platform. She wore a blue sundress, and her ponytail had been brushed out. Her long hair framed her pretty face.

Sarah slipped off her flip flops and started down the companionway into the main salon. "I'll give your mom a hand with the salad and setting the table."

"Tell her we'll eat up here in the cockpit," Sam called out as she disappeared below. "Too nice an evening to stay down there." He looked at Ian.

"I didn't see anything out of the ordinary, if that's what you're asking." Ian followed him to the grill on the stern. "Ready to put the steaks on?" He eyed the platter of seasoned ribeyes next to the grill.

"Lift the lid and see if the potatoes are soft," Sam said. "They went on a half hour ago so should be done."

An hour later, the four of them had finished dinner and sat around the cockpit table enjoying the wine. Ian raised his glass to Sam and his mother. "A toast to the cooks for a great meal. Can't beat a steak dinner and fine wine on a private yacht in the Caribbean."

"I'll second that." Sarah raised her glass and winked at Ian across the table.

Sam glanced at Anna who nodded approval and sipped from her wine glass. She was wearing a pair of loose shorts and a T-shirt. The cotton shirt left nothing to one's imagination about what she did or didn't have on under it.

"Sam," Anna said, turning her attention to him. "How was your day? I must not have slept well last night as I took a long nap this afternoon. I never do that. Fortunately, I got up in time to get dressed and make the salad." She turned to Sarah. "He didn't tell me you were coming to dinner until just before you arrived."

"Yep, about the time you got up." Sam laughed. Ian and Sarah laughed with him which seemed to piss Anna off.

"Make fun all you want," she said, rising to clear the table.

"Oh, sit down and have some more wine." Sam reached with the bottle to refill her glass. "No one's making fun of you. If anything, we're a bit jealous. There's nothing more satisfying, than a long nap in the middle of the day. I read once it was a regular practice for Chinese emperors. They would have a slave stand by their bed and drag their fingers slowly across their bare backs until they went to sleep." He smiled at Anna. "Another reason it's good to be the Emperor."

"Don't look at me." Anna held up her ragged fingernails. "Look what sanding and varnishing your boat has done. These would leave your back bloody if I did that to you. I need to find a place in town to get a manicure."

"I can do it for you," Sarah said, sitting up. I always do my own. A Thai friend in London worked at a nail salon. She showed me the tricks. I can come out on Saturday afternoon and—"

Anna looked at Sarah a moment like she wasn't sure how to respond. "That would be nice, dear," she said. "We'll see. But that doesn't mean I'll give Sam afternoon backrubs."

Sam laughed. "Maybe I'll give them to you. By the way," he looked at Ian. "I ran into Orlando at the machine shop in town today and learned something more about that salon door with the scribbling on it."

"What?" All three of them said, simultaneously.

"We were right about a kid being angry at his old man," Sam said. "So pissed that he slit his throat here on this boat."

"My god." Anna's hand went to her neck.

"Yep. Orlando said Don Antonio Melga was a wealthy coffee grower in Argentina and bought the boat to keep his mistress and their bastard son on in the harbor at Rio. He must've purchased

Firebird after the failed investment guy in Connecticut owned it. Anyway, the kid hated the old man and eventually killed him."

Everyone was silent for a few moments.

"Is he in prison?" Ian asked.

"They think he fled to Columbia and joined the FARC rebels. No one's heard any more about him. He could be dead."

"Wow." Ian refilled his wine glass. "I thought growing up without a father was hard. Guess there are worse things." He and Anna looked at each other till she turned away.

"Ian told me you had another encounter with the bad guys on the island today after I saw you at the cafe." Sarah changed the subject.

Sam shrugged. "Nothing much. I should've been paying more attention when I stepped off the curb near the marina. Just a close shave with a speeding truck."

Anna stared at him.

"We'll talk about it later," he said under his breath.

"Hey, I learned something else interesting." Sam said. "Met a charter captain in town who advised me on a great place to go snorkeling and have a picnic. We've been working hard on the boat, and I think we could use a break."

"Who'd you meet?" Sarah asked. "I know most the charter captains. We supply them with box lunches and snacks at the café."

"Captain Ainsley. He sails the big catamaran, White Squall."

"Oh yes, a nice man." Sarah smiled.

"White Squall takes their guests across the channel each day to Moskito Island, a small uninhabited rock with a great secluded beach." Sam continued. "His guests snorkel and have a barbecue. The captain suggested we dinghy over there one day. Even offered us lunch on White Squall if we wanted to join them."

"Sounds like a wonderful time." Sarah looked at Ian. "I can take one day off this weekend. Let's have a go at it."

"How about you?" Sam nodded at Anna. "We could relax on the beach under a palm tree while the kids snorkel and play grab-ass in the water."

"That's not funny." Anna grimaced.

"What?" Ian sat up straight in the cockpit and looked back and forth between Sam and Sarah.

"No worries, chap," Sarah said, going along with Sam's teasing. "I'll just grab at your cute lil bum."

"That's what I'm concerned about." Anna glared at Sam.

"Not to worry," Sam smiled. "If you wear that skimpy little thing you found in the drawer in your cabin, you'll only have to concern yourself with my roving hands and—"

"Hey! Hey!" Ian interrupted. "I'm sitting here! I'm sitting right here!"

"Fat chance of that." Anna took a stack of dirty dishes from the table and went below.

"Let's help her clear this stuff." Sam stood and passed empty glasses and silverware to Ian across the table.

"I'll help wash." Sarah carried a platter of leftover potatoes and salad to the stairs.

"Steaks were good," Ian said, piling silverware on an empty platter.

"Yeah, they were." Sam paused a moment to check the harbor for anything unusual. The sun had gone down now and the lights of the town sparkled across the black water. It was a cloudless night, but the full moon hadn't yet popped over the eastern part of the island. When it did, he knew it would light up the area like a forty-watt bulb.

"The key to a good steak is selecting the right cut of meat in the first place. Hard to do here on the island where good beef is scarce and infrequent. Ribeye steaks are the best when you can get 'em."

"When are you thinking about going over to Moskito Island?" Ian paused before taking his load of dishes below.

"Well. Sarah said she could get a day off this weekend." Sam slipped his feet into his flip flops. "Let's go Saturday. That gives us a couple more days to accomplish some things here on board." He thought about saying something about the arrival of the French cruise ship but didn't. He'd save that for a surprise.

"Works for me," Ian said. "I just hope my bastard of a boss will let me take the time off." He grinned.

"Ask nicely," Sam countered. "I hear he's a good sport."

"Hope Mom will go," Ian said in a hushed voice. "She didn't seem too excited about it."

"Yeah." Sam nodded. "And I haven't said anything to her yet about the near miss in town today. I think she's also upset that Sarah came out for dinner. She doesn't know why we invited her out instead of you going to her place."

"She's gotta get over that bullshit." The corners of Ian's mouth dropped down into a frown. No one invited her to the island. She can't just show up and start telling me how to live my life. Who I can see and who I can't, or shouldn't—"

"She's your mother," Sam interrupted. "Have some respect. Just know that she'll always be your mother and wants what best for you. Doesn't mean she's always right, but you have to respect that."

Ian went silent for a moment. "We'll see," he said. "I'm not sure what a real mother is like. We've been more like squabbling siblings. She's not that much older than me."

"You never knew your dad?" Sam asked.

"He was killed six months before I was born," Ian replied. "Always looked to my grandfather as my dad. They were both engineers. Both graduated from Cornell before joining the navy. My grandfather flew fighters in the Pacific and came home when it was over. My father flew Tomcats. A great aunt told me they were out of the same pea pod—mirror images." Ian grew silent for a moment.

"I don't think my grandfather ever got over the death of his only son. He did all the right things for me a father should do like guiding me into Boy Scouts and university and all, but there was always something missing. No chemistry, none of the bonding you'd expect from a real father. I don't think he knew how, or maybe he didn't want to after his loss. We never discussed it."

"Why didn't your mom remarry?" Sam asked. "She's a smart, attractive woman, and I think—"

"You'll have to ask her," Ian said. "She dated some, but I never met any of them. It was like she lived a secret life. Everything about it was secret, wasn't discussed. My grandfather wouldn't touch the subject. Sometimes I felt sorry for her. Could see her hurting with no one to talk with about it. My grandfather sent me off to his old boarding school in Connecticut when I entered high school, so I didn't have to deal with her unhappiness every day. I only saw Mom during holidays and in the summer and was happy to go back to school when the break was over. I guess what I'm saying is, I don't think we have a normal mother and son thing going. Not sure what normal is, but what we had wasn't anything like what my school friends had with their moms. I'm still trying to figure it out."

Sam watched Ian a moment in the dark. "Hey, this is all too deep and real for such a beautiful night," he said, trying to lighten the mood. "Let's get these dishes below. There's still time for you to get lucky with Sarah. I suggest not taking her to your cabin but stay up here on deck. Maybe grab a sail bag to sit on at the bow. Much cooler, more romantic up there, plus further away from your mom. Suggest to Sarah that she stay the night. We can run her into shore early in the morning so she can get to work on time."

Ian nodded.

"I'll have a night cap with Anna below and see if I can get agreement on the excursion Saturday to Moskito. We'll need to let Sarah know before she leaves so she can inform her boss about taking the day off."

Ian nodded again. "You're right. Let's see what mom says."

# CHAPTER 26

Saturday Morning

"Firebird, Firebird, Firebird. This is Virgin Cay Marina. Over."

Sam left his room to pick up the mic to the VHF radio at the Nav Station. "Virgin Cay, this is Firebird. Turning to channel twelve. Over."

"Virgin Cay going to channel twelve. Out" the voice said.

Sam turned the knob from channel sixteen to channel twelve.

"Firebird, Firebird, Firebird. This is Virgin Cay Marina. Over."

"Good morning, Virgin Cay," Sam responded.

"Good morning to you, too. We have a young lady here in the office who needs a ride out to your boat. Over."

Sam smiled. "Tell Sarah we'll be right there. Thank you very much. Over. Firebird Out."

"Virgin Cay back to channel sixteen. Out."

Sam went up the stairs to the deck, pulling on a T-shirt. He saw Ian barefoot and in shorts at the bow. "Hey! Your girlfriend's here. She's waiting at the marina office to be picked up. I'll take the dinghy to get her if you'll help your mother pack for our trip to Moskito. I'm not sure she knows what all to—"

"Got it," Ian called back. He dropped the bow line he was curling onto the deck and joined Sam in the cockpit. The morning sun was just coming up over the eastern mountains. "I still can't believe you talked Mom into this."

"I think she's not too keen on us taking the day off," Sam said. "I promised we'd double up a couple of days. Finish the long list of things we need to do before going to Saint Thomas. She insists on making the cushion covers for the salon while I argue the fabric shop in town can probably do them for a fair price. We've got to finish varnishing in your cabin and the fourth cabin. Polish all the stainless rigging one more time here on deck. I think we can do it in the weeks we have left, so I say let's have some fun. We're here on an island in the beautiful Caribbean." Sam slapped on his ballcap and sunglasses.

"What did she say about Sarah?" Ian asked, rubbing a hand across his hairless chest.

"Nothing after the fire flew out of her eyes." Sam laughed. "She harrumphed around but didn't veto it. Speaking of Sarah, I better go get her. Tell Anna to pack lots of sunscreen and beer for me, and whatever the rest of you want." He unhooked the gate to the boarding ladder and went down to untie the dinghy.

"What about a bathing suit?" Ian called down to him.

Sam looked at him and grinned. "I'll wear it on the dinghy ride to the island. If we're lucky, we won't need them."

"What?" Ian saw Sam push away from Firebird and start the outboard motor. Wonder what he means about that, he thought watching the dinghy glide through the harbor toward the marina.

Sarah waited at the dock wearing a white tennis outfit. It didn't totally hide the string bikini underneath. An overflowing beach bag lay at her feet. Sam killed the engine as he drifted toward the pier.

"Good morning." He stood to grab the cleat and wrapped the painter around it. "How are you this morning?" He looked up at Sarah.

"Nervous and excited," she said, picking up her bag and handing it to him. "This is my first excursion off Saint Sebastian."

"It'll be great," he said. "Trust me." She handed him her flip flops and sat on the dock to slide her bare feet onto the inflated pontoon. Sam held her hand to balance as she boarded. "All in?" he asked.

"All in," she responded.

He turned around to start the engine when a shadow crossed the stern.

"Hello there." The marina manager stood on the dock holding the day's mail. "Nothing in the post here for you, Sam. We won't have another delivery till Monday. You folks working hard?"

Sam sat on the seat and looked up at Charlie. "Not today. We're taking a little R&R and going over to Moskito for a picnic and some snorkeling."

Charlie chuckled. "Should be a good day over there. I saw the French cruise ship is in, and White Squall has started loading passengers. Make sure you take sunglasses and plenty of sunblock."

"Yep." Sam laughed. "The sunglasses protect the eyes. Keeps everyone from knowing just where you're looking."

"My point, exactly." Charlie grinned. "Look who's here." He nodded toward the marina parking lot where the black Jeep was parked in the front space. "Be careful. They're there at least once a day if not more often and never get out. They sit for a while and then drive off. Sometimes they're here in the mornings, sometimes in the afternoons. No pattern to it that I can identify."

Sam stared at the Jeep but couldn't see who or how many were inside. His stomach turned over. "Thanks for the heads up." He reached behind him to start the motor. "Let me know if anything changes."

Charlie waved as Sam turned the bow away from the dock and headed back out toward Firebird.

After a few moments, Sarah turned to him. "You still worried about them?" she asked over the engine noise.

"Have they bothered you in town?" Sam caught her eyes.

"A little," she said. "They give me wolf whistles. Sometimes they glare at me in in the café. Once they followed close behind me when I walked home after work and parked outside my apartment for an hour."

"Was it the Haitian?"

"Couldn't tell with the dark windows. He never comes into the café. Just his thugs."

"Let me know if it gets worse. We'll be outta here before long and then things should ease up."

"I know." Sarah turned back to look at Firebird over the bow. "I'll miss him when you guys leave."

Sam didn't say anything more as they approached the boarding platform. I know exactly what the Haitian wants, he thought to himself. *He wants Anna.* He saw Ian waiting for them at the rail.

"Gosh, you look great," Ian gushed, taking Sarah's hand and helping her onto the boarding platform from the dinghy.

"Why thank you, sir." She tiptoed up to kiss him on the cheek. "I thought it very colonial."

Sam handed up Sarah's bag before stepping out of the dinghy. "You guys packed? We need to get away soon. Beat everyone there so we can have our pick of spots on the beach."

"How are we on gas for the dinghy?" Ian asked, going up the stairs to the deck behind Sarah.

"We have a full tank," Sam said, following them. "Topped off yesterday at the fuel dock."

Just then Anna appeared from below carrying a beach bag. Sam stared. Her red hair was tied back in a ponytail under one of his baseball caps, and she wore tan shorts and the orange bikini top. He wondered if she had on the thong bottom that went with that bikini under her shorts. A plastic cooler sat on the cockpit table.

"We've got sandwiches, chips, beer, water, and a bottle of wine." Anna ignored Sarah and looked at the boys. "I have a blanket for the beach, but each of you should take a towel."

"I'll get mine and Sam's." Ian headed down the salon stairs. He was soon back with a plastic bag containing two bath towels.

"Grab the other end of this cooler," Sam said. "We'll load it first, then the girls. I'll drive while you sit up front to balance the load."

When the dinghy had everything and everyone on board, Ian pushed away from Firebird while Sam started the motor. Even with the added weight, the inflatable still rode high in the water.

Sam steered toward the mouth of the harbor and when they cleared, Moskito Island appeared in the distance. He glanced at his watch and saw it was nine-thirty. They were half an hour ahead of White Squall and the other day sailors. "Hold on," he said. The inflatable picked up speed and headed across the channel toward its destination a couple miles away. At first, water splashed into the boat at the bow but then abated as their speed increased.

"Hold on to your caps," Sam said, pulling his own down hard over his brow. "We don't turn around and go back for lost hats. He saw Anna grab hold of her seat with her left hand and her ballcap with the other. Her ponytail was sticking straight out in the breeze.

Moskito Island began to take shape first as a gray, then green mountain poking up out of the blue water. As they neared, its peak, palm trees, and a long white sand beach looked worthy of a magazine cover. There were only a couple of small private sailboats anchored in the bay when they arrived, and no one was on the beach. Knowing the catamarans with their guests would probably take the middle of the beach, he angled for the right end where several large granite boulders and a small cluster of palm trees marked the boundary. He noticed Anna had a big smile on her face and her eyes were darting about, taking it all in.

"Wow," she murmured. "It's beautiful."

Ian watched Sarah with a grin plastered on his face. She had a tight grip on his hand.

Passing close by one of the sailboats flying a Dutch flag, Sam saw a young couple enjoying the sun on the forward deck. A little hammock swinging under the boom held a napping toddler. The man lifted his head and waved to them as they slowed to minimize the wake.

"Oh, the Europeans," Sarah said, laughing. "They sure know how to enjoy life."

Sam smiled.

Approaching the beach in shallow water, he killed the engine as their forward motion coupled with a wave on their stern pushed them up onto the sand. Ian pulled the motor up and jumped into the water with the painter in hand, dragging the dinghy further up on the beach so everyone could step out on dry sand. Sam then helped maneuver the inflatable higher up and away from the water, securing it for the day.

"I like this spot." Ian said, standing on the high side of the beach sheltered from the wind by a boulder and shaded by palm trees. "Let's put the blanket down here and make this our base camp."

"Works for me." Sam brought the cooler up and set it on the blanket being spread out and anchored by the two girls. "Those rocks spilling out into the water there should provide us some fun snorkeling," he said.

"Look." He nodded toward the first of the big catamarans approaching the island. "Doesn't take them long to get over here."

Ian turned to watch the catamaran head into the bay and took off his T-shirt leaving him wearing only shorts. "Sarah, let's walk the beach before everyone gets here."

Sam watched him take her hand. They kicked off their flip flops and barefooted it down the beach. "So, what do you think?" He looked at Anna on her knees, smoothing the sides of the blanket.

"About what?" She paused to look at him.

"About this spot. About the day. About Ian and Sarah." He nodded towards the young couple strolling along the beach, holding hands.

"I think the spot is okay, the day's just beginning, so I'll reserve judgement. The boy is still young. This is just a phase." Anna looked away from him.

He smiled. "Well, I think this is the best spot for us. The day is sunny and beautiful, and the boy is gob smacked over Sarah. Maybe you call that a phase. Others call it love and write poetry and sing songs about it. Surely, you've experienced that at least once?"

She didn't respond and started oiling her bare arms. "Better put some sunscreen on or you'll broil in this sun."

He caught the tube of lotion she tossed and removed his T-shirt. He was already as tan as a walnut but had known several people he worked with over the years die of melanoma.

"Put some on my back." She turned around and lifted her ponytail from her neck.

Sam squirted lotion in his hands and smeared it over her neck, shoulders and down her back. "That bikini looks good on you," he said running his hand underneath the strap. "You wearing the rest of it?"

"Maybe." She glanced back at him. "We'll see."

The lead catamaran dropped anchor a few yards off the beach, and Sam saw Captain Ainsley's catamaran coming in not far behind it.

The first boat dislodged its passengers who were all dropping towels and coolers on the beach. Some brought colorful umbrellas that dotted the sand like Christmas tree ornaments. When White Squall set its anchor beside the other boat, the beach swarmed with attractive women in tiny string bikinis and men in thong bottoms, all speaking French. Sam saw many of the women doffing their tops. If the good Captain Ainsley was right, the bottoms would soon follow. He noticed Anna had stopped what she was doing to watch.

"Yep. Sure looks like it's going to be a good day," he said, lifting his ballcap and running his hand through his thick hair. He set his hat back and pulled it low over his brow. He glanced at Anna.

"Sam, I know you think I'm embarrassed by this, but I've spent many an hour at the clothes optional beach on Martha's Vineyard. This isn't anything I haven't seen, so you can stop worrying about it."

He grinned and looked back out over the sea of humanity beginning to reveal itself in all its oiled glistening glory. One couple was already humping each other under a beach umbrella, and it wasn't even lunch time. "Are you going to—" he started to ask when he turned back and saw the orange bikini top on the cooler. Now he didn't know where to look.

"Tell me if you see the kids heading in this direction," Anna said. She was on her back on the blanket with her ballcap pulled over her face to block the sun.

"Has—" Sam started to ask again.

"No, Sam. He never accompanied me to that beach at Martha's Vineyard. My best friend, Louise, and I went there every summer to get a tan and keep it."

"And—"

"And none of your business," she said, sounding exasperated. She pushed the cap up off her face and leaned up on her elbows. She turned to look at him. "So, how about you? What kind of experiences have you had hanging out nude in mixed company? I mean, if we're playing twenty questions here."

He looked up from the fixed lock he had on her bare breasts, removed his Ray-Bans and scanned the crowd for Ian and Sarah. "I've probably had more experiences than I can remember," he said. "They say alcohol kills the brain cells and reduces one's inhibitions. I haven't kept count or a list, but I'll probably not surprise you by saying I haven't lived a monk's life while roaming the Caribbean as a pirate and a friendly drunk."

"Tell me about it," she said, looking at him and smiling. "That describes my life except for the pirate part. Are you going to join the fun?"

"Thinking about it," he said. "Not sure, yet. I only have my shorts to take off."

"Don't worry." She chuckled. "It's nothing I haven't seen at least a couple of times on board since I've been here."

He looked at her on the blanket. Her bare breasts rode high and full on her chest. Her toes were painted a coral color which accented her tan. She's a lot of woman for a mother, he thought. *I need to tread carefully here.*

Two young women approached and stopped just a few yards away to spread their towels. Sam didn't understand what they were saying, but everything in French sounded sexy. Neither of them wore tops, and without any shyness, tugged off their bottoms before running down to the water.

Anna winked at him.

He chuckled nervously and undid the buttons on his denim shorts and let them fall to his ankles. "As they say, 'When in Rome.'"

Anna stood up and tugged down her orange thong then tossed it on top of the cooler.

"Hmmm. No tan lines," he said. "Must have been a good summer at Martha's Vineyard."

She glanced down to see what he was referring to. "It was, but I definitely need a refresher, and could use a razor. Again, do you see the kids?"

Sam looked out over the crowd. "Nope. My guess is they're wondering the same thing about us. Ian's probably asking her the same question. She seems more liberal about this than him."

"That's what I'm afraid of," Anna said, not smiling. "His grandfather is a strong, committed Irish Catholic. And Ian was an Alter Boy in the grandest cathedral in Boston. Do you think they. . . .?"

"I'd be worried about the boy if they hadn't," he said, looking back at her. She was bent over brushing sand off her legs, and he looked away. "Ian's twenty-two and has all the right parts. I don't know exactly how old Sarah is, but that's close and besides, she's from England which is adjacent to the continent. You can see in front of us that Europeans have different attitudes about such things."

"And you?" Anna stood and turned to face him, her hands on her hips.

He felt a surge of blood hit his groin. *Definitely a red head*. Her sunglasses hid any sign that she had noticed.

"You should see someone about that," Anna teased.

"You recommend anyone?" Sam played along.

"Just look out over the beach and take your pick. It looks like a buffet."

"Speaking of eating," Sam said, with a laugh. "It's approaching noon, and the good captain of White Squall invited us out for a free lunch. What do you say? Go or stay?"

"I packed sandwiches," Anna said, "But the kids can find them when they return. It'd be fun to mix with some different people." She picked up her bikini from the cooler lid and started putting it on." She tugged the thong up into position and looked at Sam with a raised eyebrow.

He shrugged and stepped commando style into his shorts. "I

see the boat's in shallow water, so we can wade out to it." He extended his hand and Anna took it. He led them down the beach, detouring around groups of French folks spread out on towels enjoying the Caribbean sun.

# CHAPTER 27

"Hello, White Squall! Request permission to come aboard," Sam called to the uniformed captain standing on the catamaran's pontoon bow, scanning the beach with binoculars.

Captain Ainsley turned to see who hailed him. "Yes, Please, do." He waved at Sam. "Let them come aboard," he called to a crew member beside the boarding ladder.

Several couples waited in front of them in various stages of undress. A fully nude, slim woman in her 50's or 60's – Sam found it hard to tell with French women, climbed up just in front of him. He didn't dare look, and Anna nudged him in the ribs.

"I want a full report when she gets up," he whispered.

Captain Ainsley met them on deck and shook Sam's hand. "Glad you made it. There's an open bar on the stern, so take full advantage of it, and lunch should be ready shortly. It's a buffet, so eat all you want." He smiled at Anna. "And this lovely. . . ?"

"Anna Neeson. Anna, let me introduce Captain Meredith Ainsley. We met last week at the marina, and he graciously invited us to lunch today." Sam thought the Captain held Anna's hand a bit longer than necessary, but so what. It's a free lunch.

The captain leaned down and whispered in her ear. "Haven't we met before?"

"Have we. . . .?" She squinted up into the captain's face. "I don't remember."

Sam stopped a waiter going by with a tray of rum drinks.

"We have a mutual friend," the captain continued under his breath. "Remember that evening at the villa when—"

"Here's one for you." Sam handed Anna her drink. He thought he saw her hand shake a little before she grasped the glass with both hands. "And one for you." The captain took his drink. "And one for me. Cheers to all!" The three raised their glasses to each other.

"Let's eat. I'm famished." Sam said, leading Anna toward the buffet on the stern. "Thank you, Captain," he said, looking over his shoulder. "I want to return your hospitality on Firebird someday."

"What was that all about?" he asked Anna when they stopped at the loaded buffet table and scanned the contents.

"You heard?" Her bottom lip quivered.

"Couldn't help it." He put his arm around her. "It's okay. Just tell me what happened."

"That's just it." She bit her lip. "I don't know. I don't remember him, but there was time at the villa that I don't remember anything. The captain mentioned meeting me there. Sam, I'm scared."

A middle-age, nude couple stepped up beside them at the table and began filling their plates. The woman, definitely a brunette, touched Sam's arm and pointed at his shorts, saying something in French.

"Oh, we're Americans," he said, smiling. "No speaka the Francais."

The woman stared at him a moment, a confused look on her face, then began laughing. God, he thought to himself, even their laugh is sexy.

The woman then spoke something to her partner who smiled and nodded.

"I think she's commenting on your big feet and big hands," Anna said with a glimmer of humor in her eyes. "I had a little French in Catholic high school."

"Thank you." Sam turned back to the woman. "Merci."

The woman smiled and nodded, then left them to chat up a sophisticated looking gray-haired couple who seemed to know everyone on the boat.

"This has been fun," Sam whispered to Anna, "but let's eat and get off this tub. Let's go back to the blanket to watch and enjoy our individual fantasies. It's not as much fun when it gets personal in a crowd like this."

Anna looked up at him. "What do you mean?"

"Look around. Do you see an erection anywhere?"

"No," she said. "And I don't have to look around."

"That's what I mean," Sam said.

They finished their plates and handed them to a waiter traversing through the crowd picking up dishes. It looked like he didn't care who he touched or where, *or maybe he did*. Sam couldn't decide.

"I don't want to say goodbye to the captain," Anna whispered as they approached the boarding ladder. "You can, and I'll meet you back at the blanket."

Sam watched her step down the ladder rungs and into the shallow surf. The bottom of her thong crept up. Her tight, honey-brown cheeks disappeared in the crowd surrounding the boat. The air was sweet with the aroma of coconut oil.

He made his way through the throng around the captain and tapped him on the shoulder. "Thank you, Ainsley. We have to get back ashore, but I owe you one."

"And where's your lovely lady?" Captain Ainsley winked at Sam. "She's a pistol if I say so myself."

"Uh, she had to go ahead. Her son is with us and—"

"She has a son?"

The question caught Sam off guard.

"I didn't know, she's so—"

"Right," said Sam. "She's young looking to have a twenty-two-year old son in college. He's helping me restore Firebird and get her in shape for the charter show in Saint Thomas."

"Yes, well, good luck with that, my man. See you on the island." The captain turned and embraced a chesty French woman who left two equal oil stains on the captain's starched white uniform blouse.

It was two o'clock when Sam arrived back at the blanket. No one was there. He dropped his shorts to blend in and pulled a beer out of the cooler. He saw the sandwiches were gone and turned to look out over the beach. There was still a good crowd in the water and fewer people on the beach. Some napped in the afternoon shade of their umbrellas while some were strolling up and down along the water line enjoying the surf and sand. Most were nude, but there was nothing particularly sexy about it. He checked himself. Maybe it's my age now that I'm over forty, he thought. *Sad. I probably look like some old Iguana lizard sunning on a rock*. He picked up his shorts and put them back on.

He was sitting on the blanket with his second beer in hand, wondering how the captain knew Anna. She approached from the water wearing a T-shirt over her bikini and carrying snorkel gear.

"It's wonderful out there around those rocks. Ian was right. The parrot fish are beautiful. The manta rays are numerous and friendly, and there's even a small barracuda lurking near that far rock." She tossed the gear onto the blanket and plopped down beside him. "They say they're territorial. He didn't like me coming too close."

"Want something to drink?"

"That would be lovely." She brushed sand from her legs while he got up and took a green Heineken bottle from the cooler.

"We need to do this more often as long as we're here in the tropics," he said and popped the top of her beer. She took a long swig.

"Ah, that gets the salt out of my throat." She smiled at him. "Lord knows I swallowed enough saltwater out there. I think my mask leaked, but it was too much fun to stop and change it."

"Have you seen Ian?" Sam took a drink of his beer. "I told them we wanted to leave before four o'clock to beat the catamaran crowd back to the harbor."

"Should we be worried?" Anna's brow furrowed. "I walked the length of the beach before snorkeling and didn't see them. Doesn't mean they weren't there. I was reluctant to look very hard with so many bare bums and—"

Sam laughed. "Know what you mean. Sometimes you don't want to necessarily find what you're looking for. I'll go check on them if they don't show up in the next half hour."

After a few more moments of silence, she looked at him. "When you left, did the captain say anything more about—"

"Nothing," he said, shaking his head. "Nada. Not a thing."

Anna took a few more sips of beer and stared out over the small cove. "Sam, I'm afraid. I—"

"It'll be okay." He reached over to stroke her back. "Don't worry. It'll be okay. I promise."

# CHAPTER 28

"Hey there. Ready to go back?"

They both turned to see Ian and Sarah approaching from the line of palm trees behind the beach. "It's about that time," Sam said. "The big cats will be leaving in half an hour or so."

"Where have you two been all day?" Anna checked out Ian and then Sarah.

"You miss us?" Ian deflected the question.

Anna glanced at Sam for help. "I walked the beach a bit ago and didn't see you anywhere. I was worried."

"We found a trail that goes up over a ridge and comes out on the other side." Ian pointed. "There's another protected beach over there. The cove is too rocky and shallow for a boat to anchor, but it was the perfect place to spend the day enjoying the sun in total privacy."

"So, you missed all the fun over here when the cats came in with their French guests?" Sam grinned. "The beach is emptying now with everyone clamoring back aboard for the trip back. We have some time. They'll serve drinks and snacks before pulling anchor."

"Sarah and I walked up on the ridge and checked out the crowd. I thought the view was much better on the other side." Ian grinned.

"Yeah, I bet you did." Sam chuckled.

Ian went over to the cooler and pulled two beers out of the ice. He handed one to Sarah who wore her bikini. They were both barefooted, their flip flops in their bags.

"You were right about the snorkeling being terrific out around those rocks." Anna pointed. "The fish were plentiful, and the water was crystal clear."

"Maybe next time," Ian said. "We should definitely come back here." He grinned at Sarah.

"Let's pack up and head back to the harbor ahead of those catamarans," Sam said. He grabbed the blanket and shook it out while Anna put her snorkel equipment in the tote and picked up her sandals.

"Uh, did you guys get naked or anything," Ian asked with an embarrassed laugh.

"I mean, it was the thing to do it seems. Looked like everyone else was—"

"Don't ask your mother questions like that." Sam cut him off.

"Sorry," Ian said as they lifted the cooler and carried it to the dinghy. "I just thought that—"

"Don't think." Sam tossed his bag in by the motor and went to the bow to pick up the painter that had been staked in the sand. "There are some things a son shouldn't want to know about his parents, especially his blessed mother." Sam dragged the bow of the dinghy around until it faced down the beach towards the water.

"Here." He tossed the line to Ian. "Pull while I push on the stern. It's much easier going downhill than coming up. We'll turn it around again at the water and back into the surf motor first. You hold the painter while we finish loading the girls. I'll get the engine down and started, then you jump in."

At the water line, the dinghy was turned, and the incoming waves lifted the pontoons while they easily pushed it into deeper water. Sam helped Anna and Sarah climb in and followed. After he started the motor, Ian gave the bow a big push into the surf and clambered in while Sam reversed away from the beach.

"That's how it's done." He nodded at Ian. "Good work. Is everyone okay?"

"Ten toes and ten fingers in," Sarah said with a big smile on her face. "My daddy always used to say that whenever we did something adventurous on his little sailboat off the coast of Dover."

An hour later they were stowing snorkel gear on Firebird when White Squall and the second catamaran motored back into the marina. Sam watched the two boats with their sun burned guests, tie up and unload. The cruise ship folks looked like a line of ants as they filed down the dock and into town where they would board their ship and eat the evening meal in the dining room while it threw off lines and headed out to sea to its next destination.

"Where're they going?" Ian followed Sam into the cockpit. The girls had gone below to shower and start dinner. Ian had requested spaghetti.

"Probably Saint Thomas," Sam said. "It's only twenty miles away, but they'll stay a few miles out in the ocean circling around till dawn before going into Charlotte Amalie and tying up at the dock. There's a joke around here that the most asked question by cruise ship guests is 'What island is that?' The answer most given is 'Saint Thomas.'" They both laughed.

"So, how did your day go at that little private beach with Sarah?"

"I don't kiss and tell." Ian nudged Sam with a knuckle to the rib cage.

"That good, huh?" Sam laughed. "You be careful, now. She's smarter and cuter than you are. My old man would've called her a heartbreaker."

Ian shrugged and didn't reply. They watched in silence as a brown pelican dove into the water next to the boat after a school of sprat. It popped up, swallowed its beak full of small fish, and soared off to repeat the dive.

After the third dive, Ian stood. "I'm going below to wash off the sweat and sand. Can I bring you a cold one or something?"

Sam sat up and placed his cap on the seat beside him. "We haven't cranked the engine for over a week. Now that the generator charges the batteries, we won't need to run it that often, but it's been a while. Let's start her for a bit to clear all the fuel filters and pump fresh water through the cooling system. Mind giving it a crank before going below?"

"Sure," Ian said, stepping to the helm and turning on the ignition key. He held the diesel warmer button in for about five seconds, then turned the ignition key all the way over.

There was a partial crank followed by a clunk and an electrical pop. Ian turned off the ignition, waited a moment, then tried again. The starter motor made an effort, but the main engine remained silent. He looked back at Sam.

"Try it again," Sam said, his stomach full of butterflies. "This doesn't look good."

Ian waited a few moments, then turned the ignition key. The starter motor gave out a high-pitched whine that could be heard throughout the boat.

"Turn it off! Turn it off!" Sam grabbed his ballcap and headed for the stairs. "I gotta see what's happening. Stay up here and do what I tell you." He took the stairs down to the salon two at a time. He didn't acknowledge the questioning look on Anna's face as he passed her in the galley on his way to the engine room. The smell of burned electric wire filled the inside of the boat.

When he opened the door, smoke poured out into the passageway. There was no flame visible, but something terrible had gone wrong. His knees felt weak as he stood over the smoking engine and stared at—what? He didn't know.

The smoke finally cleared, and he studied the hot mess in front of him.

Ian appeared in the haze. "Saw all the smoke and thought you needed some help down here. I worried you might be battling a fire or something."

"Or something," Sam said. He put his hands on his hips and shook his head. "I'm flummoxed. She ran perfectly last time we started her. And these old Ford marine engines are bulletproof. We don't need this right now!" He turned and slammed his fist into the bulkhead. "Not now. Not just weeks before Saint Thomas. We're so damn close!" He stormed out of the engine room.

Ian looked over the engine and inspected the starter motor. He could see several burned connecting wires but nothing else made sense.

"He went back on deck," Sarah said when Ian stepped out of the engine room and into the salon. "Is it bad?" She glanced at Anna and back at Ian. Anna was stirring the pot of tomato sauce on the gimballed stove.

"Not sure," Ian said. "Could be." He went up the stairs to find Sam.

"Dinner will be ready in a bit," Anna called to him.

Sam stood alone at the bow, staring toward the mouth of the harbor, his mind wandering through all the options facing him. He didn't hear Ian come up behind him.

"What do you think happened?" Ian held on to the furled fore-sail and sat on the stainless bow pulpit.

"Not sure." Sam shook his head. He turned to face the boy. "I'm not an engine expert, especially a big diesel like that one, but it doesn't take an expert to tell me it's not good."

Neither of them spoke for a minute. The brown pelican hit the water a few feet in front of the boat, barely missing the mooring lines.

"Maybe this was just a crazy thing to do, anyway," Sam said, rubbing the scar on his arm. "I don't know why I thought this might work. My old man always said I had a habit of taking on more than I could do. Maybe he was right."

"We don't know that, yet," Ian said. "It may be nothing, it may be something, but we can handle it. If I learned anything from you since I've been here, it's that hard work and commitment beats skill and bad luck. First, we need to determine what the problem is. Then we can evaluate our options to fix it."

"You realize a new motor costs fifty-thousand bucks, at least?" Sam checked the setting sun on the stern and continued rubbing the scar on his arm. "That's fifty-thousand I don't have. If I'd known in Puerto Rico that the engine was blown, I would've walked away from this tub. Hell, I would've run."

"Dinner's ready!" Sarah's head peeked out from the companion way. "Anna wants to eat down here."

"Be right there," Ian called back to her. "Let's eat and make a list. I think if we divide up some of the items left to do, we can begin knocking them off."

"There's only a few weeks left to the show," Sam said. "We can't run a charter boat without an engine. No one will pay to vacation on a boat that sits on its anchor. Even if it's a fancy-ass yacht." He removed his cap and rubbed his forehead. "I don't know. Maybe we should sail it out and sink it."

"That's called insurance fraud," Ian said, laughing.

"You have to have insurance for it to be fraud. At least I'd get three 'hots and a cot' for free in prison." Sam said. "Let's eat some dinner and work on that list."

# CHAPTER 29

"First thing tomorrow, I'll go to the engine shop and see if they'll send a mechanic out to look at the motor." Sam wiped his mouth with a napkin and looked at Ian across the salon table next to Sarah. "We might as well find out right away what we're dealing with. If we can't fix it, there's no sense in finishing the varnishing and cushion covers. I'll try and sell it as is, but without a working motor, don't know if anyone would bite."

Anna put her hand on his arm. "I'm sorry about this, Sam. You've worked so hard and had high expectations."

"Yeah, but maybe my expectations were too high." He entwined his fingers with hers on his arm. "You'd think I'd learn. My whole life has been like waking on Christmas morning and finding a manure pile on the living room floor and believing there was a pony in it somewhere. There never was. There never will be."

Anna dropped her hand to his thigh. "Maybe the mechanic will have good news. Maybe it's something small. Let's keep faith in this old girl." She smiled. "I'm getting to like her. She's been my home for a month, and I would miss her."

"Me, too," Sam said, covering her hand with his own. "We'll keep our fingers crossed."

"So, big boy," Sarah turned to Ian. "Let's wash these dishes and then you can run me ashore. After taking the day off from work, and it was a wonderful day, Sam and Anna." She smiled at them. "My boss will expect me at the café early tomorrow morning to get ready for the Sunday breakfast and brunch crowd."

Ian began picking up plates and silverware. "Great spaghetti, Mom."

"Sarah made the salad," Anna said. "And set the table."

"Thanks. . .for everything." Ian leaned over and did a quick lick of Sarah's ear while she filled the sink with soapy water. "And I mean everything."

Sam saw this and at the same time felt Anna's fingers caressing the hair on his upper leg. He put his arm around her shoulder and pulled her into him. *She feels so tiny. Like a china doll that will break if I hold her too tight.* He whispered in her ear, "Shall we have some more wine, or would you like something stronger?"

"Hmmm, something stronger sounds nice," Anna said squeezing his leg. "A rum punch or even a vodka on ice."

Sam got up from the table and mixed their drinks at the counter while Ian and Sarah finished cleaning up. "You can take Sarah home when you're done," he said to Ian before walking the drinks to the table. "Just be careful. If you don't come back tonight, be sure and lock up the dinghy motor at the dock. We can't afford to lose that either."

Ian nodded and went back to drying dishes. He looked at Sarah and winked.

"One for you and one for me," Sam said, setting two cocktail glasses on the salon table.

Anna still wore the bikini under the T-shirt that she had on at Moskito Island. "Vodka on ice is my favorite." She smiled. "It reduces stress.

Sam scooted in on the cushion beside her. "I know some other stress reduction secrets," he said under his breath so the kids wouldn't hear.

"And you'll need them if this motor thing isn't fixable." She stifled a smile.

"Damn. You had to ruin the moment." He leaned away and a grim look settled on his face.

"Oh, there was a *moment*?" She teased. "I wasn't aware. Sorry."

Sam sat in silence, watching Ian carry Sarah's beach bag up the companionway.

"Thank you both for a wonderful time," Sarah said, standing by the steps. "I can't remember when I've had such fun. We should do it again one day before Firebird sails off with you sweet people aboard."

"That would be fun," Anna said, her coral lips reflecting the overhead salon light.

"Let's go," Ian called down from the deck. "I've already started the engine."

Sarah smiled again and then ran up the steps.

"Will he be back tonight?" Anna looked at Sam.

He shrugged and took a deep drink of vodka. "Dunno. Not if he's lucky."

"Oh, you men." Anna punched him on the arm. "As his mother, maybe I should say, if she's lucky."

"Let's just agree they'd both be lucky to not have to sleep alone tonight in this big ole' world." Sam finished his glass and got up to refill it. "How about you? Ready for another?"

"Certainly. It's my drug of choice. Thank God, it's still legal."

Sam carried both of their drinks and led her up on deck to sit under the stars. It was a warm night and a gentle breeze blew in off the sea. They sat in silence for a while in the cockpit. The only noise was a loose halyard gently banging on the aluminum mast and the tinkle of ice in their glasses.

"Are you okay, Sam? You look a little glum."

"Guess this vodka ain't doing its job," he said, looking across the cockpit at her.

"And that is?" she asked.

"Relieving my stress. I was hoping it'd make me forget about this busted motor business." He paused for a moment. "I also hoped it would make me look sexy, more muscular, and handsome tonight so you couldn't keep your hands off me. You didn't seem to have a problem with that today on the beach when all my goods were showing."

"You expect the woman to make the first move?"

"I've known a few who did." He couldn't see the expression on her face in the dark.

Anna took a drink from her glass and said nothing.

"You want another one, or is this one going to work?"

"What do you mean?"

"Am I getting more sexy?"

Neither of them said anything for a few minutes. A siren came across the dark water from somewhere in town.

"Ah, the excitement of big city living," he said in an effort to lighten the mood. He finished his drink and thought about getting another one. Maybe a rum and coke this time.

"Sam?"

He set his empty glass on the cockpit table and looked at her. Something had changed. He couldn't decide what.

"Sam, I'm scared." Anna cupped her drink with both hands.

"Scared?" He leaned forward. "Of what? About what?"

"Of everything. About everything, I think." She wiped her cheek with the back of her hand.

"My life seems to be careening out of control. I came here to find Ian. Then I thought maybe this was a chance to take back my own life and move forward, but it just looks like everything is upside down. I don't even trust myself anymore." She wiped her nose on the bottom of her T-shirt.

"I think being in control of everything is overrated," he said. "Maybe because I've never experienced that myself. Not sure anyone has. I can see it might be good for a while but then you'd start fearing losing control again, and that would become your biggest fear. Sounds like a vicious cycle."

"Sometimes I think you're full of it," Anna said, wiping the tears away with her fingers. "But I'm glad you are. You make me laugh."

The buzzing sound of an outboard motor could be heard in the distance, and Sam looked toward the marina to see if it was Ian. "Nope. Not him," he said as the sound faded away.

"Let me ask you a hard question," he continued. "Or maybe it's an easy one. Who knows? But, have you ever been in love?"

She looked at him a moment. "Once, I think. A long time ago. So long ago it doesn't seem real anymore."

"Ian's father?"

"Yes, if it was truly love." She paused another moment. "I was a poor Irish girl from South Boston, and he was a Brahmin of Beacon Street. He was home on leave when we met at Clancy's Bar on the wharf. I was with a girlfriend who had taken her big sister's fake ID's and we were going to. . .I don't really know what we thought we were going to do. But that night, I danced with Lieutenant Daniel Neeson in his white navy aviator's uniform, and I felt like Cinderella in the prince's arms at the ball. Only this time, it wasn't a fairy tale, and we dated for the next three weeks before his leave ended. A month later, he asked me to marry him, and that summer, Turloch Neeson, his father, gave us a big fancy wedding reception at his estate in Cambridge. My mother had been a housekeeper for a family in the same neighborhood and was speechless the whole weekend. I never knew my father. Three months later, I was pregnant when a navy officer with a chaplain came to the door to tell me Daniel had been killed in an accident."

She ceased talking and the silence became heavy. A harvest moon crested over the eastern mountains, and the night was less dark. Sam saw her face streaked with tears. He leaned forward to take the glass from her hands and set it on the cockpit table. He held both of her hands in his own and said nothing.

"My life stopped at that moment," she went on. "After I had the baby, Daniel's father brought us home from the hospital to his mansion and from that moment on, I've felt like a jellyfish in the ocean, floating through the years controlled by the wind and the waves. I'm sure Ian thinks. . . ."

She began to cry, and Sam moved across to sit beside her. He grappled for something useful to say. Failing that, he put his arm around her shoulder and pulled her against him. He leaned down and kissed her forehead. She turned her face up to him with her eyes closed.

# CHAPTER 30

Sun streaming through the porthole, warmed the bedding. Sam opened his eyes. The room looked unfamiliar. The body next to him stretched cat-like, and he remembered where he was. . . and with who.

"Good morning, sleepy head." Anna reached up and ran her hand through his hair. She grabbed a handful and pulled his face down to her open mouth.

Sam broke the kiss and leaned up on one elbow. "Uh. . . What time is it?"

"You got a bus to catch?" She ran her fingers over his chest and whispered in his ear. "I like a man in the morning." Her wet tongue gave it an exclamation point.

"This is nice," he mumbled, pulling her against him. "But books written by experts on business management say the boss shouldn't screw the help. It pollutes the work environment and confuses the professional relationship."

"I'm not confused," she said. "Are you?"

"Not sure. Oh God. Your tongue in my ear starts my motor."

She did it again.

"Oh, God," he gasped. He pulled her on top of him. "How are you not confused? I'm having trouble remembering what day it is. What day is it?"

"Today's Monday. And just like yesterday, you're still the captain and I'm crew."

"I've never made love to my crew before."

"Did we make love or did we just screw?"

"What's the difference?" He rolled them over and stared

down at her. *God, she's beautiful in the morning.*

Anna looked away without responding.

"I mean," Sam said. "Is there a difference? I've never—"

"I was trying to remember the last time I made love," she said to the bulkhead. "My wedding night for sure, and just before Daniel left for his last flight, but. . . ."

"Surely there've been other men in your life?" He lay on his back beside her.

"I'm 40 years old, Sam. You don't have enough paper and ink on this tub to list all the men I—"

"No. No, I mean didn't you ever have feelings for someone after Daniel? Did you come close to marrying again? Giving Ian a real father?"

"No, and No," she said, and went silent a moment. "I was a virgin when I met him, and it was four years after he died that I was with another man, or boy. He was twenty-one and I was twenty-two. The son of my father-in-law's business accountant. He asked me out on a date. We went to a movie and then made out in the back seat of his car. He said he was experienced, but I didn't know the difference. God, it seems like a thousand years have passed since then."

Sam stared at the ceiling of her cabin. He'd never really paid any attention to it. The cabin was on Firebird's port side and morning sun streamed in through the porthole. His own cabin was on the starboard side, facing West in the harbor and rarely got morning sun. He hadn't thought about it before. It was getting too warm with two people in the bedding. "Okay then," he said, swinging his feet off the mattress and onto the floor. "We just screwed and didn't make love. I can deal with that. I'd go again right now but it's getting hot in here. My cabin's much cooler if you still—"

"I'm good," Anna said, getting up on her knees on the bed. She reached for a thin robe and slipped it on before stepping off the bunk. "I need a shower before starting the day. I'll set up that old sewing machine I found on board and see if it works. I may not be a domestic goddess, but I want to show you I can at least cover a pillow. You'll be happy to let me make the covers for the salon cushions when you see my work."

Just then they both heard the coughing sound of an outboard motor coming near.

"Guess it's a good thing Ian didn't come back last night." Anna looked at Sam standing naked in the cabin door. "Please get something on before he sees us. I can't believe this is happening."

Sam winked at her. "At least we just screwed and didn't make love, so no harm, no foul." He bent down to grab his shorts and T-shirt from the floor and closed the cabin door behind him.

"And how was your night?" Sam stood on the boarding platform holding the dinghy line while Ian killed and tilted the dinghy motor out of the water.

"Not bad." Ian's grin spread from ear-to-ear. "Took two showers last night before I got the sand out of all the crevices and creases. We had sand in places you wouldn't think you could get sand. How about you?"

"Worrying about that blown engine kept me up most of the night," he lied. "I'll go to the shop after my coffee, get one of their mechanics to come check it out."

"I plan on spending the day putting Naval Jelly on the rigging and lifeline stanchions," Ian said, following Sam up the ladder to the deck. "Removing rust from the stainless and polishing should make it look new. That job will take me at least three days."

"Let's see what the mechanic says before investing more time and money in this tub," Sam said. "If we wind up sinking it to make a reef, not sure the fish will appreciate rust free, sparkling, stainless steel rigging."

Anna called up from below. "Coffee's on the galley counter."

"Be right there." Sam leaned into the companionway. He turned to look at Ian. "See anything interesting in town?"

"Too early in the morning." Ian shook his head. "Nothing was moving in town when I walked from Sarah's apartment back to the marina. Their vehicle wasn't at the marina."

"Let's grab some coffee and breakfast and get this engine looked at," Sam said. "The suspense is driving me nuts."

Ian went below while Sam walked to the bow to check the boats in the harbor. Everything looked benign. The sun was beginning to sting, but the morning trade breezes had picked up, making the heat tolerable. He wanted to think about the previous evening with Anna but didn't have time. Perhaps later, after he found out if Firebird's engine had killed the dream.

Steve Baxter, supposedly the island's best diesel mechanic, stepped out of the engine room into the main salon, wiping his hands on an oily rag. The expression on his face gave no clue as to his findings. Sam leaned back against the galley sink with his arms crossed over his chest. Ian sat at the salon table across from his mother. No one spoke.

Finally, Steve looked up and saw his anxious audience. "I think your only decision," he said slowly, "is whether you want a burial or cremation. She's done, fini, kaput, dead."

The butterflies in Sam's stomach all tried to get out at the same time. He felt like vomiting. He shook his head and stared at the floor. "How much?" was all he could squeak out.

"Fifty dollars for my time today, but at least fifty-thousand or more to replace that power plant. Probably more," Steve answered. "This ain't no cheap yacht. Takes a monster motor to push around eighty-four feet of floating tonnage."

"What do you mean *dead*?" Sam asked. "Can it be repaired or overhauled, or something that doesn't cost so damn much?"

"The pistons are frozen. Must've been extreme heat at some point. Crankshaft is busted, and the block is cracked. Without opening her up, I can't tell how that happened. I can see she's been rode hard over the years. A new one'll cost an arm and a leg. It'll take at least six weeks to get here after you order it from a dealer. Cost to install would probably be another fifteen-thousand and take two weeks to complete. Maybe you can get a hundred in scrap value for the old motor."

No one spoke while Sam stared at the floor. After a few moments, he looked up. "At least I'm good for the fifty," he said, stepping forward and handing the cash to the mechanic. "Thanks for coming on such short notice."

The mechanic stuffed the money in his pocket. "Wish I had better news. Let me know if there's anything else you need."

Sam and Ian stood by the rail watching him motor away toward the industrial dock in town. Ian looked at Sam "Should I still derust and polish the rigging?"

"I wouldn't," Sam said and headed below. "You heard the man. I'm going to take a nap. When I wake up, maybe I'll find this was all just a crappy dream."

# CHAPTER 31

Anna also retreated to her cabin and closed the door. Sam's reaction to the blown motor caught her by surprise. That he would give up so easily worried her. Was it really that big of a problem? Even dream killing? She could hear Ian working at polishing the lifeline stanchion just above her port. Hadn't Sam said it wasn't necessary if the engine report was not good?

She crawled on the bunk and hugged a pillow to her breast. *Now what am I going to do?* She closed her eyes. Sleep was an escape, and she was an expert at it. A flurry of images and memories flooded her thoughts.

She hadn't been truthful before with Sam about meeting Guy Mont Violet. He had been so dangerously dark and handsome when she first saw him at the airport after arriving on Saint Sebastian. He had watched her waiting in baggage claim and followed when she stepped outside to look for a cab. He didn't say anything as his driver loaded her bags into his Jeep. He didn't have to. She was used to men taking charge. Wordlessly, she got in the back seat next to him and didn't respond when his hand roughly grasped her leg and pulled her against him. He knew. How he knew, she wasn't sure, but it wasn't the first time something like this had happened. A girlfriend in Boston said it was the scent she gave off. She blamed pheromones.

When they pulled into the motor court at the villa, he turned to look at her. "This okay?"

She stared into his smoldering eyes and felt a shudder deep in her core. Not trusting herself to speak, she nodded.

Her memory of the next two days was foggy and a smattering

of blurred, confusing details. A kaleidoscope of faces, drugs, and orgasms so many and powerful that afterwards she could only lay on the bed gasping for breath, ran over and over in her mind like a broken movie reel. She remembered the first time he stood naked before her, a dark Adonis, a da Vinci drawing, veins extended, throbbing. His muscles sleek, oiled, and powerful like a racehorse.

Towards the end of the second day, things turned rough. Too rough. Three times she thought she would suffocate with his hands gripping her throat. It scared her. When he cut another line of drugs for each of them, she'd gone into the bathroom and flushed it down the toilet. He was asleep on top of the covers when she returned, and she saw the rope and cuffs on the dresser. She had dressed and slipped over the wall. Thank God, I ran into Ian before Guy found me, she thought.

It was warm in the cabin and she found it hard to sleep. Anna got up and removed her shorts and T-shirt. She crawled back on the bunk and turned on her back, eyes open, staring at the ceiling. She thought about the night before with Sam. He'd been so different from her other lovers. She smiled when she remembered him getting up.

"I've gotto go and get a. . .you know. From my room."

"Don't." She'd grabbed his arm and pulled him back to bed. "I took care of that a long time ago." She didn't say anything about the young medical student in Boston who'd booked her into his hospital to have her tubes tied on her thirtieth birthday as a birthday present.

Thinking about last night made her draw her knees up to her chest and her toes curl. She grabbed a pillow to hold and rolled onto her side. She thought again about how close she had come to getting in real trouble with Guy Mont Violet. She shuddered to think what Turloch would have done. *What if Ian found out?*

She closed her eyes and finally drifted off to sleep. In her dream, she lay next to Daniel on their wedding night in the Bridal Suite at the Ritz Carleton in Boston. The champagne bottle on the room service cart sat empty. She felt complete. Safe. She felt his strong arms wrapped around her, and the aroma of his cologne filled her senses. She was now the wife of a dashing young military officer.

She opened her eyes when she heard an outboard engine fire up. She quietly slipped through the main salon trying to not wake Sam napping in his cabin and went up the stairs to the deck. She saw Ian motoring toward the marina.

Sam felt the mattress sag, evidence someone had joined him. He lay on his side on top of the covers. The small oscillating fan on the wall above the bunk gave some relief to the afternoon's heat. He opened one eye to check his watch. It was five o'clock in the afternoon. A hand slipped under his arm and caressed his chest.

"You okay?" she whispered. "I'm worried about you."

A few moments passed while he thought about her question. "Where's the boy?"

"He went ashore. Didn't say where he was going." She pressed her breasts against his bare back.

"Probably to look for another job," Sam said. "I think this one's done."

"Is it really that bad?"

Another minute passed before he answered. "Yeah. I think it's that bad."

"What will you do?"

"Don't know." He grasped her hand and held it. "Not a lot of options. Guess I can go back to Puerto Rico. Get a job on another freighter."

Anna sat up. "Are you giving up? I thought you were a fighter. I thought—"

"You thought wrong, missy." Sam sat up with his back against the bulkhead. Seeing her nakedness, he turned away to look out the porthole. "I'm a realist and I know when I'm beat. It'll cost close to seventy-thousand dollars or more to get this boat moving again. I don't have it, nor any chance to get it unless you have a sugar daddy or a rich father-in-law to tap." He regretted it as soon as he said it. "I'm sorry, I—"

"He wouldn't, and I won't ask," Anna said. "I have some jewelry we could pawn or sell, but it wouldn't come close to that much." A moment of silence passed and then she said, "Would you really go back to work on a freighter?"

Sam turned to look at her. He hurt inside but didn't want her to know just how bad. "I was a fool for thinking this would work out. And like I said, there's not a lot of options. If I'm lucky, maybe I can get a couple thousand bucks for this shell of a boat. Everything works onboard except the engine, but that's like selling a. . .a. . .I don't know what. Might not be able to find a buyer. The dinghy's worth a few hundred. It's more salable, but that's it."

Nothing else was said for a few minutes. "I need a drink," he said, moving off the bed and padding barefoot into the salon. "You want something?"

"A glass of white wine," she said, following him. "There should be an open bottle in the fridge. Cold white wine will taste good in this heat."

Sam removed the cork from their second bottle of Chardonnay and poured a glass for her and then himself. The alcohol had lightened the mood. He wondered if he was feeling a wine buzz or if the crashing of his dream had come as more of a relief. Whatever. They were both sitting bare ass at the salon table, on his boat, at least for the time being, and he'd never been one to *not* take advantage of such a situation.

He studied her a moment. Their day at the beach had deepened her tan. Her bare shoulder was dotted with freckles. Still no visible tan lines. Her red hair was piled on top of her head with dangling tendrils framing her pixie face. She wore silver earrings and two silver bracelets on one wrist. He watched her fingers turn the stem of her wine glass around and around. Her manicured nails had just the right length to give a man a good back scratch. Her toes rubbed the hair on his leg under the table, and he looked up at her. A sheepish smile creased her face.

"Okay," he said. "You want to make love this time, or what?"

“The kids aren’t here, and we have the place to ourselves,” she teased. “We can do whatever we want.” She reached for his hand and leaned forward to lick his open palm. “Do I have to choose?” She ran her tongue over his palm one more time and smiled at him.

# CHAPTER 32

Sam reached to turn on the reading light over his bed and checked the time. He pushed himself up to look out the porthole at the boarding platform where the dinghy should be. "Shit. He's not back, and it's almost midnight."

"What?" Anna turned over and squinted in the light. "What's wrong?" She pulled the sheet to cover herself.

"The boy's not back, yet." He found a pair of running shorts and pulled them on. He grabbed his ballcap and left the cabin. Up on deck, the night was still and warm. There was hardly any breeze. The boats around them in the harbor floated slack on their mooring lines. All was quiet. He looked across the water toward the marina, but it was too far and too dark to see anything at the dinghy dock.

"Are you worried?" Anna stepped out, tying the sash to her robe.

"What did he say when he left?" Sam turned to look at her.

"Nothing. He said nothing to me. He was in the dinghy and gone before I could ask any questions." She crossed her arms over her chest and looked out across the dark water. "I thought he was probably going to see Sarah. I don't know, but I'm guessing they did more at that private beach on Moskito Island than build sand castles."

"Good guess," Sam said, looking out to the lights in Drake Town. "Let's hope he's with her and they're okay. We can't do anything about it without a way to get ashore. It's too late to call the marina office."

Anna stepped next to him at the rail. Sam put his arm around her and drew her close. Neither said anything as they gazed out into the night, each lost in their own thoughts about the day's events. All of them.

"Virgin Cay Marina. Virgin Cay Marina. This is Firebird. Over." Sam looked at Anna in the doorway to her room. Sunlight behind her made the long T-shirt she wore look almost transparent. "It's eight o'clock," he said. "Someone should be in the office."

"This is Virgin Cay." The radio crackled. "Go to channel twelve. Over."

"Firebird to channel twelve. Over" Sam dialed the VHF to the new channel.

"This is Virgin Cay. Go ahead. Over." Came the response.

"Thanks, Virgin Cay. Just checking to see if my inflatable is there at the dinghy dock. Over."

"A moment while we check." There was a long pause and some static while he waited.

"Not here, Sam." He recognized Charlie's voice.

"Is it supposed to be?"

"Ian went ashore yesterday afternoon, and we haven't heard from him," Sam replied. "Has anyone there seen—"

"Before I left the office last evening, I saw him and some guy I didn't recognize get in your Zodiac and motor toward the industrial dock. It looked all friendly like, and I didn't think there was a problem. Want me to come out and get you? I've got some time before my meeting this morning at the bank and—"

"That'd be great, Charlie. Thanks." Sam saw the frightened look on Anna's face.

"Be right there. Virgin Cay back to channel sixteen. Out."

"Firebird back to sixteen. Out." Sam placed the mike in its slot on the navigation station and looked at Anna. "It's probably nothing," he said. "I'll find him."

Sam stepped off the boarding platform and onto the marina's launch. Charlie backed away from Firebird and looked at him. "Where to?"

"The industrial dock in town if you're headed that way," Sam said.

"No problem." Charlie pushed the gear into forward and gassed it. "The bank is just down the street. Beats walking from the marina."

Sam's eyes scanned the pier and commercial dock, looking for his gray Zodiac as Charlie glided the launch into the area. There were several small freighters entering and leaving, and a big Windjammer tied up at the town dock loading supplies. Sam nodded at several guests on the Windjammer deck who waved to them.

"See anything?" Charlie glanced at him as they floated toward the concrete dock.

"Not yet," Sam said, picking up a bumper and line in preparation of docking. He stood up in the bow and jumped onto the pier as Charlie idled then killed the engine. A few figure eights on a cleat with the line held the launch parallel to the dock while Charlie looped a stern line around a post.

"Thanks for the ride over," Sam said. "I'll let you know what I find."

Charlie nodded and picked up his briefcase. "I'll be at the bank for about an hour then back at the marina. Meet me there if you need a ride back."

Sam walked to the far end of the pier, looking at all the hard-bottom inflatables tied up, one behind the other. His Zodiac was not among them. He glanced up and saw Sarah's café. Maybe she's got the lunch shift, he thought to himself and headed in that direction.

"Yep. She's working today but ain't here yet." A bus boy sweeping the sidewalk in front of the café informed him. "Not till eleven."

Sam checked his watch. It was only ten o'clock. Scanning the cars in town, he saw the Haitian's black vehicle parked just down the street in front of a lawyer's office. He found a wooden bench on the waterfront and sat to wait and watch. After a while, several men in suits stepped out of the office and got in the Jeep. Guy Mont Violet was not with them. He watched them start to drive away and stood to follow. Just then, he spotted Sarah crossing the street to the café.

"Where's Ian?" Sam met her at the corner.

Sarah frowned. "I haven't seen him since late yesterday afternoon. He stopped by my apartment around five o'clock to tell me the bad news about the fried motor. He ranted that the Haitian and his men probably had something to do with it."

"He didn't stay with you last night?"

"No. He wanted to get back to the boat and help you figure out a solution." Sarah reached for his arm. "Have you not seen—"

"Not since noon yesterday. If he hasn't been with you, where would he go? The dinghy's not at the marina, and Charlie says he hasn't seen it." Sam saw a look of panic on Sarah's face. "Don't worry. We'll find him. This island's not that big. Surely, someone saw him."

"I'm sorry, Sam, but I have to get to work." She looked like she was about to cry. "I wish I could help right now, but the café is shorthanded and—"

He put his arms around her and gave her a big hug. "Don't worry. I'm sure he's all right. I'll let you know as soon as I find him. If you see him first, tell—"

"I'll know exactly what to tell the bugger for giving us such a fright." Sarah's chin trembled.

"I'm sure." He smiled as he dropped his arms. "Call me on channel sixteen if he shows up. Anna's out on the boat and can get your message. I'll check around the harbor before heading back to see if I can find our Zodiac. He knows I'm pretty upset about the main engine and may be giving me some time and space to cool off." That wasn't the case, but he didn't want to frighten Sarah any more than she already was.

"Should we notify the constable? I mean—"

"Not yet." He shook his head. "I don't trust anyone in that office. Maybe later."

"I'll be at the café today till three o'clock," Sarah said and started in that direction. She turned around and walked backwards. "Keep me posted, and I'll do the same."

He nodded and watched her turn into the café's front door. A couple of early lunch customers followed her in. Sam paused a moment to gaze out over the harbor and think. A few boats were coming in and a few were going out. It looked like a regular day on the island. No one seemed to be in a hurry. Everyone and everything was on *island time*.

He bought a pulled pork sandwich and a bottle of water from an umbrella cart on the waterfront and ate his lunch while walking the breakwater around the entire harbor. There were hundreds of inflatables and hard bottom dinghies along with a scattering of small fishing boats and private crafts tied to docks and piers jutting out into the water. His Zodiac was not among them.

It was three in the afternoon when he returned to the marina. He opened the door to the airconditioned office to see if Charlie had heard anything.

"Your cute girlfriend called here on the VHF about a half hour ago looking for you." Charlie came around the counter and met him at the door. "Said to tell you to get your ass back out to the boat as soon as you showed up."

"She mention anything about Ian?"

"Nope." Charlie shook his head. "I assume you need a ride."

"Yeah." Sam nodded. "You have time to run me out?"

"Get in the launch. Any luck on finding your dinghy?"

Sam shook his head. "The boy was here on the island yesterday afternoon late with his girlfriend but left, and no one's seen him since." If the Haitian's got him, Sam thought, I'll—"

"Maybe his mother heard from him." Charlie turned the key and fired up the launch's inboard.

"Maybe." Sam looked out toward Firebird as they left the dock.

# CHAPTER 33

As the launch neared Firebird, Sam recognized his gray Zodiac tied to the boarding platform. A large unfamiliar barge was also secured to the starboard side with lines running to the bow and stern. The barge was cushioned against Firebird's hull by several black rubber tires used as bumpers. What in the world is going on? Sam thought.

Charlie put the launch in reverse to reduce speed and drifted up behind the dinghy. Sam stepped off onto the boarding platform and pushed the launch's bow away. "Thanks for the ride. I owe you one."

The marina manager waved and eased the throttle forward. Sam watched a moment then turned and went up the ladder. Just as he stepped onto the deck, Ian appeared out of the companionway, followed by a smiling Anna, and an older stranger he didn't recognize. The man was obviously an islander, brown and grizzled by life in the sun. His floppy straw hat covered long gray hair and hung low over his eyes, but his white teeth showed in a big grin, like a Cheshire cat, Sam thought.

"Sam." Ian grinned from ear-to-ear. "This is Bobbie Parker from Virgin Gorda. He owns a salvage business next to the marina at Spanish Town. A man here in town stopped me yesterday and said he heard we'd lost the engine on Firebird. Word gets around fast on this island. Anyway, he suggested I go over to Virgin Gorda and see this man. That he might help us with a replacement."

Sam looked at the old fellow nodding his head up and down. His teeth flashing white in the afternoon sun. "And did this mysterious person in town say where we could get a loan to buy this replacement? I'm sure Mr. Parker here doesn't give 'em away to charity cases."

Ian looked at Sam a moment then turned to his mother. Anna was dressed in khaki shorts and a pink T-shirt. They smiled at each other. "That's the good part," Ian said. "Mr. Parker here has an engine that can possibly work. We'll have to check with Palmer Johnson, but he'll sell it to us for five hundred dollars."

Sam swallowed hard. Had he heard right? "Five hundred, huh?" He looked at the old gentleman who still nodded like a bobblehead.

"Five hundred," repeated Ian. "Trust me. But we have to check and see if it'll work. It's smaller than the old Ford Lehman down there now, but no less horsepower. It's a Perkins 240 diesel built by Caterpillar. Only six years old, so its newer technology. Smaller, faster, more powerful, but also way more efficient."

"And where's this engine now?" Sam asked, confused as to why they were being offered such a good deal when the engine shop in town assured him it would take most, if not all, of a fifty-thousand-dollar bill, if there was such a thing.

"Here on the barge," Ian said, leading the way to the rail. "We brought it with us."

Sam looked down and saw an engine in a wooden crate sitting on the barge's deck.

"Mr. Parker told me that one night two years ago the Commodore of the Annapolis Yacht Club ran his custom Swan 85 onto the reef at North Sound. Mr. Parker salvaged the engine and some other stuff. The motor's all that's left. Said he's had trouble selling it since it's so large. Most private boats around here can't use one that big. He wants to get it out of his shop and is asking five hundred dollars. What do you think?"

A smile crossed Sam's face. The first one in two days. "You want to know what I think? I think we can't let him take that motor back to Virgin Gorda," he said almost in a whisper. "I've got five Benjamins in my cabin. I hope we can make it work, but if we can't, it'll make a good anchor. Hell! Even a real anchor for this boat costs more than five hundred bucks."

Ian turned to the old man. "You got a deal, Mr. Parker. I'll loosen a halyard and bring it down to the barge. We'll put a chain around that crate and wench it up on deck."

He looked at Sam. "Hope this works."

"Me too, son." Sam looked at Anna, beaming with pride in her boy. "Me, too."

After setting the heavy engine crate in place on deck behind the main mast, Sam and Ian stood together in the bow, watching Mr. Parker's barge pass through the harbor entrance and make a left turn back toward Spanish Town. Anna had gone below.

"You have some explaining to do, boy." Sam turned to Ian. "You scared your mother almost to death and nearly gave me a heart attack. When you weren't here this morning, we figured you'd drowned, or run afoul of Mont Violet's thugs, or something. What did I say about going ashore by yourself?"

"I know. I'm sorry." Ian ran a hand through his blonde hair. I was pretty upset yesterday after we learned the motor was shot. I just know those thugs came on board while we were on Moskito and did something. When you went below to nap, I took the dinghy to go looking for them."

"You crazy?" Sam scowled.

"Didn't find them. They weren't at the marina, and they weren't in town. I stopped at Sarah's apartment to tell her the bad news about the motor. I was walking back to the marina when this guy I've never seen stopped me and asked if I was from the big Palmer Johnson ketch out in the harbor. He said something about it being too bad the motor was shot. I figured he'd heard it from someone at the engine shop. He suggested we contact Bobbie Parker over on Virgin Gorda. Thought he might be able to help."

"But why didn't you come back to the boat last night?" Sam said. "I mean—"

"I was too wound up. The Visitor Center near the commercial dock in town was still open, so I asked to use their phone to call Mr.

Parker. The girl in the office said he was her uncle and didn't have a phone. That he lived in a shack behind his business, and the best way to reach him was to go over there. I thought about coming back to get you but it was late, so I headed up the channel to Virgin Gorda."

"But that's sixteen miles at least." Sam crossed his arms over his chest.

"Yeah, I know. But I knew you were real worried, the gas can was full, and I hauled ass over there."

Sam shook his head. "That was a risk by itself with no navigation lights on any of the rocks out there."

"There was a full moon," Ian replied. "Almost like daylight on the water. When I got to Spanish Town, I tied up at the marina and went looking for Mr. Parker's place. There were no lights on, and I figured he'd already gone to bed, so I went back to the marina and slept in the dinghy."

Anna called up from the galley, "Dinner's ready. I'm not going to wait on you."

"I found him this morning," Ian continued as they headed to the companionway. "We loaded the Perkins. You know the rest of the story." The sun had now dropped below the mountain, casting the harbor in cooling shade.

Sam studied Ian across the dining table. The boy was digging into his second plate of pasta and meat sauce.

"This is great, Mom," Ian said, swallowing a mouthful and reaching for another piece of bread. I haven't eaten anything since lunch yesterday."

Anna looked at Ian, then at Sam and smiled. "Every mother likes to see her child appreciate her cooking. I rarely had that opportunity living in your grandfather's house."

"Any word from him?" Ian asked, before forking another mouthful of pasta.

"Not yet," she said, "but I expect to soon. I'm sure he's seen the credit card bill and knows where we are."

"So, you think the thugs in town ruined our engine?" Sam took a sip of his wine and set the glass back down in front of him.

"They could've." Ian looked at him. "They had opportunity when we spent the day on Moskito. The motor ran fine the last time we started it."

Sam looked away. The boy was right. And if he was right, what if anything could or should they do about it?

"Do you think he did it for revenge?" Anna reached for Sam's hand.

Sam shrugged.

"Who?" Ian took a drink from his water glass. "Revenge for what?"

Anna got up and started clearing dishes.

"Just more guy stuff between me and the Haitian," Sam answered the question. "It got personal one day in town. I don't think he's that dangerous—or that stupid."

"I thought they were all bullies," Ian said, looking hard at Sam. "They've been bullying everyone in town, and then they got into it with me and you on the dock that day." He grinned. "You kicked their asses. But I didn't know it had gone beyond that."

"Not sure where it is, now." Sam looked for a reaction from Anna at the galley sink. "But you're right about one thing. There's just no good explanation for how that motor burned up."

Sam heard his cabin door open and close in the dark. He had been lying in bed for over an hour in a sleepless fit, his mind going a million miles an hour, sorting through the day's events. He felt the mattress sag.

"You really think it was Guy?" He heard Anna's voice near his ear. "I'm worried that—"

He rolled over and kissed her. Her mouth opened, and he felt her tongue between his lips. Her breath was fresh. Her perfume made him weak. "I'm not sure," he said. "But we won't take any chances. We'll have someone on the boat at all times."

"I'm so relieved that Ian's back. I was worried sick."

“Me too,” he whispered in the dark, “and if this motor works out, he saved our whole effort.” He felt her lips on his throat and her tongue searching for his ear. *Oh. God. She found it.*

Afterwards, she slipped out of his bed and returned to her cabin. He could still smell her in the sheets. Yep. That was making love, he thought before drifting off into a deep sleep.

# CHAPTER 34

"I'll phone the engineering department at Palmer Johnson in Wisconsin this morning and see what they can tell me about replacing the old motor with this new one. Or at least new to us," Sam said to Anna, sitting across the table from him eating a bowl of instant oatmeal. He was on his second cup of coffee when Ian came in to pour himself one. "Hey. Good morning sleepy head. How'd you sleep last night?"

"Almost never got to sleep," Ian said, shaking his head. "Did a storm come in last night?"

Sam looked at Anna who kept her head down. "Yeah. I felt those rollers coming into the harbor as well. Must've been some wind out there."

Anna looked at him and winked.

"Good thing it wasn't like that the night before," Ian said, putting the cream back in the fridge. "It could've swamped me on the way to Virgin Gorda."

"Yep." Sam stifled a laugh. "Good thing."

"After I call Palmer Johnson I'll stop by the chandlery and get some more Naval Jelly." Sam stood in the inflatable still tied to the boarding platform. Can you think of anything else we need?"

"Nope." Ian said, leaning over the lifelines. He wore a pair of ratty shorts and was barefooted. "Except Mom said maybe some more sun block, and varnish, and sandpaper."

"Call me on the radio at the marina office if you come up with anything else," Sam said. He started the motor and untied the dinghy. "Leave a message if I'm not there. I'll be back before lunch. Oh,

I saw more rust on the stern pulpit. And on those stanchions by the port side gate."

"Got it." Ian waved.

"I'd like to speak to the engineering department," Sam said when the Palmer Johnson operator answered his call. He leaned back in Charlie's office chair and put his bare feet up on the desk. The marina manager had stepped away to assist an incoming charter yacht.

"What?" Someone on the other end answered abruptly.

Sam dropped his feet to the floor and leaned forward on the desk. "Yes, I'm the owner of a Palmer Johnson ketch named Firebird. I think she was built sometime in the sixties. I'm down here at Saint Sebastian near the Virgin Islands and have some questions about the engine. I need to—"

"I'll transfer you to Mr. Langley, our chairman," the voice said.

"No. No. Please." Sam turned to look out the window at another boat coming into the marina. "I'm sure he won't want to talk with me. Is there someone—"

"Bill Langley here." The next voice carried the tone of authority.

Sam gave a quick explanation for his call and waited for the blow off response.

"Well, I guess I'm the right guy here at the yard to speak with. I was a welder in the boatyard when we built Firebird back in the sixties, and probably the only guy still around that remembers her. You say she's on Saint Sebastian?"

"Yes, sir," Sam said. "I found her in pretty bad shape over in Puerto Rico and am restoring her for the crewed charter business. I have a specific question I'm calling about but would also appreciate any background or history you can give me."

There was a long pause on the other end before Mr. Langley spoke. "We don't keep records like that on the yachts we build. I remember it was a sad day Mr. Blaylock died. He was Chairman of Blaylock Industries, the big maker of ball bearings in Gary, Indiana. We'd just had a launch party and poof, he was gone. A damn heart attack. Not sure who all has owned her. I think the family sold it to some investment banker. I lost track after that."

"That's more information than I had before," Sam replied. "Helps fill in some blanks. At least gives me her genesis."

"What's your specific question?" Langley said. "I've got a customer meeting in fifteen minutes and—"

"The old Ford Lehman engine has frozen. The diesel mechanics down here say it's not fixable so I'm looking at replacing it. I've obtained a slightly used Perkins 240 and wonder if it will fit?"

"Plenty of power there," Langley replied. "Caterpillar owns Perkins, and you can't get better quality than that. As I recall, that Ford engine sits level. The prop shaft is directly below and attached to the fly wheel by a pulley system with belts. That allows the prop shaft to stay level through the stuffing box. It was a new development back then. Still used on larger yachts today. Much more complicated if the prop shaft angles up into the transmission like they do on smaller craft. Just need to make sure the replacement is installed with new motor mounts as the Ford was a bigger engine. Properly place the engine directly above the pully system and you should be good to go. Any mechanic that's worked on large yachts will know that system."

Yeah, Sam thought to himself. That's what worries me since the boy, and I are the mechanics.

"Uh, good luck with that project. Send me some photos when you can. I have fond memories of working on Firebird back when I was young, flat bellied, and had more lead in my pencil. If you know what I mean. . . ."

Sam hung up the phone and studied the brass boat clock on the wall over Charlie's desk. Easy peasy, he thought. A seventy-thousand-dollar engine problem solved for five hundred bucks and maybe another five hundred for installation parts. *I'm a very lucky man. The dream is still alive. But it's also too damn easy.*

He was still looking at the clock and thinking about what Langley had said when Charlie returned to his office. "Get what you needed?"

"It'll work," Sam said. "The new engine should be an easy install. Palmer Johnson was very helpful. It was a good call."

"Great," Charlie said. "So, you think you will still be out of here by Thanksgiving? I'm getting calls for moorings for the coming season and we need your spot."

"The charter show on Saint Thomas is the week before Thanksgiving, so we should definitely be gone by then." Sam stood to let Charlie have his desk back. "And Charlie, thanks for everything."

"We can get those new motor mounts in about three business days." Steve Baxter was looking at the catalogue in the engine shop with Sam standing over him. "I can't believe you found a workable motor over at Parker's Salvage. Hell, if I knew he had that engine out of the Commodore's fancy Swan, I'd have bought it myself. What'd you pay for it? I'd a given him fifteen, twenty thousand. Hell, I know two people on Saint Thomas who'd buy it from me for twice that."

"I'll be back in three days to pick up those mounts," Sam said, anxious to get away. He was still struggling with why Parker sold him the engine for such a cheap price. Based on Baxter's comments, the old man's story of unloading it for lack of interest didn't make sense.

On his way back to the marina, he saw the black Jeep roll to a stop at the intersection. He couldn't see inside. He wondered if the Haitian was watching him. Probably, but screw him, he thought. *I'm sure the bastard was behind the sabotage of my engine, and he'll pay. One day, he will pay.*

Back aboard Firebird he found Anna below at the sewing machine. She was completing a cover to one of the salon cushions.

"What do you think?" She held up her handiwork. The material was a cream-colored terry cloth. "I think it's clean looking and practical. It brightens up the dark room and can be thrown in the washing machine with towels and sheets."

Sam nodded. "Looks nice. Does it fit?"

She picked up one of the cushions, pulled the cover over it and reset it on the settee. “Like a glove.”

“Does freshen up the place.” He smiled. “Good work. Just six more to go.”

“Actually, more than that,” Anna said. “The fabric store in town ordered me additional material. I took all they had for the main salon here but also want to cover all the cushions in each cabin. This light color against the freshly varnished wood makes it look like a new yacht.”

“That’s what we want our paying guests to think,” Sam said. “Where’s Ian? I’ve got some news.”

“In the engine room. Said he was going to start dismantling the old one. I’ve heard banging and clanking in there for the past two hours.”

Sam opened the door to the engine room and saw Ian bending over the block. Parts littered the floor. “Take a break and meet me on deck. I’ll buy you a beer. Got some good news today from Palmer Johnson. That motor you found is a winner.”

The harbor buzzed with the sound of small craft crisscrossing open water between all the boats on moorings. Sam waited in shade under the cockpit canopy while Anna and Ian put their work away and joined him. After relating everything that Bill Langley told him about replacing the old motor, he paused and took a big swig of his beer. “Based on that, we should have the job finished by the weekend. Maybe a delay of four days but not more. We’re back on schedule.”

Anna reached for Sam’s hand and squeezed it.

“It was Ian who saved our bacon.” Sam nodded at the boy. Ian looked embarrassed, and Anna wiped a streak of grease off her son’s face.

“If you hadn’t taken the initiative and found that new motor, I hate to think about what we’d be doing right now.”

“My grandfather has a saying,” Ian said. “‘Nothing ventured, nothing gained.’ Other than possibly flipping the dinghy going across the channel at night, there was no real risk.”

"Langley also told me something interesting about Firebird's original owner," Sam said. "His name was Blaylock. He was a rich mid-western industrialist and died of a heart attack right after they christened her in the boatyard."

"Wow," Ian said, shaking his head. "That's too bad. He never got to sail her in a magical place like this. You realize every past owner we know something about has met a bad ending?"

"Yeah," Sam said and finished his beer. "I thought about that, too."

"Maybe we've broken the spell, or at least the trend," Anna said, surprising them both.

"How?" Sam asked. "In what way?"

"Well, she could've already been a reef for the fish in Puerto Rico, or even here at Saint Sebastian. Now she has a new modern engine, a rebuilt generator, polished stainless-steel rigging, freshly varnished cabins, new covered cushions, new filters, belts, and pumps, a reconditioned deck, and a captain and crew who love her and want to take care of her. She has a bright future."

Sam lifted both bare feet up into Anna's lap. "And a first-class masseuse on board that gives fantastic foot rubs to rich charter guests."

Anna pushed him away. "Let me know when you have a rich charter guest." She stood up in the cockpit. "I'm going below. There's more sewing to do before dinner. Ian, make sure you wash and clean up before you come to the table. You look like you've been wrestling a grease monkey, whatever that is."

"And lost." Sam winked at Ian across the cockpit table.

At dinner, Ian's hair was still wet from his shower and he smelled of soap and Old Spice.

"I can tell you've been into my cologne." Sam said. "What's the occasion?"

"Thought I'd see Sarah tonight after she gets off work." Ian reached for another slice of bread.

"I hope you two use protection." Anna didn't look at either one of them. Her eyes stayed glued to her plate. "I mean—"

"I know what you mean, Mother." Ian stopped eating and sat back in the settee.

"Uh, there's some, uh, a box of, a supply in my—" Sam started to say.

"Don't worry. Sarah takes care of that." Ian interrupted him.

After a long pause, Sam said, "Then be back early in the morning. We need to finish dismantling the old engine. That will take us at least two days. We'll want to label all the electrical wires and filter tubing and be prepared to install the new motor as soon as the new engine mounts arrive."

Ian stood and bent to kiss his mother on her cheek. "Okay if I'm back by eight? I promise to return in time for breakfast." He looked at Sam. "And I'll be careful." He glanced at his mother. "In every way."

Sam nodded and watched him take the steps two at a time up to the deck.

# CHAPTER 35

"Mind some company?" Anna sat on the cushion across from him in the cockpit. She held up a glass in her hand. "Gin and tonic. Want one?"

"Thanks, but I'm working on my own here." He raised his rum and coke. The night was calm and quiet. He could hear harbor water lapping gently at Firebird's hull.

"I heard the dinghy leave and come back. You take Ian to shore?"

"Yep." Sam nodded. "Didn't want him to leave us stranded out here again. We agreed I'd meet him at the dock at nine in the morning."

"Nine? I thought he said eight—"

"They're two young adults with raging hormones. Remember what that was like? I told him to eat before he came." He watched Anna for some reaction. Her lips turned up in a soft smile, but that was it. Several minutes passed with neither of them saying anything.

"So, Sam." Anna broke the silence. "What are your plans?"

"Get the new motor installed and—"

"That's not what I meant. I mean long term? I assume you think this refit is going to work out and—"

"I don't make long term plans," Sam said. "I did that once, a long time ago."

"I need to know, Sam." Anna took a long sip of her drink.

He saw she was barefooted. Her toenails painted a bright red color matched her nail polish. She has beautiful hands, he thought. And sexy feet.

"I need to know," she continued, "for Ian's sake. My original purpose in coming here was to get him to return home to finish his senior year at Cornell. Then we got involved in your project." She glanced over Firebird's deck. "It looks like there's an end time scheduled and I, rather we, need to make our own plans."

"What do you mean 'end time?'"

There was a long pause while she stared out over the dark harbor. "You plan to be finished with the work here and take Firebird to Saint Thomas for the charter show in November." She looked back at him. "That's four weeks from now. I assume you will schedule some bookings and will be cruising the Caribbean for the winter season."

"And?" Sam leaned forward and put his hand on her knee.

"And, Ian and I need to start making our own plans. I need to know what's next." Anna put her hand on top of Sam's. "Living day-to-day in Turloch Neeson's house wasn't the best, but everything was taken care of. I know it was a gilded cage, but. . . ."

"I thought you and Ian would stay with me this first season," Sam said, squeezing her knee. "I thought we were in this together. I'm sorry if I never made that clear. Sometimes. . . .I'm sorry but. . . ." He found it hard to finish the sentence.

"Have you said this to Ian?"

"No. Guess I should, huh?"

"Who knows what the boy's thinking?" She laughed which broke the tension. "He could be a typical guy only thinking with—well, you know what I mean."

"You're right on, for at least this evening. If everything goes right." Sam winked at her.

Another moment of silence passed while neither spoke. Anna stared at the drink glass she held in her lap.

"So, what do you think?" Sam finally asked. "I mean what do you think about being my partner and first mate on this classy charter yacht for the next season?"

"Is that a proposal?" She smiled. "Or is it a proposition?"

"More of a job offer?" Sam leaned back in the cockpit seat and laughed.

"Good thing." Anna stood and reached for his empty glass. "Want another drink? I'm empty."

"But what about—"

"I have to speak with Ian before I can give you my answer. Don't go away. I'll be right back." She disappeared down the steps to the salon.

Sam looked across the way to the marina and saw it was shutting down for the night. The office lights were turned out and the night watchman walked the dock checking boats in their slips. The conversation with Anna had unnerved him a bit. Talking about plans, and the future, and commitments always did this to him. He wasn't very good at it. The last twenty or so years of working freighters that left the dock on Monday and didn't return for weeks at a time had prevented any real planning. It's Firebird's fault, he thought to himself. The bitch has bit me. He felt the smile crease his face. Maybe it's time.

Anna brought up two fresh drinks and sat next to him. "I'm sorry if I upset you by not answering your question," she said in the dark. "I worry a lot and I know my father-in-law is looking for us. It won't be long before he finds out where we are."

"Then what?" Sam asked. "I mean what do you think he'll do."

"I don't know." She took a sip of her drink. "He's a nice man. I don't fear him. He probably just wants the best for Ian and me. He would be considered overprotective by some."

Above the hill beyond Drake Town, they saw fireworks light up the sky. A few seconds later, the sound of crackling and booming caught up with the colorful light show.

"Looks like some event going on at Wesley Cay,' Sam said. "Probably the yacht club there celebrating something." Another long silence followed while they watched the fireworks.

"Tell me about the last long-term plan you had?" Anna said after the final explosion sparkled out.

He turned to look at her. "What do you mean?"

"You said you made your last plan a long time ago."

"Yeah," he muttered, and took another drink of his Cuba Libre. "It was a long time ago." He looked back out toward town. "I was eighteen. Just graduated from high school in Texas City. My *plan,* as you say, included marrying Darlene Maxwell, the daughter of the Assembly of God preacher in town, and my high school sweetheart, and then living happily ever after. Like all fairy tales."

"You loved her?" Anna asked.

"'Bout as much as any eighteen-year old boy can love a seventeen-year old girl who let him go to third base and then. . . Well, you get the picture. Isn't that how most marriages started in the seventies?"

Anna didn't say anything.

"The thing I didn't plan on was her running off a year after we were married with my so-called best friend. I was a fool to have missed the signs. They were there all along. She loved him. Not me. When it happened, I went after her, thinking I could change her mind. Like most Texan's, I thought I'd never give up. We will fight to the last man like at the Alamo. We don't surrender."

"Did you?" she asked.

"Did I what?"

"Did you surrender?"

He stared out over the harbor a moment, not responding.

"Only after I learned that they had been driving a hundred and twenty miles an hour to get out of Texas and into Louisiana away from me and wrapped her Ford around a Cypress tree just off the interstate. The coroner said she was four months pregnant. He self-consciously rubbed the red scar on his bicep.

A few moments passed while he let that soak in. "I got in my truck after the funeral and started driving. Didn't stop till I got to Ward County out in West Texas and signed on with a drilling company, poking holes in the Permian Basin. Two months later an accidental explosion at a rig gave me a concussion and removed a chunk of muscle on my upper arm. Four weeks recuperating in a hospital in Midland gave me plenty of time to think. After my discharge, I started running, and I've been running since. Sam stopped talking and took a deep breath followed by another gulp of his drink.

Anna watched him closely. She put her glass on the table and reached for his free hand.

He flung his glass over the side of the boat. It disappeared in the darkness and was followed by a splash. "I'm sorry," he said. "But it's damn hard to talk about. I can't remember when I last told someone."

"Maybe this is a good time." She squeezed his hand. "My therapist told me that keeping stuff like this bottled up didn't make it better, just delayed and powered the eventual explosion."

"Yeah. They tried to get me to see a shrink." He wiped his eyes and looked at her. Then one day, I jumped on a freighter to Central America. Rode freighters for the next twenty years until I found Firebird in Puerto Rico. She looked like she'd had a life at least as hard as mine and was also in need of a fix. Was never sure I should or could do it, so here we are."

"We think no one has problems bigger than ours," Anna said quietly. "You said you had plans before all that?"

"Yeah. A fantasy more than a real plan." Sam paused a moment and thought about what he would say next.

"I hoped for a family. A couple of kids. Maybe a boy and a girl. I wanted to go to college. Maybe Texas Tech. Get a petroleum degree or business degree. Then get a good inside job where I had to wear a suit and tie. A brick home somewhere in Houston or even Fort Worth. I always liked Fort Worth when we went up to visit my dad's brother. Two cars in the garage and maybe a boat for water skiing. A lot of my friends in high school went water skiing with their families. Sometimes they invited me to go along. But the biggest thing I wanted was to join a country club and learn to play golf. My best friend, Donny Taylor, once invited me to spend a Sunday with his family at their country club. We swam in the pool and then I walked with him while he and his big brother played golf. Man, I thought that had to be the peak of success. We went into the clubhouse and he showed me the card room where his dad played poker with his club buddies. That was a life unknown to me. I made it my plan. I even wrote it all down. It got lost somewhere after Darlene died."

"Is that still something you want to do?" Anna asked. "If you could start all over tomorrow on that plan, would you?"

Sam paused a moment before answering. "Maybe parts of it. Too much water has passed under the bridge. The train's already left the station."

"What do you want to do now?" The look in her eyes was almost pleading. "I mean, Ian and I need to figure out our own lives and right now, like it or not, we are impacted by what you do."

"I didn't ask for—"

"Right. I know that. But you and Firebird need us and. . . ." She didn't finish the sentence.

Sam stood and walked to the railing. The lights in town glittered with life. He heard laughter from a nearby boat and saw a woman appear on deck and dive into the dark water. She was soon followed by a man. They swam to each other and floated, giggling, and whispering. He turned to Anna. "Let's go swimming."

Afterwards, Sam helped her out of the water and onto the boarding platform. Their clothes lay in a pile on deck. "You are one spontaneous puppy," she said, squeezing the water out of her hair. "It's warmer than I thought it would be."

"Part of my charm." Sam stood behind her. He wrapped her in his arms and pulled her back against him. He playfully bit at her bare shoulder."

"Oooh, I like that," she said in a throaty whisper.

"What?"

"Everything. Just don't stop."

"That's my plan."

# CHAPTER 36

"Wake up, sleepyhead. It's almost time to get Ian."
Sam opened his eyes and saw Anna on one elbow looking down at him. Her eyes were bright as was the glowing smile on her face. "I'm awake. I'm awake," he said, hunching forward when her fingers found him. "But I dunno if I can."

"Appears you can." She planted her lips on his.

"Arg," he growled and rolled them both over.

"You're too heavy." She tried to push him off. "Besides, you were insatiable last night."

"What is it they say about big hands and big feet?"

"Wasn't your hands or your feet." She giggled.

"You thought that was not a scientific fact?"

"I've been around men in my life with big hands and feet, but. . . ."

"I love it when you talk dirty." He toyed his tongue around her ear lobe.

"God, that turns me on. Stop it." She pushed him away and sat up. "We don't have time."

He looked at his watch. "Damn! You're right." He slid off the bed and reached for his shorts on the floor. "By the way," he turned back and grinned. "After last night, I'm thinking about giving you a promotion and doubling your pay."

"Oh?" She smiled and rolled over in the bedding. "What's two times zero? And is there a new plan working in that little brain?"

"Maybe." He pulled a clean T-shirt from the bag in his closet. "Can you finish covering the cushions in the main salon by the time we get the new motor installed?"

"Maybe." She swung her legs out on the other side of the bed, stepped into the head and closed the door. "Can you take me to the fabric shop today? I need more material."

"I'll bring Ian back out and get him dismantling the old engine. Then I'll run you into town. You want coffee?" He stopped by the cabin door. "We have time."

Ian waited on the pier at the marina. He tossed his bag in the dinghy and stepped down as Sam swung the nose of the inflatable back toward Firebird.

"So?"

"What?" Ian didn't crack a smile.

"So, how was your evening?" Sam said it again, slowly. "How. . .was. . .your evening?"

"Screw you." Ian looked away and tightened his lips to keep from grinning.

"Yeah, right." Sam laughed as the dinghy bumped into the boarding platform. He grabbed a cleat to hold close to the platform while Ian disembarked. "Tell your mother I'm waiting here. She wants to get more fabric for the salon cushions."

The morning rush hour, such as it was, had subsided when Sam and Anna walked into town from the marina. The early ferry from Saint Thomas had just arrived and unloaded twenty or so tourists. A ferry would arrive every hour on the hour until noon. It looked like the T-shirt vendors in town were going to have a good day.

"You should come in with me," Anna said when they stopped in front of the shop on Captain Cook Street off the main square.

"Aren't you just getting more of that cream-colored terry cloth you used on the first cushion?" Sam asked.

"Did you like it?"

"Yes. Told you I did."

"I know, but men don't always mean what they say or say what they mean. I'll be a few minutes."

Sam looked around the street and towards the town center. He still thought the Haitian and his men had something to do with sabotaging their boat engine. If true, they probably wouldn't be happy that he'd found an even better fix.

A fat tourist in a wool suit and sweating profusely passed by. "It's a hot one today." He nodded at Sam. "Hot. Hot. Hot. Hot."

Sam took off his baseball cap and ran a hand through his bushy hair. Time for a haircut, he thought. Don't want officials on the island thinking I'm some drug smoking, rock and roll hippie. Wonder if Anna can—"

"Sorry to keep you waiting out here in the heat," she said, stepping back outside. "It's just as warm in there. Doesn't anyone on this island believe in air-conditioning?"

"They're used to it," Sam said, picking up the pace beside her. He saw she wasn't carrying any bags. "Didn't they have what you wanted?"

"Yes. but most of it is at their warehouse. They'll cut it for me and bring it out to the boat."

"Don't I need to pay them?"

"Did already. Used my own credit card. The one where the bill goes to my P.O. Box, not to Turloch."

"I'll pay you back. How much is it?"

"Here's the receipt." She stuck a piece of paper in his hand and stepped up the pace. "*Whenever* works for me."

"Hey. Hey. Hey. Slow down a moment." Sam was breathing heavily. "What's the damn hurry? I mean—"

"Shut up, Sam. Guy's car turned on the street behind us when I came out of the store. Did you not see it?" She looked at her watch and kept walking. "Don't turn around."

That moment, the Jeep revved its motor and squealed to a stop beside them. The rear door flew open and Guy Mont Violet stepped out. A silver chain on his chest showed inside his open shirt, and the rings on his fingers flashed in the bright sunlight. He smiled.

"We have unfinished business." Guy stared at Anna. "Get in."

"I think that's a no." Sam stepped up between them. He could feel her fear. It was primal. The Haitian was slender but muscled.

Sam stood a good bit taller. He glanced inside the Jeep. The driver stared straight ahead over the steering wheel.

"I told you once, this doesn't concern you." Guy puffed up his chest and reached for her hand.

When his fingers touched her wrist, Sam exploded on him. Guy's back was pressed into the door with Sam's hand clinched around his neck. Sam's other hand was balled into a fist. "Get back in and get the hell out of my face or I'll—"

"Don't, Sam." He felt Anna tug at his arm. "Don't. This is all my fault."

"Takes two to tango." Sam didn't take his eyes off Guy's contorted face. He was obviously having trouble breathing. *Good.*

"You comprende? She doesn't want to dance anymore?" He lifted the thug off the ground by his neck till his feet were barely touching the pavement. "Do you?" Sam jerked the man one more time, and he emitted a short squeak.

"I'll take that for a yes," he said, letting Guy slide down the door until his feet were on the ground. Sam released his grip and the Haitian went to his knees. "Let's go." Sam grabbed Anna by the arm and started toward the marina. At the corner, he turned around and walked backward to watch the driver help his boss up off the sidewalk and into the back seat. He kept the car in his vision until it turned on to the side street and headed up the mountain.

# CHAPTER 37

Neither of them said anything until they arrived back at the marina. All the way, he kept turning around to see if they were being followed. He was untying the dinghy when the marina manager stepped out of the office. "Can I speak to you a moment?" The worried look on his face told Sam it was important.

"Sure. What's up?" He left Anna in the inflatable holding on to the dock and met Charlie in front of the open door.

"Got a call from the Customs and Immigration office this morning. They said a lawyer from Boston representing a Turloch Neeson contacted them inquiring about the whereabouts of an Anna Neeson."

Sam looked back at Anna. "Yeah? What'd you tell them?"

"The truth. Said there was no one of that name registered in the marina. That seemed to satisfy them. I think they were just going through the motion of following up on that phone call from the states and didn't really care what the answer was. Typical Island bureaucrats."

"Thanks," Sam said. "I owe you one, or is it two or three by now? Let me know if they call again." He started to say something about his run-in that morning with the Haitian but decided against it. No need to worry Charlie about it, he thought.

"How's that new engine coming?" Charlie stepped behind the counter and handed Sam a stack of mail.

"Waiting on new motor mounts and then we'll get her installed. We're taking apart the old motor now and getting ready." Sam glanced at the mail in his hand and saw it was mostly junk.

"I need that mooring ball in four weeks," Charlie said.

"I know." Sam opened the office door. He felt the day's heat rush into the cool air-conditioned space. "I know. You'll have it. We'll be over at Saint Thomas by then." He stood on the dock by the dinghy to finish sorting through the mail. He saw the envelope from the charter show and ripped it open. His application had been accepted, and they had assigned him a slip at Yacht Harbor, the main marina in Charlotte Amalie. He tossed the rest of the mail in a nearby trash can and jumped in the Zodiac to start the outboard.

"Guess I need to show you how to start this in case you have to take the dinghy sometime by yourself," he said, looking at Anna on the seat across from him as they motored toward Firebird.

"That would be nice." She smiled. "All the times I've watched you, I still haven't a clue what you're doing when you flip switches, push buttons, and pull ropes."

Sam could tell she was still shaken by the morning's events in town. "I think we've seen the last of him," he said, reaching for her hand. "He knows now that it's over, whatever it was."

"I hope," she said almost in a whisper. "But I don't think so."

When they stepped on Firebird's deck, Sam noticed a pile of engine parts by the mast. Pumps, gaskets, belts, filters, the engine head, and bolts and nuts and boxes of other parts littered the deck. Everything but the block. Just then, Ian came up from below carrying a bucket of waste oil. "This needs to be taken on shore," he said when he saw Sam and his mother. "I'm sure the engine shop can tell us where to dispose it. They have to do it every day."

Sam took the bucket and set it by the mast. He nodded toward the pile. "Looks like you've made good progress."

"You won't think so when you look in the engine room." Ian took off his ballcap and lifted the bottom of his T-shirt to wipe sweat from his face. "There's a lot of shit—uh, sorry Mom—stuff still to be brought up. We have the heavy engine block down there. I unbolted it from its old rubber mounts, but we'll need to remove the deck plate here and winch it up with a halyard. The same way we'll need to get the new engine down."

"Looks like you've got it all figured out." Sam grinned. "You don't need me to finish—"

"Oh, no you don't." Ian laughed and put his cap back on. "I need your back and muscles even if I've done all the thinking work."

Sam saw Anna standing alone up in the bow, her arms crossed defensively over her chest. She stared across the harbor at the two catamarans headed out with their guests. Her gaze was fixed on White Squall, captained by Meredith Ainsley.

Later in the afternoon, Sam and Ian were on their knees, unbolting the deck hatch to pull the engine block out when Sam heard an outboard buzzing toward them. He looked over Ian's shoulder and saw a man at the helm of an open bow Boston Whaler approaching.

"Ahoy there. Firebird, ahoy." The man called out.

Sam met the man down on the boarding platform where he was passed two bolts of cream-colored terry cloth.

He knocked on the door to Anna's cabin. "Special delivery for Ms. Anna Neeson." A moment passed before the door opened.

"What do you want, Sam?" Her face was swollen, and her eyes were red.

He cocked his head toward the bolts of fabric leaning on the bulkhead in the salon. "They just dropped it by."

"What time is it?" She wiped a tear from her cheek.

"A little after three. Ian and I are about to bring up the engine block. Hoping to get it done before dark. You okay?"

"What do you think?" She wiped another tear and looked up at him. "I've put you, my own son, and Firebird in danger with my irresponsible behavior.

"But—"

"No. It's true," she said, her voice barely above a whisper. "And you know it. I wish I knew how to turn it all off. How to start over. How to stop hurting so much." She burst into sobs and closed the door on him.

Sam pushed open the door and stepped into her cabin. She lay face down on the bed crying quietly into a pillow. Her shoulders shook with her sobs. It was killing him. He sat on the bed and rubbed her back, searching in his mind for something to say. "We'll beat them," he finally said, surprising even himself. "They can't win if we fight together. . . you, me, and Ian. They haven't got a chance."

Anna turned on her back and gazed into his eyes. His heart stuck in his throat, making it hard to breathe. At that moment, she was depending on him. Her safety and her happiness, maybe even her life, were in his hands. He bent down and kissed her. Her lips tasted salty.

"The old me would be on a plane headed back to Boston and the safety of Turloch's castle," she said after breaking their kiss. "But it's too late for that. You're stuck with me."

He kissed her again, and she slipped her arms around his neck and whispered in his ear, "I'm scared. I need you so much. Ian and I, we both need you so much."

# CHAPTER 38

"Hey Sam. You in there?"

He pushed himself up off the bed. "Yeah. What is it?"

Anna opened her eyes and watched him. She had drifted off for a few minutes in his arms. After the trauma of the morning with the Haitian, he hadn't wanted to wake her.

"I put a chain around the engine block and hooked it to the main halyard," Ian said when Sam stepped into the salon. "Ready to hoist it out whenever you are." He nodded at the closed cabin door. "Everything alright?"

"We had a little encounter with the head thug in town today," Sam said, leading Ian away from his mother's door. "Scared her a bit, but it's all over now. I don't think they'll be bothering us again. The little shit probably still has my fingerprints around his throat."

Ian glanced at the door but turned and followed Sam up to the deck.

"How do you think we should do this?" Sam studied the rope halyard leading down through the open hatch into the engine room.

"Thought I'd go below and guide the engine block up while you crank the halyard out here on the mast," Ian replied. "It's not a straight shot up and out, so I'll have to muscle it backwards a bit to fit through the opening. It's the way Palmer Johnson designed the engine room to move a motor in and out. I'm sure it will work." He stood barefoot next to Sam with his legs spread apart and his hands on his hips. "The winch here is self-tailing, so all you have to do is crank. Shouldn't be that difficult."

"I probably can handle that." Sam grinned at the boy's seriousness. "This ain't like building the pyramids in Egypt."

"Well, yes. It is kind of like that." Ian grinned. "Pulleys and levers, and rope and muscle were all the tools they had to move those heavy stone blocks in place. My grandfather took me to Egypt to see the pyramids at Giza when I graduated from boarding school. He hoped that'd inspire me to be an engineer."

"Did it?" Sam looked at him.

"Not really." Ian shook his head. "Made me want to be an artist. The design and decoration lit a fire in my belly. Pissed the old man off when I told him on the plane back to Boston."

Sam tugged a couple of times on the halyard.

"He said I was going to Cornell like he did, and like my dad did, and I'd major in engineering like they did." Ian laughed as he mimicked his grandfather's Irish brogue.

"So, he was first generation?" Sam looped the halyard around the winch drum on the mast.

"His mother cleaned and cooked for the Bishop in Dublin. Never knew his father. He stowed away on a freighter to Boston when he was fifteen. A plumber hired him as an apprentice, and he worked his way through Cornell repairing pipes in faculty housing on campus."

"Sounds like a stud guy." Sam peered down into the engine room to see how much clearance they had to get the block through the hatch.

"Yeah, he is." Ian turned quiet. "I owe him an apology for putting him through this shit. I didn't tell him I was leaving school, and he has no idea where I am."

"Oh, that might surprise you." Sam picked up the winch handle from its pocket at the base of the mast and turned the winch a few times to take the slack out of the halyard. "I'm ready when you are. Let's get this block out and clean and prep the engine room for the new motor. Hopefully, the new mounts will arrive tomorrow, and we can get this puppy back on schedule."

"What do you mean 'might surprise' me?'" Ian asked. "You know something I don't?"

"Not really." Sam glanced at him out of the corner of his eye.

"Just sounds like a good tough guy that's concerned about his family. Can't see him just giving up. Not knowing. Not caring."

"Me neither. And that worries me." Ian disappeared down the stairs to the engine room.

"That should do it this evening." Sam unhooked the rope halyard from the chain after they set the old block on deck. "The shop said they'd take all the scrap metal off our hands. At least we won't have to pay someone to haul it away."

Ian stood by the crate containing the new motor. "Are you ready to rig this one to the halyard?"

"Let's do it first thing tomorrow. It's getting dark, and your mother's waiting dinner. Do me a favor and don't mention the problem she and I had in town today."

Fire flashed in Ian's eyes. "Did that rat bastard touch her?"

"No. No." Sam shook his head. "We had some words. I pushed him around a bit. Threatened his manhood if he bothered us again, and he and his buddy took off."

"Why do you think he's—"

"He's a bully," Sam said. "Alligators bite and bullies bully. I'm new on the island and he's testing me. Charlie, at the marina, thinks the same thing."

Anna set back at the salon table, watching her son. She took a sip from her wine glass. "When are you seeing Sarah again? I mean—"

"I know what you mean, Mother." He winked at her. He finished his plate, cleaned the remaining sauce with a wad of garlic bread and reached for his water glass. "I don't know when I'll next see her. We didn't make any plans when I left her apartment this morning, we had a little spat. You might say it was a big spat."

Anna looked at Sam and smiled. "A lover's quarrel. I didn't realize my son was old enough to have a lover, much less quarrel with her."

"It's not funny." Ian pushed away from the table and refilled his water glass. "It came out of nowhere this morning when I was getting ready to leave. I don't know what to do."

"Women are like that, aren't we, Sam?"

He looked up from the book he was reading—instructions on how to install a filtering system for diesel fuel. "Uh. . .yeah, whatever." He went back to studying the schematic drawings.

"And men are just like *that*." Anna rolled her eyes at him and raised her wine glass to Ian before taking another sip.

Ian put his glass in the galley sink and went up on deck.

Anna watched Sam still reading his manual. "Thanks for your support today in town. I kind of lost it there a bit."

Sam looked up. "No problem." He smiled. "I'll think of a way you can make it up to me."

"Yes," she said. "I'm sure you will figure something out." She didn't take her eyes off him while sipping the rest of her wine.

He lifted his chin toward the stairs. "Think I need to go see how he's doing? He didn't look too good when he was down here."

"His little girlfriend is just toying with him." Anna pushed an errant strand of hair behind her ear. "Been there. Done that."

"Hmmm. . . ." Sam put the manual on top of the table. "You think she's just being a bitch?"

"Is that what you call it?"

"Yes, if she's screwing with his mind for no good reason." Sam realized he had raised his voice. "I'll go up and chat with him. The kid could probably use some advice."

"You're not his father," Anna said, twirling her wine stem with her fingers.

"I know." Sam stood up at the table. "I'll do the dishes and clean up down here when I come back. Leave everything for me."

"Oh, I will," she said. "I most certainly will."

"You okay, son?" Sam found Ian lying on his back in front of the main mast. Twinkling stars littered a black sky. He sat down beside him, drew his bare knees up to his chest and wrapped his arms around them. A few moments passed before either of them said anything.

"Girls are crazy," Ian finally said. "Bat shit crazy!"

"Welcome to the club." Sam said.

"What club?"

"The Man Club."

Another few moments of silence passed. "Your membership card will come in the mail. We know you have a million questions. All newbies do. The funny reality is there are no answers. Just more questions. If you think you've figured out an answer, just know it's wrong. The secret of the fellowship of man is that there are no real answers to such questions. When and if you have sons of your own, it will be your responsibility to pass these secrets on to them."

"You're so full of shit, its coming outta your ears." Ian laughed and sat up with his back against the mast. "I almost believed you there for a moment. You are good, man."

"Not so much shit there as you think." Sam watched him in the dark. "One day, you'll think I'm smart and wise like that little troll in that movie. . .uh, Star Wars?"

"You mean, Yoda?" Ian laughed. "Yeah, you're my Yoda and I'm Luke Skywalker."

Sam looked away. "You know, Luke didn't have a real father, either. He had a stepfather in the desert who was killed early in the first movie, but young Luke was basically alone. Obi Wan Kenobi and Yoda trained him into the man, the Jedi Knight, he became."

A few moments of silence passed while they listened to halyards clanging against metal masts on boats in the harbor.

Sam interrupted the quiet. "What happened this morning between you and Sarah?"

"That's just it." Ian drew a bare foot up under him and rubbed it. "I wish I knew. I'd apologize if I knew what I did wrong. We had a good night, at least I thought it was pretty good. We didn't get to sleep till almost two in the morning. I was worn out, but she seemed to have trouble falling asleep. Can't understand it. I know how to make a woman. . .a girl. . .well, let's just say I've never had any complaints. Just the opposite."

"So, you got up in the morning, had your coffee—"

"Kind of like that. She was cold to me the whole time after we got up. Whatever I said, whatever I did, seemed to piss her off. She isn't one to yell or cuss. She just goes silent. When I got dressed and went to the door, she didn't even kiss me goodbye. She just sat staring out the window. I knew something was wrong. Her eyes were all red and puffy. She'd obviously been crying. I shut the door behind me, thinking she might run after me, but nothing. I don't know what to think, or what to do."

A long silence passed between them. A million things flew through Sam's head. He thought of every saying he'd heard growing up, every pithy comment, even a few verses he'd learned the summer his aunt took him to her church's vacation bible school in Houston. Nothing worked. *What would Yoda say?*

"Women." Ian sighed, shaking his head.

"Yep," Sam agreed. "Can't live with them. Can't shoot 'em."

Later that night, while Anna lay sleeping in the crease of his arm, he decided he would stop by Sarah's apartment first chance he got and have a chat. *The boy's too worked up about it, and I don't have enough information to give good advice. What would I say if he were my son? Wait. What?*

# CHAPTER 39

"Let it down, now! Set it down easy," Sam called over his shoulder to Ian, operating the halyard winch on the mast. Sam guided the old engine block into the dinghy secured alongside Firebird. "There. That's it. Now, ease it out." The heavy iron block settled onto the dinghy floor, and the halyard went slack. The dinghy's two pontoons sat low in the water. "I'll untie it and you pass down all those old parts by the mast."

Breakfast had been coffee and a quick bowl of Cheerios. They had all overslept which he thought was getting to be a bad habit, and the sun was already nearing its zenith. Anna still hadn't appeared out of her cabin for the day.

After handing down all the parts and boxes of items from the old engine, Ian looked at Sam, standing by the outboard. "How much do you think they'll pay for all this?"

Sam laughed. "The cost of all these items new was probably thousands of dollars. We'll be lucky to get a hundred for all of it. Maybe enough to buy you and me a good lunch over at Sarah's café. Main thing is we get this heavy junk off the boat and get our new engine installed."

"Do we have time to lower the new motor into place before we go?" Ian held up the halyard to show he was ready. "We're on a roll here with me cranking and you guiding the motor."

Sam checked his watch. "Good idea. Let's don't stop for lunch. We'll eat onboard after we uncrate that mother and get her into place." He looked around the deck for Anna. *Maybe she would like to go ashore with us later?*

Being smaller than the old one, the new Perkins engine lifted easily out of its crate and off the deck. After several tries, Sam guided it down through the hatch into the engine room. "Let's keep the halyard attached until we get the new motor mounts installed," he said. "Hope they came in today. We'll need to lift the engine again to maneuver it over the new mounts. Steve Baxter at the engine shop said they should be in no later than tomorrow but could also come in this afternoon's delivery. Let's eat something then go into town and see."

Ian stood in the dinghy, holding the line taut, while Sam stepped up onto the town's industrial dock. He saw the machine shop across the road and checked his watch. It was already four o'clock.

Orlando stepped outside and turned to lock the door for the night. "Someone's been busy," he said, eyeing the pile of scrap iron.

Sam tied the dinghy line while Ian scrambled onto the dock. "We're working hard to get the old girl moving under her own power again. Getting the new motor installed will help, as will getting rid of dead weight on board."

"Leave it all by our loading bay door," Orlando said. "I'll have the guys weigh it tomorrow morning when they come in. Everyone's already gone. We closed early today so everyone can watch the cricket team play Saint Croix this evening over at the park stadium. How is that new engine? Steve told me you were damn lucky to find it."

"Looks great in the engine room." Sam said, "but we'll know more when the motor mounts get here, and we can install it."

"Oh!" Orlando snapped his fingers. "The engine shop closed early today for the game, and Baxter dropped your mounts over here. Said he was closing tomorrow also, and knew you needed them." Orlando pulled the keys out of his pocket and opened the door. "The register's locked so come by another day to settle up. I'll hold the check for the scrap iron for you."

"Thanks," Sam said, picking up the box of new motor mounts. "Say, what do you hear about that Haitian thug up on the mountain? He still causing problems for folks in town?"

Orlando shrugged his shoulders. "Dunno. Why do you ask?"

"No reason, really," Sam said. "I had a little run in with him and his *Ton Ton Macoute* when I first arrived here on the island. Haven't seen him around lately," he lied.

The shop manager studied him a moment like he knew more than he was willing to say, then ushered him outside and locked the door. He nodded toward Ian unloading the inflatable. "Stop by again sometime and we'll talk about it. Come alone. That's not a good subject right now."

Ian steered the dinghy as they headed back across the harbor toward Firebird. "Now that we have the mounts, I think we can get that motor installed this evening. At least we can get it bolted into place. It'll take two days or more to connect all the hoses and the electrical bridle, plus the alternator, filters, water pumps, and belts."

Anna met them on deck. She had showered and wore a short sundress that showed off tan legs. She smelled of shampoo, and her toenails had been freshly painted.

Sam stayed with her while Ian took the new mounts down into the engine room.

"Haven't seen you all day." He bent to kiss her forehead. Her hair was still damp.

"Miss me?"

"Haven't seen you in this sexy dress before," he whispered.

"And you haven't seen my panties before, either."

"Are they new?"

"I'm not wearing any."

"Ah. Commando," he hissed.

"Hey, up there!" Ian called through the hatch from the engine room.

"I'm here," Sam responded. "What's up?" He winked at Anna. "Besides me," he whispered.

"After I install these last two bolts, we can lift the engine onto the mounts."

"Ready when you are." Sam smiled at Anna.

"I sewed the new covers for the salon cushions this afternoon," she said, following him to the mast and handing him the winch handle for the halyard. "I think you'll like them. I only have the cushions in my cabin and your stateroom left to do. Since we'll use Ian's cabin as our room when we have charter guests, I decided to wait to recover those when we have more time. You don't see them anyway when the bedding is on."

Sam leaned against the mast, put an arm around her waist and pulled her to him. Her hand lifted the bottom of his T-shirt and caressed his bare abdomen. Her hand felt warm against his skin. "Come to my room tonight," he whispered into her hair.

"We'll see," she said. "Maybe he'll spend the night with his little girlfriend."

"Let's hope," Sam said.

"Ready!" Ian's voice called from below. "Take slack up on the halyard!"

Ian swung the new engine into place while Sam lowered it with the halyard. Darkness had set in and the lights in the engine room blazed, making the work of fitting the puzzle pieces back together go quickly.

"How's it going in there?" Anna stood at the engine room door. "Dinner's on the table."

"I'll wash up and be right there." Ian grabbed his T-shirt off the floor and walked bare chested, bare legged, and bare footed toward his room.

"Yep, he's turned into a fine specimen of a young man," Sam said when Ian closed his door.

Anna looked at him. "You should wash your face and comb your hair before coming to the table. Maybe we'll skinny dip after dinner if he goes ashore."

Anna sat down after ladling up everyone's second bowl of vegetable soup.

"Soup and sandwich is my favorite meal," Sam said. "Besides steak and potatoes, spaghetti and meatballs, and—"

"Is there much left to do on the engine?" Anna interrupted. "I didn't hear one curse word out of either one of you all the time you were working in there."

"Knowing what you're doing and having the right tools makes all the difference," Sam said, putting his spoon down. "Or something like that."

"I think the captain of a fancy charter yacht should at least wear a clean T-shirt to dinner." She folded her napkin in her lap and turned to smile at Sam who had come to the table bare chested after his shower. She wore a sundress and added gold loop earrings and a matching chain necklace.

"Uh, I'll be right back." He slipped out of the seat and returned moments later in a pair of khaki shorts and a light blue island shirt sporting parrots of different flaming colors. A splash of Old Spice introduced his arrival.

"You're right." He looked at Anna before sitting down. We need to freshen things up around here if we're gonna entertain high paying guests."

Ian looked away, trying to stifle a laugh.

"You look nice." Anna touched Sam's hand. "I like that shirt. Haven't seen it before. Cute parrots." She ran a coral fingernail across his palm.

"Are Old Spice fumes flammable?" Ian grinned at Sam. "Can we open a porthole? It's overwhelming."

"Shut up and finish your dinner," Sam said, picking up his sandwich. "I'll buy you your own cologne. You've about used mine up. What's Sarah's favorite?"

"Anything but Old Spice. She likes Polo by Ralph Lauren in that dark green spray bottle. The girls at college liked it, too. Yeah. That'd be great."

"But that's damn expensive as I remember and may not be sold here on the island. I'll check around. Not surprised that debutantes liked it on rich, college boys." Sam winked at Anna. "Might have to settle for an after shave like Aqua Velva. We used it in the oil fields. Bought it cheap at the pharmacy. Yep. It was said

Aqua Velva worked magic in the bars and clubs around Odessa and Midland."

"I love Polo." Anna squeezed his hand.

He returned her squeeze. "I'll see what I can come up with."

# CHAPTER 40

The morning sun had just cleared the harbor entrance when Sam put his empty coffee cup in the sink, grabbed his cap and went on deck. It was going to be another hot day in paradise. He had slept the night in his own bed since Ian stayed onboard instead of going to see Sarah. Anna's offer of skinny dipping after dinner was postponed.

He planned to go ashore to the machine shop to see what Orlando had to say about the Haitian. He also wanted to drop in on Sarah before she left for work to get some answers for poor Ian. He was surprised to find the boy on his knees on the foredeck with a white, silky, nylon sail spread out from mast to bow.

"Hey! Good morning." Ian lifted the head of the sail. "Look. I found this cool spinnaker in the sail locker. It's in great shape. Just needs some stitching of the seams and a good cleaning. No mildew or rips that I can see. Evidently wasn't used much. And check out this faded red Phoenix in the middle. Probably twenty feet tall or more. Must be quite a site flying this beauty downwind. Can't wait to see it in action."

"Yeah. I saw this soon after I bought the boat." Sam picked up the sail luff and studied it. "The Phoenix is also called a Firebird. Figured one of the owners had it made."

"You headed in?" Ian leaned forward, smoothing wrinkles out of the sail.

"Got a few errands to run. Need anything from the chandlery?"

"A couple rolls of white Duct Tape," Ian said. "Some sails have frayed luffs, and the extra mainsail has a small rip."

"Hear anything from Sarah?"

"Not since two days ago when I left her apartment."

"You worried?"

"Don't know. Should I be?"

Sam shrugged. "That's one of those unanswerable questions I referred to the other day." He stepped toward the ladder going down to the boarding platform. "Coffee's still hot. Your mom's getting ready to make more cushion covers. I saw the sewing machine on the salon table, and it looked like she had cut the patterns."

"I'll see if she needs any help." Ian stood up and stretched. "Coffee sounds good right now."

As Ian bent to roll up the big spinnaker and slide it into its sail bag, Sam studied the boy's broad shoulders, strong legs and narrow hips. If I did have a son, he thought, he'd look just like that.

On his way into town, Sam stopped at the marina office to see if Charlie had heard anything more about his run in with Guy Mont Violet. He also had time to kill as it was too early to go by Sarah's apartment. She might not be up, and he wanted to catch her just before she headed to work—usually around ten thirty.

"Yeah, I heard about it two nights ago over at Pussers," the marina manager said. Sam sat in a chair across the desk from him. "A couple of his enforcers were at a table with one of the island constables. One of 'em said something about the bastard on the big boat out in the harbor. Knew he was referring to you."

"You think they're getting the authorities involved?" Sam leaned forward in his chair.

Charlie laughed. "Not really. My take is they were just gossiping. They were snickering like little kids and making fun of the Haitian. One said the boss had to change his pants when his driver got him back to the villa. Then they all died laughing, including the constable. Those muscle-headed jerks are a bunch of snakes if you ask me. Wouldn't trust any of them. Neither should the Haitian."

"What's their game?" Sam asked. "I mean it takes money to support an organization like that."

"Who knows? Your guess is as good as anyone else's on this island. There's a lot of speculation, but no evidence that I know of."

"Drugs? Money Laundering? Smuggling?"

Charlie shook his head. "No clue."

"Thanks for the info." Sam pushed himself out of the chair. "I'll be curious if you hear anything else."

"Just be careful." Charlie followed him into the reception area. "How's that new motor install going?"

"It's going," Sam said. "The engine is in place. It'll take a couple of days to put everything back together and crank her up. I'm hoping in two days the old girl's heart will be ticking like new, and we'll be ready to motor anywhere. I'd like to surprise the crew and take the boat out to Moskito for a couple of days. Do some sunning, some snorkeling, and scrape the barnacles and moss off her bottom."

"Sounds like fun. Maybe I'll take a couple of days off and go with you."

"You can have the owner's stateroom. We'll treat you like a paying guest," Sam said as they stepped outside on the marina dock. In the lot across the way, he saw Guy Mont Violet's Jeep parked in the shade of a tree.

Charlie saw it, too and shook his head. "Like I said, be careful." He turned and went back into his office.

Sam knocked on Sarah's apartment door and stood back to watch some kids kick a soccer ball around on the asphalt. The boys wore dark blue pants and light blue shirts with white sneakers, the uniform of the Saint Sebastian public schools. A few moments passed before he knocked again. *Maybe she's already left for work.* Just then he saw the black Jeep turn and stop at the end of the street. He waited a few more moments and knocked a third time. He was about to leave when the door opened. Sarah looked like she hadn't slept in days. Her eyes were sunken and red, and her tangled hair lay flat against her head. She pulled a loose robe around her and wouldn't look him in the eye.

"Good morning." Sam smiled. "Uh, I don't want to bother you but. . . ." He didn't know what else to say.

"Come in," she whispered, and stepped back from the door. All the blinds were shut, and the curtains drawn, making the room dark and foreboding. A musty body odor hung in the air. Sarah shut the door behind him and sat on the couch, her socked feet pulled up under her, while he remained standing. She still wouldn't look at him.

"I thought maybe you had already gone to the café," he said, glancing around for a place to sit. He moved an empty pizza box off the only chair and sat down.

"I quit," she said, barely above a whisper.

"What?"

"I quit," she said again. This time her voice was stronger. "Quit my job at the café. I told them yesterday."

Sam took off his cap. "But why? I mean what happened? Did someone threaten you?" He thought of Guy's goons at the end of the street.

She shook her head. A moment passed without either of them saying anything.

"Isn't this rather sudden? I don't think Ian knows about this. What do you plan to do?"

Sarah put her arms around her knees and pulled them to her chest. She was hurting, and Sam's heart went out to her. She finally looked up at him for a moment, wiped tears streaming down her cheeks, and looked away.

"Is there anything I, we can do? I mean. . .I don't know what's happening, but whatever it is, it's killing Ian. He thinks he did something."

"Ian didn't do anything. It's not his fault. It's all mine." Sarah buried her face in her hands and started to cry.

Sam put his cap back on, leaned forward in his chair with his elbows on his knees and clasped his hands together. He never knew what to do when a female cried in his presence. "Can you tell me what this is about?" he said softly. "I don't want to pry into what's none of my business, but maybe I can help. I'll do anything I can. I will."

"There's nothing anyone can do." Sarah wiped her eyes with the back of her hand.

He wanted to say something but remained silent.

After a long pause, she continued. "It's not only me, but dear sweet Ian who will get hurt in this. That's what stings my heart the most." She covered her face with her hands and started to cry again.

After a bit, the sobs subsided, and she took several deep breaths. "I'm leaving on the last flight out this afternoon to Puerto Rico. I'm going home. My parents are waiting for me in London."

Sam swallowed hard. "Why? How come this happened so quickly? Three days ago, you and Ian were so happy together. Does it have anything to do with Guy Mont Violet or his thugs? If it does, let me assure you. . . ." He stood up and balled his hands into fists. A car horn sounded somewhere outside. She looked so frail. So sad.

"I'm pregnant," she said, looking up at him.

"What?"

"I'm pregnant—with child—and must go home." The car horn sounded again.

"But how do you know? I mean, you and Ian have only—"

"I'm pregnant. And he's not the father."

# CHAPTER 41

Sam stepped to the window, pushed the curtains back and opened the blinds. Sunlight streamed in through the slats. The Haitian's men were nowhere in sight. He took a deep breath. It felt like he had been punched in the chest. He stared out the window. "You going to tell Ian?"

"I. . .I don't know. Haven't decided. Was thinking maybe I'd leave him a note."

"It'll kill him," Sam said. "He acts tough, but he's a fragile kid. Maybe I should tell him. It'd be a lot harder hearing it from you in person." He looked at her for confirmation.

"She glanced away. "I don't have enough time. Perhaps you. . . ."

"But what do I say? What can I say?"

Sarah left the sofa and stood beside him at the window. "Tell him the truth. Tell him before he arrived, I met a young man from New Zealand who was traveling the world before settling down to career and a family. We spent time together, and he left." She paused a moment like she was collecting her thoughts. "Then sweet Ian arrived, and my world turned upside down. Tell him I love him. I don't know if he loves me. He never said. I won't expect it from him. We were both here to explore the world and ourselves. I blame no one."

She put her hand on Sam's shoulder. "My mother assured me the baby would be welcome. The doctor here on the island said I am between two and three months. My parents are strong Catholics, so there's no other option. I'm fine with that. I just hope Ian doesn't hate me."

"Does he know how to reach you in London?" It was all Sam could think to say.

"No. I wouldn't want him chasing after me. I don't want or need anyone's pity. That's the one thing I can't stand."

Sam looked at his watch. Can I do anything today to help? I mean—"

"Just don't tell him until after four this afternoon." She wiped a tear from her cheek. "My plane will have left by then." She went up on her toes and put her arms around his neck. "Thank you for everything you did to make me feel like a member of your family, or should I say, crew. I'll miss you all, including Firebird."

Sam gave her a quick hug. "You take care and drop me a note when the baby comes. Send it to the Marina Manager at Virgin Cay. I've made arrangements with Charlie to forward my mail."

"Ms. Neeson will hate me for leading her son astray and then hurting him."

He saw color had returned to her face. "Don't know about that," he said. "She's a mother lion protective of her cub, but there's a soft side to her as well. It may take a while, but I believe she'll only wish good things for you." He kissed her on the forehead. "I know I do." He opened the apartment door and started to step outside.

"Promise me you won't tell him until after I'm gone," Sarah said. "I don't think I could leave if I saw him again."

Sam nodded. "I promise."

# CHAPTER 42

It was eleven o'clock when he made his way back to Firebird. The tropical sun was already making the deck too hot to walk on in bare feet. Ian was working in the engine room, and Anna had finished covering another cushion at her sewing machine in the main salon.

"Looks great," Sam said as she held it up for his inspection. "You're making real progress."

"Only a few more to go," she nodded. This light color brightens all the cabins. It also makes the interior look larger."

"Yeah, but will show dirt and—"

"Easily removed and washed with the bedding and towels between each charter," Anna said. "It's terry cloth, remember? The same material that towels are made of." She folded the cushion cover and set it next to the stack she'd already completed.

Sam poured a cup of coffee and went to check on Ian. He stood in the engine room doorway watching the boy wipe down the new motor.

"We should be ready to fire this baby up by late this evening," Ian said. "It's taking longer to install the electrical bridles than I thought. Thank god they're color coded or I'd never figure out this wiring rat's nest."

The new motor gleamed in the decluttered engine room. "Is the transmission linkage connected, and how about the fuel lines from the tanks to the filters and the filters to the injectors?"

"Done, done, and done," Ian replied. "I've already bled the air out of the fuel lines. We get the batteries hooked up, and we can try to start her."

"Don't count on first turn of the key." He patted Ian on the back. "It never works on the first try. There's always something left off or not connected correctly."

"My bet is on the first try." Ian stood and stretched his back muscles. "Give me a few more hours after lunch to wrap this up and we'll see."

Anna stepped up beside Sam and slipped her arm around his waist. "Ian, I never knew you were so skilled with motors and things," she said. "Where did you learn how to do all this?"

"Grandfather wants me to be an engineer. Remember?" Ian smiled. "Three years at Cornell in engineering left its mark. But also spending every summer at the yacht club crewing and racing sailboats with my friends didn't hurt. You pick things up messing around in boats."

Sam checked the time. "Let's eat lunch and then get back and finish this up. If we can get it completed today, I thought we might take her out to Moskito Island for a couple days of fun."

"Can Sarah go with us?" Ian looked from Sam to his mother and back again.

"Let's see if we get it running before you ask her." Sam nodded, knowing the truth would break the boy's heart. "It won't be all fun on anchor at Moskito. We still have a lot of work to do and not much time left to get it done. I want to scrape the bottom clean and put a new coat of varnish on the teak toe-rail. Eighty-four feet is a lot of bottom scraping and it hasn't been touched since I left Puerto Rico. We won't have time to haul her and put on new bottom paint until after the show on Saint Thomas. Remind me to call over there and get that scheduled."

"I'll get this baby running on the first try and go ashore tonight to see Sarah," Ian said. "She'll want to tell her boss at the café tomorrow morning that she'll be away for a few days."

"Better than that," Sam said, trying to stay ahead of the train that was coming at him. "Let's get it started and while you clean up, I'll go ashore this evening and bring her back out here for dinner."

"But what will we eat?" Anna removed her arm from around Sam. "I'm not sure if we—"

"Make a list and I'll pick it up when I go for Sarah." Sam was scrambling. "I know we have steaks in the freezer we can take out to defrost. Just salad makings are all we probably need. I'll stop at the market by her apartment."

Anna smiled. "Another trip out to Moskito sounds like fun. It's just what we need after the drama of the blown engine."

"Is this the weekend for the French to be in port?" Ian had turned back to connecting the wiring to the engine starter. "Hope so."

"Me, too," Sam said, and yelped when Anna pinched him on the arm.

It was late afternoon, and Ian was still busy in the engine room when Sam took the grocery list and went ashore. He hadn't yet figured out how to tell the boy about Sarah's departure from the island. It wasn't going to be easy.

He stopped by the market near the marina and picked up the things Anna had jotted down. He went by Sarah's apartment to confirm that she had actually gone. He looked at his watch. It was six thirty. She should have flown out two hours ago.

Approaching the apartment, he saw the drapes were open but there was no light inside. It looked dark and empty. A good sign. He started to turn away when he saw a white envelope taped to the front door. He looked around; there was no one on the street. Maybe a note for her landlord, he thought. But, maybe not.

He went up the steps and looked at the envelope. It was addressed to Ian. Peeling it off the door, he turned and headed back to the marina. *So, she decided to write him after all.*

Ian was waiting at the rail when Sam tied the dinghy and came up the boarding ladder. The boy's hair was still wet from his shower. Sam smelled the Polo cologne he had recently bought him.

Ian looked confused. "Where's Sarah?"

Sam saw Anna come up the stairs from the salon carrying a tray of gin and tonics. "Uh." He looked at Ian. "I went by her apartment, but it was dark and didn't look like any one was around. When I went up to knock, this note was taped to the door with your name on it." He pulled the envelope from his pocket and handed it to him."

Ian opened it on his way up to the bow. He stood for a moment reading, then looked back at Sam and Anna. "She's gone." He turned to stare out over the harbor. "She's gone and she's not coming back." After a moment, he sped past Sam, almost knocking the tray out of Anna's hands and disappeared down the salon stairs. The door to his cabin slammed.

Sam looked at Anna. It was obvious she had no idea what was going on.

"I thought you went into town to buy groceries and bring Sarah back for dinner. He was counting on her being here. It was all he could talk about when he stopped working on that damn engine and went to clean up."

"Got the groceries," Sam said, holding up the plastic bag. "Didn't get the girl. Sarah wasn't there."

Anna frowned a moment then looked back at the stairs where they had last seen her son. "Want one of these?" She nodded at the tray of drinks.

"I'll take two." He dropped the groceries on deck and took a cocktail glass in each hand.

"I'll join you." She set the tray on the cockpit table. You going to tell me what's going on?"

"I'm guessing he got a Dear John letter," he said, taking a sip of his cocktail. "Her apartment was all locked up and looked abandoned."

Anna studied him a moment in the evening's waning light. A speed boat passed by at full throttle, its wake causing Firebird to rock on her mooring. "My little boy has just had his heart broken." She sighed. "And it probably won't be the last time."

Sam took deep swig of his gin and tonic and gazed across the harbor toward town. He wondered what Sarah had said in her letter. He hoped she hadn't mentioned talking to him. "I'll fry those steaks on the stove top," he said, finishing off the first drink. He picked up the grocery bag in one hand and the second cocktail in the other and went down the steps to the galley. He glanced in the passageway to Ian's room and saw the envelope on the floor. He set the produce in the sink and went to retrieve it.

*Dear Ian,*

*I just received word that my father is deathly ill and could pass at any moment. Mum requested I come home. There is a flight to Puerto Rico in two hours with a connection to London, so I'm going for it, even though it means I can't tell you all this in person.*

*Believe me when I say it pains me to do this so suddenly. I had a wonderful time with you these past weeks and will never forget you. I hope you find whatever it is you are looking for. Your mum was very nice and Sam, well, what can one say about Sam.*

*I hope you have a happy life and remember me fondly.*

*Love,*
*Sarah*

Anna sat on the salon steps watching him read the note. "Can I see it?" She held out her hand.

"Yeah, but we need to talk later." He passed her the envelope.

She finished her drink and opened the note. She looked up at him. "It's a lie, isn't it?"

He poured olive oil into the hot skillet and salted three steaks. "Do you want to make the salad, or should I?"

# CHAPTER 43

Ian didn't come out of his room to eat, and Sam wrapped his dinner in foil and put it in the fridge. He took Anna's hand after they had cleaned the dishes and led her up to the deck. A cool breeze blew in from the sea. and they sat on the cushions in the cockpit. She snuggled back against him, and he put his arms around her. He kissed her just under her ear making her moan.

She turned and found his mouth with her own. "God, that feels good," she said, breaking the kiss. "But my son's in pain and—"

"Let's live dangerously," he spoke against her throat. "Like making out in the living room when you were in high school and your parents were in their bed, listening to every sound."

"Not in my house." She laughed. "My Irish Catholic parents would've never left me alone with a boy, especially in their own home."

"Okay, just fantasize it," he whispered hoarsely. "Be the bad girl. Let loose and fly." He nipped her ear lobe with his teeth.

"Slow down, slow down," she whispered. "You'll rock the boat."

# CHAPTER 44

Sam sat shirtless at the salon table nursing his second cup of coffee of the morning and watched Ian come out of his cabin. No sign of life had come from Anna's room since he had deposited her limp body on her bed late last night.

Ian stooped to pick up the envelope on the floor by his door containing Sarah's note. "You read this?" He dropped it on the table and stepped to the counter to pour a cup of coffee.

"Can I?" Sam asked, not sure of what to say.

Ian shrugged. "Might as well. Won't change anything."

He opened the note and pretended to read before slipping it back in the envelope. "I'm sorry," he said, watching the boy. "Did you have any idea?"

Ian sat at the table and stared at his cup. "I had a feeling something was going on but couldn't figure out what. I told you she was upset about something. I thought maybe because I hadn't said anything about our future. I thought she would think I was rushing things. Maybe she knew this about her father and didn't know how to tell me."

"Maybe." Sam nodded. "Do you know how to get in touch with her?"

"Nope." Ian shook his head and looked up at his mother who had just appeared in the salon. "Never thought I'd have to, so didn't get any address or phone number in London. Maybe the manager at the café will know something."

"Maybe," Sam said. Anna's hair was wet indicating a fresh shower. Her khaki shorts fit loosely around her hips and her skin glowed. "And good morning to you." He smiled. "Did you have a good night?"

"What's this?" Anna picked up the envelope.

"Read it," Ian said. "We need to get that engine running today if we want to get out to Moskito Island this weekend."

Sam watched him walk barefoot back to his cabin. "Better put some shoes on if you're gonna work in the engine room."

"How's he taking it?" Anna held up the note. "What did he say?"

Sam shook his head. "Wants to see if he can get in touch with her. Doesn't look like it's over, yet."

"You didn't answer me last night when I asked if this was true. Is she lying to him? What's the real reason she left the island?"

"You'll have to ask her," he said, pushing himself up from the table. "It's none of my business. And did I say you look great this morning?" He bared his teeth at her. "I could gobble you up in one bite."

"Oh, cripes," she said, heading to the salon steps.

"What?" He watched her cute little bottom as she went up ahead of him.

"My dress," she said over her shoulder. "It's still in the cockpit."

"Almost done here." Ian looked up at Sam watching from the engine room door. "I need to clean things up, wipe oil off the engine, collect tools, and we're ready to fire this mother up."

"Want some lunch first? I think your mom could use a break. The salon and cabins are beginning to look like a brand-new yacht with the new cushion covers."

"Let's go eat in town. I want to ask at the café about Sarah's contact info. Let me finish up here." Ian wiped his hands on a grungy towel. "I guess we can postpone the suspense of whether or not the engine works a bit longer. I can't think of any reason she won't run when we crank her."

"You know," Sam dreaded going by the café just yet. "Your mom was fixing something special for lunch to reward us for getting the engine installed. Let me check."

"I can make soup and sandwiches." Anna said when he caught her in the galley. "Vanilla ice cream in the freezer and chocolate syrup to put on it."

"Done." Sam grinned, feeling relieved. "We'll eat here."

"Okay, I'm ready when you are." Ian put his spoon down and wiped his mouth with the back of his hand. He looked across the table at Sam. Anna was busy washing the lunch dishes. "Let's fire this baby up. I can't take the suspense any longer."

Sam watched Anna at the sink. Her hair was piled up on her head and she wore a thin ribbon headband to keep it there. He smiled remembering the night before when she bit the back of her hand to keep from crying out when he did whatever he was doing, just right.

"Hey," Ian said. "Get your mind back on business here and help me start this motor."

Sam looked at him sheepishly. "Okay, okay. Hold your horses. Did you check the diesel level in the tanks?"

"Over half full," Ian looked like he was talking to a child. "We have enough to run to Puerto Rico and back a couple of times. Why are you stalling?"

"Not stalling, making sure we have all our t's crossed and our i's dotted."

Flanking the big engine, the two of them stood in the cramped room. "Turn on the fuel supply," Sam said, "and open the saltwater valves. It will take a couple of cranks to draw fuel into the cylinders and get the cooling water moving through the manifold." He watched Ian follow his instructions and then connected the positive cable to the start battery. The fuel pump hummed and then shut off automatically. A starter button was on the wall behind him, and he reached to push it. The engine cranked a couple of times and stopped. He pushed it again and the motor cranked twice and fired once. On the third try, it fired and sputtered to life.

"Give it some fuel." He nodded at Ian who had his hand on the throttle.

The throttle moved forward, and the new engine began to purr.

"Quick, check the exhaust for water coming out," he called out as Ian disappeared up to the deck. "If not, we have to shut it down."

"All's good," Ian called from above. "Exhaust water is coming out just fine."

"Check the amp meter on the helm. Is the battery charging?"

"As expected, and the water temperature and oil pressure gauges are all in green."

Sam smiled. The engine seemed to be running smoothly and all the systems were operating properly. It was almost too much to ask for. Something always goes wrong at a time like this, he thought. Meanwhile, the engine hummed.

"Mom, check the hot water at the galley sink." Ian yelled down the salon steps. "Let's see if the engine is creating hot water."

"It's steaming," Anna responded.

"Damn," Sam said under his breath. "Too perfect."

"Shall I check the transmission?" Ian had appeared beside him in the engine room. They stood a moment in silence watching and listening to the heart of the boat beating a smooth rhythm.

"Yeah, let's do that." Sam nodded. Go up to the helm and put her in forward to see if the prop works and moves the boat. Don't overshoot the mooring ball. If it engages and moves okay, then put it in neutral and try reverse. I can't believe we didn't screw something up putting this all back together."

Ian grinned. "My grandfather will just shit when he hears what we did."

Sam heard a clank in the transmission as Ian shifted. The prop shaft turned clockwise, and he felt the heavy boat moving forward. After a moment he heard two clangs as Ian went to neutral and then to reverse. The prop shaft reversed direction, and Firebird slid backwards until Sam felt her go taut on the mooring line.

"That's good," he called up to the helm. "Let's idle her for an hour and keep an eye on all the systems. I'm still waiting for something to come undone."

After ninety minutes of uninterrupted operation, he killed the ignition at the helm, and all went quiet. "Check one more time below for water or oil leaks." He turned to Ian. "I was thinking we'd wait until Saturday to take her on a maiden motor trip over to

Moskito. If everything is as good as it looks, maybe we'll leave tomorrow, and beat the crowd."

"We need some things from the store before we go," Anna said. We're short on bread, cereal, and beer."

"I'll get it." Ian looked at Sam. "I want to go by the café to get Sarah's address in England." He ran a hand through his shaggy hair. "I hope she got home okay."

Anna glanced at Sam, but he didn't see any way to stop the boy.

"Tell the marina we're going out tomorrow for a couple of days to clean the bottom," Sam said. "Charles won't be surprised. Also, stay away from the Haitian and his thugs. We leave in two weeks and don't need any more trouble."

"Gotcha." Ian took the grocery list and raced down the ladder to the dinghy.

Anna stood next to Sam watching the gray Zodiac pull away. "You still haven't answered my question."

"What question?"

"Why did Sarah up and disappear so quickly? Why did she break my son's heart?"

"You read the same note I did," he said.

# CHAPTER 45

Motoring out of the harbor the next morning, they watched the French liner easing its way up to the cruise ship dock in the middle of town. Her rails were crowded with passengers waiting to disembark and see the sights.

The trip over to Moskito Island was busy with Sam controlling the helm, and Ian running up and down the stairs to the engine room watching things. Sam put the big yacht and her new engine through multiple checks. So far, everything passed with flying colors. The engine ran quieter, cooler, more efficient, and more powerful than the old one.

"It's a much nicer ride for our guests," Sam said to Anna. She stayed in the cockpit with him, wearing a big floppy hat. "The other motor made so much noise, you could hardly hear one another up here."

Approaching the island, Sam picked a spot on the left side of the bay in clear water close to a large rock. It would give the day catamarans plenty of room at the beach.

Ian stood in the bow, watching the anchor chain play out while Sam handled the helm. "Ten more feet and I'll lock it," Ian called back. "This is a good spot." The clear turquoise water revealed a white sandy bottom about twenty feet below the keel. They were the second private boat in the bay.

Sam felt the chain seize and the ship snag on its anchor. He revved the throttle a bit to ensure a good grounding, then shifted to neutral. The heavy boat slid forward a bit, then settled on the chain. With the anchor in place, he let the engine idle while he went forward.

Ian stood in the bow holding on to the furled genoa and looking out over the lush, green island. "I can't get over how beautiful this place is. Looks like a movie set."

"The tourists books say there've been several movies filmed here," Sam said. "I think Clark Gable hung from fake pirate spars swinging his trusty cutlass at a brigand or two."

"What's a 'brigand,'" Ian asked.

"Not sure. Probably British for a bad guy." Sam laughed.

"Uh. . . .Wow! Look at that." Ian's eyes got wide.

Sam turned to see a couple walking on the nearly deserted beach not far away. They stopped, and she went up on tiptoes to kiss her paramour. The man grabbed a handful of butt cheek and laughed. They kissed again before turning around and walking in the opposite direction.

"Um, well, no arguing this is a sexy island." Sam winked at Ian who still watched the couple. "By the way, did you find out how to contact Sarah?"

"Nope. Nothing." Ian shook his head. "They had no information at the café other than she was from London. I think the manager was lying. One of the girls wouldn't look at me. Her boss said he'd tell Sarah I was asking if he heard from her, but he wasn't expecting to. We've got the rest of the day to do some work," Ian said, changing the subject. "What's first on your list."

"I want to operate the water maker for a couple of hours while cleaning the bottom," Sam said, as they walked back to the cockpit. "We'll tie a couple of lines to the stanchions and toss them in the water. We can hang off them while scraping the barnacles. You take the starboard side, and I'll work the port. Scrapers are in the cockpit locker. Be sure to wear rubber gloves."

They went below to put on swim trunks and came back on deck. "Masks and flippers are in the starboard locker," Sam said. "We'll start at the stern and work our way forward to the bow. Scrape downward from the water line to the top of the keel. I'll hire a diver back in town to clean the keel. Tomorrow we'll play, and on Sunday we'll finish scaping if we're not done before heading back to the harbor."

"What about me?" Anna said, stepping up out of the salon. "What can I do to help?"

The white string bikini she wore caused Sam to go blank. Ian had already gone over the side and was working his side of the hull. "Uh. . .we'll need you to be alert in case we need help with something." Sam coughed.

She grinned. "Okay. I'll lie here on deck in the sun so just call out when you need me."

"I need you. God, I need you." He raised an eyebrow at her.

"Not now." She laughed. "When you really need me to do something."

"Oh, I definitely need something." Sam laughed and turned to the deck box to grab a pair of gloves.

It was late afternoon when he and Ian knocked off from their scraping job. The boy had cleaned much more of the hull than Sam had and let him know it. "Don't expect me to help on your side," Ian said. The three of them sat in the cockpit nursing beers and watching the sunset. More boats had come in during the afternoon and in the dusky light, flames from grills on stern rails could be seen around the bay. "I know you're the captain, but you've got to carry your own weight."

"Don't worry about me." Sam laughed. "I'll have my side completed before its time for us to leave on Sunday. Besides, there's no rush to get back and we can even leave on Monday if I choose, since I'm captain and all."

Ian took a long swig from his beer bottle. "Tomorrow, I'm playing. The day sailors will be in here with their French passengers, and I don't want to miss anything."

"Don't talk like that in front of your mother," Anna said. winking at Sam across the cockpit.

"Sorry, Mom, but I'm twenty-two years old and. . . ."

"I know how old you are," she said, rising to go below. "Like I said, don't talk like that in front of your mother. Dinner will be ready in half an hour."

After eating, Sam and Anna sat at the table finishing their wine while Ian washed dishes at the galley sink. Sam pulled out a piece of paper and a pencil. "Okay," he said. "I think we're nearing the goal line on finishing Firebird. There's not that many days before we leave for Saint Thomas so let's review where we are and make a list of the things that need to be done. Anna, what's your first thought?"

"The upholstery here in the salon and the mattresses in the cabins are all done. We need some nice colorful throw pillows down here to make the décor pop."

Sam wrote *pillows.* "What else?" He looked at Ian.

"The sails have been inventoried and repaired. At least the main ones that we'll be using. They are dirty and need a good soap and water bath. That's a lot of sail square footage and is a bigger job than it sounds."

Sam wrote Sails Cleaned. "What else?"

"A good detailing down below and on top," Ian added. "Maybe new bedding for the cabins and new towels. High thread count sheets and blankets. That's what customers come in contact with first. That'll cost money but—"

"Let me worry about that," Sam said. "You're right. What we have now is not even good enough for boy scouts much less charter guests. I think we'll have to defer acquisitions of things until we get to Saint Thomas. The selections on the island here are rather slim."

"Agreed," Anna said. "I can do the shopping when we get to Charlotte Amalie."

Sam looked at his list. "What about things we can do with some elbow grease while we're still at Saint Sebastian? Time and muscles are our best resources until we leave for the charter show."

"All the stainless on deck can use one more polishing." Ian rinsed a dish and put it in the rack. "It can shine like fine silver. I took off the heavy corrosion when we first started the project. Now it's a final polishing before the show."

"Anything more?"

"Menus," Anna added. "What do you want to feed your guests?

A week's charter will have seven breakfasts, lunches, and dinners, not to mention snacks and cocktail hours."

Sam frowned. "I don't know diddley about that stuff except for cheese and crackers and peanut butter. Maybe I'm in over my head."

She laughed. "Don't you worry about it, Captain. You keep us from sinking and get us safely to each destination. I'll take care of the passengers and their cuisine, both acquiring and preparing. Trust me. I know more than making spaghetti and salad."

"Then you can never leave," he said, smiling at her.

"We'll see." She finished off her glass of wine. "We'll see."

"What else?" Sam looked at them. "I mean, we've done a lot these past months. A rebuilt generator, a new hot water system and water pumps. New covers for all the cushions and new varnish on all the wood down below."

"And a new engine," Ian said, sitting down at the table with them.

Sam nodded. "That was the biggest improvement and most difficult project but added the most value. We're in good shape if we clear most of the items off this list in the next nine or ten days."

Something bumped the side of the boat, and she rocked on her anchor chain.

"Ahoy, there. Firebird. Ahoy."

Sam didn't recognize the voice and looked at Ian.

Ian shrugged and took the salon steps two at a time. After a minute he called back down. "It's Orlando from the machine shop with his wife. They invited me over for a drink on his trawler. They just dropped anchor and were surprised to see us here."

Sam went up on deck and noticed it was already dark. Lights flickered from the boats in the bay. "So, you own a stinkpot?" he said, seeing Orlando standing in his dinghy and holding on to the toe rail.

"Sailing's too slow for a working man who charges his customers by the hour." Orlando reached up to shake Sam's extended hand.

An attractive woman in a tiny almost nothing bikini sat in the dinghy. He remembered Orlando once saying he and his wife liked to come to Moskito when the French were here.

He waved at her. “Nice evening.” He turned to Ian. “Have a good time and don’t wake me when you come back. After the afternoon in the water scraping the bottom of this big tub, this old man is exhausted and plans on hitting the sack early.”

Anna came up and watched with Sam as Orlando’s inflatable motored away toward his trawler on the other side of the bay. “What was that all about?” She slipped a hand under his T-shirt and caressed his bare back.

“Not sure,” he said. “But I think it means the kids are out of the house tonight and. . .oh God. Don’t stop.”

“How much time do we have?” she whispered.

He lifted her chin to gaze into her eyes. “The rest of our lives, if we do it right.”

# CHAPTER 46

Sam woke and saw Anna sleeping beside him. He smiled and turned toward the bulkhead. It had been a good night. Even better than his best night with Darlene. *Crap! Why am I thinking of her?*

"Good morning, Captain."

He turned over and saw Anna looking at him. She was so damn cute he couldn't stand it. "It's better than *good*." He smiled at her. "It's damn great!" He leaned over and kissed her.

"It's Saturday morning. Do you want to get up or are we not done?"

"I'm game if you are. Is it my animal magnetism or. . . .?"

"No, no," She giggled. "It's just that, you know. . . ."

"Why you little tart!" He laid back and looked at her.

"I'm sorry." She covered her face with the sheet. "I'll have to say a thousand *Hail Mary's* when I next go to confession."

He couldn't take his eyes off her. *How did this happen? Not that long ago we couldn't stand each other.*

The familiar sound of an inflatable bumping the hull grabbed his attention. He slipped on a pair of shorts and went up on top. Ian stepped onto the deck and waved at Orlando who shoved off and headed back to his trawler.

"So, a sleepover?" Sam teased when Ian turned around and saw him.

"I wish," Ian said without smiling. "Don't think anyone did much sleeping, especially me."

"What?"

"Nothing happened, much to his wife's disappointment." Ian said. "Let's sit under the canopy in the cockpit. The sun is blinding."

"Can I get you boys some coffee?" Anna called up from below.

"Please," Sam answered.

"Make it two?" Ian said.

"So?" Sam asked. "Did you maybe misunderstand?"

"Hard to misunderstand 'Do you want to bang my wife?'"

"Is that what he said?"

"Not exactly. It was more like *she thinks you're hot. Do you want to make it with her?*"

"And?"

"I just stared at them a minute without saying anything. Orlando then said, 'we'll take that as a maybe.' The next thing I know, they're both going at each other right in front of me, like I wasn't even there."

"And?"

"We were in the salon of his trawler. I went outside and tried to sleep on the aft deck. I thought he'd come up to give me a ride back to Firebird, but I guess they stayed at it until morning. At least that was the first I saw of him."

"The Caribbean brings that out in people," Sam said, wondering what he would've done if he'd been there instead of the boy.

"You okay?"

"I'm fine." Ian shrugged. "Never had anything like that happen before."

"Here's a little something for breakfast." Anna sat a tray in the cockpit with toast, jam, grapefruit sections and slices of pineapple. "Coffee's almost ready. I'll bring it up." When Ian turned and reached for something to eat, she blew Sam a kiss before going back down to the galley.

Loud laughter coming across the bay made them both look up. The two big day catamarans loaded with French passengers were racing toward the beach. Captain Ainsley's White Squall arrived first and anchored in shallow water just off the sand beach. The other one nestled in close beside it. Anna came up on top with their coffee and stopped cold when she saw Ainsley's boat.

Sam took the cups from her and handed one to Ian. "Thanks," he said.

After a moment, she turned and went back down the steps.

Later, he and Anna were talking quietly in the salon while Ian went back into the water to finish scraping his side of the bottom. "I don't understand," Sam said. "What's your problem with Ainsley?"

She looked away, and he saw a tear run down her cheek. "I don't really understand it myself," she said, her bottom lip quivering. "He knows Guy and spends time at the villa. I remember him being there, but I don't remember the circumstances or any specifics about it. Guy was generous with his drugs and everything he thought belonged to him. It was whatever his guests desired. My mind goes blank when I try to recall details. It wasn't good. Whenever I see Ainsley, a cold wind blows through me, and it scares me."

# CHAPTER 47

By Saturday noon, the beach was dotted from one end to the other with festive umbrellas provided by the cruise ship. Sam stood at the bow with his binoculars checking out the crowd as well as the other boats anchored in the bay. He paid particular attention to White Squall. He could see her uniformed captain chatting on deck with his guests. Most were barely clothed and drank from glasses of island punch. The catamaran's crew moved about the deck with trays of drinks. Sam caught the aroma of grilled meats wafting his way. Every now and then he saw the captain gaze out at Firebird. Wonder what the bastard's thinking, he thought. Whatever happened between Ainsley and Anna still puzzled him.

"I'm done working for today." Ian stripped off his wet bathing suit on the forward deck. "I scraped the whole port side of the hull. Your side still looks like an herb farm."

"Showing off the goods, eh?" Sam tossed the boy a towel draped on the lifelines. One could say it looks like you're trolling."

Ian wrapped the towel around his waist and picked up his wet suit. "I'll do that at the beach. If you troll, you go where the fish are."

Sam nodded at the oiled human masses on the island. "Looks like plenty of interesting fish over there." It was awkward chatting with the boy about sex, even if just teasing. Their relationship was in flux, at least as far as he was concerned. At some point he and Anna needed to come clean with him. They'd tried to be discrete. But Sam was surprised how quickly it had evolved.

"Uh, your mom and I will stay out here this afternoon. Maybe get a little sun, do some work on the boat. You've put pressure on me by finishing your side of the hull." He saw Ian smiling at him.

"Yeah, right." Ian shook his head and headed to the salon stairs.

Sam could tell he was trying to hide a grin.

"I'll go to the beach and give you two time alone out here."

Sam was resting under the canopy out of the mid-day sun and nursing a cold beer when Anna stepped out on deck wearing his favorite white bikini. "Are we going to the beach?" She looked at him."

"He knows," Sam said.

"Who knows? Knows what?"

"Have you spoken to your son about us?"

"About what? I have no idea what you're talking about."

Sam stood and led her to the bow. "The boy's down in his room getting ready to spend the day at the beach. He knows about us. He knows we've been sneaking around."

Anna studied his face a moment. "What did he say? What did you say?"

"He told me he would leave us alone out here while he went ashore. Said he'd give us some time alone. That's exactly how he put it. I didn't say anything. Neither confirmed nor denied."

Anna looked down. "I've gotten by for twenty-two years without having this conversation with him. Guess maybe it's time. We're in too close quarters to keep it a secret. Or—we can cease all together."

Sam took her hand and pulled her to him. He looked down and placed a kiss on each eye lid. "I love you," he said. "I really do, and it pains me to see you troubled by this. I'm forty-two years old and haven't loved anyone since I was eighteen. And that was probably just teenage lust. My old man accused me once of being a bag of hormones in sneakers."

Anna raised her lips to his and kissed him. "Are you sure? I've felt for some time now, that we were headed in this direction, but I didn't know how to bring it up. God knows I love you, too." She leaned her oiled body into his while kissing him.

"Excuse me." Ian stepped out on deck in a fresh bathing suit. "Think I'll swim to the beach. I'll take a waterproof bag to carry a towel and sunscreen." He smiled at his mother's embarrassment.

"Take the dinghy if you want." Sam held Anna's hand. "We plan to stay on board."

"Thanks, but I'd rather swim." He picked up his bag and jumped from the rail, making a big splash next to the boat.

Sam and Anna watched him swim with graceful strokes toward the crowd on the beach. "He's become a handsome strapping boy," she said almost in a whisper. "A young man. It happened so quickly. Guess I wasn't paying attention."

"That went well. Easier than I thought." Sam put his arm around her shoulder as they watched Ian step out of the water and head up the sandy beach. His strong legs, broad chest, and blonde hair made him look like a surfer god.

"What went well?" She looked up at him.

"Your talk with your son about us." He kissed her forehead.

"But, I didn't—"

"I know," he said, laughing. "But now he knows, and that's the point."

"I'm sure he has some questions." She slipped her hand down into the back of his bathing suit.

"They always have questions," he said, pulling her hand out of his trunks. "The questions are easy. It's the answers that are tough."

He led her back to in front of the mast and spread a towel on deck. "You sun here while I finish cleaning the hull. I didn't plan to do this today, but the boy made it a competition. Oh, he'll win, but I don't want to make it look too easy." He put an open mouth kiss on her and went to the stern to get his flippers out of the deck box.

Two hours later, he stood over her dripping water on her bare back.

"You already done?" She opened her eyes and pushed up on one elbow. Her oiled body glistened in the sun. "I dozed off. The rocking of the boat and the warm sun is like a—"

"An aphrodisiac?"

"No. I was going to say—"

"Works that way for me," he said, dropping his wet suit on the deck.

"I can see," she said, smiling up at him. "You finish cleaning the bottom of the boat?"

"All done and smooth as a baby's butt," he said. "It's so clean, the fish can eat off of it."

"Now you're being silly."

"Maybe." He squeezed sun block out of a bottle into his hand and rubbed it over his shoulders. "I work fast when I'm motivated."

"And?"

He leaned forward and kissed her, his tongue tracing her lips. God, she tastes good, he thought. "I was motivated knowing you were up here waiting for me." He leaned forward to kiss her again.

# CHAPTER 48

It was late afternoon when Sam stepped back out on the deck. He had donned a clean pair of running shorts after his shower. The beach crowd was streaming back to the two catamarans. He noticed Orlando's trawler was gone from the bay. He scanned the island for Ian. The colorful umbrellas were being folded and left on the beach for the next day's visitors. Several people from private boats stayed late enjoying the end-of-day sun.

"You missed a spot down here."

He looked down over the lifeline and saw Ian treading water.

"I cleaned it for you. You're welcome." Ian tossed his waterproof bag up to Sam. "The bottom looks good. We should haul her after the show at Charlotte Amalie and put on new bottom paint." He pushed away from the hull and swam around to the boarding platform.

"Anything interesting happen today?" Sam asked. He picked up Ian's bag and spread his wet towel on the lifeline to dry.

"Nothing really." Ian stored his mask and flippers in the deck box.

"I met an older couple from Boston who know my grandfather. One lady I met on the beach was the mother of a classmate of mine at Cornell. Where's Mom?"

"Below taking a nap. I think the sun got to her."

"By the way, I ran into that captain of White Squall, Captain Ainsley or something like that. Nice fellow. Offered me a rum punch and spent some time chatting. Said he'd met you and mom the last time we were out here."

"What else did he say?" Sam frowned.

"He said that he thought Mom was a looker, and he asked a few questions about my father. Stuff like that. Seemed curious about Firebird. Asked when we were leaving the island and where we're going."

"What'd you say?"

"Nothing really. Just that you were planning to operate her as a crewed charter yacht and were scheduled to attend the show over on Saint Thomas. I'm going below to get out of this wet suit. Can I bring you up a cold one?"

Sam watched White Squall backing away from the beach and point her pontoons toward open water. Guests lined the rails, waving at each boat they passed. "Yeah. That'd be good."

Ian started down the salon steps. "Should I run the engine to charge the house batteries?"

"Good idea," Sam nodded. "Also bring up a cold bottle of Pinot Grigio from the fridge. Your mom will want that." A few moments later he felt a slight vibration and heard the hum of the engine at idle.

Anna passed him a snack tray containing several cheeses, crackers and some red olives. He set the tray on the cockpit table and opened the wine Ian brought up with three glasses. The sky had grown overcast, and he felt the wind increasing.

"With the clouds we won't be able to see the sun set," Anna said, taking a glass from Ian. "There's a green flash just as the sun drops below the horizon. You have to watch closely. Blink, and you'll miss it."

"Have you seen it?" Ian asked.

"A few times." Anna lifted her glass to him. "It was beautiful. A bright green flash like a tiny explosion."

Anna gazed at her son while turning the stem in her fingers. "How was your day at the beach? Looked like a good crowd from the cruise ship."

"And a lot of private boats were here as well, Ian said. "I staked out a spot and spread my towel. A couple of times I jogged to the far end of the beach and back before diving into the water to cool off."

"How was the view?" Sam smiled, knowing he was asking a leading question.

"The French are the French," Ian said. "I think I was hit on a couple of times by some French women but didn't understand the language so wasn't sure how to respond."

"That probably wet a couple of bikini bottoms." Sam laughed and then groaned when Anna's foot caught him on the shin under the cockpit table.

"Maybe," Ian said. "If they were wearing bottoms."

"You two are terrible." Anna looked away as Sam guffawed. "I thought the reason we came over here was to do some work."

"Right. And we did, and I mean we are." Sam rubbed his shin. "But you knew the French ship was in and—"

"Enough." She frowned. "I don't want to hear any more about the French."

"Right." Sam looked at Ian. "Me neither. Ouch," he yelled when her foot once again connected with his bare leg.

Just then a strong gust pushed Firebird back hard on her anchor chain.

Sam looked at Ian. "Maybe we should rethink spending the night here with that storm building."

# CHAPTER 49

Black clouds boiled in the sky over the mountain when they settled back onto Firebird's mooring in the harbor at Saint Sebastian.

"Looks like we beat the storm." Ian returned to the helm after securing the line to the bow cleat. "I thought sure we would catch hell on the way back. Good thing we left when we did."

"My fault." Sam turned to see another bolt of lightning flash across the dark sky. Large drops of rain began to hit the deck around them. "I hadn't checked the weather report for the last two days. This late storm caught me by surprise. Make sure all the hatches are closed, and let's go below." His words were almost drowned out by the crashing of thunder and lightning, and the curtain of rain that now engulfed the boat and everything around them.

"Here, put some of this aloe on me." Anna turned her back to him in the salon and raised her hair off her shoulders. "I knew I was getting too much sun this afternoon but with a cool trade breeze, you don't feel like it."

A wave rolled Firebird, slamming her back taut on her mooring line.

"Wow!" Ian's eyes got big. "That was one powerful gust. Maybe I should go up and check things out."

"It'll blow by." Sam smeared the cooling gel on Anna's back and over her shoulders. He leaned forward and blew a kiss in her ear. The sound of the hard driving rain grew louder, neutralizing all sounds in the harbor. It suddenly stopped, and they could hear the creaking and moaning of nylon lines being stretched and spars being slapped by loose halyards as Firebird bucked and jumped on her mooring bridle. "See?" Sam put the aloe down on the salon table and bounded up the stairs to the deck.

The water in the harbor churned from the passing storm, but Firebird's mooring lines were holding. He gazed across to the mainland and saw Charlie at the marina, untangling several inflatables that the storm had woven together. Over at the town dock, he saw the two catamarans secured to the pier, their French guests back on the cruise ship probably getting dressed for the cocktail hour and dinner.

"How does it look?" Ian joined him. "Any damage?"

They walked the rail together, finding everything in order.

"She looks great." Sam paused to look up and down the main and mizzen masts. "Rigging and sails are okay, and other than everything being wet, looks in perfect condition."

"I liked the way the new motor sounded on the way back," Ian said. "She hummed and never coughed once even though we were gunning it. I thought the wave action would have stirred up some dregs in the fuel tank, but she didn't miss a beat. I checked the filters after we got here, and they were clear and clean."

"When we finish that punch list of things to do down below, we'll have ourselves a real fancy charter yacht." Sam slapped Ian on the back. "If those things get done this week, we'll have a free week to get ourselves over to Saint Thomas."

"Yeah, I wish Sarah was here to see. . . ." Ian's voice trailed off and his words died in the light breeze.

"Yep—me, too." Sam nodded, his lips tightening into a line. "Me, too."

"Why do you think she. . . .?" Ian's brow creased into a frown.

"Don't know." Sam looked away. "Maybe you can talk to her about it one day."

"Yeah, maybe."

After an awkward moment, Sam turned to the salon steps.

"So, what about you and Mom?" Ian's question halted him in mid stride.

"What do you mean, what about us?"

"I know something's happening." Ian's face turned serious. "You and she are whispering and giggling like a couple of school kids when you think I'm not paying attention. But I am."

Sam returned to the settee in the cockpit and studied Ian's face. "I'm not sure what's happening," he said. "What do you want to know?"

Darkness had enveloped the island, and streetlights were on in town. "I don't know what I want to know," Ian said, almost in a whisper. "I mean sometimes I feel like she's my responsibility. That I'm the adult and need to look after her. Not sure she's capable of looking after herself. Both Granddad and I over the years. . . ."

"I love her," Sam said, hoarsely. "I love her, and I think she loves me. I hope she loves me."

"And what exactly does that mean?"

"Don't know, yet." Sam stepped to the rail. The lights in town reflected off the water's surface, doubling their number and intensity. "We haven't talked much about it. There's no agreement. No plan."

"What do you want to happen?"

Several moments passed before Sam answered. "Fair question." He ran a hand across his chest and caressed the scar on his arm. "I guess the answer is I don't want her to leave. To go back to Boston or wherever."

"What does that mean?"

"You're going to make me say it, aren't you?" He smiled.

"Don't know what you are talking about," Ian responded, the serious look still creasing his forehead.

"Do you think she would?" Sam lost his smile and looked at him.

"Would she what?"

Sam shook his head and looked away. "Marry me. Would she marry me if I asked?"

"You going to ask her?"

*Damn, he's sounds like her father.* "Should I?"

"Do you want to?"

"I don't want her to leave. I want her to stay and help make

Firebird the most successful charter yacht in this part of the Caribbean. And if marrying me is the way she wants to do it, then yes, I want to. I want to ask her to marry me."

Ian dropped his gaze to the deck and shook his head. "Was that so hard?" He looked back up at Sam.

"Yeah, it was." He slapped Ian on the back. "After over twenty-years of being alone and getting used to my own company, it was damn hard. What do you think she'll say?"

Ian reached down to rub something off his bare foot. "Don't know." He straightened up and looked at Sam at eye level. "We'll never know until you ask."

"And what about you?" Sam studied Ian's face. "Do I have your permission?"

"Yeah." He grinned. "You have my permission to ask. When do you plan to do that?"

"When the time is right." Sam said, following Ian down the stairs to the salon. "We'll see."

# CHAPTER 50

The three of them ate dinner in silence. Sam kept looking at Anna, and she would divert her eyes. She'd fried chicken breasts and added a can of mushroom soup as a sauce.

"This is good." He winked at her. "The gravy makes it."

"Nothing special," she replied, not looking up from her plate.

Sam looked at Ian across the table. "I'd say this is pretty special. Dinner for me until I met your mother was usually something out of a can and crackers."

After the table was cleared, Sam poured two glasses of wine and asked Anna to join him on deck. He saw Ian watching them.

"Okay, I'm exhausted," Ian said, taking the hint. "Think I'll turn in early. Maybe start a new book. I picked up a Tom Clancy novel in the lending library at the marina."

"Let me see it before you take it back," Sam said. "Tomorrow morning we'll go over the final punch lists of things to do before we leave for Saint Thomas. Nothing major on that list. Just a lot of little things to clean up. With the new engine and all systems working well, I now see real light at the end of the tunnel. The most important thing I think on the list is that we rip the bottom seams out of our sail bags and replace them with strong Velcro. The sails are too big for Anna to lift and put into a bag, With Velcro, we just open both ends and slide the bag over the folded sail like a sleeve. It can then be left on deck till I can help her store it below in the sail locker."

"Where'd you get that idea?" Ian asked. "I wondered how Mom could handle those big sails."

"Charlie at the marina suggested it. He's seen it on other large yachts."

Anna picked up her wine glass. "Let's go up," she said to Sam. "Cooking on the stove always makes it so hot down here."

Sam followed her up the steps, watching her little bottom sway in front of his face. *God, she's one beautiful woman.*

A car horn sounded in the distance, amplified by the stillness of the water around them. The storm had passed, and the deck was wet from the rain. It felt cool to Sam's bare feet. He had on khaki shorts and a clean T-shirt he had donned for dinner. His sandy hair had turned almost blonde in the sun these past weeks. He felt the warmness of her body against him as they stood together at the rail looking at the lights in town.

"It's beautiful here," she said, almost in a whisper.

"So are you."

She turned and looked up into his eyes. "You're just horny."

He slipped his free hand around her waist and pulled her against him. "Always, but this night is different."

"And how is that?"

He remained silent for a minute, not knowing how to begin. "Uh, different in that it's been a lot of years since I've had a conversation like this."

"And how is this one different?"

He took a deep breath and closed his eyes. *Here goes.* "I know we've spoken in the past about you joining me as first mate on Firebird as she turns into a beautiful charter yacht."

"You make her sound like a butterfly coming out of her cocoon."

"I think she is," he said, turning her around in his arms and pulling her back against him. "And so are you."

Another moment of silence passed.

"And?" she said.

He kissed her cheek and whispered in her ear. "And I want you to do that. To come with me. But I also want you to do it as my partner. My business partner as well as my mate. My wife." He felt her stiffen.

She turned around and stared up into his face. "Are you sure? I mean, have you thought this through, or do you just want to get me in your bed for the night?"

"Yes, and yes." He grinned and set his wine glass down so he could hold her with both hands. A shudder ran up his spine as he gazed into her eyes. "I spoke to the boy about it. Asked his permission."

"And?"

"He said I have his permission—to ask."

Anna turned around and gazed out over the water.

Sam spun her back to face him and knelt on one knee. "Will you marry me, Anna? Will you marry me, and Firebird?"

She looked at him at eye level with her. "Do you want an answer now, or can I take some time to think about it? I mean—"

"How much time?"

"I'm not sure. I can answer right now about joining you as partner and First Mate on Firebird. The answer to that is, yes. Definitely, yes. Marrying you is the second part of that question. Are you sure that's where you want to take this? Did you think I'd require marriage to accept the first part?"

"Maybe." Sam stood. "I'm not sure. I meant it as one question."

Another car horn sounded from up on the mountain, followed by two more closer to town.

"So, where are we?" Sam asked. "I love you. You've said you love me."

"I do." She put her arms around his neck and went up on tiptoe to kiss him. Her lips were full and sweet. "I do. I do," she breathed into his mouth. "I will."

After everyone had retired for the night, Anna lay on her bed in the dark with her eyes open. Sam had said something about taking a shower and had gone into his own cabin. So much had happened. So much that she never counted on. This wasn't her plan when she left Boston in the middle of the night and came down here to find her son. *Who am I kidding? I didn't have a plan.*

Ever since Daniel's death made her a young widow and single mother at eighteen, she'd floated through life on her father-in-law's money and protection. And like a jelly fish in the ocean, she'd ridden that ocean current wherever it took her. Meeting Sam was much like when she met Daniel at that bar in Boston. It just happened, and her life took a turn she hadn't expected, hadn't planned on. *So, am I ready for this?*

Sam had asked the question and she had accepted. She could have said *no*, but her son had now grown into a strong, intelligent, independent young man. He didn't need her anymore. Sam did need her, and it was time to start living her life. She'd waited too long. And besides, she loved this man.

She rolled over and hugged a pillow to her breast. *This smart, funny, handsome, sexy man.*

# CHAPTER 51

"Wow! It's a beautiful morning," Sam exclaimed, surprised to find Ian up and working at the mast. He had a sail bag across his lap and was cutting the threads with a sail knife, opening the bag's bottom seam.

"Thought I'd get started on these," Ian said. "You think the Velcro will keep the bottom closed with such a heavy sail in it?"

Sam picked up the roll of white Velcro tape that sat next to the sail bag and examined it. "Charlie was surprised to see how much weight it could hold. He said a big sailing yacht was moored here one season with an all-female crew, and the skipper turned the sail bags into sleeves that could be slid on and off the sails by just one of the girls. They'd then dragged the bag across the deck and dropped it through the hatch into the sail locker."

"Makes sense to me." Ian spooled out a long piece of Velcro tape and applied it to the bottom of the bag. "I'll hand stitch the Velcro to the nylon to make sure it doesn't peel off."

"We only need to do it to the main and foresail bags." Sam watched Ian thread a needle and start stitching. "That's the bag for the genoa you're working on. Then there's the 100% jib bag and the storm jib bag. Your mom will appreciate this. It'll make it easier for her and for me."

"So?" Ian looked up at Sam while pulling another stitch through the sail bag.

"So, what?" Sam grinned, knowing full well what he was asking about.

"You guys must have talked. I know you stayed in her room most of last night. What did she say?"

"She said she loves me," Sam teased.

"And?"

"I told her I love her." Sam started to walk away.

"Okay, okay." Ian tossed the sail bag aside and stood up. He was bare footed, wearing an old T-shirt and a faded pair of gym shorts. "What else?"

Sam saw him smiling in anticipation. "I asked her to marry me."

"And?"

"She wanted some time to think about it."

The smile left Ian's face. "She didn't?"

"She did."

"Damn it!" Ian banged his open palm against the aluminum mast and stepped to the rail. He stared down at the harbor water lapping up against Firebird's hull. "How much time does she want?"

"Oh, she took a long fifteen seconds, then said, 'yes.'"

Ian turned around and looked at him. A grin creased his face. "She did? She accepted?"

"She did."

"She didn't!"

"Believe me. She did. She said 'yes, I will.'"

Ian turned to look out at the other boats in the harbor. "I can't believe it. After all this time, she—"

"Yeah. Me, too." Sam put his hand on the boy's shoulder. "It's been a lot of years for both of us. Feels surreal, like it's a dream and not really happening, but here we are, talking about it."

"Is she up?"

"She's getting dressed."

Sam remained on deck while Ian disappeared below. He watched a couple of freighters leave the mouth of the harbor to start the workday and wondered how this news would change his relationship with the boy. Before this, he was his employer. Now he wasn't sure. Was it, friend? Mother's boyfriend? Mother's lover? *Dad?*

Sam looked toward the town dock and saw the French cruise ship had already departed. They usually set sail before the sun came up, so they could serve breakfast to the passengers while at sea on their way to their next destination. In this case, he knew it was only over to Saint John, just twelve miles away.

Captain Ainsley's catamaran sat in its berth awaiting passengers for their daily snorkeling and picnic trip to nearby islands. Sam started to go below for coffee when he saw the captain step out onto the deck and greet what looked like an arriving passenger or crew member. The two moved to the stern of the big cat and huddled in private conversation. Sam looked closer and there was no question. It was the Haitian, and they were both looking at Firebird.

# CHAPTER 52

As he started down the stairs, Sam saw Ian in the salon surrounded by laundry bags.

"Hey! I need a hand here. Mom wants these taken over to the marina. Says our sheets are getting moldy. I told her mine were just the way I want them—smelling like sweat and Polo, but she insisted."

"Pass them up," Sam said. "Let's not get in her way when she's cleaning."

After the bags were stacked on deck, Sam went down and poured himself a cup of coffee. "You know there's a closet in the galley that's plumbed for a washer and dryer?" He looked at Anna doing dishes at the sink. "When Firebird was built, no expense was spared. Right now, the space is used for storage and is full of parts and cleaning equipment. We've got a good generator producing electricity, and propane provides heat for the dryer. Just don't have the bucks right now for the unit. Maybe one day after a few good charters."

"So, you told him?" She glanced at Sam.

"Yeah. He knows. And approves. Did he say anything to you?"

"Gave me a big hug and mumbled, 'It's about time.'" She dried her hands on a towel before slipping her arms around his neck and laying her head against his chest. "Oh!" She wrinkled up her nose and pulled away. "Take off that smelly T-shirt and put it with the laundry."

"Ah, you just like to see my bare chest," he said, pulling the T-shirt over his head. "Any excuse to get me out of my clothes." He slipped his thumbs in the waist band of his shorts and started to push them down.

"Your shorts are okay." She slapped his hands away just as Ian stepped out of his cabin and entered the salon..

"I'll run the laundry over to the marina and get it in the washers," Ian said. "There's so much with clothes and bedding that it could take all morning."

"I'll go with you," Sam said. "Let me get a clean shirt and I'll meet you on deck. I want to see if there's any chance to schedule a haul out at the boatyard to put on new bottom paint before we leave. Thought about doing it at Saint Thomas after the show, but a new red bottom during the show would make her sparkle."

It was mid-morning by the time they tied up at the dinghy dock and unloaded the five bags of laundry. Sam saw the marina manager, come out of his office.

"Looks like the dirty laundry brigade landed." Charlie shook Sam's hand.

"Yep," Sam replied. "Necessary action to prevent the First Mate from mutiny and leaving the ship."

"The worst job on a crewed charter yacht, I've been told," Charlie said. "You ought to put a washer and dryer on that old tub. I'm sure you have the space for it. I know you have a generator."

"Everything but the cash," Sam said. "Not high on the priority list right now."

"Maybe. But check out the bulletin board in the office. Folks from time to put things up there for sale. You might find a bargain."

"Will do," Sam said, picking up three laundry bags and tossing them over his shoulder. "Bring those others," he said to Ian, "and let's get going, It's just not a high priority, Charlie." He winked at the marina manager and headed down the dock toward the marina laundry.

"Do we really have a space?" Ian looked at Sam after they had loaded up all the machines and still had a bag left over.

"We do." Sam started putting quarters into the machines and pushing the start buttons. "But—"

"I know. I heard you. But I'm not sure Mom can do this every week and still play hostess to customers."

"We all make sacrifices and do what we have to do," Sam said. "And that includes your mother."

"What would a unit cost?"

"One designed for a yacht like Firebird would probably cost a couple grand or more. Right now, I need that money for other things."

After the machines were all sloshing, Sam stepped to the laundry room door. I'm going over to the yard to see about that haul out. If we paint the bottom ourselves, it will reduce the cost big time."

"I'll watch the laundry here." Ian nodded, looking at his watch. "This will take the rest of the morning. I'll see you when you get back."

On his way, Sam saw the marina manager chatting with a man standing by a car in the parking lot. "Hey Sam!" Charlie called to him. "Want you to meet someone. This is Bill Decker, the Chubb Insurance rep here on the island. He was asking me about Firebird. Bill, meet Sam Berrenger; owner and captain of that fine yacht in the harbor."

Sam shook the man's hand.

"A unique boat to say the least," Bill said. "Have you thought about insurance? It'd cost a pretty penny to replace her if, God forbid, something happened."

Sam looked out at Firebird. "Insurance? I barely have the money to—"

"Speak to someone who lost a boat and they'll tell you they can't afford not to have insurance. You'll also need a good liability policy if you have charter guests. One unfortunate accident, and your guest could own your boat, your house, your car, and your savings."

"I don't know." Sam hesitated. "I haven't budgeted—"

"Here's my card," the broker continued. "I'm in the Chubb office in town across from the cruise ship dock. I'm sure we can create a workable payment schedule, so you can make an initial payment, and regular monthly payments as you generate charter bookings. Of course, we'll need to get a current survey to confirm her value and condition. There's a fellow in town that we use. Just let me know and I'll get him scheduled."

As he headed on toward the boatyard, Sam looked at the broker's card. He knew he should have insurance. Even the charter show folks said they would require proof of liability insurance when he arrived at the show. He had some money in the bank and another monthly pension check due in a week. He could use that to make the first payment. "Damn!" he hissed under his breath. *Just like a fancy lady, Firebird's already draining my bank account.*

# CHAPTER 53

It was past 2:00 o'clock in the afternoon when Sam arrived back at the marina. Ian and the laundry were nowhere in sight, and the dinghy was gone. He had stopped for a bite to eat at the sandwich shop in town and spent an hour with Bill Decker at his office going over insurance options. He had settled on a plan that he could afford. Basically, a liability policy that would satisfy the charter show management and a replacement policy if Firebird was ever totaled. He also insured the sails and equipment for theft or loss but decided not to take the hull repair option, deciding he would just have to roll up his sleeves and do the work himself—if *God Forbid*—something happened that didn't total the boat. All that was left was to get Firebird surveyed, and Decker said he could schedule that when they arrived in Saint Thomas for the show. Sam looked at the thick parcel of insurance papers in his hand. Oh crap, he thought. Now, I'm definitely back in the establishment.

"So?" Ian looked at his mother and Sam across the salon table. He had not only folded all the laundry and put it away, but after going back for Sam at the marina, had made dinner for them.

"It's good," Sam nodded, lifting another forkful of lasagna. "Tastes great, especially the garlic bread." He held up a buttered slice.

Ian shook his head. "I mean, *so*, when are you two pulling the trigger—getting married? When's the ceremony?"

Anna glanced at Sam and twirled her glass of red wine in her fingers.

Sam saw her smile and knew she wanted him to respond. "Uh, good question." He looked at Ian. "We need to discuss, uh—"

"Sorry," Ian said, picking up his wine glass. "Didn't mean to intrude but just thinking about my schedule. I should let Cornell know I intend to return in January. I'm also sure Granddad would want to know I'm coming back to school. Just trying to fill in the blanks."

Sam saw Anna hiding her mirth at his discomfort behind her wine glass and shrugged, "Why wait? The sooner the better, if you ask me." Her smile went away, and he grinned.

Ian turned and cocked his head at his mother. "And you?"

"Uh. . .No big hurry. Why the rush? It's been over twenty years for all of us. We need to think about this some more. Maybe I want a small family wedding, or maybe I want a high mass wedding at Boston's cathedral. The Archbishop once told me that—"

"But I'm not Catholic," Sam interrupted. "Doesn't that make a difference in these things? I guess I'm protestant. My mother had me baptized when I was ten. Probably the last time I was in church."

"See?" Anna looked at her son. "Your grandfather would come undone if he were here and heard this conversation. We need to discuss this more—in private." She turned and looked hard at Sam.

"Uh, yeah. More thought and discussion." Sam chugged the rest of his wine. Like insurance, he thought to himself. *Like damn insurance.*

"What did you learn at the boatyard?" Ian changed the subject. "About hauling Firebird?"

Sam shook his head. "No can do. They don't have a lift large enough to take her out. Eighty-four feet and almost sixty tons is too big for anything on Saint Sebastian. They say the only one in the area big enough is at Saint Thomas, and they're booked months in advance. Especially as we're approaching the season."

Ian shrugged. "We can do a bottom scrape every few weeks until then. That should keep the barnacles to a minimum. But at some point, we'll need to put on a coat or two of anti-fouling paint that's copper based to repel them."

"When is sailing fun?" Anna glanced around the table. "I thought sailing was supposed to be exotic and fun. All you talk about is hard, sweaty work. I mean, if I'd taken the laundry bags to the marina and spent all day in that hot, humid room, I might be on a plane back to Boston right now."

"And that's why I asked about when you guys are getting married." Ian reached across the table for his mother's hand. "I have a surprise. A wedding present being delivered to the boat tomorrow."

Sam met Anna's gaze. "What do you mean, a 'present being delivered?'" He turned back to Ian beside him.

"After taking in that mess of laundry today, I knew Mom wouldn't want to do it on a weekly basis, especially for charter guests she doesn't even know. It's different doing it for your son and the man you love."

Sam looked at Anna. "You'd do that?"

She winked at him and turned her attention back to Ian.

"I found a deal on a washer and dryer today in town. Basically brand new. A couple had ordered it for their yacht, but he drowned in a diving accident. She sold the boat and went back to Miami. I bought it from the chandlery as a wedding present for you both. It's being delivered in the morning. We can get it installed before we have another load to do." He looked at his mother and smiled.

"I don't know about letting laundry put pressure on us to set a wedding date." Sam said to Anna. "What do you think?"

"I think my son loves me very much." She blew Ian a kiss across the table. "It's every girl's dream to get a washer and dryer as a wedding gift. But actually—" She looked at Sam. "I think he had your best interest at heart. He knows I wouldn't last long here if I had to schlepp laundry ashore every week. Thank you, Ian, and I'm sure Sam, really, really, thanks you."

"Good job," Sam nodded. "It'll make all our lives easier around here."

By the way," Ian said." Any sign of the Haitian or his thugs when you were in town today?" He refreshed his mother's glass and refilled his own.

Sam shook his head. "Nope. All was quiet." He didn't say anything about seeing Ainsley and Guy Mont Violet together that morning on White Squall. "Maybe they've forgotten about us and are making someone else's life miserable."

"Let's hope." Ian drained his wine and stood up. "What's left on our punch list? I finished Velcroing the bottoms of the sail bags. Tried it on the working jib. Works great. With the white Velcro strips, you don't even notice it's there, and its plenty strong to hold over a hundred plus pounds of sail."

"I want us to try and get away in five days." Sam took his dinner dishes to the galley sink. "I circled the boat today in the dinghy and she looks great. All the sanding and new varnish is making the bright work on top and below look brand new. The stainless lifeline stanchions and rigging sparkle after all our polishing, and all the new cushion covers in the salon and bedding in the staterooms make us look like photos in Better Homes and Gardens. Speaking of photos, Charlie is coming out tomorrow to take pictures for a brochure we'll need at the Saint Thomas show. I told him I had some taken with an old Brownie camera, but he said his Nikon would make them look professional. He said we can take them with us, and the show staff will print up the brochures on our first day."

"There really is light at the end of this long tunnel," Ian said, setting his dishes in the sink. "Is it okay if I take the dinghy and go ashore this evening? I want to try and call Sarah in London. A friend of hers at the café where she worked gave me a number. I have some things I need to say to her and—"

"I'll go with you," Sam said, grabbing a flashlight from the nav station. "I want to pick up a few things at the market and call the boatyard at Saint Thomas to leave a message about getting on their schedule. "Plus, I don't think it's a good idea for anyone on this boat to be alone in town at night. The marina office is already closed for the evening, so we'll have to use the public phones by the ferry dock."

After the dinner dishes were done and put away, they met on the boarding platform. Sam stepped in and held the dinghy while Ian got in and started the motor. After pushing away from Firebird and heading across the harbor toward the marina, Sam worried about

Ian's call to Sarah. *Must be way after midnight in London. Maybe she won't answer or hopefully, he was given a wrong number.*

With flip flops in hand, Ian jumped onto the dock after tying the dinghy line to a post. "I'll head over to the phone booths in town while you go to the market," he said. "I'll meet you in town so you can use the phone."

Sam watched him disappear into the night thinking maybe he should go with him. What if Sarah told Ian that he knew why she left? There wouldn't be much I could do about that then, he thought.

He checked Anna's grocery list and headed across the dimly lit parking lot toward the small island market that stayed open late. He nodded at a young couple walking past him into the marina.

Car tires squealed in a residential neighborhood he skirted to get to the market. He started to step off the curb when a van screeched to a halt in front of him. Before he could react, three men leaped out with guns drawn and pulled a bag over his head. He felt a sharp pain in his arm and heard himself yell out before all consciousness melted away to blackness.

# CHAPTER 54

Sam opened one eye and squinted into blackness. He seemed to be sitting in a chair, but his body felt numb and immobile. His head ached like it was squeezed in a vise. Slowly he realized he was in a bad place. Something had gone terribly wrong, but he couldn't figure it out. He closed his eyes and dropped his chin to his chest. He took a few deep breaths and tried to wipe liquid from his face but couldn't raise his hand—move any part of his body. It hurt. Everything hurt. He opened his eyes, pulled in a deep breath and sucked rough canvas against his open mouth. *Something's over my head. Where am I? What's going on?*

He heard rustling in the room—someone or something crabbing along the floor. It brushed against his leg. "What is it? Who are you? What's going on?" he spoke in a hoarse whisper.

"Sam? Sam, is that you?"

He recognized Ian's voice.

"Sam, are you okay? Where are we? I'm tied up and—"

"Me, too. Can't move and something's over my head. Can you—?"

"Looks like a small storage room," Ian said, lowering his voice. "My hands are tied behind my back, and it feels like duct tape around my ankles."

"I'm in a chair and can't move," Sam said, the ache in his head beginning to throb. "You get a look at who did this?"

"Not really. Got jumped from behind. They put a rag over my nose, and I guess I passed out. No idea how long ago or how long we've been here."

"Is there a window? Any light coming in?"

"There's a small one about chest high. Light's coming through some ratty curtains." Ian braced his back against Sam's legs. Looks like iron bars on the window. Now that's strange. Why would—"

"Push back against me. See if you can stand and see outside. Find out where the hell we are, and what's. . . .Damn, my head's killing me. Must have a concussion." He felt pressure on his leg as Ian wriggled his way up to his feet. A moment passed, then he heard him hop to the window.

"Don't see anyone around. Okay—it's a villa with a center courtyard. I see a water fountain and a driveway that enters through a gate. Oh crap!"

"What?" Sam whispered.

"A guard," Ian spoke in a hushed voice. "Two. One outside the door and one by the driveway gate. Both with automatic rifles."

"Get a good look at them?"

"Yeah. We know 'em. They're the two creeps that tossed me in the harbor."

As Sam began to regain feeling in his body, he realized he was lashed to a wooden chair. He struggled to loosen the ropes on his wrists to no avail and the same with the ropes or duct tape, he couldn't tell which, on his ankles.

"You're quiet over there."

"Just thinking. Why is the Haitian doing this?"

"Man, I can barely hear you," Ian said. "Let me get that bag off." He hobbled to Sam's side and grabbed the black canvas bag with his teeth. It was a struggle as the sack kept hanging up on Sam's chin, then his nose, but finally came free and dropped to the floor.

Sam shook his head and opened his eyes. The room was dark except for an orange glow coming from the small window. Ian leaned against the wall next to it. "I was saying," Sam said. "Why is the Haitian going to all this trouble over a little feud with us nobodies?"

"But we're not sure this is his villa," Ian said. "How do we know—"

"His goons are outside. That's how we know."

"Your face is all bloody." Ian sounded alarmed. "Are you—"

"I thought it was just sweat in my eyes. They must've cracked me pretty hard on the head." Sam glanced around the small room. It looked like a garden shed. There were bags of grass seed and fertilizer stacked in a corner. The room had a dank musty smell, like wet dirt and chemicals.

"Wait," Ian crouched down and peeked out the window. "Some men just came out of the main house. They're standing on the lawn. I see him. You're right. It's the Haitian."

"Recognize anyone else?"

"There's the fat constable, but I don't recognize the other two. They're wearing suits and ties." Ian ducked down from the window. "Oh crap. They looked this way."

Sam closed his eyes as a wave of nausea rolled over him. The blood on his face had dried, and one eyelid felt stuck. He was out of ideas. *Why? What does Guy Mont Violet want from me? He has everything, and I have nothing. Except for Anna.* He felt the strength go out of his body as bile rose in his mouth.

He glanced around the darkness for anything they could use to break free. Other than a few bags of gardening supplies, and the chair he was tied to, the room was empty.

"Wait," Ian was back at the window. "Somethings going on."

"What do you see?"

"They're looking up like. . . . Damn! Hear that?"

A low rumble seeped through the cracks around the garden hut door and the light coming through the window curtain brightened and pulsated like a strobe. Dust descended from the ceiling. Sam exhaled hard through his nose. The noise grew louder and became unmistakable. *A helicopter! A damn helicopter!*

# CHAPTER 55

The blast from the helicopter's propellers threw up a dust cloud as the craft swerved over the villa's outer walls and hovered over the courtyard. Sam could feel the throbbing vibration in his chair. It felt and sounded like the villa had come alive and had a pulsing heartbeat. *Fromp, fromp, fromp.* He saw Ian's mouth move but heard nothing.

The engine noise subsided, and Sam heard men yelling.

"They're putting blocks behind the tires. Someone's walking to the chopper door." Ian's low husky voice sounded like he was describing action at a golf tournament. "I don't recognize—oh yes I do, it's that captain from the catamaran. What's—?"

"Ainsley. Captain Ainsley." Sam spat. "Shoulda known he had something to do with this."

"Wait!" Ian swung away from the window. "The Haitian looked in this direction. Someone got out of the chopper."

"Who?"

"Tall. Wearing a suit and tie. A businessman or something." Ian moved back and peered over the windowsill.

Sam wriggled his wrists, trying to loosen the ropes. He winced, feeling them cut into his skin. "Damn. I'm stuck here."

"Looks like he's in his fifties, maybe sixties," Ian continued. "Well dressed. There's a couple of new guys standing with him that also got off the helicopter. The Haitian's gesturing and talking up a storm."

"What's he saying?"

"Can't hear. The rotors on the chopper are still moving. There—they shut down." Ian swung away from the window. "Everyone's coming in this direction."

Sam heard men's voices, still too muffled to understand what they were saying. One sounded familiar. Definitely not the captain's British lilt or Guy Mont Violet's rolling French accent. Crisp. Punctuated. More Spanish. Familiar, but he couldn't quite place it.

"I think they're going into the building next to us." Ian peeked through the covering on the dust covered window. "A lighted stone patio's next to us and they're stopping. Two of the thugs are bringing out trays of drinks. Looks like a celebration."

"Wonder what's going on. I mean why did they waylay us in town, bring us up here and. . . ." Sam stopped when he heard the familiar voice again.

"We have a boat ready to take the goods from the island. We took care of that a few months ago."

Sam and Ian looked at each other. Sam recognized the voice of Jerry Diaz, the harbormaster in Puerto Rico that introduced him to Firebird and talked him into buying her. It was even his idea to bring it to Saint Sebastian.

. "It's worked out well. No one suspects," Diaz continued. "She's in perfect shape and the right size for what we need. The cargo is being loaded now down at the cove below us."

Damn! Sam thought. *The bastard knew all along. It was a set-up!*

Ian's eyes flashed anger. "They must have Mom with them. The sons-of-bitches have her!"

"Shhhh!" Sam shook his head at Ian. "What else are they saying?" He worried about Anna, too, but they couldn't miss any of this conversation.

"When will you depart?" The voice of the head man had an edge of urgency to it. "My sources say a federal team is in San Juan preparing to raid this villa in the next couple of days. We're probably being watched right now."

"Don't worry about that," the harbormaster replied. "My man is putting that team together. He says it will be the weekend before they're ready. We'll have a three-day head start."

"Loading should finish in a few hours," the Haitian chimed

in, a hint of deference in his voice. "We'll be away before sunup. Besides me, there are two others coming along to provide security and crew the boat. Should I tell them the nature of the cargo? I think—"

"Hell no! The fewer that know, the better," the head man said. "A snitch already reported that we're selling nuclear triggers on the black market. My firm can't take the risk. The vessel and cargo must be destroyed if you're in any danger of losing control. Our clients are already crapping their pants. We've guaranteed them that everything's safe. You damn well make sure it is!"

Sam made eye contact with Ian and mouthed the words, "*Nuclear what*?"

Ian shrugged and shook his head.

"What about the woman?" Sam recognized Ainsley's voice. "What's going to happen to—"

"Woman! What woman?" The visitor's voice went up a few decibels. "What woman? Guy, what is he talking about?"

"And the other two as well?" Ainsley added.

Sam kept trying to loosen the bindings on his wrists as he watched fear growing in the boy's eyes.

"They're the crew on the boat we took for this project," the Haitian said. "That problem will be taken care of at sea. The ocean is big and hides many secrets. Not to worry."

"Make sure of that," the visitor mumbled. "Make sure. What's the name of the vessel?"

"Firebird," Ainsley answered. "An old sailing yacht built in the sixties by Palmer Johnson."

"Interesting," the visitor replied. "My father-in-law owned a boat by that name."

Sam raised an eyebrow.

"We should go before our presence here is noted," the lead man continued. "Keep me informed and make sure you get everything off the island and to its destination. Any trouble and you know what to do."

Dammit! Sam thought. The boy's right. They have Anna. She's

probably scared to death. They better not have. . . .He wrenched the bindings on his wrist and felt the sting of them cutting further into his skin. He had to stay calm. Something would happen to create an opening for them. It had to.

It was too dark in the room to see Ian's face in detail, but he had to be worried about Anna, about themselves.

The helicopter's engine started up and drowned out the men's voices.

"What are they doing?"

Ian peeked out the window. "Three men are getting in the chopper. Ainsley and the Haitian are standing by the door talking to the head guy."

"You get a good look at him?"

"Good enough. I'd recognize him if I ever saw him again. Oh wait. There's a decal on the side. Says Blaylock something. Someone just stepped in front of it. Can't make it out!"

The rotary blades turned faster, and the noise evolved into a loud throbbing pulse as the craft lifted and swung away toward the sea. In a moment, all was silent outside and in the storage room. Ian with his back against the wall, slid to the floor. "What now?" he whispered. "What—"

"Shhh." Sam heard voices approaching. He nodded toward the door.

Ian looked up at the window. The sound of men speaking grew louder. "Everyone ready?" The Haitian's heavy French accent was unmistakable. "You know what to do!"

A key rustled in the lock and the wooden door burst open. Guy Mont Violet stood silhouetted in the light from the courtyard. He first looked at Sam in the straight back chair and grinned. Nothing friendly in that smirk. He turned to Ian and nodded to one of his henchmen. The thug stepped forward and reached out to cover the boy's face with a white rag. Ian struggled a moment then went slack.

*Did the bastards kill him? What—?*

"Now my friend here." The Haitian nodded at Sam.

"So, it's you, you low life scum." Sam tried to stand but couldn't with his feet taped to the chair legs. He fell, toppling forward as the thug caught him and pressed the rag to his face. His thoughts of fighting back evaporated and everything went dark.

# CHAPTER 56

He opened his eyes in darkness, his face pressed against a fabric of some kind. A wave of nausea swept over him. Other than a splitting headache and some dizziness, he seemed to be okay. Nothing felt broken or out of place. His wrists were still bound behind his back, and he lay on a hard floor in a fetal position. He felt confined. He lay quiet, trying to remember. Before blacking out, he had seen the smirking face of Guy Mont Violet. *How long ago was that? How much time has passed? Where the hell am I? Where's Ian and Anna?*

He raised his head and his face brushed against what felt like nylon. He lay back, trying to organize his thoughts. The Haitian had said they would get rid of their hostages at sea. Sam felt a little roll under him like on a boat. He closed his eyes and rested his head on the floor. He must be on Firebird, and they were already under way. No engine vibration, so they were sailing. How was Ian? And Anna? A pit crowded his stomach thinking how terrified she must be.

His mind cleared and the ache in his head waned. He became aware he was breathing warm stale air. He tried to move and realized he was inside a bag of some kind—a large bag, a nylon bag—*A sail bag!* That was what he felt on his face. The floor lifted slightly and rolled again. *Definitely sailing.* He wondered if Ian was nearby. Maybe they were both in the sail locker.

"Hey!" he said in a hushed voice. "Anybody here?"

Something brushed against his leg.

"Wha. . . .? Who?" replied a muffled voice. "Sam? Sam? That you?"

"Keep your voice down," Sam hissed. "Yes, it's me. You okay?"

"Where are we? My head hurts and I ache all over."

"I think we're in sail bags, and aboard Firebird. Maybe in the sail locker. Haven't heard any voices. Have you?"

"Nothing. How about Mom? I'm worried and—"

"Me too." Sam stretched out his legs and his bare feet touched the bottom of the sail bag. He pushed harder and heard the unmistakable sound of Velcro ripping. He pushed again and felt his feet go through the bottom. "Hey," he whispered. "Check the bottom of your bag. I think I'm in one of those we Velcroed the seam." He heard a rustling, then more rustling, followed by the unmistakable sound of Velcro separating.

"I'm out!"

Sam felt Ian's body roll against him. He began thrashing his own legs and feet until he got his body clear of the nylon sail bag. Moonlight streamed through the porthole. *Definitely Firebird's sail locker.*

Ian blinked his eyes, trying to clear his vision. They both had their hands bound behind their backs and duct tape around their lower legs and ankles. "God, your face still has dried blood all over it."

Sam watched Ian roll over on his stomach and try to wriggle the ropes off his wrists.

After a fruitless effort the boy turned around. "So, what do we do?"

"Good question. We probably don't have much time."

Ian sat up. "Let's turn our backs to each other and use our hands to untie one another."

"Worth a try." Sam pushed himself to a sitting position. The boy scooted up behind him and Sam felt fingers working the ropes on his wrist. He reciprocated, but they kept getting in each other's way. "You go first," Sam whispered. Ian's hands brushed against his back as fingers furiously tugged and pushed at the ropes binding his wrists.

"Got an end loose," the boy said. "There, I've untied the knot."

Sam felt the binding loosen but it was still too tight. After waiting a few more moments while Ian worked at it, he pushed and pulled his arms back and forth till he felt one hand go free. "That's it," he whispered. "I'm done."

A loud thump in the companionway outside the door made them stop.

"What. . . .?" Both froze and waited. Minutes passed and nothing else was heard.

Without further talking, Sam untied Ian's hands.

Another loud thump in the companionway startled them. In the faint moon lit locker, Sam saw alarm in the boy's eyes. Another metal-on-metal bump reverberated through the cabin walls.

Sam let out a relieved breath. "It's the boom with the heavy mainsail moving at the mast. The sails are all up and the wind's increasing the further we get from land." Just then, the boat lifted on a large wave and slammed back down. They were heading away from the Caribbean into the Atlantic.

"What's the plan?" Ian stood. "How do we find Mom and how do we take out these bastards?"

"Don't know, yet." Sam glanced around the inside of the locker for a weapon, an idea.

"At the villa, there was talk about blowing up the boat if they lost control." Ian looked out the porthole. The surface of the ocean had settled and was flattening. The whitecaps were spaced wide apart.

"Yeah." Sam pushed a sail bag out of the way and stepped to the port. "They must have explosives on board. Maybe C4, dynamite, or even a rigged artillery shell."

"The weather's easing," Ian said. "The boat's steadying under sail."

Sam nodded. "We don't have a lot of time. They'll want to get rid of us as soon as possible."

"Where do you think they have Mom?" Ian asked.

"Probably in my cabin." Sam tightened his lips into a line. "I could be wrong but. . . ." He put his hand on the boy's arm. "If they haven't hurt us yet, I'm sure she's okay." Ian nodded, but Sam could tell the boy was eaten up inside with worry.

"How long have we been away from the island?" Ian changed the subject. "How much time do we have?"

"All good questions." Sam shook his head. "Like you, I was out and don't know when we left."

Ian looked at his wrist. "The assholes took my Seiko."

"There's a deep trench in the ocean floor about twenty miles off Saint Sebastian," Sam said. "That's probably where they'll dump us."

"Lucky putting in those Velcro seams, huh?" Ian said, picking up one of the sail bags and examining it.

"Yeah, lucky," Sam said. *Really lucky to be out here on a boat we rebuilt, taking us to our graves.*

# CHAPTER 57

The boat heeled and Sam heard the sails flop. "Wind's picking up and they're jibing." He looked behind Ian and saw the empty spinnaker bag on the floor. "They're flying the chute. Means they're planning on going downwind for a while."

Something on deck clanged, and a voice called out. "Furl the genoa! Too much headsail!"

Sam looked at Ian. *Guy Mont Violet.* They heard footsteps running across the deck and activity at the bow. The vibrations of a luffing foresail could be felt throughout the yacht as the large sail was rolled up. Under main and spinnaker, the boat settled into a steady seam and everything grew quite except for the sound of water slipping by under the hull.

"How many?" Ian mouthed.

Sam shook his head. "The Haitian told his boss there would be three. Two others counting him but could be more. I don't trust him."

"So, what do we do?"

Sam gazed out the porthole at the position of the moon. "We wait until they go to bed. They'll leave a helmsman on watch. Makes our odds better. We'll also have the element of surprise on our side."

Ian pulled opened a drawer in the locker chest and lifted two stainless steel winch handles. "At least we each have a weapon," he said. "More than just our bare fists."

Sam hefted the heavy object in his hand. "Better than nothing." They both were in the same clothes they wore off the boat to go into town. T-shirts and shorts. His Top Siders and Ian's flip flops had been lost somewhere along the way.

"They have guns?" Ian asked.

"What do you think?" Sam nodded. "Maybe we'll be lucky, and they won't be carrying them on board. Salt spray can screw up a pistol or rifle real quick."

"I hope Mom's okay."

"Me too," Sam grimaced. "Me too."

"Do you think they—"

"Don't know." Sam didn't wait for the boy to finish. "Hopefully, they've been too busy." He pressed his ear to the locker door to listen, not showing Ian he was worried sick about Anna. He knew the Haitian and what the Haitian wanted.

He heard two male voices in the main salon. One was Guy Mont Violet. The other, he didn't recognize. *One of his thugs.* The Haitian was telling him to sleep up on deck in case the helmsman needed assistance. He would relieve them both at dawn. Then all went silent.

Sam stared at the floor in thought. "We lucked out." He saw Ian watching him. "Pretty sure there's only three of them. It sounds like two on deck and the Haitian below. Let's give it time for things to settle down, and then we'll make our move."

"And what's that?" Ian asked.

"Don't know yet." He slid back down on the floor. "Gotta think about it."

"Is the door locked?" Ian asked.

"Haven't tried it but think not. Never had a key to any of Firebird's cabins."

Ian stepped to the door and turned the handle. The door creaked open a couple of inches, and he closed it.

"What time do you think it is?" Sam asked, lowering his voice.

"Looking at the position of the moon, definitely after midnight," Ian said. "Getting close to dawn."

Sam noticed the boat felt steady—minimum heel and side slippage through the sea. "We should move soon. The head man said the boat was to be blown up if they lost control. Any idea how they'd do that?"

Ian shrugged. "Explosives wouldn't be hard for those dudes to get hold of."

"Where would you put it? How would you rig it?" Sam asked. "I mean if we go out there and do what we have to do, they could blow us all to smithereens if we don't know how to stop it."

"Firebird's an over-engineered boat," Ian said. "Maybe she can withstand—"

"I doubt it." Sam rubbed his raw wrists. "I'm guessing they put it in the bilge. Maybe blow off the keel, put a big hole in her middle so she quickly sinks. The Haitian probably carries a remote control."

Ian picked up the empty spinnaker bag on the floor and tossed it on a pile of sails. "A remote trigger would be easy to set up. Grandfather uses them all the time in highway construction. Probably has a delay on it, so the Haitian and crew can get away before she blows."

"Bet he keeps it in his cabin – or *my* cabin. The prick is too vain to take one of the smaller state rooms." Sam opened the locker door a few inches and peeked out. The bright white overhead lights were on in the salon. Not the red lights used to protect night vision when at sea. He could see the salon had been stacked floor-to-ceiling with cardboard boxes. Must be the contraband from the villa, he thought.

No one was around. Suddenly, he heard--*Anna's voice! Where is she?* He couldn't make out what she was saying, but there was fear and urgency in her tone. He heard the Haitian's angry French reply and saw the door to her cabin was ajar and the light was off.

He turned to Ian. "I know where and how many, at least I think I do. Two are up on top, one steering and the other standing watch. The Haitian's in my cabin with Anna. I've got a plan. We'll divide and conquer."

# CHAPTER 58

Sam slipped down the hallway toward the main salon with the boy following close behind. Passing Ian's old cabin, Sam saw the door hanging open. A backpack had been tossed on the bunk; its contents scattered on top of the quilt. Must belong to one of Guy's thugs he thought. He started to go on but turned back to the room. He almost missed it. A holstered pistol lay partly covered with a pair of men's briefs. He looked at Ian and nodded toward the bed.

"Got it," Ian mouthed the words and retrieved the weapon.

Sam continued into the main salon, pausing at the navigation station. The room was so well lit their movements could be seen by whoever was on the helm in the cockpit. He flicked off the overhead lights and switched on the red ones by the nav station.

"Thanks, boss," came a voice from on top. "We were flying blind. Couldn't see shit up here with those bright lights on."

Sam paused a moment to see if the Haitian would come out of his cabin to check what was going on. An empty tequila bottle sat in the galley sink. The VHF radio and Ham radio were both turned off. He doesn't want messages coming in or going out, Sam thought.

A few moments passed, and nothing happened. He opened a drawer underneath the nav table and grabbed the flare pistol he kept for emergencies. The box next to it held two flares which he put in his pocket. It could cause a devastating fire if he shot one off inside the boat, but bullets through the aluminum hull could also sink them. Either way, he and Ian were armed and still held the element of surprise.

Ian nodded toward the top of the stairs going up to the deck.

They could see a pair of legs standing at the helm and the back of another person lying on the starboard settee cushion.

Sam looked at him and *mouthed,* "You take those two. I'll take the bastard down here." He watched Ian unholster the pistol and check the magazine. The boy cocked and loaded and nodded his understanding. *Knows his way around a gun.* "Kill 'em if you have to," he whispered. "Otherwise disarm and hold them till I can join you. If something happens to me, kill 'em all, and take care of your mother."

Ian crept up to the top of the steps and crouched down. He looked back at Sam, waiting for a signal.

Sam looked at the door to his old room and took a few deep breaths. He heard muffled sounds coming from inside, but couldn't make out what was being said, or who was saying it. He hoped the door wasn't locked from the inside. Should he break it down? That would take precious seconds and dilute the surprise advantage. He reached for the handle and turned. *Not locked.*

He slowly pushed open the door and froze, trying to understand what he was seeing.

The Haitian stood naked at the foot of the bed holding a half-full whiskey bottle in one hand. He swayed on his feet and stared at Sam with blurry eyes. It took a few moments for him to register what was transpiring. During that time, Sam saw Anna laying face up on the bed, tied spread eagle with a gag in her mouth. Naked with only a towel across her middle.

At that moment, a pistol shot rang out and Ian's voice yelled at the two thugs to get down on the deck. Guy Mont Violet flung the bottle at Sam and dove for an automatic rifle on the dresser.

Sam dodged the bottle, leapt towards the Haitian, grabbed one bare foot and pulled him away before he reached the weapon. They fell to the floor at the end of the bed with Sam on top. Guy Mont Violet cursed in French as Sam attempted to subdue him with a wrestler's head and shoulder lock. Fortunately, Sam had a forty-pound advantage on the Haitian and held the wide barrel of the flare pistol pressed up against his temple.

When Guy stopped struggling, Sam started to get up and saw Guy's hand reach under the bed and return holding something that looked like a remote-control device. "Shit!" He fell back on top of the Haitian who in one big push flipped them both over onto their backs with Guy locked in Sam's arms and Sam's legs wrapped around his waist.

Attempting to knock the remote control out of the Haitian's hand, Sam flailed at it with his flare pistol and somehow, the gun sailed out of his hand and slid across the room.

Mont Violet pushed up with his feet, attempting to wrestle free. Sam held on while the Haitian drove them backwards till Sam's back hit the cabin wall.

Something dug into his back between him and the bulkhead. It was the whiskey bottle. He grabbed it and brought it around in front of the Haitian's face. Guy gave out a loud grunt and Sam jammed the neck of the bottle into his open mouth, causing him to gag and flail.

With both hands, Sam held the base of the bottle and pulled it down into Guy's throat, cutting off all air through his mouth. He felt the glass bottle breaking through vocal cords and crushing small bones in the larynx and neck. The Haitian flopped like a fish out of water, his struggles weaker. With the bottle lodged tightly in the throat, Sam covered Guy's nose with his hand, cutting off all oxygen.

The body in his arms went limp and Sam waited a few more moments to be sure. After his past experience on the island, he didn't trust the bastard—even dead.

# CHAPTER 59

Sam heard sounds from the bunk and pushed the lifeless body away. Anna struggled to get free, her eyes wide in fear as she stared at him.

"It's okay," he said, brushing hair away from her face. "He's dead. He won't hurt you anymore."

Her eyes moved frantically from him to the door and back.

"Ian's got a gun on them on deck. We're in control of the boat. Let me do that." He untied one of her hands and began working the bindings at her ankles. He saw the raw marks on her skin and figured she had been tied up for hours.

"What took you so long?" Anna sputtered after taking the gag from her mouth. "Where have you been?" She started to cry. "I thought you were all dead." She freed her other hand while Sam pulled the ropes away from her feet.

"Got here as soon as we could." He looked at her. "What happened to you?"

She sat up on the bed, rubbing the marks on her wrists. She took a moment to wipe tears from her face with the pillowcase. "I was at the stove in the galley cooking dinner when I sensed movement. I turned just as two men grabbed me." She put her bare feet on the floor and looked at Guy Mont Violet's lifeless body at the foot of the bunk.

Sam took her hand and pulled her to him. She wrapped her arms around his neck. "I'm so glad you're here," she whimpered. "I was so afraid both of you were—"

"Did they. . . .?"

"No." She paused a moment. "I thought that's what it was all about, but they just tied me up and dumped me on the bunk in your cabin. I don't know how much time passed, but I could tell they were motoring somewhere out of the harbor. I was worried sick about you two."

"Yeah." Sam reached down and picked up the remote-control off the floor. "They hijacked Ian and me in town. Knocked us out and took us up the mountain to the villa. We overheard their plans to use Firebird to take some illegal stuff off the island that the Feds were after. They were planning to dump the three of us at sea." He studied the device in his hand. "Oh crap!"

"What?" Anna saw the alarm on his face and looked at the object.

He glanced at the top of the stairs. "Get some clothes on. We've got to get off this boat!"

"But we're miles away from land and—"

"Get dressed. Now! We don't have much time." He showed Anna the face of the remote control. The digital dial glowed red and revealed what looked like a timer, counting down the seconds. If he was right, there were less than five minutes remaining.

"Ian," he called out, taking the stairs two at a time to the deck.

At the top of the companionway, he found Ian in the cockpit with the pistol in his hand. The two thugs lay face down on the deck with their hands bound with duct tape.

"I heard Mom's voice. She okay?" The moon sat high over the calm sea, bathing everything in soft gray light.

"Yeah. Okay." Sam glanced around the deck. He didn't know what he was looking for—just an idea. He looked back over the stern and was surprised to see they were towing a twenty or so foot inflatable with a large Mercury outboard engine. Must be the Haitian's, he thought.

"Pull that big inflatable up to the stern. We've got to get off this boat. She's rigged to blow in a few minutes."

"What. . . .?"

"Do it, now!" He grabbed a couple of life jackets from the deck locker and started putting them on the two trussed up thugs. He turned around and saw Anna step out on deck carrying a backpack. She was wearing one of his shirts and a pair of jeans.

"I grabbed our passports and boat papers," she said, seeing the question in his eyes.

"Great." Sam pulled the two men to their feet and guided them to the stern where he tied nylon lines to the top of their life vests and pushed them forward, dropping them into the cold sea.

"Hey. We're gonna drown. . . ." One called out before his head went under and then bobbed back up above water.

"Only if you keep your mouth open," Sam yelled to him. He passed the ends of the lines to Ian, standing in the big dinghy and turned to help Anna down into it. He jumped onto one of the pontoons and pushed against Firebird's stern to get some distance between them.

Ian started the motor, put it in reverse and backed away, pulling the two captives through the water away from the big ketch.

"Why. . . .?" Anna started to ask, nodding toward the two men floating behind them in life vests.

"Don't want those snakes on board with us. Too dangerous in these close quarters," Sam said. "They can think about their sins while we tow them back to Saint Sebastian."

He pulled the remote control from his pocket and held it out for them all to see. He looked up and estimated they were about a hundred yards away from the drifting Firebird. In the glow of the full moon, the figure of the scarlet Phoenix in the middle of the silky white spinnaker tugged against its lines as a light breeze pushed the ketch further away. "Stay at this distance," he said to Ian at the wheel. "I think we're far enough away to be safe."

"Oh, no." Anna turned from watching the glowing red digits counting down on the remote. "Not my beautiful Firebird. Not the gorgeous cabinets and doors I worked so hard to sand and varnish. All the cushions I reupholstered. All the—"

A buzzing sound emitted from the remote device when the digits hit zero. The three of them stared at their home for the past months, all their sweat and labor, their hopes for the future, drifting slowly toward oblivion. Her sleek lines never looked so graceful, so beautiful.

A bright flash of light came from the bow of the ketch and the night ripped open with a loud boom. In slow motion, a glowing ball of fire rose up from the deck, consuming the white nylon spinnaker and its Phoenix.

# CHAPTER 60

Sam stared as the blinding fire of the explosion slowly extinguished. He expected to see Firebird ripped to pieces, its remnants scattered across the ocean's surface. Instead, in the gray of dawn, a ghost ship appeared out of the smoke and haze. The boat drifted slowly and quietly about seventy-five yards away – still intact. Only the foresail and the spinnaker were gone. From the halyard at the top of the mast, a burnt tattered sail remnant fluttered in the light breeze. The main and mizzen sails still full of air, pushed the big yacht along at an easy pace.

"Wha. . . .?" Anna put her hand on Sam's knee. "What just happened?"

Sam grimaced. "I think the proper term for that is—it was a dud. The explosive device must have been placed at the bow, allowing the blast to dissipate up and away from the deck. The fireball tells me they probably used some plastic explosive to blow up propane tanks from the galley." He shook his head. "We're damn lucky they didn't know what they were doing. If they'd put that below decks where the explosion would've been contained, we'd be missing one yacht right now."

Ian stood in the bow of the dinghy, looking across the water at the bobbing heads of their two captives. He pulled the lines, drawing them closer. "What do we do with these rats?"

"Keep them on the line!" Sam throttled forward and steered back to Firebird. He bumped the tender against the hull and held it fast while Ian jumped on deck and secured the painter to a stern cleat.

Rays of sunlight began streaking across the water's surface, announcing the new morning. Sam helped Anna up on deck and went forward to check the damage. Ian pulled the two thugs near Firebird's hull and looked down at them. "So, which one of you two geniuses rigged the bomb?"

His question was met with steely eyes.

"Okay, let me know if you see any dorsal fins. We need to save one of you to testify in court."

"We lucked out," Sam said, turning to Anna and Ian as they joined him at the bow. "In addition to the loss of the spinnaker and the genoa, we have some scorched spots on the deck and up the main mast. Nothing that deck cleaner and oil along with some touch up paint won't fix. We should still be able to make a good showing in Saint Thomas."

Anna took his hand and squeezed it.

"You okay? I mean, after all the—"

"You are my hero. Both of you." She put her free arm around Ian's shoulders. "Just like in the movies, the cavalry arrived before anything bad happened. It was close, but your timing was perfect."

"Hey! Hey!" The two thugs started kicking the side of the hull. "Hey! Somethings in the water here and—"

"Curious dolphins." Ian laughed. "They may tickle them to death." He went back to the stern and pulled the men to the boarding platform. He stepped down to drag them out of the water, their hands tied behind their backs.

"Bring them up on deck and secure them to the mast," Sam called to him, then went to help.

"Are we returning to Saint Sebastian?" Ian asked after they left their guests at the mast. "I mean, it's—"

"No." Sam shook his head. "Too risky with the compromised authorities there and Guy's men still on the island."

"How about Puerto Rico? It's only about fifty miles."

"You heard them say their man was putting the federal team together in Puerto Rico. We need to go where they're not in control of the show. I'm thinking Saint Croix."

Ian stepped to the lifelines and looked out over the open

sea. The morning sun rose, bathing everything in a golden glow. "Without a foresail, I'm guessing our boat speed at two knots. It'll take all day and all night to get to Saint Croix at this rate."

"About seven hours if we crank up the engine," Sam replied. "Seven hours at seven knots. Let's give that new engine a workout. If all goes well, we should be at Christiansted by mid-afternoon."

"Should we radio them we're coming?" Ian started untying the sheets to furl the mainsail.

"No." Sam watched Anna going down the stairs to the main salon. "They're probably monitoring radio traffic. Let's make it a surprise."

# CHAPTER 61

Sam stood at the bow beside Ian, watching a blue police launch powering toward them from the town dock at Christiansted. He looked at his watch. "Exactly seven hours. We made good time." They had tied to an available mooring ball in the harbor and called on the radio to the marina to ask if there was an FBI office on the island. A quick conversation with an agent and they were assured that someone would be right out.

"Sounded like he knew what I was talking about when I mentioned Saint Sebastian and a dead Haitian." Sam turned to see Anna in the shade of the cockpit holding a beer.

Their two captives, sitting cross-legged in the sun, slumped forward, their chins resting on their chests. Sam heard one of them snoring.

"I told the agent the cargo was still on board."

"Did he ask what it contained?" Ian asked.

"Nope. I figured he already knew since he asked about it." Sam looked at Anna. She turned from watching the police boat approaching and smiled. He winked at her.

The sun was setting when the launch roared away with boxes stacked and secured to its deck, and the two thugs handcuffed and sullen-faced guarded by uniformed officers. Guy Mont Violet's body had been wrapped in a sheet and taken onboard on a gurney.

Ian brought a tray of rum drinks to the cockpit, surprising Sam and Anna. "I've always heard that sundown is cocktail time on all classy charter yachts," he said, smiling at his mother.

"I've heard that." Sam reached for a glass. "But I don't have personal experience since this is the first classy charter yacht I've ever been on." He clinked Anna's glass. "We'll start the tradition on Firebird."

"What did the agents say before they left?" Ian looked at Sam. "Can we leave tomorrow for Saint Thomas? That would put us back on schedule, and—"

"Probably day after tomorrow." Sam nodded. "They're coming back in the morning to take a statement from each of us. We can leave after that. That'll put us in Charlotte Amalie a few days before the show starts. We'll need time to clean up the mess at the bow. I'll call my insurance company to see if we can get some monetary relief for a new spinnaker and genoa. Those two sails alone would cost at least ten thousand to replace."

"Too bad there's not a reward for—"

Sam took another swig of his drink. "There might be. The agent alluded to it. He wasn't sure, but said he'd let us know tomorrow when he's out here."

Anna rose from the cockpit seat and stood next to him. He put his arm around her, and she leaned into him "If there's any reward you, dear lady, should get every penny of it for what you went through."

"No. No." She smiled and nuzzled her nose against his throat. Her arms went around his waist and her hands slipped in the rear pockets of his shorts. "Who knows what would've happened if you hadn't. . . ." She turned her gaze out over the harbor at the marina. The sound of halyards clanging against aluminum masts carried across the water like church bells. "Anyway, it's over and we're safe."

"What about that, Sam?" Ian put his empty glass back on the tray. "Did the agent say anything about the Haitian's gang on Saint Sebastian and the others in Puerto Rico?"

"He said they had a warrant for the head guy in the helicopter. Turns out, he's the Chairman of Blaylock Industries. They're the big maker of bearings for the auto industry, but he said they also have an electronics division that manufactures nuclear triggers for the

U.S. military. Who knew? On the subject of small worlds, it was his wife's father that built Firebird a long time ago."

"Ian looked surprised. "Did they know when they—"

"Nope. Pure serendipity," Sam said. "I remember the chairman of Palmer Johnson telling me about Blaylock when we discussed the new motor."

Sam paused a moment to reflect. "Oh yeah, and the agent said they've picked up his men in San Juan and the ones left on Saint Sebastian. He wasn't sure how cooperative the island authorities there would be, but with the FBI having the Haitian's body, the contraband, and our statements, they have all the evidence they need."

"Let's hope," Anna whispered. They watched in silence as the setting sun touched the western horizon.

"Let's go ashore for a celebratory dinner and then call it an early night?" Sam said. "A lot has happened. We can all use the sleep before dealing with the feds again tomorrow morning."

# CHAPTER 62

After returning to Firebird from a great meal at an upscale restaurant in downtown Christiansted, Sam stood outside Anna's cabin door unsure of his next step. He raised his hand to knock but stopped when Ian entered the salon.

"Thought I'd get a bottle of water out of the fridge before turning in," Ian said. "When can we really leave for Saint Thomas?"

Sam grabbed a Heineken and sat at the table with him. "Depends on how much time the authorities take getting our statements tomorrow."

They sat in silence. Sam wasn't sure where this was going. The boy had something on his mind.

"So, you're still going to do this charter thing?" Ian took a drink from his water bottle and screwed the cap back on.

Sam nodded. "I am. You have another idea?"

"Nope." Ian held the plastic bottle on the table in both hands. "But. . . ." He paused a moment.

"But what?"

"I'm going back to college, to Cornell, in January."

"I know. You've said that."

"I wasn't sure you still knew that was my plan."

Sam grinned. "I'll miss your handsome boyish face, but I'm not surprised. It's the right thing for you to do. How long do you plan to stick around here?"

"You've got my mind and muscles until after Christmas." Ian glanced at the door to his mother's cabin. "You tell me how long you want me to stay."

Sam lifted his beer and took another drink. "We could use your help through the holidays. We'll get the cosmetic repairs done on deck to cover up the fire damage and order the new sails before the charter show starts. I can use help during the show entertaining agents attending and touring Firebird. We'll get matching khaki shorts and white crew shirts and show this fancy yacht off. I'll need some good bookings for the winter season to pay for all this."

"Have the events of the last forty-eight hours changed yours and Mom's plans to—?"

"I was hoping to speak with her about it tonight," Sam said.

Ian's mouth turned up into his signature grin. "So, what do you want to happen?"

A long silence passed while Sam scraped the green label off the Heineken bottle with a fingernail. "I still want her to marry me," he said, looking up. "That hasn't changed. I'm in love with Anna like I've never been in love before."

"What do you think she'll say?"

"Not sure." Sam shook his head. "She accepted my proposal once, but after all this drama, I thought maybe I should ask her again. What do you think?"

Ian's teeth flashed white behind his smile. "You've got my permission, again." He stood to reach across the table and shake Sam's hand. "I'll try not to interrupt." He went down the passageway and disappeared into his cabin.

"Come in?"

Sam pushed open the cabin door and saw Anna in a long T-shirt, standing by her bunk pulling back the quilt. Her blue eyes, so big they almost made her little nose disappear, nearly took his breath away. She looked more like a school girl, getting ready for bed than a forty-year old mother of a grown son. He felt Firebird rise and settle back on her mooring line, like heaving a sigh of relief. "Hi." He smiled. "Can we talk?"

Anna closed the door behind him and melded into his arms.

He smelled her freshness, her sweet essence, and buried his face in her hair. "I'm so glad you are in my life," he said.

# CHAPTER 63

Sam stood at the starboard rail, watching the government launch spin away from Firebird and head back toward Christiansted's town dock. The sun was directly overhead. They had spent the morning with three FBI agents, telling them everything they could remember about being taken hostage and Firebird's hijacking. Not much was said about the contraband—boxes of electronic triggers used to detonate atomic bombs. What little Sam knew, he had overheard the kidnappers discuss at the villa.

He felt a presence beside him and turned to see Ian cross-armed, watching the motor launch grow small in the distance.

"Can we go? We free to leave?"

"Whenever we're ready." Sam looked up at the sun. "The lead agent said they had everyone in custody on Puerto Rico including Jerry Diaz, the harbormaster. I never knew he was dishonorably discharged from the coast guard and spent a couple of years in prison. The head guy was picked up at his company offices in Indiana. The thugs on Saint Sebastian fled back to Haiti. He thought they'd be easy enough to find. Interpol's already on it."

"Mom has lunch made in the salon if you're hungry." Ian picked up a piece of tattered sail that had fluttered down from the halyard. "I'll start cleaning up."

Sam paused before leaving the deck. "There are two pieces of news I learned before the agents took off."

Ian looked at him. "What?" He wiped his hand on his shorts.

Sam took a deep breath. "Your grandfather sent a message to the marina office here that he's meeting us in Charlotte Amalie. The agent was kind enough to relay it to us."

Ian shook his head. "Not sure how Mom will react to that."

"The other news is that the agent says the government's offering a reward that we may qualify for."

"Ian stared at him a moment. "But, that's terrific news. You deserve it, Captain."

"Wait." Sam said. "If there's a reward, it's for all of us. I mean if we even get it and—"

"Whatever it is," Ian said, "I don't want any of it. When my grandfather passes on, if the stubborn cuss ever does, I'll become another useless rich playboy in Boston." He grinned and ran a hand through his unruly blonde hair.

Sam smiled. "We'll see. Maybe we'll learn more when we get to Charlotte Amalie. It's a long shot. Let's get out of here. We can make the harbor at Saint Thomas before dark if we motor sail." He looked up to check the wind direction. "Maybe sooner since we'll be on a broad reach with the main and mizzen deployed. You can clean up the sail scraps and wash the smoke off while we're under way. If we're lucky, we should be there by six, no later than seven o'clock."

"Tell Mom the good news, and I'll tend to the mooring line." Ian picked up the boat hook bungeed to the mast and headed to the bow. Sam watched him a moment before going below. The boy had matured the past four months. His shoulders were broad, and his muscles were well defined. His legs looked strong and sturdy as tree trunks. He moved with a confidence he didn't have when he first arrived on Saint Sebastian. Sam smiled. *A son any father would be proud of.*

Sam paused at the salon table to pick up a sandwich from a platter and leaned in to kiss the back of Anna's neck. She stood at the sink washing dishes, her hands gloved in ivory soap bubbles.

"Oh, you surprised me," she said, putting a blob of bubbles on his nose.

They heard the engine fire up.

"We'll be in Saint Thomas before you know it." Sam wiped soap off his face and took a bite of sandwich.

"I need to put things away down here," Anna said. "I didn't know we were leaving so quickly. I—"

"It's okay." He put his arms around her. "It'll be an easy trip with minimum heel. We'll motor with the wind mostly on our stern. You could take a long nap on the way. I bet you can use the rest."

She kissed him on his nose. "I'll finish these dishes and make sure things down here are secured. We don't need broken bottles on the floor. Why the rush to leave?"

"Oh, there's a million reasons," Sam said over his shoulder as he went back up the salon steps. I'll give Ian a hand. Come up and join us when you're done."

# CHAPTER 64

Morning sun warmed Firebird's deck when Sam stepped outside after his shower. He rubbed the scar on his arm and across his chest and gazed across the harbor at the town of Charlotte Amalie covering the mountainsides and surrounding the waterfront. Two giant cruise ships had come into the dock during the early morning hours. He had felt the vibration of their big screws when they maneuvered sideways into tight spots against the pier.

The morning stillness came alive as residents of the capital city of the U.S. Virgin Islands started moving about the island. Cabs honked and delivery trucks with diesel engines spewed black smoke into the air.

"Another beautiful morning in paradise."

He turned to see Anna, looking lovely in a white gauzy sheath—almost angelic.

He smiled. "And you are the most beautiful woman in paradise."

"I bet you say that to all the girls." She reached for him.

Her hand felt tiny in his. He pulled her to him and kissed her. She ran her fingers through his hair.

"I don't remember," he said, looking over her shoulder.

"Remember what?"

"I don't remember all the girls," he said almost in a whisper. "It's hard to remember anything before I met you."

"Right answer." She put both arms around his neck and went up on her toes to give him another long kiss.

A sleek powerboat roared by on the starboard side, its big wake causing Firebird to rock. Sam took Anna's hand and walked her to the bow.

"Sure, you want to do this?" he asked, looking into the blue pools of her eyes. "You really want to marry me, this vagabond, a drifter who hasn't done anything socially redeeming with his life? I don't deserve you. But I love you and will love you more than you can ever imagine."

"Are those the vows you've written for the ceremony?" She smiled. "If they are, they're lovely."

"I thought all I had to say was 'I do.'"

"That's enough." Anna leaned backed against him, taking his hands and wrapping his arms around her.

"I have no memory of the vows I took with Ian's father." She stroked his hands. "It was so long ago. So many days. So many months. So many years."

Sam kissed his favorite spot on the back of her neck.

Ian joined them on deck holding a steaming cup of coffee. "Good morning. When do we move into the marina for the show?"

"Registration opens Monday morning at nine o'clock," Sam said, releasing Anna from his embrace. "We can move Firebird in as soon as we pick up our packet. I figure they'll put us stern-to at the main dock since we're the largest boat entered. There's an Oceana 80 and a couple of Irwin 65s from Tortola expected."

"So, what's the schedule for the next few days?" Ian sipped his coffee. "There are some scorched spots on the mast and at the bow that need some white paint."

Sam moved them back to the cockpit. "I radioed North Sails here on the island. The new sails will take a couple of weeks. Chubb insurance said there would be no problem getting us a check. Their agent here on Saint Thomas wants to survey Firebird after we get her set up in the marina. He wants to make sure she's still in good condition after our little event."

"Any word yet from Grandfather?" Ian glanced at his mother.

Sam nodded. "Got a message from the show director that a Mr. Turloch Neeson will be arriving on the island later this afternoon and requested a launch to bring him out to Firebird."

"Yep. That'd be him." Ian grinned. "Still ordering people around. What about the reward?"

Sam shook his head. "Heard nothing about it. Maybe—"

A fast-approaching speed boat came toward them. Two men in suits and ties stood in the bow holding briefcases. The launch slowed and slid sideways against Firebird's port side, cushioned by the big rubber fenders Sam always set out when in an active harbor.

"Ahoy!" One of the men wearing a baseball cap with FBI on it in white letters waved. "Permission to come aboard."

"Come ahead," Sam said, moving to the railing. Ian and Anna waited in the cockpit.

Two other men stepped forward from the rear of the powerboat. One held a notepad and introduced himself as a reporter from the AP. The other said he was the executive director of the charter show.

"Sam saw the FBI agents standing aside, waiting their turn.

"Oh, no problem with us," the older guy with the cap said. Sam had already pegged him to be the team leader. "We would like to do one last search of your boat to see if we missed anything when you were at Saint Croix."

"You folks are all over the papers and television back in the states," the reporter said. "This is the first chance we've had to catch up with you. Can I get a few minutes? The world is waiting to hear your story, what you have to say."

"Be my guest," Sam said to the agents, then directed the reporter and the show director to the cockpit shade. "What do you mean we're all on the news?"

Half an hour later, the reporter closed his notebook. "Think I've got everything I need. Sounds like you and your crew are real heroes just like they're saying on CNN."

"CNN! You, kidding?" Ian looked at Sam. "This could make getting dates on campus a lot easier this next semester."

"Like you need any help with that." Sam winked at Anna.

The show director stood and shook Sam's hand. "Everyone associated with the show is very excited that you and this beautiful yacht are a part of it. If there's anything we can do to make your visit any better, please ask. My office was overwhelmed this morning with travel agents from some of the best firms in the states calling for more information about chartering Firebird this coming season."

Sam's ears perked up. "Uh, I need to meet with someone on your staff to get some marketing brochures printed," he said. "We'll have to get some film developed for the photos we need but—"

"Ride back to the office with us, and I'll introduce you to my marketing director. We have a template to make it easy and quick. She'll need to get your charter rates and other pertinent information."

Sam looked at Anna with a helpless, puppy dog face.

"Let me change and get my things, and I'll be right there," she said and left the cockpit.

The two federal agents finished their inspection and rejoined Sam and Ian on deck. "It's a beautiful yacht," the one in the baseball cap said. "We didn't find anything else. Where did the fight take place that—?"

"In the captain's cabin," Sam answered.

"And you crammed a whiskey bottle down his—?"

"Down the bastard's throat. Yessir." Sam's mouth went into a tight line. "He was about to—"

"Yeah. We read the report." The junior agent nodded. "I want to shake your hand, Sir. God knows what could have happened if those devices had gotten into the wrong hands. I'm from Indiana and very familiar with Blaylock Industries. My uncle retired from there a few years ago. It's hard to believe such an established company would be involved in such a thing."

"Blaylock," Sam said. "The original owner of this boat was a Blaylock who died right after building it. I—"

"No kidding." The young agent jotted something in his notebook.

"Probably a coincidence," said the baseball cap. "The guy arrested was. . . " He checked papers he carried in a folder. "A Delvin Prouty. His wife is the major stockholder in the company. It's causing a lot of shake up in Washington as Blaylock Industries was also a major manufacturer of electronics for the defense department."

"He sounded like a real asshole to me when we encountered him at the villa on Saint Sebastian," Sam said. "That's who told the Haitian to get rid of us. We never got a good look at him. Hope they throw the book at him."

"The U.S. Attorney on the case will be contacting you about that." The two agents shook Sam's hand and then Ian's.

Anna stepped out on the deck in a sky-blue sundress and strap sandals, carrying a small canvas briefcase. Her hair was pulled back in a ponytail. She looked like the girl next door. "I'm ready to go meet with your marketing person," she said to the show director.

# CHAPTER 65

Sam and Ian watched the launch head back toward Saint Thomas's Yacht Haven Marina. Anna had already charmed all the men on board. The AP reporter was in serious conversation with her on the settee in the stern, and the show director had brought her up a drink from the galley.

"What do you think?" Sam looked at Ian.

"I think your first mate is going to be a great social director," Ian said, watching the launch cross the path of a freighter headed out of the harbor. "She's already got them wrapped around her little finger."

Sam laughed. "Yep. I agree with all of that, but what else?"

"Like what?" Ian turned to look at him.

"Like your grandfather arriving in a few hours. Like maybe a reward might or might not be ours. Like travel agents vying to book Firebird for charters. Like, you leaving us soon."

Ian laughed. "Well how about, like what did my mother say when you asked her about marrying your ass again?"

"She didn't say, 'yes.'" Sam paused a moment. "She said, "HELL, YES!'"

"No, she didn't," Ian teased.

"Damn sure did! Your mama knows a good deal when she sees it."

"And you're the 'good deal'?"

"Better than a Blue Light Special at Kmart."

Ian studied his feet in his Reef sandals and wriggled his toes. "Should we take the dinghy ashore to pick up my grandfather?"

"What do you call him?"

"Granddad. Or Grandfather. He's old school."

"I'll call him Mister Neeson," Sam said. "What do you think he'll say?"

"Good question." Ian nodded. "Hard to guess. I was never close to him. I think he kept a distance to keep from getting hurt again. Mom said it almost killed him when my dad died. I saw the old man basically as an institution. He set my goals, oversaw my grades, paid my tuition and expenses, and managed my mom. He wasn't abusive. Just distant, impersonal, and controlling. He'll either hate you as an intruder into his domain, or he could embrace you as a solution to a problem, or a number of other things. I hope I get the chance to speak with him first. I'm sure he's upset with me dropping out of college and disappearing. He's got a right to be angry about that."

"Maybe you should take the dinghy to the marina and a cab to the airport to meet him." Sam sat in the cockpit and put his bare feet up on the opposite cushion. "That'd give you guys some private time. I'm sure he'll have different issues with Anna and me."

Ian checked his watch. "I'll need to leave pretty soon."

"Let's finish this conversation," Sam said. "What do you think about the other subjects I mentioned?"

"I'll turn those same questions back to you," Ian said. "Like what do you think about the reward, booking charters, and me leaving for college?"

"That's fair," Sam said. "As to the money, we made our plans without it. If it comes, great. If it doesn't, our plans are still in place, and Anna and I'll have a great life. Especially if we get lots of good-paying charter guests because of our notoriety. We need to work out how to give them a fun time that ensures return customers. Your mom is my secret weapon for that.

"And as for you leaving us for college. . . ." He paused a moment and gazed out over the harbor. "Well, don't let the door hit you in the ass!" He ducked when Ian threw a sandal at him.

That evening after Anna returned from her meeting with the

marketing director and Turloch Neeson had concluded his reunion with his family, Sam stood at the rail watching the stern light on the dinghy fade as Ian drove his grandfather back to shore. The old man had booked a room at a boutique hotel on the island and said he was flying back to Boston early the next morning.

Sam was surprised at how easy everything had gone with him. Turloch had seemed genuinely happy to see his family and had bent over backward to accommodate Sam in the family discussions. He had of course worried about his grandson and daughter-in-law and was relieved to see they were safe. He said he was thrilled to hear his only grandson was returning to Cornell to finish his engineering degree. What Sam couldn't discern in the short time they hosted him on Firebird, were his thoughts and feelings about Anna marrying him.

He had given his approval and congratulated them when Anna told him, but Sam had detected a hesitation behind the man's twinkling Irish eyes. He decided to give him the benefit of the doubt and assume he was somewhat satisfied to not be responsible for her anymore.

"Are you okay?"

Sam turned to see Anna on deck. Her white silk sarong exposed a bare shoulder and long, tan legs. Her hair was up with curls brushing the top of her ears and gold loop earrings with a matching necklace, framing it all.

"Wow! You have a date or something? I mean, you look. . . .delicious."

"A girl can hope." She smiled.

"We'll have to swim if we go anywhere. Ian took the dinghy and I don't know when he'll be back."

"So, we're all alone? For a change?"

Sam crooked his finger at her. "Come here, you lovely vixen. My heart's beating so fast, you're about to give me a heart attack."

A whistle sounded somewhere on shore, and the lights of Charlotte Amalie cascading down the hillsides, sparkled like diamonds against the blackness. The night air felt warm and humid as he took her hand, her beautiful hand, and brought it to his lips. His eyes stayed locked on hers. "My gosh, I've never seen you so lovely."

"You clean up pretty good yourself, big boy." She moved siren like into his arms.

He breathed against her cheek and she closed her eyes. Her lips parted and her tongue wetted them.

"Are you really going to marry me?" he said, almost in a whisper. "I mean this is like the beauty and the beast. I never thought I'd get to wed a fairy princess."

Somewhere in the harbor, a passing boat sent a small wake that lifted and gently rocked Firebird.

"I think maybe the old girl's jealous." Anna nibbled his ear lobe.

"Who?" Sam leaned back and looked at her. "Who's jealous? I promise there's no other—"

"I know, silly." Anna laughed. "I'm referring to Firebird. I think she can sometimes be a jealous mistress."

"Oh, but I'm sure she loves you as much as I do," Sam said. "Listen to her hull hum. Almost like a cat purring."

"That's the water pump you're hearing, you nincompoop." Anna pulled his head down and kissed him. "See. It just switched off."

"Must be a leak somewhere." Sam played along. "I'll check that out. It's a demand system."

"So, when are you going to marry me? Make me an honest woman, as they would say back in Boston." Anna turned away from his embrace and stood at the rail looking towards the festive lights of the big cruise ships at the town dock.

He moved beside her. "They say that in Texas City, too. And you're already the most honest woman I know."

"Did Turloch ask if you could give me the life I want and deserve?"

"No, and if he had, I'd have told him the truth."

"And that is?"

"I would've said that he can be comfortable knowing you are with a man that loves you more than life itself. Who would move mountains for you and protect you to his last breath."

"Why would you say that?"

"Because I think that's what your father-in-law has been doing these past years. The only thing he couldn't do was make you happy, and that probably hurt him more than anything."

Anna took a deep breath. "Did he say that?"

"No, not really. But a guy knows."

She put her finger to his mouth and traced his lips. "I'm so glad you're a *guy*."

Another mystery wave rocked Firebird back on her anchor. Anna grabbed him by the waist to steady herself. "Yes. No doubt about it. I think the old girl's jealous."

He pulled her snug against him. "There's more than enough of me to go around."

She went up on tiptoes and kissed him. They broke the kiss, and she leaned against his chest. "You know a lot of lives have been saved by you on this adventure. You're starting out new with a woman that loves you. My son found the father figure he always wanted. And I. . .I have someone to love and who loves me for me, for who I am. You also rescued Firebird from being sunk for a reef and gave her new life." She looked up at him and smiled. "We're a big happy family but instead of a family pooch, we have a big beautiful sailing yacht that looks after us."

"You're one sweet, romantic woman with an over-active imagination." He kissed her forehead. "How about marrying me before Ian goes back to school?" He paused a moment. "Let's do it right after the show next week. We'll get a local priest and sail over to Norman Island in the BVIs for the ceremony. They say it was the model for Robert Louis Stevenson's Treasure Island. I'll ask Ian to be my best man." He had his hand on Anna's back and felt her shiver.

"Are you sure? I mean—"

"Why wait? Nothing is forever. A life-ending comet or asteroid could hit the earth next week or next month and—"

She looked up into his eyes and smiled. "If you're that ready for this then let's tell Ian tonight."

"I'm definitely sure about this." He smiled. "Are you?"

Anna nodded. "I am. Yes, I am."

"Hey," Sam called out, spreading his feet apart to steady them both.

"What?" Anna looked up at him.

"Feel that? The vibration in the hull? Sounds like the water pump came on again, and the old girl's rocking on her anchor. I think she's telling us to do it!"

CPSIA information can be obtained
at www.ICGtesting.com
Printed in the USA
JSHW020015250920
8226JS00001B/1

9 781977 225283